A Private Man

A Private Man

by Chris Laing

Seraphim EDITIONS

This is a work of fiction, and the characters in it are solely the creation of the
author. Any resemblance to actual persons – with the exception of historical
figures – is entirely coincidental. When historical figures consort with fictional
characters, the results are necessarily fiction. Similarly, some events have been
created to serve fictional purposes.

The publisher gratefully acknowledges the financial assistance of the Canada
Council for the Arts.

 Canada Council **Conseil des Arts**
for the Arts **du Canada**

Library and Archives Canada Cataloguing in Publication

Laing, Chris, 1936-
    A private man : a novel / by Chris Laing.

ISBN 978-1-927079-09-6

    I. Title.

PS8623.A395P75 2012   C813'.6   C2012-904912-3

Editor: George Down
Author Photo: Michèle LaRose
Design and Typography: Julie McNeill, McNeill Design Arts
Hamilton street scene courtesy of Janet Forjan, www.hamiltonpostcards.com

Published in 2012 by
Seraphim Editions
54 Bay Street
Woodstock, ON
Canada N4S 3K9

Printed and bound in Canada

To Michèle

"For Sentimental Reasons"

CHAPTER ONE

JULY, 1947. AND HOTTER THAN hell in Hamilton.

But it sure felt good to be back on my old stomping ground. Felt good? Well, hell, it felt great. I didn't think I'd get back alive. After five long years in war-ravaged Europe, count me among the lucky ones who survived.

Now I was back on Civvy Street – and if you believed the folks at the Rehab Centre, I was becoming a productive member of postwar society. But I say the jury was still out on that score.

I boarded a Belt Line streetcar on King Street, followed by a couple of soldiers in uniform toting duffel bags. Must've been on leave, judging by the big grins on their mugs. They reminded me of that old song from the last war: "Pack up your troubles in your old kit bag and smile, smile, smile."

Not always easy to follow that simplistic advice. But after three operations, the shrapnel wound that blew out my right knee was on the mend. Sure, I still limped, but so did a lot of other guys who'd survived the German shelling. And I was a helluva lot better off than my comrades who'd stayed behind under the Normandy sod.

At the Ferguson Street railway tracks, the motorman clanged his bell and stomped on the brake when a market truck loaded with cucumbers veered toward us. Our sudden stop jolted the pole on the streetcar's roof from the line above in a shower of sparks. When the driver walked behind the tram and returned the pole to the overhead cable, he shook his fist at the truck driver. That earned him a round of applause from his passengers, me included.

I swung off the streetcar at John Street and limped across King to the Wentworth Building, which housed the one-man agency I'd bought a few months ago, determined to prove that my so-called disability wouldn't stop me being the best damn private detective this side of Philip Marlowe. So what if this was Hamilton?

And my job today? Hire a new secretary.

Down the hall on the third floor I unlocked my office door; the frosted glass panel still lettered W. J. JEFFRIES INVESTIGATIONS. For the umpteenth time I puzzled over what to replace it with. Something snappy. Maybe VETERANS INVESTIGATIONS or ... MAX DEXTER MASTER DETECTIVE. No, not quite right. I'd think about it later, as usual.

I flipped on the lights and tossed my grey fedora onto the filing cabinet by the door. In front of the window facing King Street, three worn club chairs hunkered around a low table like old soldiers in a retirement home. The secretary's desk and type-writer stand guarded the door to my own office in the opposite corner. The lease referred to this layout as a two-room suite. Washroom down the hall.

I ignored the Mount Everest of paper on my scarred wooden desk, crossed to the window and forced it open a few inches. Muggy air crawled over the sill, carrying with it the stench of car exhaust from below. Another day of record-breaking temperatures in Southern Ontario, which meant too damn hot. Annoyed by the traffic noise, I closed the window, opened the bottom drawer of the desk and sat down, using both hands to place my right leg across the drawer.

"Ahhh," I said, out loud. "Contrary to popular opinion, there is indeed rest for the wicked."

"I beg to differ with you, Young Man," a stern voice boomed from the doorway. "As far as I can see there's been far too much rest taken in this office."

I gaped up at a middle-aged woman standing tall and straight-backed before me. She wore a severely-cut black suit and her coarse grey hair was so closely cropped it conformed to her head like a pewter helmet. For a panicky moment I was back in Grade 6 and Sister Theresa was targeting me with her X-ray vision. I put my hands behind my back to avoid a blow across the knuckles from her ruler.

I snapped back to the present, withdrew my leg from the desk drawer and sat upright. It took me a moment to dig through the pile in my pending basket until I extracted the list of interviewees for the secretary's job. "Ah, yes, you must be Miss Higgins. In response to our notice in *The Hamilton Spectator*."

"Well, of course I am. We made an appointment for nine a.m. sharp this morning. And it is now nine a.m. sharp."

I flicked my eyes to the wall clock. It read oh-nine-thirty but I couldn't remember the last time I'd wound it. I glanced back at Miss Higgins but her eyes had followed mine and her lips were now pinched in a prune-like frown. If my years of training in the Canadian Army had taught me nothing else, it was the hard-won lesson of when to abandon an unwinnable position. I could spend the next hour being lectured by this officious woman or I could save us both a truckload of aggravation.

I gave Miss Higgins a tight smile and lifted my leg back across the desk drawer. Hands behind my head, I squeaked back in my chair and cocked my head toward the wall clock. "I'm sorry, Ma'am, but the success of this business is measured by the punctuality of its staff. And arriving a half-hour late for your job interview has disqualified you as a candidate."

Her face became a purple mask and a wormy vein crawled along her forehead. She sputtered but couldn't speak. Then she turned and puffed through the still-open door like a cartoon steam engine.

I sighed with relief, not realizing I'd been holding my breath. Judas Priest! Miss Higgins' scornful scowl at the disarray in my office had pushed my guilt button and I hung up my jacket, rolled up my shirt sleeves and began to clean away the clutter. My former secretary had worked twenty years for old Jeffries and when she'd quit last month she delivered a short, but impassioned, speech: "You take the cake, Mr. Dexter," she'd said, "for the world's messiest man."

At the secretary's desk, I plowed through the mound of accumulated paper, advertising flyers and other junk. I'd filled three medium-sized boxes with trash and I still hadn't reached the desktop when the scent of too much perfume wrinkled my nose.

I looked up at a skinny woman in a sagging red dress as she peered at me from behind a veil of dark hair. She closed the door without a sound and crept a timid step forward, clutching a black purse and a newspaper against her flat chest. "The ad," she whispered. "Miss Jones."

I waved her toward a chair beside the desk and she sat. When she raised her eyes and brushed her hair from her face with long, bony fingers, I realized Miss Jones was just a kid, probably wearing one of her mother's dresses.

"Well, Miss Jones, tell me about your work experience," I said. "You're familiar with typing and filing, arranging appointments and keeping accounts?"

Her eyes widened and her mouth dropped open as if to answer but not knowing what to say. "I'm just starting out," she finally squeaked.

I smiled and lowered my voice. "What's your real name?"

Her lower lip pouted and her shoulders slumped. When her eyes met mine, she said with a tiny grin, "Linda Jaworski."

I pushed back my chair and stood. "Whaddya say we go next door for a Coke, Linda?"

We took a booth in the White Spot, where Linda told me her parents didn't understand her because they were too old to remember that high school was an "utter waste of time". So she planned to move out, get a job and her own apartment. Show them she was old enough to live on her own. She was 16, after all.

"War's over, Mr. Dexter. Boys are back from overseas and there's lots of jobs. Jeepers creepers, I don't want to be left behind, miss out on all the fun."

After she ran out of steam, I got her to promise she'd call a friend of mine, a counsellor at Central High. And she'd consider giving her parents another chance. After we waved goodbye I felt better about her prospects. I hoped she did too.

Back in my office, a young guy with an armload of newspapers breezed into the room. "Hot off the press, Max." He flapped an early edition of *The Hamilton Spectator* on the desk, lowered his voice and glanced around as though he were selling risqué postcards. "Ya shoulda seen the glamourpuss I seen downstairs. Whatta gorgeous dame. Slinky like Betty Grable, but even sexier. Like Lana Turner."

I laughed and gave him a light punch on the arm. "What d'you know about dames, Rick? Now beat it. I'm busy."

Back to my cleanup of the secretary's desk. I glanced at the *Spec*'s front page – the good news: RATIONING OF COFFEE, SUGAR & BUTTER TO END THIS YEAR; the not-so-good news: REMOVAL OF WARTIME PRICE CONTROLS SENDS PRICES SOARING.

I riffled through the new mail. Bills for electricity, rent and office supplies. No cheques for services rendered. A full-colour flyer proclaimed: *COMING SOON The All New 1948 Studebaker Starlight Coupé: Manufactured Right Here in Hamilton*. I sighed as I pitched it into the wastebasket; I couldn't afford to replace my Model A Ford. In fact, I was just making ends meet on a disability pension from the government and a few new accounts I'd managed to acquire. And I retained the credit and background checks that Jeffries had serviced, but I planned to reduce the amount of that boring work in favour of more interesting cases. I hoped my new secretary would help me become more efficient and, maybe someday, make a profit.

In my own office, I retrieved the interview list for the morning, crossed off Miss Higgins' name with a shiver and glanced at the wall clock. Still oh-nine-thirty. I stroked off the next name as well ... the rebellious Miss Jones/Jaworski, a sweet kid. Maybe she'd stay in school but somehow I doubted she'd resist the tidal wave of hopeful excitement now flooding Hamilton after years of rationing and anxiety caused by the war.

Next on my list was Isabel O'Brien. What was that old saying? Bad luck comes in threes? Was it just an old wives' tale? That thought teased me when I heard a firm knock on the door and looked up to admire a striking redhead striding into my life. Her flaming hair, cut in a shoulder-length curl, contrasted with her green tailored suit, its skirt falling just below her knees, accentuating her hips. Nifty. She glided right through into my office and extended a velvety hand across the desk as I scrambled to my feet.

"Good morning," she said, giving my hand a firm shake. "You must be Max Dexter. I'm Isabel O'Brien, your new assistant."

Her dazzling smile pulled you right into her orbit. But what did she mean, she was my new assistant? She'd skipped over secretary and promoted herself already? My mind was spinning its wheels.

I was still standing, still shaking her hand, still mesmerized by her green eyes and the sprinkling of freckles across her nose, still deciding what to say, when she walked back to the outer office and returned with a small man dressed in a sombre three-piece suit, twirling a homburg in his left hand. Everything about his appearance, from his spit-shined shoes to his pencil-thin moustache, shouted I'm a successful man of commerce and I've no time to waste.

Isabel slid her arm through his and drew him closer to the desk. "Max, I'd like you to meet our new client, Mr. H. B. Myers."

Lord love a duck, now she's calling me Max. Everything about this dame knocked me off balance. I hadn't spoken a word to her yet and she's hired herself, promoted herself and brought in a new client, all in the space of two minutes.

I reached across the desk and shook Mr. Myers' hand as though I were the one in charge here. "Happy to meet you, Sir. Please have a seat."

Isabel relieved him of his hat. "I'll hold all your calls, Max, and see what's keeping the coffee."

My eyes widened but I gave her a brave smile. And I made a battlefield decision not to resist her superior firepower as she captured my unfortified office. So I said, "Thanks, Iz," and she strode out the door.

I turned my attention to Mr. Myers: a prissy little guy, taking care not to crease his tailored suit and sitting forward on the edge of his chair with an anxious-to-leave look on his pinched face. "I'm a busy man, Mr. Dexter; time is money, you know."

"Yes, Sir, and I'm eager to know how I can help so you can be on your way."

"Good, good." Then he explained that he owned a successful brokerage firm occupying an entire floor of the Pigott Building and he suspected one of his accountants of embezzling funds from his company.

"How much is missing?" I asked him.

He shrugged. "About fifty thousand."

I fought hard to keep my eyes from bugging out. Holy mackerel, fifty thousand! At a time when the average annual wage is about two thousand bucks, this banty little businessman mentions losing fifty grand as though he might be discussing his bar bill at the Hamilton Golf and Country Club. I swallowed my anger, or envy, or whatever I was feeling and soldiered on. "So ... What did the police say when you reported this?"

His pixie nose tilted upward. "Nothing. I didn't report it." Then he leaned forward, wagging a delicate finger. "And I don't intend to. You can imagine the loss of confidence this news might provoke among our customers. Large amounts of money are handled by my office, you see. And I'm in the business of selling trust in my company's ability to invest a customer's money for a satisfactory profit. So I want this problem solved on the q.t." Then he straightened in his chair and tugged on his monogrammed shirt cuffs, flashing his gold links.

A tap on the door announced Isabel's entrance. She set a tray on the corner of my desk, poured coffee from an insulated jug bearing the circular White Spot monogram and left without a word.

"Nice to see an efficient operation," Mr. Myers said. "Perhaps you'd be good enough to explain how you'd propose to solve my problem?"

I considered his question for a moment and tried to don my professional detective's face. "Alright. A number of things we can do right away. First of all, we'll learn all we can about your accountant – background checks, how he spends his free time, is he a gambler, for example, who his associates are, and other info which might be pertinent. Maybe do some surveillance or even place someone undercover in your accounting department."

"Only one problem with that," he said.

I waited.

"He's missing."

I took my time screwing the cap back onto my fountain pen and pushed aside the pad on which I'd been making notes. My chair squeaked as I rolled it back, and I gave my new client a hard look. I noticed a thin line of perspiration sprouting along his receding hairline, or maybe I only imagined the power of my hard look. In any case, he seemed like a smart guy, successful in business, and ten-to-one he lived in one of those mansions along Aberdeen Avenue. But, goddammit, the last thing he tells me is the first thing he should have told me. And it occurred to me, not for the first time, that this agency of mine would be a helluva good business if it weren't for the stupid customers.

"Since when?"

"Friday."

Hell, today was only Wednesday. Maybe the guy hadn't bothered to phone in sick. But with fifty thousand clams missing … I needed a break from this chowderhead before I jeopardized the transfer of some of his money into my account, especially now that it appeared I had an assistant on the payroll. "Alright, Mr. Myers. I've got another appointment in ten minutes," I lied. "Could we meet later today? I might be able to make some time this afternoon."

I limped to the door just as Isabel opened it. Did she have her eye to the keyhole? We exchanged an intense look and if I believed in thought transference, I'd have to say that it was happening right now.

She stepped toward my new client. "Here's your hat, Mr. Myers. I'll rearrange Mr. Dexter's schedule and contact your secretary."

He positioned the homburg on his noggin just so, and patted Isabel on the arm. "Thank you, my dear. You're a very charming young lady." And he left.

Back at my desk, I propped up my leg and Isabel settled into the visitor's chair. "Well," I said with a sigh.

She grinned, or was that a smirk? "Yes … that's what I was thinking."

"Looks like you're my new assistant. Even though I'd advertised for a secretary."

"Titles are so arbitrary, don't you find?" Her green eyes sparkled as she stood and gathered up some of the papers scattered over my desk. "My job is to do whatever needs to be done here. Let's not waste any more time talking about it, Max."

I stared at her for a moment. "Mr. Myers a friend of yours?"

"Don't be silly, Max. We met in the lobby, searching in vain for your name on the directory board. I asked that nice elevator operator and he brought us up together." She placed the tray with the coffee things on top of the stack of papers, lifted them both and headed for the door. Her red curls bounced on her shoulders as she turned her head and flashed me another hundred-watt grin. "I'll fix that directory now. And maybe you could give me a hand arranging the new office furniture after lunch."

She paused then, her eyebrows raised, and I realized this was a sort of test and she was waiting to see how I'd handle it. My first thought was that she needed a swift kick. Ordering new office furniture on her own hook went way beyond the responsibilities of an assistant, never mind a secretary. But then I weighed the pros and cons. On the plus side, she was direct and decisive. On the minus side, same damn thing – she was direct and decisive. If I wanted to make every little decision, I'd have to hire someone far less competent, and to hell with that.

"Okay, then," I said aloud. "After lunch we get the new furniture then figure out how to pay for it. Meantime I'm working on our new case."

She had the grace to look surprised. "But you're not meeting with Mr. Myers 'til this afternoon."

"Iz," I said, "waiting on the client makes for a slow game. But it's my guess that you already know that."

CHAPTER TWO

JUST BEFORE NOON I PHONED to arrange a quick lunch with my best source for insider info about Hamilton's High and Mighty and their latest shenanigans. Then I stepped from my office and tried to identify the faint odour tickling my nostrils. Isabel sat behind her desk, filing her nails. The desk's surface had been cleared and, on its corner, a yellow rose sprouted from a pint-size Royal Oak milk bottle.

I limped over and sniffed the rose. "Got a new admirer already?"

She gave me a too-sweet smile. "Young Rick from the news-paper office just dropped it off. Said he'd seen me entering the elevator and knew I'd be here."

I frowned. "And how'd he know that?"

"He said all the luscious babes go up to Max's office."

I shook my head and tried to look angry. "That little wiseass, I'll fix him later." Rick had a summer job as a gofer in *The Hamilton Spectator* office next door. I tipped him half a buck a week to deliver the early edition.

I settled my fedora on my head and snapped the brim. "I'm off to lunch with one of my contacts. Want me to bring you something?"

"Oh, no thanks, I had a word with Spiro at the White Spot Grill. Because you're such a good customer, Max, he said he'd be happy to have one of the busboys run something up."

The last time I'd asked Spiro to send a sandwich up to my office he'd told me to "Get stuffed".

"Okay," I said, "see ya."

A lively lunch-hour crowd jostled shoulder-to-shoulder along this stretch of King Street, which required us slower walkers to have sharper elbows. I paused in the doorway of the Laura Secord candy shop to catch my breath. My memories of dingy and bedraggled old Hamilton before the war collided with the scene before me now. You could feel the pulse of the new mood, what I imagined prisoners of war experienced after their release. These folks flooding the downtown streets seemed to exude a contagious optimism. I marvelled at the change but I felt a pang of bitterness as well. Didn't they know what we went through on the other side of the pond? The suffering, the dying, the indiscriminate destruction of so many lives on both sides of the battle lines? Or had they forgotten already?

I closed my eyes and inhaled several deep breaths. *It's over,* I told myself for the umpteenth time. *You're damn lucky to be able to start a new life. Get on with it.*

In the next block I stumbled into Duffy's Tavern and was struck blind until my eyes adjusted to the smoky gloom. After a moment, I spotted Scotty Lyle in a corner booth, making good progress on a rye and ginger. Scotty was a reporter for the *Spec*, good for me because he knew about everything in town. He was also my uncle – bad for me, because he was a pain in the ass.

"Want one?" He held up his drink and tinkled the ice cubes.

"Bit early for me, Scotty. Need my wits about me this afternoon." I slid into the booth opposite him and answered the quizzical look on his rosy face. "Got a new secretary and she's running rings around me."

He nodded like a guy well experienced with people trying to give *him* the runaround. Then he flagged down a waitress and we ordered steak sandwiches from the grill. Scotty held up his glass. "And you'd better bring me another of these, Sweetheart."

We made short work of our lunch. He pushed away his plate and leaned against the black leatherette cushion, firing up a Buckingham cigarette. "So what are y'after, Maxie? You said on the phone that you needed a little inside dope."

"That's right." Then I gave him the bare bones, didn't want to arouse his interest too much. "New client, guy named Myers. Runs a brokerage company in his own name, offices up there in the Pigott Building and says he's got an internal problem. I just wondered if the *Spec* had any background stuff on him, maybe something that wouldn't have appeared in the paper."

Scotty Lyle had a well-earned reputation as the best investigative reporter in this town. He'd won some kind of newspaper award for his coverage of last year's infamous Evelyn Dick murder case. So in a way, I was lucky he'd married my Aunt Flo, if you discounted the problems his boozing caused her.

I'd seen a tiny flicker in his eyes when I'd mentioned Myers' name and I wondered if I'd touched a nerve. But he seemed relaxed now as he puffed on his cigarette. "Nothin' I can think of offhand," he said. "He's a big name on the society pages, serves on the boards of charitable organizations, the Art Gallery and what not. Why d'you wanna know? What'd he do to make you suspicious?"

"Well, not quite suspicious, there's just something about him. Besides being a supercilious little bugger."

"Su-per-cil-i-ous." Scotty drawled out the word, smirking. "Quite a few syllables for a private dick."

I sighed but kept my lip buttoned. As my old CO used to say, "You'll never lose your stripes if you learn when to shut up."

Scotty gave me a thump on the arm. "Okay, I'll snoop around, let you know."

I left enough money to cover the tab and shook his beefy hand. "Thanks, Unc, I'll hear from you."

When I stepped from Duffy's onto King Street the harsh sunlight hit me flush in the face and I stumbled against the doorway before getting my bearings.

"Too many martinis for lunch, eh, Sarge?"

I stopped to search the throng of office workers scurrying back from lunch, but I didn't recognize anyone who might've spoken to me.

I felt a tug at my pant leg and glanced down to find Bob, seated on his battered, four-wheeled dolly, selling his pencils, a tired army cap resting on his unkempt hair. The sight of his legless body gave me a guilty jolt – my God, that could have been me. Strike me down, I thought, if I ever complain about this limp.

Bob's grin suggested he'd caught me acting like a sergeant who'd spent a liquid lunch hour in the Legion bar.

I said, "You're a low-level comedian, Bob." And I laughed along with him, knowing I'd never have Bob's courage to smile at the busted hand life had dealt him. "But I did want to talk to you. Still living with your sister in that little place behind the cleaners on James North?"

"Sure, Sarge. Whadidya think, I moved inta the Pasadena Apartments?"

"Well, I might have a bit of work for you and Aggie. You could still use a few extra bucks, right?"

He rattled the White Owl cigar box where he kept his money and grinned up at me. "We're open for business, Sarge."

"Good." I squeezed his shoulder. "Maybe I'll drop by later this week and we'll talk about it."

I returned to my building but thought I'd gotten off the elevator on the wrong floor. Two gorillas wearing Eaton's shirts manhandled a green three-seater sofa through the doorway of my office. I followed them in and found Isabel, hands on hips, directing them to the vacant spot in front of the window. Hell's bells! This furniture looked pretty damned expensive. How could she have mistaken me for Daddy Warbucks?

"Perfect. That's just right." She was laying it on with a butter knife. "You boys could win the Strongest Man in Canada contest at the CNE."

They straightened and beamed at her, lapping up her attention like thirsty puppies. She caught my eye as I stood in the doorway, mouth half open, and she winked. "Here's the big boss now, Boys. I'm sure he appreciates all the work you've saved him, right Max?"

I was a good sport and went along with her, clapped the apes on the back with thanks and even helped them out the door with the empty cartons and wrapping material. When I offered them a couple of bucks as a tip, the bigger guy held up a callused mitt. "No, no, Mister, the little lady's smile is thanks enough."

Then the other bruiser chimed in. "And the Salvation Army will be happy as hell to get all this old junk we're luggin' outta here."

I shook my head and limped across to my new sofa, sat on the corner cushion and hoisted up my leg, surveying the office. It wasn't as fancy as the stuff in Eaton's display windows along James Street, but damn near. In front of the sofa sat a glass-topped coffee table with brushed chrome legs and, at either end, matching green armchairs. The two end tables held chrome-based lamps with green shades. Current issues of *The Saturday Evening Post*, *Life* and *Liberty* magazines fanned out beside a chromium ashtray the size of a manhole cover.

Isabel sashayed over to an armchair, kicked off her black pumps and settled herself, propping her well-shaped, nyloned feet on the coffee table. "So," she said.

"Sew buttons," I said, trying not to stare at her legs, keeping my guard up lest I become as bewitched by her charms as those mutts from Eaton's. "We need more magazines."

She blinked. "Why?"

"When you look through the glass top of the table, the crappy-looking carpeting is too obvious."

"Saturday. If there's someone here to let them in."

I almost asked what she meant, then closed my mouth and nodded. I swung my leg onto the floor and sat forward, getting her full attention. "Isabel," my voice serious and subdued, "I admire your ambition and your confidence. But I can't afford these new furnishings."

"Oh, but you can, Max. Eaton's has a terrific credit plan and you're qualified for a Veteran's loan at the bank."

"But I hate owing money."

She flipped a page in her notebook. "Speaking of money, Max, you don't charge enough. Why, your rates are the same as old Jeffries charged before the war. Do you have any idea how much the rent on this office has gone up since then?"

I shook my head.

"For crying out loud, Max, this office is smack dab in the centre of one of the hottest real estate markets in Ontario. If you don't start charging more, paying for furniture is going to be the least of your worries."

No doubt she was right, but business management wasn't my strong suit and I began to fidget.

She checked her watch. "Let's talk about this later. Mr. Myers called to reschedule your appointment. If you hurry, you'll be right on time." Then she folded a standard contract form and slipped it into an envelope. "Don't forget to have him sign it, Max. He agreed on the phone to the new daily rate."

I stood and pocketed the envelope but not before checking the contents. "Good grief, damn good thing he didn't know the old rate."

"He says it's well worth it and he's anxious to start right away. So goodbye, Max."

I walked up King Street and cut through Gore Park where the old guys dozed on the benches and fended off the pigeons. I side-stepped the splashing kids running through the spray of the elegant old fountain. From here I could see the Pigott Building, the city's one and only skyscraper just a half-block south on James, its art-deco features glistening in the afternoon sun as though reflecting the silver that was mined in its offices. Myers must have a helluva business, I thought, to occupy an entire floor there.

The sun's rays through the stained glass panels at the entrance glinted off the polished marble of the lobby as I passed from the noisy traffic on James Street into the reverential hush of this High Church of Capital. I crossed to the bank of brass-doored elevators and rode in style to the swankiest floor in the building. A Hollywood receptionist was tickled pink to direct me to Mr. Myers' suite, where her twin sister took me by the arm and guided me to the inner sanctum. There was a slight odour in the vast room, maybe incense, and I had to restrain myself from genuflecting.

"Nice to see you again, Mr. Dexter." Myers reached across a half-acre of rosewood desk and squeezed my hand as though he were rescuing me from Burlington Bay. I didn't wince but almost bit my tongue during his I'll-show-you-who's-boss handshake. I sat in one of the red leather visitor chairs and he hoisted himself back onto his high-backed executive's throne.

"I've already explained how sensitive this situation is," Myers said. "That's why you're reporting to me and to no one else." He handed me a thin file folder. "Here's young Benson's personnel record. My secretary has included a few other details provided by the manager of the accounting department. Any news of this scandal could be a big setback for my business, undermine customer confidence. So I want you to find Benson pronto."

I leafed through the file. Just what you'd expect to find: basic details such as name, address, date of birth and so on. But listed under "Next of Kin" was "Estate", not a parent or other relative. Unusual, perhaps, and I made a note to check it. Also included were details of his educational background, a copy of his university transcript and accounting qualifications. Then I found several performance reviews, the latest dated this year, and all rated Benson's work as fully satisfactory, duly signed by his manager. "Mr. Benson's been missing since last Friday?"

"He was at work on Thursday. Missed Friday and again Monday and Tuesday of this week."

"Well, maybe he's just sick. Anyone try to contact him?"

A twitch of his tiny moustache, and his lip curled. "Well, of course," he said. "His manager called his apartment but couldn't reach him."

I gave him a moment to cool down. "His fellow workers are in the dark, too?"

"That's correct." His tone less challenging now.

"When did you discover the embezzlement?"

Myers fiddled with his gold fountain pen, sliding it end for end between his dainty fingers. "After our annual audit a few weeks ago, certain ... discrepancies appeared. An internal investigation led us to suspect Benson of diverting funds from customer accounts." He set down his pen and folded his hands on the desk. "When his manager questioned him, Benson became upset, angry, and he denied everything. Now he's disappeared." He'd taken up his fountain pen again and was pointing it at me. "Only a guilty man would do that, Mr. Dexter."

I frowned at the pen aimed at my chest and wondered if he was trying too hard to convince me. "I'll need to start by interviewing your accounting manager," I said.

"Of course. He's on standby." He stroked his moustache. "But I'd like you to keep the actual theft confidential from the rest of the staff and just treat this as a missing person case."

I nodded and rose to leave, removed the contract from my jacket pocket and handed it to him. He scanned it, signed it, kept one copy for himself and passed the other back to me. Didn't even blink at my new daily rate. We shook hands and I surprised him with a bone-crusher of my own before he walked me to his office door and clapped me on the back.

"One last thing, Mr. Dexter. Wrap this job up in a week and I'll double your fee."

Jeez, I could do with more clients like this one. I touched my forehead in a mock salute and his secretary ushered me down the hall to meet the accounting manager.

Ken Thompson was a pale imitation of his boss. He too wore an expensive black business suit but the extra pounds he carried strained to escape its seams. Nor, despite being taller, did he have Myers' military bearing and brisk, efficient manner. Even his copycat pencil moustache needed sharpening. He explained that Benson was a smart young chartered accountant, hired six years ago straight from university, who showed great promise of a brilliant career. His embezzlement of fifty thousand bucks had been a shocking surprise. The company had since revised its procedures so that a similar redirection of funds was impossible, he said. And, no, he had no idea where Benson may have fled.

I was beginning to wonder whether he'd fled at all. Perhaps there was a logical explanation for his absence from work. A family emergency, for example. Or he'd taken off on a weekend toot. So far I'd only spoken with Myers and his oversized shadow, both of whom had tagged Benson with the theft. I had no reason to doubt either one of them but in this business you became suspicious of everyone.

"What do Mr. Benson's co-workers have to say about his disappearance?" I asked him.

"I spoke to everyone in his section. They're as dumbfounded as I am. He never misses a day of work."

"Could I have a list of their names?"

"Of course. My secretary will send it to your office right away."

I opened Benson's personnel file which Myers had given me and remembered there was no next of kin listed. "Do you know anything about his family situation?"

Thompson pondered for a moment. "No, I'm afraid not. He's a very private individual."

"Well, something doesn't add up here, Mr. Thompson. Seems out of character that a clever young guy with a bright future in a successful company would commit such a risky crime. And according to his performance reviews, he's a model employee. So why do you think he became an embezzler?"

Thompson stood up and rearranged his jacket over his protruding belly. "I don't know, Mr. Dexter. That's why you were hired."

He led me over to the door and lowered his voice. "Mr. Myers would be very upset if this matter became public knowledge. No one else knows about the theft … and that's the way he wants to keep it. Just find Benson and we'll take it from there."

I left his office and since it was near the end of the business day, I decided to continue my interviews here tomorrow.

On my way back to my office I rested my leg on a bench in Gore Park; my mind was spinning and I let it go. I imagined Benson tickling his toes in the white sands of a Cuban beach, a couple of Latin Lovelies lighting his El Producto. Then gambling the night away in a swish Havana casino. No, it didn't seem probable, but after ten years in police work, I'd learned to accept that even the most unlikely people can do the damnedest things.

Then I tried to make sense of what I'd heard from Myers and his chubby manager. They claimed that knowledge of the embezzlement would damage the trust their clients placed in the company. Probably true. But was that Myers' only reason for offering me such a generous bonus?

"Oh, shit!" said a distinguished-looking gent in a dark suit. He'd been walking with a companion along the sidewalk bordering Gore Park. Holding his fedora at arm's length, he inspected the liquid splotches dripping from its brim. His nostrils quivering, he glared at the flock of pigeons fluttering beside him as if he could identify the bombardier.

"That's exactly what it is," said his partner, hiding a smile.

A group of the regular benchwarmers gathered to applaud the victim of this daily occurrence. A grizzled First War vet, his left arm missing, medals pinned to his tattered jacket, shouted at him. "Ya'd better change yer wicked ways, Commander, that's a sign from above." And a chorus of guffaws went up from his pals.

I laughed along with the old-timers as the pair of businessmen strode off toward the Hamilton Club, where, no doubt, an attendant would repair the damage from the bombing raid.

The old guy's taunt made me wonder whether my interviews with Benson's associates might reveal if the missing accountant had any wicked ways. I rose from the bench and stretched. It was only a three-block detour to Benson's apartment building. What the hell, my leg needed the exercise.

CHAPTER THREE

WHEN I ARRIVED AT JAKE Benson's apartment on Hess Street, I'd broken into a sweat and my gimpy leg complained. While catching my breath, I surveyed the two-storey building, its brick walls blackened over the years by Hamilton's smoke-laden air. Through the smudged glass panel in the entrance door I spotted a balding guy in work clothes and tool belt kneeling on the floor of the cramped lobby, studying the unassembled parts of a locking mechanism. I tapped on the glass and he held up his hand.

He opened the door by sticking two fingers through the hole where the lock had been removed. "Watch where you step, Bud," he said. "Don't wanna mess up these pieces, eh?"

I tiptoed around the jigsaw puzzle and stood out of the way. "You the super? I'm looking for Mr. Benson's apartment."

He stepped toward me, leading with his chin. "Yeah. Whaddya want him for? You a bill collector?"

"Hell, no. A friend of a friend. Seen him around today?"

He continued inspecting me, then shrugged and leaned against the wall, the lines deepening along his forehead. "Ain't seen him for a few days," he said.

"Is that unusual?"

"Kinda. I see him comin' and goin' most days. Quiet guy. But always says hello. Got no answer when I knocked on his door."

"Did you enter his apartment?"

"No reason to. Maybe on a trip or somethin'." He sharpened his gaze. "See here, Mister, what're ya really after?"

I decided to come clean. "He hasn't shown up for work since Thursday. I'm looking into it. Why don't we check his apartment? See if he might be there."

He grimaced and rubbed his unshaved chin. "Jeez. Don't think I could do that. He ain't been gone that long. And I don't even know you."

I passed him my card and he studied it. "A private dick?" he said. His shoulders relaxed when I grinned.

"How about this?" I said, the friendly detective, trying to be helpful. "Just take a quick look in his place. See if he might've had an accident. Slipped in the tub, maybe. What d'you say?"

The gears clanked in his brain as he stroked his whiskers again. "Okay. But you stay here. I'll be right back."

A few minutes later he clumped back along the linoleumed hallway and shook his head with a smirk. "Told ya the place was empty. Now I gotta get back to work. Take a hike, Mister."

Well, at least I'd tried.

When I returned to the office, I found Isabel seated at her desk, brow furrowed in concentration as she pored over a stack of ledgers and other financial records. A long table, which I hadn't seen before, also displayed a number of open files and reports. She hadn't noticed me enter and now looked up in surprise. "Oh, hello, Max. I'm calculating."

"Not many women would admit to that."

She gave me a wry grin. "Funny." Then she motioned her red curls toward my office. "Why don't you work at your desk now? I need another half hour here, then we should discuss your business affairs."

I groaned and rolled my eyes. "It's after five; you don't want to overdo it on your first day."

"And how long do you usually stay?"

"Until the work's finished."

"Right. Half an hour." She continued fingering the ancient IBM adding machine and cranking its lever. "And by the way," she called after me. "I know you won't believe it, but they're actually electrifying some of these business machines nowadays."

A message on my desk said Scotty Lyle had phoned so I called him back at the *Spec*.

"Did some digging for you, Max," he said. "But not a lot to report, I'm afraid. Like I said before, your man Myers is what the politicians call 'A Pillar of the Community'. One of those rich guys who contributes to all the right causes and greases the palms where it'll do him the most good."

"Sounds like your kind of guy," I said.

Scotty humphed. "Yeah, well, I don't trust any of that country club set. Think their shit don't stink."

I smiled to myself, well aware of my uncle's lifelong support of the rights of the working man, what he called the downtrodden and shat-upon. I decided to give his cage a little rattle, even though I agreed with him. "So I guess Myers didn't support the picketers during the Steel Company strike last year?"

He sputtered into the phone and nearly choked; I could imagine his already red face blooming into full flame. "Now don't get me going, Laddie. You know damn well those strikers were being screwed for years by their greedy bosses – guys just like your friend Myers."

I waited a moment while he cooled down. "Any thing else, Unc?"

I heard him snort then blow his nose. "No," he said and cleared his throat, taking his time before he continued. "Well, there is a story I've been digging into for the past year. And so far I've been stymied. It could turn out to be quite the scandal – and it wouldn't surprise me if Myers' name popped up."

I puzzled over that for a moment, wondering what he meant by "quite the scandal", but when I pressed him he clammed up. I figured I'd learn about it sooner or later because he loved to dangle such tidbits in front of me, hoping to get the better of my curiosity.

"Okay," I said. "Thanks for your call," and hung up the phone. For the life of me, I couldn't quite fit the words 'scandal' and 'Myers' into the same sentence, and concluded that Scotty was off on another of his crusades. If I'd had a salt shaker handy, I would've taken a grain.

I opened the file for H. B. Myers Investments Ltd. and began writing up my notes of this afternoon's interviews. Paperwork. How I loved it. It was a relief when Isabel backed through my doorway with her arms full of ledgers and dumped them on the desk.

"You're in better shape than I thought you were, Max."

I stifled a smart remark.

She drew up a chair and sat beside me. "I've been trying to reconcile your accounts receivable with your overhead and other liabilities. With my help, I think you might survive."

"Good to know."

"But your bookkeeping system is outdated; your financial planning is non-existent and most of your receivables are ninety days or older."

I smiled at her and leaned back in my chair. "Care to repeat that in English?"

She tapped my hand. "You need me to organize your business."

"Last time I looked, you were organizing my whole damn life."

She ignored my grin and pushed on. "I made a reservation across the street for an early dinner. Let's go, we don't want to be late."

By the time I'd opened my mouth to object, she'd gathered her things and bustled out of my office. And was that a smirk on her face?

CHAPTER FOUR

WE CROSSED KING STREET AT the corner of John and used the side entrance to the classy Royal Connaught Hotel, not my usual hangout since the prices were way above my pay grade. In the main dining room, my what's-going-on antenna sprang to attention when the maitre d' made a beeline for us and greeted Isabel by name. He guided us to a corner table where a waiter stood at the ready. Classical music soothed from hidden speakers.

"I only come here on special occasions," I said, trying for nonchalance.

She winked. "My treat."

The waiter brought us two martinis, took our dinner order and disappeared. Isabel leaned toward me and lowered her voice. "I guess I should tell you the truth."

"I was hoping you might," I whispered back.

She took a dainty sip of her drink and set it down. "Where to begin ..."

"How about not being a secretary?"

"Yes, I thought you might have noticed." And after a languorous sigh, "It's a long story."

"This *is* an early dinner," I reminded her.

She traced a finger along the condensation on her chilled martini glass. "Once upon a time, my father was desperate to have his son become managing partner at O'Brien Associates, Chartered Accountants. To carry on the family tradition." She took another sip. "But he didn't have a son."

"Aha."

"So he sent his only daughter to the University of Toronto for a degree in commerce. Then she followed the required program to become a Chartered Accountant and joined O'Brien Associates."

I saw the sadness in her green eyes and said, "I guess she didn't enjoy her work at Dad's place."

Her brow creased as she stared into her drink, perhaps deciding how much of her private life to reveal. "She tried her best to please her father but he's not a man who takes women seriously. And when the time comes, I don't believe he could trust a woman to take over the family business."

"A definite drawback."

"Yes, but not as serious as the other problem."

I widened my eyes and waited.

Her mood perked up and a smile played across her lips. "The practice of accounting bored her to tears."

I returned her smile and she seemed to relax.

"So last week I announced my resignation from O'Brien Associates," she said. "And today I joined Max Dexter Associates."

My admiration of her decisive manner collided with my fear of being flattened by her steamroller style and I couldn't hide the panicky spin behind my eyes. She was like a whirling dervish buzzing through my life, discovering decisions that needed to be taken ... and taking them. And so far, I liked it. Except when I didn't like it. What the hell was wrong with me? I grinned at the movie playing in my head: Isabel locked in a titanic struggle with her forceful father, no doubt another impulsive decision-maker. An action film in which I played the part of innocent bystander.

She tapped me on the wrist. "By the way, Max, the building superintendent is sending up a sign painter tomorrow, to redo the lettering on your office door."

Just then the comforting aroma of Sunday-dinner-at-home-with-the-family enveloped us as the waiter served our prime rib. We enjoyed it for a while in silence.

"I'm wondering," I said, "what possible benefit the O'Brien Associates' heiress would get from joining Max Dexter Associates?"

Her features tightened. "First of all, she wouldn't have to spend all her waking hours with greedy men who think only of profits, capital acquisitions and their pals in the old boys' network."

"Not to mention receivables ninety days or older."

"Those too." She nodded at me, perhaps surprised I'd been listening before. "And in return for the services of a first-class chartered accountant to reorganize and manage the operations of Max Dexter Associates ..."

"I can't wait for this."

"I'd like to do something more interesting. And maybe more useful as well." She leaned toward me, setting aside the spray of fresh flowers between us, and whispered, "I'd like to become a detective."

Our eyes locked and we didn't speak for a long moment.

"It's a deal," I finally said. "On one condition."

She blinked. The first time I'd seen the beautiful accountant even a bit off balance.

The waiter cleared our table and brought us coffee. "Well?" Her eyebrows did a little dance.

"I guess I also have a story to tell."

"It's *still* an early dinner," she said.

I shifted in my chair and stretched out my gimpy leg. "Once upon a time, my father hoped his only son would serve with him on the Hamilton police force. But he was involved in a shootout during a raid on a bootlegging joint on the Beach Strip and one of Rocco Perri's gangsters killed him."

Her jaw clenched and she fiddled with her coffee cup. "That big Mafia guy, Max? What'd they call him, the king ...?"

"That's right. King of the Bootleggers." But at home my old man called him the king of the bastards. And later ... well, that was later. "Anyway, as soon as his son graduated from Central High he joined the RCMP, moved out west and never wanted to see Hamilton again."

"What about his poor mother?"

"A mystery. Rumours hinted she might have been associated with one of Perri's gang members. Then after the ... my father's funeral, she moved to Florida and hasn't been heard from since."

Her eyes blinked wider, a shiny green now, and she rocked back, almost spilling her coffee. "Oh, no, Max. I'm so sorry."

I shrugged and charged my batteries with a jolt of the strong coffee. "A few years later, the son was transferred to RCMP head-quarters in Toronto. Then, in a fit of patriotic fever, he joined the newly-formed Provost Corps in 1939 and spent the war years overseas as an MP."

"And was that where he acquired his limp, Max?"

Memories I always kept under lock and key fought to escape. That battle. Those senseless deaths. The leg I almost lost. Even now, those vivid images continued to haunt me – splintered bones protruding through my torn flesh, my blood spurting out ... and the terrifying certainty that I was about to die.

Those were painful events I never spoke about. But the plead-ing in Isabel's eyes urged me to get a grip and continue. "Military Police don't have a lot of the usual crimes to contend with dur-ing wartime. Sure, there are always some thefts and assaults. Bringing drunken soldiers back to the base and pacifying the local population. And lots of irate parents claiming Canuck ser-vicemen had taken advantage of their innocent daughters and were responsible for their pregnancies."

I drew a deep breath, lost for a moment in a swirling memory of confusion, cordite and corpses. I flinched when I noticed the waiter had returned; he refilled our cups and placed a silver tray of after-dinner mints between us.

When he left, I continued. "At the battlefront, MPs are responsible for traffic control and co-ordination behind the lines ... you can imagine the shemozzle during the Normandy inva-sion when tanks and support units began piling up on those nar-row country roads in France." My knee began to throb as the memories flooded back. "It was as if you were the only traffic cop in Times Square after the New Year's Eve celebration and you'd lost your voice and your whistle. Throw in the constant bom-bardment by the Kraut artillery and you get the picture."

"And that's when it happened?"

I massaged the twinge in my leg, almost losing my nerve to carry on. "We were trying to clear a backup of supply convoys when an incoming round smacked into an ammo carrier. The explosion took out a dozen soldiers and most of them died. When I awoke in hospital back in England, two doctors were debating about amputating my leg. That's a conversation you don't want to hear."

Iz's eyes were too bright and I felt myself blinking back the emotion for both of us. "But I made it," I said, trying to sound upbeat. "After three operations, I spent another year in a rehab facility and didn't make it back to Canada until late in '45."

She reached for my hand. "And I'm glad you're here, Max."

She focused her complete attention upon me, as welcome as a warm towel after a dip in Lake Ontario. I was glad I was here, too. "I didn't mean to burden you with the story of my life, but you have to understand why my puny little business is so important to me."

"Tell me."

"My leg wasn't healing properly so I needed another operation and more rehab in Toronto when I returned. After my discharge there, I tried to rejoin the Mounties but my disability got in the way. Then I decided I'd come back to Hamilton where I still had some friends, but the local force rejected me too. So this small agency, which you've christened Max Dexter Associates, is my last chance to remain in law enforcement work. I know it sounds corny, but ever since my dad's death I've wanted to ... follow in the family tradition, I guess you'd say."

"You mean you want to avenge his murder?"

"No, no, not like that. But it's ... Well, maybe there's something worthwhile, or *just*, in serving the cause of law and order."

What was I doing? I'd only known this woman a short while and here I was telling her things I didn't discuss with my best friend. I took refuge behind my coffee cup and tried to figure it out. It must've been those green eyes which seemed to glow as they gazed into my soul, drawing out my most private thoughts. What the hell was happening to me? Could she be in league with the devil?

"Jeez," I said, "listen to me. I must sound like the Lone Ranger after rounding up the bad guys and throwing them in the hoosegow."

"No, Max, you don't," she said. "Now tell me your one condition. About me becoming a detective, I mean."

"Alright. It's this – I'm the boss. And my business will operate on my principles or it won't operate. I'm not interested in becoming rich or having a fancy office in the Pigott Building. I have a few friends, most of them veterans, who could use some work and I intend to help them, too."

I could see she wanted to say something but she bit her lip and waited me out.

"Much of this work is boring and tedious ... stakeouts are the worst. But for me, it's the best job in the world. People never fail to surprise you and there's a new challenge every day. And my life would be even better if you managed the agency's business affairs." I sent her an assessing stare. "So, if you're willing to respect the direction I've chosen for Max Dexter Associates, then I'd be happy to train you."

She exhaled with a puff and her shoulders relaxed.

"What do you say to a six-month trial period?" I asked her.

She grinned and said, "Hi-ho, Silver," and reached across the table to shake my hand.

At that moment, the waiter appeared and placed a red leather folder containing the bill between us. He glanced at me with a challenging twinkle in his eye.

Isabel snatched it first. "I'll sign for it," she said.

"Wait a minute, at least let me cover the tip." I reached for my wallet, giving the waiter a closer inspection. "What's your name?" I said.

"Longo, Sarge."

I racked my brain but couldn't place him. "You know me, huh?"

"You arrested me in England, Sarge," he said. "I got thirty days."

Iz raised an eyebrow.

"Oh," I said, "did you deserve it?"

"Well, I was guilty of liberating that truckload of boots you caught me with. But the day before, I snagged another truckload of booze and canned hams and boxes of biscuits destined for the officers' mess and you never heard a peep about it."

He took a half-step back, his face brighter than the trees in Gore Park at Christmastime, and I couldn't help grinning back.

I did remember him now. He wasn't a bad guy, so long as you understood that he'd take anything that wasn't nailed down. I also knew that he'd stolen loads of food rations – selling them to the natives had been his bread and butter, so to speak, but he'd also made a habit of giving away some of the rations to the street kids. No, not a bad guy at all. Of course, if the Connaught ever hired me to investigate mysterious disappearances, I knew where I'd start looking.

I got up and scooted over to hold Isabel's chair.

Longo bowed to her. "Nice to see you again, Miss O'Brien."

As we made to leave, he tapped me on the shoulder. "Ah, did you forget the tip, Sarge?"

"Nope ... can't tip a thief, Longo. But you're a helluva good waiter. And I'd like to talk to you later about doing a little work for me."

I heard him chuckling behind us as we walked from the dining room, the maitre d' bowing to the heiress and her limping companion. At the front entrance on King Street the doorman waved in the direction of the taxi stand. Isabel slid onto the rear seat of a Veterans cab and I closed the door and leaned through the open window.

"Thanks for everything, Iz. You might've guessed that I don't make a habit of talking about myself. Feels good once in a while."

She gave me a mock-stern look. "Now, if I could only get you to talk about your business affairs." Then she smiled. "You won't be able to put me off tomorrow, Max."

I watched the cab pull away then re-entered the Connaught. The dining room wasn't busy tonight and I caught Longo's eye as he moved like a silent shadow between the tables toward me. He was well placed here to be my eyes and ears when the occasion arose and I was certain we could come to terms.

CHAPTER FIVE

ON THE RIDE UP TO my office next morning, the diminutive elevator operator said, "She's already here. Arrived at oh-seven-thirty."

"Yeah, Tiny, she's keen as mustard. Hard to stay a step ahead," and I wiggled my gimpy knee.

"*Semper Paratus*," he said with a grin, citing the motto of his regiment, the Royal Hamilton Light Infantry, known locally as the Rileys. Then he passed me an envelope, "Johnson's timetable."

"Thanks." I tucked it away. "Maybe you could keep track of his visitors until the end of the week. And that should wrap up this case."

He tugged my sleeve and lowered his voice. "Word to the wise, Sarge. New tenants on the floor above you. Look like Japs so I'm keepin' an eye on them too."

I entered my office and flipped my hat onto the file cabinet, the sharpness of Spiro's coffee filling the room. My new assistant was up to her elbows in ledgers and tax returns and looked up to give me a brief smile. "As soon as you've had your coffee, Max, we can analyse–"

I extended my hand in a traffic-cop signal. "Hold your horses, Iz. I'm heading back to Myers' office this morning to interview some of Benson's co-workers. Maybe we could look at this guff later."

She wrinkled her brow and shook her red curls. "It's not just guff, Max. You have to help me decipher some of these mysterious entries so I can understand your operations."

"I agree it's important," I said. "But while I'm out, I'd like you to call Vera – here's her number – and review this list of credit checks she's doing for us. Oh, and ask her to start looking into Jake Benson, would you? Tell her there'll be more names later."

Her green eyes flicked between me and the page I'd handed to her before she placed it on her desk. Then she pursed her lips, tapping a ledger. "Would Vera be the V. Evans shown on your so-called payroll records?"

"Yep."

"Any relation to the P. Evans on the following line?"

"Phyllis is her daughter. She types up Vera's reports and my correspondence."

She gave me a semi-tolerant accountant's smile. "Are they hiding in your closet, Max? Or do you have another office I don't know about yet?"

I limped toward my desk, bridling at her implied criticism of my unorthodox bookkeeping methods. "Let's talk about this after lunch, Miss O'Brien." Then I stuffed my notes into my well-worn briefcase and hustled over to the Pigott Building to meet Walter Potts, one of Benson's co-workers.

Potts' office took up less floor space than Myers' desk. Filing cabinets lined two walls and an ancient Chubb floor safe occupied one corner, its massive door ajar. At a narrow table a thin pale guy who looked like Bob Cratchit worried over columns of figures in an oversized ledger. I tapped again on his open door and he peered over the top of his glasses.

"Oh, my," he said and jumped up from his chair, knocking it over. Red-faced, he righted it, shook my hand and pointed to an empty visitor's chair, which I guessed he'd just cleared of the files stacked on the floor beside it. "You must be Mr. Dexter. I was told you'd come to see me, but I'm afraid I can't help you much."

I sat and gave him my low-wattage cop's stare, not wanting to scare the pants off him. "But I haven't asked you anything yet, Mr. Potts. You're not hiding something, are you?"

"No, no, no." His eyes bugged from their sockets and his hands fluttered like falling leaves. "Jake Benson has the office next door but I don't know him well at all. We exchange small talk every day but nothing very personal. I just can't believe that he might be missing. I'm sure it's a misunderstanding."

I nodded and toned down my stare. Bob Cratchit wouldn't tell a lie and I didn't believe that Potts would either. "Okay, Mr. Potts. Any idea how Mr. Benson spends his time away from the office?"

He shook his light bulb head, calmer now. "No, Sir, we never discussed it. But the secretaries like to speculate about that because he's such a private man. In fact, one of them told me he's a jazz fan and often goes to the downtown clubs."

"Which one told you that?"

"I think it was Miss Arneson. The blonde girl at the end of this hallway."

Nothing more to interest me here, I was sure of it. This guy wouldn't say boo to a bedbug. I stood and shook his hand. "Thanks, Mr. Potts. I won't bother you anymore."

His eyes spoke his relief that I was finished and he dove back into his ledger.

I consulted the next name on my list. Two doors down, the sign on the door read C. N. Cysko, and I peeked into the office. Empty. In search of his whereabouts, I limped to the opposite end of the floor where the carpeting was plusher, the office suites were the size of backyards and the secretaries looked like *Vogue* models.

Outside Myers' office, his statuesque secretary was bent over a low cabinet replacing some red file folders. An impressive welcoming sight, even though she hadn't intended it.

"Knock, knock," I said.

She didn't interrupt her filing or look around. "Amscray, Kid," she said. "Go bother someone else with your stupid knock-knock jokes."

I noted the engraved plaque on her desk. "Morning, Miss Carlson. Sorry to disturb you."

She straightened and turned in slow motion, allowing me the full panoramic view. "Oh, hi there, Mr. Dexter. I'm terribly sorry," she said and I think she was blushing. "But I thought you were Chuck Cysko. How can I help you?"

"In fact, I'm looking for Mr. Cysko. He's not in his office. Maybe you could locate him for me."

"Of course." She picked up her phone and dialled a couple of numbers. "Hi, Doris, it's Veronica. Did Chuck Cysko call in yet?" After a brief conversation she hung up and said, "He just arrived." Then she studied me for a moment and continued, "You should understand that Chuck's a bit of a free spirit. He hasn't quite adapted to the H. B. Myers culture."

I thanked her and before I could leave she rounded her desk and slid a business card into my shirt pocket, holding her hand tight against my chest. If she were checking my heart rate she didn't seem surprised to feel it beating at double time.

For a moment I thought she must be speaking in Braille, but then I heard her sultry voice. "That's my private number, if you need anything else."

My mouth was too dry to respond so I mustered a smile and retreated to Cysko's office. He was sprawled in his chair, hands locked behind his full head of curly hair, size twelve brogues parked across the corner of his desk, whispering into the receiver wedged between his shoulder and his ear. When he spotted me in his doorway, he said, "I'll call you later, Honey," and hung up with a bang. Then he sprang upright, all six-feet-plus of him, came around his desk in a cloud of Gillette aftershave and, with a big grin, gave me a wrestler's handshake. "Chuck Cysko," a voice to wake the dead, maybe thinking I was deaf. "Sorry to miss you earlier. Have a seat."

"Thanks for meeting with me, Mr. Cysko." I chose the chair furthest from him, hoping to protect my ears. "I'd like you to tell me what you can about your neighbour – Mr. Benson."

"Hey, call me Chuck. In fact, you can call me anything but Kid." Then he laughed until he broke into a sweat and his face turned crimson. "Pretty funny, eh? Kid. Get it? The Cysko Kid."

When I didn't laugh, his expression pained. What the hell was wrong with this guy? He was trying so hard to win my friendship that I was afraid if I gave him a hint of encouragement he might try to kiss me. "Mr. Benson," I said. "Along the hall ... do you know him well?"

He settled down and shook the lion's mane on his head. "No. No, I don't. God knows I tried to be friends with him but he's a wet blanket. Just like some of these old farts around here. They don't know how to have a good time."

I recalled Myers' secretary saying this guy hadn't adapted to the culture here and I doubted he ever would. "Alright," I said. "Do you happen to know what Mr. Benson does after office hours? Girlfriends, sports, that type of thing?"

Another head shake, big clumsy movements like a bear at a scratching post. "Don't know a damn thing about him. Invited him out after work a few times, but no dice, maybe he thought I'd try to jew him out of a few drinks. Hell, I even tried to set him up with Doris Arneson down the hall but he didn't show up."

"Just a shy guy, do you think? Or is he not attracted to women?"

Cysko leaped up as if he'd been bitten on his backside and waved a sausage-sized finger at me. "Now just one minute there, Pal, I don't like what you're insinuating here. You saying that him and me ... that we're some kind of ... you know ... fruitcake couple?"

I almost laughed in his face. Miss Carlson had also said Cysko was a free spirit. But I think you could make a good case that he shouldn't be free much longer.

I slipped my unopened notebook back into my pocket and rose to leave. "If you think of anything that might help me find Mr. Benson, send me a letter, okay?"

CHAPTER SIX

DORIS ARNESON SHARED AN OPEN area with three other secretaries at the end of the hall. As I approached, her fingers were flying over the keys of an Underwood typewriter with an extra-wide carriage. She glanced up and smiled. "Help you?"

"Thanks. I'm Max Dexter. Betcha the secretaries' telegraph told you all about my investigation into Jake Benson's disappearance."

"Well, of course." She stood to stretch her back and I admired the colour of her sweater. "Let's go down to the coffee shop to talk," she said. She whispered something to the dark-haired woman typing nearby, who turned to look me over, then gave me a wink. The troops certainly seemed friendly here.

When we boarded the elevator, Doris nudged the operator as he pulled the brass grille closed. "Take us to the Ritz, Cap, and don't stop for any lights."

"Hey." He pretended to be annoyed. "That's my line."

The Ritz was a pint-sized coffee shop off the rear of the lobby. And not very ritzy. We slid into a booth and Doris waved two fingers at the swarthy guy behind the counter, fished a flat box of Virginia Ovals from her purse, selected one and lit it. "Smoke?" She held up the elegant box. "I get 'em from a friend of mine who works at the Tuckett Tobacco factory on Queen Street. So they're fresh."

I shook my head. "Maybe you could give me the lowdown on Mr. Benson."

Our coffees arrived and Doris stirred in a bit of sugar. "You're the first private detective I've met," she said. "Not what I was expecting."

"And what was that?"

"Oh, don't get me wrong. I'm not disappointed." A mischievous grin brightened her fine features, maybe Nordic with a name like Arneson. "But ... you know ... you get a certain image in your mind from the movies and the detective programs on the radio. So I thought you'd be more like Sam Spade."

I couldn't resist flashing her a smile. "And now when you see a real live detective in the flesh, he's even more handsome than Howard Duff?"

She laughed out loud and almost spilled her coffee. "Something like that."

"Mr. Benson," I reminded her.

"Sure. Jake's a nice guy, quiet, polite, treats us secretaries with respect. Not like some of the other bean-brains around here. I sure hope he's all right."

"Does he have any close friends?"

"Not in the office. He's a hard worker, stays late most nights. Keeps to himself, but not unfriendly. I suppose I talk with him more than anyone else."

"What about after hours? Did he say anything about his family, other interests? Girlfriends, maybe?"

She stubbed out her cigarette in a glass ashtray embossed with a picture of the King and Queen commemorating the royal visit in 1939. "He doesn't say very much. He mentioned once that his father was in that old folks' place run by the Sisters in Dundas."

Well, well. Here was a lead to that elusive family which nobody seemed to know about. "What about his mother?" I asked her. "Brothers, sisters?"

She shook her head. "Never mentioned any others." She paused for a moment. "And he's the kind of guy who's so driven to succeed that he doesn't make time for a woman in his life." A wistful smile. "I know," she said. "I tried."

Hmm. She tried. I filed that away and thought of Benson's father; maybe I'd visit him this afternoon. "Oh, I almost forgot. Mr. Potts said you told him Jake Benson's a jazz fan, likes to go to the clubs."

"That's right. He told me he'd drop in someplace on the way home from the office. You know, the Flamingo, the Golden Rail, one of those lounges. His way of relaxing, I guess."

I made a note to follow up with Liam Grady, the bartender at Duffy's, who knew most of the guys tending bar at the downtown watering holes. I was running out of questions but another thought occurred to me. "I was wondering, Doris, did you notice anything unusual about Jake just before he disappeared? You know, late for work, did he say anything out of the ordinary, that kind of thing?"

She went quiet for a moment, absently butting out her dead cigarette again and again in the ashtray, taking her time with her answer. "Not really," she finally said. "Everything seemed pretty normal. Jake was real busy following up on some kind of audit work he was doing. And he mentioned he had a meeting about it on Friday morning with Mr. Myers himself."

I mulled that over, noted it in my book and readied to leave when I remembered to ask, "Say, you wouldn't happen to have a recent snapshot of Mr. Benson, would you?"

A shake of her head. "'Fraid not."

We finished our coffee and I handed her one of my cards. "Would you mind calling me if you think of anything that'll help me locate him?"

"Sure." She seemed in a pensive mood now, as though speaking about Benson's absence evoked some dark possibilities. I flipped two bits on the table and we parted.

Back on James Street, a gusty wind was pushing raindrops the size of silver dollars from across the bay and I had to limp at double time back to the office. I noticed an armless man seated on a folding chair under the awning at the entrance to the Brights Wine store. He wore an Air Force wedge cap and a rumpled blue shirt with the sleeves cut off, and on his lap sat a collection box with a few coins it. Hanging from his neck was a hand-lettered sign: "I lost them for you." I dropped a fifty-cent piece in his box and said, "Thanks."

Upstairs, I dripped into my office to the amusement of my new assistant or secretary or whatever the hell she was. "Got time for an early lunch?" I said.

"Sure, Max. Just have a seat on the couch. Spiro's sending something up."

Spiro again. Another captured heart.

A tap at the door and a pimply-faced teenager entered with a couple of takeout lunch cartons. His arms had outgrown the sleeves of his busboy's jacket and two Cokes clinked in his side pocket. His pant cuffs were at half-mast, too.

"Just set that down here, Nicky." Isabel slipped him a bill.

"Thank you, Miss." His voice a choked falsetto and he blushed right up to his hairline as he hurried out the door.

"Nicky?"

"Spiro's oldest boy. I'm helping him with his Grade 10 math."

I shook my head but kept my trap shut as we unwrapped our food and she produced a bottle opener from her purse to uncap the Cokes.

"Mmmm, meatball sandwich," I said as I caught a juicy drip with my finger and licked it. "My favourite."

She rolled her eyes and ran her finger down the open page of her notebook. "L. Grady?"

"Liam. Bartender at Duffy's Tavern. Discreet and observant."

"P. Flanagan."

"Paddy. Runs the newsstand at Fischer's Hotel on York Street. Knows everything."

"H. Stone."

"Helen. Supervisor at the Credit Bureau."

"Oh, so that's her name. When I visited Vera this morning she told me you had a friend on the inside there."

I kept the surprise from my face that she'd visited Vera, who did my credit checks and other odd jobs. "You saw Vera Evans?"

"Indeed I did, Max. And a very tidy operation, too. She scoots around her little house in her wheelchair just like an Indianapolis race driver. And with the number of phone calls in and out of her place all day long, why, I'm surprised the police don't suspect her of running a bookmaking operation."

I washed down a meatball with a swig of Coke and swallowed a burp.

"Her daughter, Phyllis, was home with a cold today," she said, showing off now, pleased to know more about the situation at Vera's than I did. "So I had a nice little chat with her. A very bright young woman. Did you know that Phyllis graduates from Business College in two weeks, Max? I told her you'd be pleased as punch to have her start here full-time on August first."

I swallowed again, thinking of my dwindling bank balance. "Good choice," I said.

"And I'm only halfway through the books. I'm sure you have lots more little surprises in store for me, right?"

"You're doing fine, Iz. Did you come across the lawyers' file yet?"

"No." She gave an exaggerated shudder. "Do I want to know about this?"

"Oh, it's quite legit," I said. "And it's a part of the business I'd like you to take a good close look at."

"You're not in some kind of legal trouble, are you?"

"Nothing like that. I'm interested because only a couple of the defence lawyers in town can afford to keep a full-time investigator on staff. The other lawyers have to contract for this service, and that's the work I'd like to see Max Dexter Associates doing."

She reached for her notebook. "Tell me more."

"Well, it's a lot more interesting than the routine stuff we're doing now. It involves locating and interviewing witnesses for the defence, as well as checking the backgrounds of prosecution witnesses. And often there are leads to follow up that the police don't pursue, for a variety of reasons."

She stopped writing. "So why haven't the other private detectives here taken up the slack?"

"Because there aren't many of us and I don't think the others see the opportunity. So right now most of the work's going to Toronto guys, who aren't always familiar with the Hamilton scene."

She tapped her forefinger to her lips, maybe even thinking that I wasn't as dumb as I looked.

"You're smarter than you look," she said.

I scrutinized her face but she showed no signs of being a mind reader.

"One other point," I said.

She raised her eyebrows.

"If this area of the business expands as I believe it will, maybe we'll be able to pay the Eaton's bill as well as the new staff you've hired."

A twitch betrayed itself at the corners of her mouth. "Of course, Max. That's why we had to revise the rate structure."

Holy moley, it was hard to stay ahead of her.

I retreated to my office to write up my notes from this morning's interviews and to make a few phone calls. I found a message from Ed Zielinski, my former boss at RCMP headquarters in Toronto. It had been some time since we'd spoken and I wasn't anxious to renew his acquaintance, but I called anyway. Got the Royal Canadian runaround and left a message.

Briefcase in hand, I retrieved my hat and peered out the window. The summer downpour had almost stopped but the wind was blowing harder, judging by the number of people fighting with their inside-out umbrellas. When Isabel saw me preparing to leave, her squint asked where I was going.

"Gotta pick up my car from home," I said. My flat was on the ground floor of a three-storey apartment building on the corner of Hunter and Emerald Streets. Too far for me to walk so I drove my car to work until a couple of months ago when I'd made a sweet deal with the Veterans Cab Company. Today, however, half their fleet was being serviced so I decided to drive myself. "I'm heading out to Dundas, to visit Benson's father. Should be back about five. Think you could meet me at Duffy's?"

"Sure, Max. But I can't stay too long. I'm having dinner with my father this evening."

I drove out Main West and when I reached the unpopulated area between the city and Dundas, the wind almost howled my old Model A into the bushes. A big shiny Buick rumbled past me, a

'46 or '47 model, and it took no mind of the wind at all, thumbed its nose at it. I daydreamed about a new car, but so did a lot of folks. During the war, auto production had switched over to military vehicles and didn't start up again 'til late in'45. So most of the cars on the road were pre-war, from the twenties and thirties. And, oh my lord, the cost of the new ones. Price of the new Fords this year was $1,300 for the coupé, an additional two hundred bucks for the sedan. I thought about my bank account and laughed.

I fought the wind all the way to Governor's Road, where I pulled into the parking lot at the House of Providence. A smiling nun with a chubby face and twinkling eyes greeted me at the reception desk. Dressed in her white habit, she could easily pass for Santa's grandma. Her gold name tag read Sister Norbert, R.N.

I removed my hat and returned her smile. "Afternoon, Sister. I'd like to talk with Mr. Benson for a few minutes, if he's available."

"Oh, he's available, Young Man. But I'm afraid he can't speak with you. Or anyone else, for that matter."

Oh, nertz! Why hadn't I checked? "I'm sorry ... I didn't realize ..."

"No, I guess you didn't. Now, perhaps you could tell me why you're here."

I explained that Mr. Benson's son hadn't reported for work and his employer had hired me to find him.

The suspicion in her eyes had softened while she listened. "I'm so sorry to hear that," she said. "He's such a nice boy, spends every Sunday afternoon here with his dad. It's admirable how he talks to him as though his father understands every word he says. But, of course, it's hopeless."

"How long has he been a resident here, Sister?"

"Let me think ... yes, it was 1942. The darkest year of the war. I lost a nephew at Dieppe. God rest his immortal soul." She blessed herself. "And poor Mr. Benson has been in a coma ever since his arrival. Stroke, you understand."

"I'd appreciate any information about the family, Sister. Mr. Benson's employer and his co-workers know almost nothing about him."

"Well, I'm afraid we're in the same boat. When he visits, he spends all his time with his father. Sometimes he talks to me about his dad's condition, but that never changes." She excused herself and I could see her riffling through a bank of files in a rear office before she returned with a blue folder, which she examined. "Mr. Benson's file indicates his wife died before the war, and he has two sons. Jake, the boy from Hamilton who visits him. And another who lives in Toronto." She studied me as though judging my trustworthiness. "I forgot about this second son, because we've never seen him. I suppose I could give you his address and you might try contacting him."

I noted the details, thanked Sister Norbert and she shook my hand with both of hers. "God bless you," she said. "I'll pray that you find Mr. Benson's boy safe and sound."

I drove into the small downtown area and crossed over King Street toward Dundas Park. Near its entrance, I passed a row of neat houses, an Eaton's truck in front of one where an old icebox leaked water all over the sidewalk as two guys carried a shiny new electric refrigerator into the house. Everyone but the iceman called it progress.

The parking lot beside the concession stand was empty and I gave the Ford a rest. Despite the windy weather, several kids were squealing on the swings nearby, their bikes sprawled on the grass beside them. I sat on a bench watching them while I lapped my double-dip chocolate cone. What was I missing on this Benson case? If he had embezzled fifty grand, why did everyone, including Sister Norbert, have such a high opinion of him? Did his brother in Toronto have anything to do with the alleged theft? Something was screwy, and it wasn't only me.

I decided to drive back to Hamilton on King Street to avoid the nasty wind along Main. But it was worse: the stretch along the Desjardins Canal would've given the wind tunnel at Malton Airport a run for its money.

I blew into Duffy's a few minutes after five and spotted Iz sitting at the end of the bar, sharing a joke with two football players. How did I know they were football players? Besides being a trained detective, I saw these lugs were each the size of a Hill the Mover truck and wore football jerseys – one emblazoned WILDCATS and the other TIGERS.

I made my way through the dining area of the lounge, Billy Eckstein's soulful baritone crooning *A Prisoner of Love* from the bubbling jukebox in the corner, and Liam waved me over. "Just in time, Max, we need a referee in this game."

When I joined the group, Iz smiled at me and took a sip of something pink in a fancy glass. The two palookas were sucking Peller's Ale from the bottle and Liam poured one for me in a frosted mug.

He wiped the bar and said, "Guess you heard the scuttlebutt about merging the Cats and the Tigers, eh, Max?"

"It's bullshit," said the Wildcats guy and he turned to Isabel. "Pardon my French, Little Lady, but that's the stupidest thing I ever heard. Cats won the Grey Cup in '43 and the goddamn Tigers don't even remember what the Cup looks like."

The guy wearing the Tigers jersey was about to explode when Iz leaned across them and touched my arm. "What do you think, Max? You're a sport."

I saw the mischief in her eyes and swallowed some suds. "It'll never happen."

Big grins from the tanks as they clinked their bottles together and glugged down their beer.

"Nope," I said. "It just makes too much sense. Everybody knows that the days of the amateur teams are numbered. And in the next few years the league'll become professional whether we like it or not. So we wouldn't want to do the smart thing now and join two pretty good teams into one helluva great team and win the Grey Cup every year, would we?"

By now I'd worked up a head of steam and a few of the other patrons were looking our way. The ball players gaped at me. "Nosireebob," I said, winding up my spiel. "It just ain't the Hamilton way to do the logical thing."

Isabel had a wide smile on her face at this malarkey. The big guys slammed their empty bottles onto the bar top, glared at me and strode out the door.

"Pretty smooth," Liam said. "There go two of my best customers."

Iz raised her glass at him. "You did ask for a referee, Liam, and Max did stop the argument."

Liam pretended not to enjoy the ribbing and set up another round of drinks. "So how are things, Max? Betcha you're workin' a tough case and you need my help again, right?"

Liam was a survivor from my old neighbourhood who came up the hard way in a tough family. He kept in touch with a few guys on the shadier side of the law and helped me out from time to time. I gave him an outline of the Benson situation and, to bring Iz up to date, spoke in detail about my visit with Sister Norbert. "We've got an address for the brother in Toronto. Maybe you could track him down tomorrow, Isabel. So far I haven't been able to scare up a photo of Benson. Maybe his brother could help." I turned to Liam. "I hear he's a jazz fan, likes to visit the local clubs. With a good photo, some of your bartender buddies might be able to identify him."

"If we find out where he was the night before he disappeared maybe someone will remember if he had company," Liam said. "I could check on that, Max."

"Thanks. It would give us something to go on. I'll give you a shout when a photo turns up."

"For all we know," he said, "he might be down in Hialeah, with a babe on each arm, placing a bet on the daily double."

Isabel pushed the remainder of her pink concoction toward him. "Well, I've got a dinner date. Nice to meet you, Liam." His eyes pinwheeled when she reached across the bar and squeezed his hand. She leaned toward me and said, "Ta-ta, Max." Then she swished away, turning the heads of the other drinkers in her wake.

"Stick around, Max," Liam said. "I wanna hear more about you and Isabel. Boy, she's a real pipperoo."

I drained my beer mug and gave him my stare of steel. "Keep your shirt on, Buster. It ain't what you think."

CHAPTER SEVEN

NEXT MORNING I BOARDED THE elevator in my building and nodded to the operator holding the door for me. Everyone called him Tiny, for obvious reasons. He adopted a flat American accent with a drawn-out breathy sigh like the character on the radio. "Howdy, Bub."

"You've been listening to the Fred Allen program again, eh Tiny? That's a pretty good imitation of that farmer guy, what's-his-name."

"Titus Moody."

"Yeah, that's right." I changed the subject. "She early again, Bub?"

"Yup." He gave me a rare grin. "And so are you."

When I walked into my office the glass rattled in the door, causing Isabel to glance up from the worksheets spread across the coffee table.

"Sit here on the couch, Max. There's more coffee in the thermos."

I stirred in some milk and settled against a throw cushion I'd not seen before. "You don't have to be here at the crack of dawn, Iz."

"The sooner I get the office running tickety-boo, the sooner I'll begin my detective training," she said. "That's the plan."

Smiling at her determination, I dug a list out of my briefcase and passed it to her. "Could you give Vera a call later? I'd like her to get the lowdown on these people. Credit bureau checks and anything else she can dig up."

She scanned the names and frowned. "The Myers employees you interviewed yesterday. And I meant to ask you before, why did you include Jake Benson?"

"Detective Rule Book, Page One – Suspend judgement until you've checked."

Her eyebrows peaked. "Have you checked on me, Max?"

"Not yet." I kept my face straight, despite the zing in her eyes.

After a long moment, her gaze softened. "Suspend judgement." She repeated this, giving it some thought. "Might be a good idea, Max."

I marvelled as a few volts of energy seemed to pass between us. "How was dinner with Dad?"

She grinned at my change of subject. "Oh, the usual. He'd invited another in a long line of bachelor accountants who spent more time trying to impress my father than sweeping me off my feet."

"Maybe your dad just wants you to be happy."

"No, Max. He wants a surrogate son."

We exchanged a look ... empathy, I think.

"You never married, Max?"

"Too busy with life ... and the war." My mind drifted for a moment. "There was a nurse in England, during my rehab, but ... you know wartime romances."

She finished her coffee and made a noisy production of clearing the cups and tidying up. "You've had a call already. Detective Russo's coming in to see you at eight-thirty."

I could feel my forehead furrowing. What the hell did Frank want so early? "Okay," I said. "In the meantime, I'll finish writing up my notes from yesterday." I placed the flat of my hand on my brow in mock agony. "I stayed too long at Duffy's last night."

She chuckled and picked up her purse and notebook. "Have to see the building superintendent for a few minutes. Watch the phone, will you?"

I'd almost finished my paperwork when Detective Sergeant Frank Russo swaggered through to my office and sprawled on my visitor's chair, a hustler's grin on his mug. "Shoulda seen the luscious redhead in your lobby, Max. Sexy walk. Curves in all the right places. A real dish." He twirled an imaginary moustache and leered. "I winked at her and she almost wilted."

I gave him my "you're-full-of-shit" look. "You came in here before breakfast to tell me *that*, Frankie?"

He laughed, then sat upright in his chair and the light went out of his eyes. "Nah, it's business." He took out his notebook and flipped a couple of pages. "Met your client, Myers, this morning. We talked about Benson, the missing accountant."

What the hell? Myers had been adamant about not involving the police. I shifted in my seat, not liking the direction this was taking.

"He's been found, Max. Floating in our unofficial cemetery. Two in the back of the head."

Goddamnit. My mind whirled and I could feel the blood pounding in my ears. I'd never met Jake Benson, didn't know him from Adam, but two in the head was no way for any man to die. It was the kind of dirty, undignified death that the bastards in the rackets specialized in. "A mob hit, eh, Frank?"

"Looks like." He flipped another page. "Myers says the guy embezzled fifty big ones and disappeared. But instead of notifying the police, he calls in Sherlock Holmes."

I glanced at Frank, his dark eyes serious. "Myers hoped to work things out on the q.t.," I told him. "To avoid upsetting his clients."

"And his profits," he said.

"You're right," I said and felt the need to justify myself. "Just thought I'd give it a couple of days before I called you."

We regarded each other in silence. Frank Russo was only a few years older than I but he was one of the big guys when we were kids in a crowded apartment building on Napier Street. He lived with his parents and kid sister, Gabriella, in the flat above ours. Frank became my big brother when my dad was killed in that shootout with Rocco Perri's thugs.

He shook his head from side to side. "Oh, Maxie ... I've spent my life bailing you out of the shit. Benson embezzled a potful of money," Frank made a gun with his forefinger and thumb, jabbing it toward me, "and you didn't report the crime."

"If you believe Myers."

"What d'you mean? You think he's lying? He told me his auditors confirmed Benson's responsibility. Of course, that'll take us a little time to verify."

"It doesn't matter what I think, Frankie. The poor guy's dead now. And if it's a mob hit, then it's unlikely we'll ever know who did it, let alone why." Frank jumped when I slammed my palm on the desk with a thwack. "Shit, this stinks," I said.

He waited until my temperature dropped a few degrees. "Yeah," he said. "It could be a dead end. But Benson might've been up to his eyeballs in something. Gambling debts he couldn't pay or some damn thing."

"Mmmm ... Well, that wasn't the impression I was getting."

Frank's eyes slitted and he seemed to scowl, a lifelong habit when his brain shifted into another gear. As close as brothers since childhood, we'd learned that even under pressure we could trust each other not to reveal our confidences. Some said it was an Italian trait, and, if so, I'd absorbed it like a true *paesano*. So I was no stranger to inside police information passed my way from my big brother; when Frank gave me the nod he knew my lip stayed buttoned.

He'd been looking away and now gave me his full attention. "Well, we'll see. Doc Crandall's already on the job at the morgue. But there's no doubt about the cause of death. Two small-calibre entry wounds at the base of his skull. Doc'll dig out the bullets and find out anything else worth knowing. You know how that goes." He reached into his shirt pocket and waved his pack of Winchesters at me. "Want one?"

I shook my head. He lit up and flipped the matchstick into the clean ashtray on my desk. "Talk to me about this Myers guy. In the absence of any next of kin for Benson, I called him during the night and he identified the body at the morgue."

"How did you know to contact him?"

Frank waved his cigarette at me. "I found a business card in Benson's wallet. Then, putting two and two together, I phoned his boss, didn't I? Even a private dick could figure that one out." He leaned back in his chair with a smirk, awaiting my response. When it didn't come, he continued, "What about this Myers guy? He seem on the up-and-up to you?"

"Good question." I studied my pal's swarthy features, fatigue puffing under his eyes, the stubble on his chin bristling. "I've seen him a couple of times now. He appeared anxious to locate Benson and I've no reason to disbelieve him. Doesn't seem the type to dump bodies in the bay. But there's something ... *off* about him. Can't put my finger on it yet but you know that feeling you get?"

He motioned again with his cigarette, acknowledging his agreement as he directed a plume of smoke toward the ceiling. "Yeah. And he was a bit cagey with me about not reporting a suspected theft." He stubbed out his weed, making a helluva mess in my ashtray. "But it's too early to tell. I'll interview some of Myers' staff and get into Benson's background. You get anything on his family and friends?"

"Not much. I spoke with his immediate boss and some of his co-workers. Found out his father's at the House of Providence but he's in a coma. Has a brother in Toronto and I got an address and phone number. My assistant's trying to track him down right now." I called through the closed door, "Isabel?"

When the luscious redhead with the curves in all the right places walked into my office, Frank's mouth fell open, then he sprang to his feet.

"Well," said Iz, looking him over. "The winker."

He turned to me, his face matching the flame of Isabel's hair. "What the hell, Max? Why didn't you tell me?"

"You didn't ask," I said. Then I introduced them.

Frank scrambled to bring another chair over to the desk for Isabel. "I didn't mean to be fresh," he told her.

She gave him half a smile, then turned to me, "You shouted, Max?"

The barb registered and I paused a few seconds. "Frank's brought some sad news." And I brought her up to date on the discovery of Benson's body.

She dropped the hand which covered her mouth while I'd been speaking. "I'm so sorry to hear that. Must be why Mr. Myers wants to see you this morning, Max."

I made a note about Myers. "I told Frank about Benson's brother. Any news yet?"

"I was just working on it," she said and referred to her notebook. "His name is Simon. Benson, of course. Caught him before he went to work at the Royal Ontario Museum. He's a curator there. I told him I'd gone to university with his brother and we'd lost touch. He was reluctant to give me much information about Jake, but he said they talk on the phone fairly often and every month or so Jake travels to Toronto. In fact, he'd seen him just a couple of weeks ago."

Frank completed his notes. "Alright. We'll take over from here. I'll contact the brother. Have him come down to view the body and arrange for burial. After you've seen Myers, I'd appreciate a copy of your notes. If that doesn't violate the Gumshoe Code."

"Always happy to stepinfetchit for Hamilton's finest, Frank. We'll send you something but it might take us a while to rewrite it in words of one syllable."

Isabel grinned at his scowl. "I guess you boys must have a history. I'd love to hear it sometime." Then she escorted Frank from my office and, in a voice loud enough to annoy me, he referred to the new furniture as though he were reviewing it for *Better Homes & Gardens* magazine.

Frank's chair was still warm when I got a call from Scotty Lyle. "It's the world's best reporter, Laddie. How're y'doin'?"

"Fine, Unc. What's new on your beat?"

"You tell me. Seems you've been holding out on your old uncle. Just got a tip from the cop shop that a body was recovered from the bay during the night."

"I see."

"I'll bet you do. Quite a coincidence the dead guy worked for a broker called Myers. Remember you asked me the other day if I had inside info on a broker called Myers?"

"That is quite a coincidence."

"C'mon, Max. Cough up. What's goin' on?"

"I'm telling you the truth, Scotty. You know as much as I do. The dead guy's name is Benson, an accountant. Last week he disappeared and I was hired to find him. The cops just told me, not two minutes ago, that his body had been pulled from the bay."

"You've gotta know a helluva lot more than that. How'd he die? You're not saying he drowned, are you?"

Shit, I was caught in a double bind. Frank had always trusted me not to blab about inside dope from his job. And I'd agreed with Myers to keep mum about the missing money. As much as I wanted to give Scotty a scoop on this story ... well, I couldn't. "Sorry, Unc. I've got no details. Your sources are a lot better than mine anyway. So I hope you let *me* know."

His reporter's manner became conciliatory. "Max, my favourite nephew. I don't like to call in a family favour–"

"But under the circumstances ..."

"Well, yeah ... they're special circumstances because this could be a big story. I've got a guy snooping around at the morgue, and I'm trying to get in to see Myers but I can't get past his secretary. She says he's distraught, for Chrissake. Why did this guy disappear?"

"Honest to God, Scotty, I just don't know. I was trying to answer that very question and now ... he's dead."

"You must have a theory. Did he run off with someone's wife? Was he consorting with criminals? In trouble at the office?"

All good questions and I wished I'd had good answers. "Scotty, I just began working on the case two days ago. No theories. No nuthin'. Myers wants to see me today and I'm sure I'll be off the case since it's now a police matter. End of story."

I didn't enjoy bending the truth, and when I rang off I paced between my cluttered desk and the window. I peered through the grimy pane. It seemed the future of this case was as bleak as the view of the pigeon-streaked wall next door.

The squeak of my door interrupted my gloomy reverie.

"Your appointment with Mr. Myers is at eleven," Isabel said. "I told him you'd be there."

I nodded and continued to stare through the window.

"Still upset about Jake Benson, Max?"

"I guess so. It doesn't make any damn sense. The people he worked with saw a hard-working, ambitious young guy."

She approached and stood beside me. "You also told me they'd said he was a very private man, Max."

"So private that no one had even suspected he might also be an embezzler?" I said. "Or a gambler? Or involved with organized crime?"

"Sounds contradictory to me too." A long pause, then she asked me, "Do you think your friend, Detective Russo, will get to the bottom of this soon?"

I turned from the window and, seeing her lips tightened with concern, I was reluctant to tell her the details. But more often than you'd think, the detective game is played on a deadly field and she'd have to learn that, too. "Not likely," I said. "Frank's a damn good cop but it appears that Jake Benson was the victim of a mob killing." Then I described how Frank had found the body, washed up on the shore of the bay, two bullets in the back of the head.

She raised a hand to her mouth, drawing in a sharp breath, the colour draining from her cheeks. I guided her to a chair and she took a moment to compose herself. "I'm fine now, Max. Tell me the rest."

"That type of death is a Mafia trademark. What they call a professional hit. Often to avenge a death or settle some other score. Sometimes it's a demonstration to others of what could happen if you welsh on a debt. And such murders are almost immune to prosecution. No witnesses. Nobody talks. It's a family thing."

She stared at me, shaking her head as though I were describing an alien world. And in her experience, I guess it was. "But this can't be happening in Hamilton, can it, Max?"

Like most law-abiding citizens, Isabel had no idea of the extent to which the Mob had infiltrated the city's life. I gave her a brief rundown, beginning with the booze trade during Prohibition and the ever-widening reach of Rocco Perri's gang and others into gambling, loansharking, prostitution, extortion and narcotics from Buffalo to Toronto. "And the RCMP believes that, someday, Hamilton mobsters could control the sale and distribution of drugs for the entire province. By any measure, it's a criminal empire."

She paid close attention, some of the time open-mouthed. "I've heard rumours about criminals and such," she said. "But I thought that was all in the past. Isn't that right?"

"No, Ma'am. Old Rocco went out of business in '44. Disappeared. Some say he met the same fate as Jake Benson in Burlington Bay. But competition for control of his empire has resulted in gang wars and multiple killings that continue to this day. Seems all the police can do is keep a lid on it."

"My God," she said in a whisper. "That's hard to believe."

"But true," I said. "That's why the police won't spend a lot of time investigating Jake Benson's death. We're lucky that Frank's been assigned to the case – he'll do what he can. But the pressure will be on him to wrap it up fast and file it away as just another Mob killing."

"That's why you're so frustrated that the police have taken over the case?"

"Not to mention that Myers will now cancel my contract."

"I don't believe that's your main concern."

"No, it isn't. I'm just mad as hell that Jake Benson occupies a numbered drawer in the basement vault at the morgue and I'll be off the case while he remains a mystery man." My eyes drifted again toward the window, my spirits slumping. "And we may never know why he was murdered."

CHAPTER EIGHT

AS I LEFT MY OFFICE to see Myers at eleven, I saw Tiny holding the elevator door open for me. I limped into the car on the double and spotted a dog-eared paperback of Damon Runyon stories on his stool.

"What's new with Nathan Detroit?" I said.

He shook his head. "Crapped out again," he said. Then he picked up the book, withdrew an envelope stuck between its pages and passed it to me.

"Your report's not due 'til next Friday," I said.

"It's something else, Sarge. Snooty bastard in a grey chauffeur's uniform told me to deliver it right away."

I glanced at the envelope: plain white, my name typed on the front, sealed. I stuck it in my pocket.

"Thanks, Tiny. Did he give you a tip?"

"You kiddin'? Damn guy was so tight I could hear him squeak when he strutted away."

I stepped out of the Wentworth Building onto King Street and spotted Bob beside the entrance selling his pencils. "How's it going, Champ?"

"I've been waiting to see you, Sarge. Got a spot of bother, as the Brits used to say. Having trouble with the disability people ... and Aggie and I need the money–"

"Say no more, Bob. I'll call them after lunch. If that doesn't work I'll go in and jump on the manager's desk."

Bob's usual grin returned.

"By the way," I said, "you notice a chauffeur leaving the building?"

"Not five minutes ago. Stiff-assed-lookin' guy. Drove off in a black Caddy with a small dint in the right rear hubcap. He was double-parked and the driver he blocked off was threatening to ram him outta the way. Chauffeur just sneered at the guy as though he wasn't even there."

"Seen him before?"

"Seen the car, but the driver's new."

Bob didn't miss much. "Thanks. If you spot him again ..."

"Sure, Sarge. I'll let you know." He wheeled himself along King Street and set up shop at the entrance to the Capitol Theatre, his usual station.

From my jacket I withdrew the white envelope Tiny had slipped me and gave it the nose test – not a love note – then opened it. A business card:

J. B. O'BRIEN
PRESIDENT
O'BRIEN ASSOCIATES

On the flip side in neat handwriting: Mezzanine Bar, Connaught, today at six.

What the hell? Why would Isabel's old man issue me this terse command? I was about to rip the damn card into pieces when I stopped myself – what's this guy's angle? Doesn't even know me, so it has to be about his daughter. But what about her? I decided it might be in my interest to meet the bugger.

I pocketed O'Brien's card and cut across Gore Park toward Myers' office; the weather had turned a bit cooler and smelled of rain again, so there were fewer kids splashing in the fountain today. But just as many old guys gossiped and watched the pigeons pecking like chickens along the sidewalk. I crossed James Street to the Pigott Building and rode the elevator in style once again.

As I approached her desk, Miss Carlson pushed her chair back and rose to her full height in slow motion. My eyes blurred and in a magic moment she became Rita Hayworth and slithered toward me, hips swaying, arms outstretched, and led me into Myers' office. It took me a moment to descend to earth and, damnit, there was Myers shaking my hand and inviting me to have a seat. Erect behind his enormous desk, he resembled a little king. "I appreciate your coming this morning, Mr. Dexter. Such distressing news about young Benson. We're all in shock here."

"Yes, Sir," I said and waited.

He seemed to gather himself, then continued. "I spoke at length with Detective Russo at the morgue. But I don't suppose there's any way to minimize the bad publicity this situation will generate ... any ideas about that, Mr. Dexter?"

"No, Sir, I don't. It's hard to minimize two bullets in the head."

He shot me a sharp look. "Yes." Then he stood, came around his desk and motioned me to join him at the large window overlooking the bustling downtown. For several moments we watched the silent motor traffic and the toy-sized people scurrying beneath us. Even from this height you could almost feel the accelerated pace of the city. And as a bonus for the rich, the stench of the exhaust fumes didn't rise to the high-rent suites. "We're on the doorstep of the postwar boom, Mr. Dexter, and everything is expanding at quick time. Even the crime rate, I'm afraid. Why do you think Benson was killed?"

"I've no idea, Sir. And with the police now investigating I'll have a tough time finding out. Recovery of the missing money may not be possible either."

Myers rocked back on his heels, hands in his pockets. "I've thought about this all morning, Mr. Dexter, and I'm reconciled to the loss of the funds since the insurance company says it's not covered under my policy. As to my former employee, well, there's nothing I can do to help the police." He turned to me and softened his tone. "I know it's a frustrating situation for you, Mr. Dexter, because our contract is ended."

I was stunned by his cavalier attitude toward one of his own people, not even referring to him by name but merely as a "former employee". And his assumption that the end of our contract was my main concern.

"As for the bad publicity," he said, "well, I've hired a public relations firm to develop what they call a communications plan." He stood a little taller, almost to the height of my shoulder and spoke now with a firm resolve. "It's a messy business for the company but I'm confident we'll weather this storm, Mr. Dexter. I believe our clients will understand this could have happened in any financial business. It's not as though we're to blame."

I felt like wringing the little bastard's neck – someone murders one of his employees and his main concern, his only concern, is the well-being of his goddamned company. The shit!

I realized I was becoming wound up tighter than one of those picketers at last year's Steel Company strike, and probably for similar reasons. A deep breath, released in slow quiet puffs, cooled me down. If I wanted to succeed in this business I'd have to ignore some of this crap, take it in stride as best I could. It took a helluva lot of effort but I held my tongue.

Myers turned away and pressed a button under his desk. Miss Carlson entered and as she handed him an envelope they exchanged a look which I couldn't decipher. He passed the envelope to me and clapped me on the back. "I'm very pleased with your services, Mr. Dexter, so I'm paying you the bonus we'd discussed." He walked me to the door. "After all, it wasn't your fault that the case ended so soon."

When he shook my hand all I could think to say was, "Thank you." True, he was a heartless little twerp, but by hauling back on the reins of my working class tendencies I could keep Max Dexter Associates afloat. See, I told myself, a little tolerance pays off. Besides, I could afford to be magnanimous because I'd probably never see this guy again, would I?

Miss Carlson hooked her arm through mine and guided me to the elevator, the seductive aroma of her perfume reviving my fantasy and she became Rita Hayworth once more. I'd had a crush on Rita since seeing her in some silly Hollywood musical during the war along with a bunch of hooting Brits in a Men's Canteen. And here she was now, close enough to be real.

She squeezed my arm and whispered, "Toodle-oo, Mr. Dexter. Maybe I'll see you some time."

I stepped aboard the elevator and admired her through the polished brass grille. She puckered up to blow me a kiss and my heart went thumpety-thump as I whisked back down to earth.

CHAPTER NINE

WHEN I RETURNED TO THE third floor of my building, the scent of fresh paint led me to examine my door. MAX DEXTER ASSOCIATES was displayed in two-inch letters on the frosted glass panel. Nice.

As I entered I was greeted by not one, but two attractive women seated behind the desk, both eating tomato sandwiches, both making I-can't-talk-now-because-my-mouth-is-full gestures. Isabel was the first to swallow and take a sip of her lemonade. "Sorry about that, Max. We're too busy to go out for lunch so Phyllis and I are working through."

I'd never have recognized Vera's daughter. She looked nothing like the gawky teenager I remembered from my last visit to her mother's house. When she set her sandwich on its wrapper and stood to greet me my eyes popped. Boy, was she a humdinger: her dazzling smile was so magnetic that, at first, you didn't notice her six-foot height.

"Wowski," I said, shaking her extended hand and gazing up at striking features. "Long time no see, Phyllis. You've grown ... up."

"I'm so glad Isabel convinced the school that working here until graduation could count as my final job placement."

Iz gave me an impatient toss of the red curls. "Don't look so worried, Max. Phyllis isn't on salary until next month." She shuffled through a pile of phone messages and dealt me a hand. "There's a sandwich on your desk," she said. "Maybe you could return your calls while Phyllis and I finish up here. Then you and I are meeting at the security company at two. Your regular get-together with the owner 'to exchange information of mutual interest', he said. Sounds very mysterious." She pronounced this last word in a Tallulah Bankhead drawl.

Jeez. Invited herself along to the meeting. I felt a spark of annoyance, the steamroller heading my way. But how she's going to learn the business if she's not involved?

I took a moment to settle at my desk because I couldn't remember the last time I'd seen it cleared of clutter. The faded blotter had been replaced by a fresh green one, on which sat a tray containing a wrapped sandwich, a glass of lemonade and two Niagara peaches. The detritus from my desk made a neat pile against the wall, a note on top of the heap saying, "Phyllis, start here." I creaked back in my chair and let out a long breath. I liked to organize myself and be faithful to the Boy Scout oath. But I hated to be organized. Did it make any difference? Organized was organized, right? So why did I feel like a dog and my tail was wagging me?

I finished my lunch and riffled through my messages, noting that Ed Zielinski from the Mounties had called back. He answered on the first ring.

"Long time no talk, Max. How're things down there in Hamilton? Still think you'll make a go of that business of yours?"

He spoke in a brusque manner and just hearing his voice set my teeth on edge. Ed had been my supervisor when I'd been assigned to RCMP Regional Headquarters in Toronto before the war. I'd learned a lot while working for him in the organized crime unit and we'd gotten along well enough. But he never let you forget who was boss.

And when I announced my intention to leave the Mounties to join the Provost Corps, he became hostile, even belligerent. Later, one of my former colleagues informed me that he'd planned to groom me to become his deputy and I'd upset his plans. But he was the strong, silent type so I didn't know what the hell his plans were. In any case, I wouldn't have remained with the force because I had a war to fight.

"Yeah, Ed. Things are going well here. What can I do for you?"

"Listen," he said, "I'll be in town for a couple of days next week. You free for dinner Monday?"

I took my time checking my blank schedule. "Sure, I can fit you in." I didn't always like myself for it, but I could be as snotty as the next guy, especially when I felt challenged.

I knew the RCMP brass always stayed at the Connaught, no second-class digs for them, so we agreed to meet in the dining room there. "What brings a high mucky-muck like you all the way from Tronna?" I asked him.

"Not on the phone, Max." he said. "See you Monday."

I hung up and recalled how uncooperative he'd been when I attempted to rejoin the RCMP after the war. In fact, I heard from a friend there that he'd done everything he could to block my return. And it worked. Did Zielinski's autocratic attitude remind me of my father's, causing an additional strain on our relationship? Well, maybe. But that, too, was ancient history. It did me no good to dwell on that crap.

Tap-tap-tap and Phyllis peeked around my door. "Sorry to disturb you, Mr. Dexter–"

I extended the palm of my hand. "Mr. Dexter was my grand-father. Call me Max, please."

She stepped into the office and I imagined her stretching her impressive height and leaping in the air as she scored the win-ning basket for the Max Dexter Associates team over the Harlem Globetrotters in Madison Square Garden.

"Did you hear me ... Max?"

"Of course I did. What did you say again?"

She gave me that female eye-roll. "Isabel's ready to go now and I'll be just fine on my own for a while."

I stood and brushed the bread crumbs from my pants. "That's what I thought you said."

CHAPTER TEN

ISABEL AND I CROSSED OVER King Street and picked up a Veterans cab at the Royal Connaught. It was a fifteen-minute ride to the east end, during which she opened the file on her lap and asked me about the owner of the security company, George Kemper.

"He was one of my instructors during my RCMP training," I told her. "Like me, he was raised in Hamilton. And since he'd known my father ... I guess you'd say he took a special interest."

"So he retired from the RCMP?"

"Yep. Put in his twenty years, then became a partner in a security company here. They have a small army of security guards, most of them veterans and retired cops, in various factories and office buildings. It's a growing business, not to mention very lucrative."

"Has Mr. Kemper tried to hire you, by any chance?"

"I knew you were a mind reader."

The taxi turned off Kenilworth North onto Beach Road near the Dofasco plant and squeaked to a stop in front of an enormous Quonset hut. Beside the front entrance, a half-dozen panel trucks lettered WENTWORTH SECURITY SERVICES were lined up, as though awaiting inspection by a visiting general.

George Kemper slapped me on the back and made a big fuss over Isabel, led us into his spacious office and settled us around an oak conference table surrounded by a half-dozen leather armchairs. A picture window allowed us a front-row view of a vast parking area, behind which a mountain of scrap metal reached for the sky. Beyond the dead cars and twisted girders, the slag heaps and puffing smokestacks of the city's backbone steel industry completed the industrial landscape.

"View is still spectacular," I said.

Kemper stared at me stone-faced. His wrestler's brawn, flat-top haircut and drill sergeant swagger had caused more than one RCMP recruit's sphincter to tighten, including Yours Truly. He turned to Isabel and I watched her eyes widen until he burst out in a great guffaw of laughter. "That's what I always liked about Max, Little Lady. His subtle sense of humour."

A shake of red curls accompanied her smile at the boyish behaviour of grown men.

"So, Max." His luxurious leather chair seemed to enfold George like a grandmother's hug as he leaned back. "If you want to bring your new assistant with you when you join my company, it's okay with me. Could you both start on Monday?" And he grinned like a fox with a key to the henhouse.

"You know damn well that I'm as independent as you are," I said. "So my answer's still the same. And since I'm such a generous guy, I've got two leads for you." I slid a piece of paper across the table's rink-sized surface and he stopped it with a goalie-stick hand. "First name's a plant manager," I said, "who suspects a couple of his delivery guys are making unauthorized drop-offs. Could involve surveillance of their routes and maybe an undercover driver. Second name's a farm equipment dealer, worried about his inventory disappearing. He also asked me about a personal bodyguard."

Kemper made a few notes as I spoke. "Why's he need a bodyguard?"

"Dunno. Not my line, so it's over to you."

"Much obliged, my friend, I mean that. Now, I've got something for you. Know anything about Oriental Imports Ltd.? Office is in your building."

"Nope." I remembered Tiny, the elevator operator, saying something about Japs in our building. "Don't know anything about it."

"Well, one of my clients has a problem. He married a Chinese woman before the war and it sounds like she's being scammed by this outfit. Seems these guys might be involved in the illegal immigrant business. Anyway, here's my client's name and number. I told him you'd call."

I took the information and thanked him. Then we discussed Isabel's background as a chartered accountant and her interest in detective work, some of which he must've already learned when he'd called my office to arrange this meeting.

He wagged his index finger at her. "I figured right away you had a lot more than movie-star looks." Then his smile faded and his bushy eyebrows lowered as he leaned forward and folded his hands on the table. "I'm dead serious about this job offer, you know. Some of our corporate clients have reported a big increase in what they call white-collar crime. So with a C.A. on staff, well ... And you, Max, I've told you before that my partner would like to retire soon. He sweet-talks the clients and drums up more new business than we can handle. A real smooth operator. Just like you. And that leaves me free to hire the troops, train 'em and keep 'em in line." He gave us both a long stare. "I want you two to give my offer serious thought."

George dipped his head as though sealing the deal, rose from his chair and escorted us out to the parking lot. "There's one other thing, Max. I hesitated to mention this before, could be nothing at all, but you know that golfing buddy of mine, Jimmy Nolan? Well, he met a guy in the clubhouse bar who tried to interest him in an investment deal that sounded fishy and you know how cautious Jimmy is. Said that half a dozen other members there at the Glendale club may already have jumped on board. So he asked me to look into it and, well ... since it's more in your line, I thought maybe you–"

"Sure thing. Who's the guy?"

He fished a business card out of his shirt pocket. "He gave me the guy's card, and I wrote Jimmy's number on the back, in case you need to call him. Thanks, Max."

I pocketed the card and shook his hand as a Veterans taxi arrived in a spray of gravel. Isabel inhaled a deep breath of industrial air and deadpanned, "Say, George, I bet it smells great here on those days when you don't need a gasmask."

He was shaking his head, staring after us as the cab pulled away.

"I can understand why you're tempted to join your friend in business," she said.

"Well, I can't deny that the financial security is attractive, but I think I'd be bored to death. To me it sounds like a sales-man's job. And I wouldn't be my own boss."

"I think you're right, Max. And I hate wearing nose plugs."

Still chuckling at her remark, I glanced at the card George had given me. Holy shit! What's going on here? I read it again to make sure.

C. N. (CHUCK) CYSKO
INVESTMENT COUNSELLOR

CHAPTER ELEVEN

THE CABBIE DROPPED US AT the Federal Building at the corner of King and John Streets. Isabel crossed over to the office and I went in to raise hell in person about Bob's disability pension.

I pushed through the brass revolving doors and joined a throng making its way across the marble expanse of the lobby toward the elevators. I was still thinking about "Call-me-Chuck" Cysko's possible scheme and wondering if it might tie in somehow with Jake Benson's disappearance. That's why I was slow to notice someone calling to me.

I scanned the people in my vicinity. Didn't see anyone trying to get my attention. Some folks were hurrying toward the lineups at the post office; others peeled off for the elevators to Customs and Excise, Immigration, or the Veterans' Affairs offices upstairs.

"Hey, Mister." I traced the voice to the operator of the newsstand in the corner and limped over. "If you're looking for the post office," he said, "it's through those doors straight ahead."

I'd heard about this guy, and studied him as I approached. Maybe in his late forties, ordinary-looking character, average height, but dumpy – didn't look like he got much exercise. He seemed to be gazing my way but he'd tilted his head upward, not focusing on me. Or anyone else, because he was blind.

One of the secretaries in the insurance office on my floor told me the Institute for the Blind had taken over the newsstand and this guy, Rudy, was its first operator. "He's pretty smart," she told me. "You can't fool him."

He stood calmly behind a counter crowded with candy bars and snacks, hands resting alongside a small wooden bowl; his blue shop coat looked straight from the cleaners. Newspapers and magazines were displayed in neat self-serve racks and, along the back wall, cigarettes and tobacco.

"You called me?" I said.

"I sure did. I heard you moving toward the elevators, thought you might be daydreaming and missed going straight for the post office. Where you usually go."

I stared at him. A tiny smile on his puffy mug and I noticed he'd missed a few spots shaving this morning. "How do you know where I usually go?" I said.

"Your limp's the giveaway," he told me. "Right leg sort of drags when you bring it forward. Every limp has its own characteristics, you know."

I laughed. "Sure, I guess it does. So what else do you know about me?"

He still wore his small grin. "Not too much, because you haven't stopped here before. But you've gone through to the post office quite a bit, probably for your small business. Small, because you don't send someone else to mail things and buy stamps. So you're probably a one-man show, selling insurance or bookkeeping, something like that – office nearby because you can't limp too far."

"Not bad, Sherlock. Anything else?"

"Probably wounded in the war and you're still recovering. And since you're not a bigwig businessman you probably weren't an officer. But you do have your own business, shows some initiative, so I'd guess you were a sergeant. How's that?"

I shook my head and laughed again. "Pretty damn good," I said. "Your name's Rudy, eh?"

"Yep." He extended his hand, waiting for me to shake it.

I pumped his arm and said, "My name's Max. Got business upstairs today so, if you don't mind, I'm gonna use the elevator. But I'll stop by on my way out."

I got off on the third floor, marble hallways, golden oak doors and trim. The frosted glass door at 301 was lettered "Department of Veterans' Affairs" and I entered. Inside, the decor was inoffensive government blah.

A well-rounded middle-aged woman greeted me at the counter, the movie version of everybody's Aunt Tillie. "Help you?" She sounded like Aunt Tillie, too.

"Yes, Ma'am." I explained Bob's problem with his disability payment, adding that I had spoken to the manager last month about the same difficulty.

"I see." She walked to the manager's cubicle at the rear of the large room and returned with a file smelling of chili sauce. From the corner of my eye I noticed the manager's bald head slowly appear as he rose from his chair to glare at me above the opaque section of the glass panel surrounding his office. His noggin reminded me of a harvest moon rising, but the man in this moon looked as sour as a peck of lemons.

"Mr. Ducharme's in good form today," I said to her, "but why's he hiding from me?"

She grinned and looked me straight in the eye. "He's pouting," she said. "Retires tomorrow and hates having to relinquish his crown of office. At home he'll be right under his wife's thumb, and you know how much authority he'll have there."

"My, my."

She tapped Bob's file. "There's nothing the matter with your friend's paperwork. I'll look after this right away and let him know."

"Thank you," I said. "But I'm still puzzled. Why did Mr. Ducharme hold up payment?"

She sighed and her gaze slipped away for a moment. "Maybe because he could," she said. "Such a shameful way to treat a veteran. Or anyone, for that matter." Her grey eyes flashed and her cheeks became rosier. "You know, some people in the public service just don't accept that their job is to serve the public. As if they didn't know that you and your friend pay our salaries, for Pete's sake."

I shook Aunt Tillie's hand in both of mine and thanked her again for solving Bob's problem. "With old Ducharme's retirement, I suppose you'll be the new manager, right?"

"Now, now, Mr. Dexter," she said, withdrawing her hand. "Don't be such a tease. You know very well the government will appoint a man to fill the job. Why, it's common knowledge that men are more capable managers than women and, besides, men have families to support." She leaned closer and lowered her voice. "Of course, I'll be expected to train him with no additional pay."

I knew she was right and I shook my head. The system was out of whack and it probably wouldn't change for a long time, if ever. "Nobody said life was fair," I told her.

Back in the lobby, I headed for the newsstand and waited while Rudy finished with the customer in front of me. I watched the man tuck a copy of *The Toronto Evening Telegram* under his arm, scoop his change from Rudy's wooden bowl and stride away.

"How're you doin', Bud?" I said.

He turned his head toward me and said, "Well, hello there, Max." Bugger recognized my voice already.

"Watched you make change for the guy with the newspaper," I said. "How did you know what denomination the bill was?"

He smiled. "Obviously, I didn't know. But most of the customers just tell me, it's a two or a five, or whatnot."

"And those who don't?"

"I ask them."

"No one tells you it's a ten and slips you a one-dollar bill?"

He gave a little chuckle and said, "I'm often asked that question, Max. And since you're so nosy I'll tell you how it works: My wife does most of the work for me. Drives me downtown every morning, opens up the booth here, sorts and stacks the newspapers, then sets me up with my cash box. I start out with the coins and bills arranged in a certain order and try to keep them that way. Coins are easy because they're different sizes. But I have to take the customer's word for the bills. And here's the funny part: I've never been cheated. In fact, I often end up with more than I should. You know, someone puts a five in my change bowl and says it's a one."

"I'm surprised," I said.

Rudy was nodding as though he knew some secret that I didn't. "I'll tell you something," he said. "Deep down, people are generous. It's human nature, Max."

Well, maybe Rudy's people were generous but in my world human nature was a helluva lot meaner. And somehow I felt Rudy was well aware of that. "Betcha listen to all those detective shows on the radio," I said.

He bobbed his head. "Sure do. And I'd be a great gumshoe if it weren't for this one slight drawback."

We shared a laugh at that. Then I leaned forward and lowered my voice. "It's not out of the question, you know. I'll bet you hear a lot of gossip about what's going on around town. Looks like you're pretty busy here and you're a good listener so people open up to you. Am I right?"

Rudy fidgeted with his change bowl, twirling it clockwise and back again several times. "I guess so, Max. When you can't see, you have to be able to listen. And I hear a lot."

"I'll bet you do," I said. "And when I was upstairs did you happen to hear what I do for a living?"

"Well ..." a hand-in-the-cookie-jar look on his face. "I might have asked one of the postal clerks on her break about the guy limping toward the elevators."

"Of course you did," I told him. "A guy needs to know these things. And when you learned I'm a private detective you thought you might like to get involved by keeping your ears open for me. Am I right again?"

I smiled when I saw his cheeks redden. His little change bowl was spinning double time now.

"Yeah," he said at last. "I'd like that. You have anybody I should be keeping an eye out for?"

After a stunned silence, we both laughed out loud. "You know what I mean," he said.

I grasped his right arm and shook his hand. "I'll think about it," I said. "Talk to you soon."

CHAPTER TWELVE

I WAS CROSSING KING STREET as a streetcar jerked to a start, the driver clanging his bell while I hustled out of his way at double limp. I caught a glimpse of his satisfied grin when I shook my fist at him.

Back at the office, I found my new employees packing up for the day. Phyllis was twisting backward, her skirt hoisted high while she straightened the seams in her nylons. "I can't wait 'til those new seamless stockings come down in price," she said to Isabel and cast an envious glance at her unseamed legs.

I backed out the door unseen, waited a moment, then made a loud entrance. Phyllis snapped a silvery compact closed and smiled at me with freshly-painted lips. "Today was fun," she told me. "I want you to know I'll do my best for you, Max."

I held the door for her and smiled as Iz linked arms with her. They chattered their way toward the elevator like long-lost sisters. Back at my desk I finished my notes for the day, setting aside the info from George Kemper about Oriental Imports Ltd. I'd call his client later, but I planned to refer that case to Tommy Huang, who specialized in immigration matters. Cysko was still on my mind and I stared at his business card with the name on the back, wondering how best to follow up on him now that Myers had paid me off.

I phoned George's golfing buddy, Jimmy Nolan, hoping to learn more about the investment deal Cysko had offered to his fellow club members. Jimmy recalled a boozy session in the club's lounge with Cysko, who had laid out his plan to assemble a group of investors in what sounded to Jimmy like a get-rich-quick scheme. "Something to do with investing in a European reconstruction program," Jimmy said. "Claimed investors would make a piss-pot full of money, most of it tax-free. Sounded like horseshit to me and I told him so."

"But some of the other members did invest?"

"That's what Cysko claimed, but who the hell knows? And what kind of name is that? Cysko? Sounds foreign, for sure, so maybe he's a Jew or a communist. Anyway, I'm certain he's a con artist. And he wouldn't tell me the names of the other investors until I'd joined the exclusive circle, as he called it."

I thanked Jimmy for his information, told him I'd look into the matter and rang off. I stuck Cysko's card in my notebook and creaked back in my chair, staring up at a plaster crack in the ceiling which resembled a question mark. What the hell was Cysko's game? Maybe his buffoon act was his cover and in reality he was the scheming SOB that Jimmy Nolan believed him to be. Whatever the answer, I considered it a good sign that his name should pop up again. A sign of what, I couldn't say, but you can't have everything.

I glanced at the wall clock: damn, still oh-nine-thirty. But my stomach said eighteen hundred so I limped across to the Connaught to meet the chief of O'Brien Associates. I hadn't mentioned this command performance to Isabel. Thought I'd meet the old bugger first.

It might have been James Cagney who waved at me from a table in the corner of the mahoganied bar. A shortish man, curly red hair streaked with grey crowning a round face supported by a strong chin, well on its way to becoming double. I'd seen similar Irish faces in the Corktown House where I stopped after work sometimes for a Guinness with the micks. But his eyes weren't their eyes: his were steel ball bearings that read me like an X-ray. And like James Cagney, I imagined, O'Brien had the ability to play the role of a song-and-dance man one minute and a gangster the next.

He half rose, shook my hand and bobbed his head toward the empty seat across from him.

"Sorry I'm a bit late," I said. "Traffic was heavy."

He didn't even crack a smile at my weak joke, waved away my apology and lifted his red-grey eyebrows at me as a waiter appeared at his elbow. I nodded at O'Brien's drink. "Same, please." We sat in silence for thirty seconds until the waiter reappeared and I raised my glass in response to O'Brien's toast and sipped the smoothest, mellowest whisky I'd ever tasted.

"The only thing the Scots do well," he said as he savoured his single malt.

I studied him; he wasn't smiling, so his Scots remark wasn't a joke. "Why did you summon me, Mr. O'Brien?"

He swirled the golden liquid, admiring how it adhered to the sides of his glass. "It's my daughter, Mr. Dexter. I thought it fair to warn you." Now his hard eyes riveted me. "She's a beautiful girl, the picture of her mother, God rest her soul. And like her mother, Isabel has a *joie de vivre*, an enthusiasm for life that's hard to resist. But her interests are short-lived, I'm afraid. And all this nonsense about becoming a detective is just a pipe dream. If she stays with you for a month or two I'd be surprised."

My head spun. Were we talking about the same woman? Everything I'd learned about people told me this rich business-man and widower was full of baloney. I believed Isabel had made a considered, difficult decision to change her career despite her father's opinion. But was that because I wanted to believe it?

"What would you like me to do?" I asked him.

"Nothing at all. Just a word to the wise, my boy. In a few weeks my daughter will come to her senses and return to the firm. In due course, I'll find her a suitable husband and she'll leave the business to raise a family. It's a woman's proper role, Sir, as God Almighty ordained."

I nodded my understanding, which I presumed he read as my agreement with his old-world views. For a long moment I examined the hotel's lion logo imprinted on the coaster under my glass. The refracted light distorted Leo's features, sort of like how O'Brien's attitude was at odds with my impression of his daughter's character.

"I don't know how to say this without offending you, Mr. O'Brien." I paused to sip my drink. "I believe that Isabel is an intelligent, thoughtful and determined woman who'll succeed at whatever she chooses to do. I think you'd do yourself a favour if you stopped trying to control your daughter's life, Sir."

The colour drained from his face and his jaw muscles twitched as he stared right through me. I concluded my impromptu homily. "You might take a father's rightful pride in how well Isabel is prepared for her future life, whatever that may be."

He signed for the drinks, rose from his chair and whispered in a raspy voice, "Good day, Mr. Dexter." Then he strode away, erect and proper.

I sat back and let my mind settle. A piano player, surrounded by a half-dozen drinkers, was at work in the opposite corner of the bar. The familiar refrain of *Stardust* came tinkling my way and eased the image of O'Brien's controlled anger. Was I wrong about Isabel? I hated to think so, because I'd already begun to depend on her to lift the burden of the agency's administration from my shoulders. But in my rush to pass off this responsibility, had I misread her intentions? Was her current enthusiasm for detective work just a lark?

I finished my drink and, as I left, the pianist slid into a slow version of *Smoke Gets in Your Eyes*. Was he a mind reader, too?

Walking past the dining room I heard, "Pssst," and spotted Longo, the good thief waiter I'd arrested in England, standing near the entrance. I backpedalled a few steps.

"Jeez, Sarge. Haven't seen you for three years and now it's twice in the same week."

"Yep."

"First with the beautiful daughter and now the old man."

"Right again."

"So I figure you got somethin' pretty good goin'."

"But not what you think," I said. "You see a lot of the old man in here?"

"You betcha. He's a regular." Longo pursed his lips and peered down his aquiline nose at me. "And he's a big tipper."

"Ouch." I grimaced at his jab and he chuckled. "Who do you see O'Brien meet with? Other businessmen? Women?"

"Most often with other big honchos. But never alone with a woman. Why d'you ask?"

"I'm interested in him. Maybe if you notice him with anyone ... unusual, you might let me know."

His eyes slitted but he nodded. "Roger that, Sarge."

CHAPTER THIRTEEN

I LEFT THE HOTEL AND was standing at the corner of King and John waiting for the traffic light, not because I was overly law-abiding but I'd learned my lesson. With my gimpy leg I didn't stand a chance against those kamikaze streetcar drivers. I noticed Scotty Lyle among the pedestrians crossing toward me; he waved, giving me no chance to avoid him and his pointed questions about Jake Benson.

"Just the man I want to see," he said, grasping my arm and propelling me back toward the John Street entrance to the Connaught Hotel. "Don't look so panicked, Laddie. I just want to buy a beer for my favourite nephew."

My antenna quivered whenever I became someone's favourite anything.

Inside, we didn't go into the main part of the hotel but entered the Men's Beverage Lounge at street level beside the Coffee Shop. Downstairs you could get a haircut and a shoeshine. The Beverage Room was a loud and smoky place which smelled like the bottling floor at Peller's Brewery. Scotty guided me toward the far corner where five or six tables were set apart from the others to form a private area. Well, sort of private.

"Guys from the newspaper and the radio stations often drink back here," he told me. "There's some loose talk about incorporating a Hamilton Press Club but these bums can't agree on what day of the week it is so I'm not holding my breath. Damn radio guys aren't real journalists anyway."

We snared an empty table and before we were seated a waiter with a loaded tray of draft beer slapped one down for each of us. "Ten cents apiece," he said, in a hurry.

Scotty took his time sitting down and, giving the waiter the evil eye, dug out some change and slid a quarter and a nickel toward him. "Buy one for yourself," he said, but the waiter wasn't listening as he snatched the money and made for the next table.

I put on a show of surveying my surroundings, nodding in mock approval. "Nice place, Unc. Welcoming atmosphere and pleasant staff."

He ignored my remark and clinked his glass against mine. "Cheers, my boy." He took a long swig, belched and sat back. "I guess it wouldn't surprise you if I had a few questions."

I jumped in first, cutting him off. "And I've got one for you."

He took another slurp of beer and moved his chair closer. "So go ahead, Lad. You first."

"When we met for lunch the other day I asked you for background info on Myers, now my former client."

"Yeah," he said. "What about him?"

"Well, you got me wondering. You mentioned you were investigating some sleazy business and it wouldn't surprise you if Myers' name popped up. What did you mean by that?"

He aimed a beefy finger in my direction and said, "Why do you want to know, if he's no longer your client?"

"Just curious," I said.

He leaned way back in his chair, almost tipping backward, and gave me the long stare. Then he rocked the chair forward with a bang and wagged a stubby finger at me. "No, no, Max. None of that stuff. I give no tit if I get no tat."

I took a moment to consider my real interest in Myers. Why should I care if he were involved in some scandal or whatever? Not my client, not my worry, right? Well, almost right but ... something niggled away in the back of my brain about him – I was having a helluva hard time accepting his cold-blooded response to the gangland killing of one of his employees as normal business practice. But it sure wasn't my ambition to become Hamilton's Moral Crusader.

Scotty fixed me with a patient stare and waited. I thought I might deflect his questions about Jake Benson's murder by shifting his focus to Myers but I saw that wouldn't work. No choice now: I'd have to comply with Scotty's Law – some tit for some tat.

I leaned forward in my chair, trying to ignore the guys at the next table bitching about Hamilton's City Council. "Let's just say I've got a hunch about Myers," I said. "Sounds goofy, I know, but he just doesn't feel right to me."

He grinned as he delivered a soft punch to my arm. "That's my boy," he said. "It runs in the family, you know. We're all nosy buggers. It's in our genes; we've just gotta know why." He finished his beer and twirled his finger toward the waiter for another round. "Now tell me about Jake Benson."

I had no intention of revealing details which Frank Russo trusted me to keep to myself. But Scotty said he had someone snooping around the morgue and it wouldn't be long before the cause of Jake Benson's death came to light. So I didn't see a problem talking to Scotty about that.

"You already know the body was recovered from the harbour," I said, my voice lowered. "It was a trademark Hamilton killing. Shot in the back of the head, dumped in the bay."

He slapped the table, jiggling our glasses, spilling some of his beer. "Thought so," he said. "It's what my guy at the morgue figured too. He's known Doc Crandall over there for years and there were some pretty strong hints. We're hoping for some official word today, but if not, I'll attribute my story to 'usually reliable sources'. How's that sound?"

"Fine by me."

"So it's a Mob hit, then. But the question is, Why? C'mon, Maxie. I gotta know the juicy details." He extended his hand, wiggling his fingers. "Gimme, gimme."

I gave him a vague outline of what I'd learned about Jake Benson's family background and fought off his questions about possible motives for the sudden death. "Honest to God, Scotty, I just don't know. I was on the case for three days and now I'm off it. I'd tell you more if I could, but I'm still in the dark myself."

His skeptical scowl told me what he thought of my response. "Okay," he said. "Dunno why you're clammin' up here but I guess you've got your own sources to protect. How about we meet in a couple days and talk again?"

"No," I said.

"What d'ya mean, 'No'? We're pals. You're my nephew, for Chrissakes."

"I mean," I said with a little spunk in my voice, "no, I'm not leaving here until you give me a little tit for tat. So what's this investigation of yours that might involve Myers?"

For a long moment I was on the receiving end of a Scotty glower, his flabby cheeks a Supertest road map of spidery veins, his jowls spilling over his too-tight collar like rising bread dough. But when he grinned, those fleshy features disappeared and his face became the picture of a charming leprechaun.

He was grinning now, scootching his chair closer to mine and grasping my arm as though he were about to reveal the secret plans of the Manhattan Project. "You're a cunning little bugger, Laddie. It's why I love you like a son."

I covered his hand with mine and whispered. "Try to keep your emotions in check, Unc. Just tell me about Myers."

His guffaw momentarily drew the attention of the crowd at the next table and he exchanged a few jibes with them before settling himself. Shedding his elfish guise, he became the serious newsman. "I told you I've been workin' an angle for close to a year now, right? And I'm trustin' you to keep mum about it."

He sipped his beer, waiting for my affirming nod.

Then he surprised me when he asked, "You're familiar with the Evelyn Dick case, eh?"

Evelyn Dick, my God. Who didn't know about Hamilton's most notorious citizen? Last year she was charged with the murder of her husband and the death of a newborn child; her trial had captured the attention of Canada and beyond. And it wasn't just the murder of her husband that had titillated the public's imagination. No, it was the dismemberment of his body, incinerating some of the body parts and tossing the remaining torso from the top of Hamilton Mountain. How could such a young and beautiful woman-about-town do such a thing? That was the question on everyone's lips then. And when they talked about it today, it was still the question.

In fact, I hadn't been discharged from the military when *The Hamilton Spectator* broke the shocking news in March of '46 that some local children had discovered that bloody torso while hiking on the mountainside. And when I returned to Hamilton last summer Evelyn's stunning story was still riveting everyone's attention as each sensational tidbit of her forbidden, seductive life was revealed in the newspapers and on the radio. It was understandable why the public's appetite was so voracious. Hamilton folks had just endured five years of wearying war news, local soldiers killed and wounded and a nationwide rationing program which brought shortages of damn near everything. So the public was primed for something different, a welcome diversion. After all, who could resist a tale of murder, sex and intrigue?

I blinked as Scotty waved a hand in front of my eyes. "You still with me, Laddie? I asked you about the Evelyn Dick case."

"Yeah." I shrugged myself back to our conversation. "Yeah, of course I remember. And spare me that tired joke about 'How could you Mrs. Dick?' So, what's the latest?"

"Well, she's still in Barton Street Jail but rumour has it she's finally being transferred to the Women's Prison in Kingston in the next few days."

"So that's the end of it, huh?"

"Hell, no," he said. "We'll be yacking about Evelyn for years to come. There was so much conflicting evidence at the trials that we still don't know who actually killed her husband. And the way things worked out we probably never will."

"So what's your interest, Unc? You don't really think there's a connection with Myers, do you?"

He rubbed his neck muscles as though to relieve some pain while he scanned the adjoining tables, making sure no one was paying us any attention. "Well, maybe," he whispered. "Remember early on in Evelyn's trial there was talk of her Black Book? Supposed to contain names and addresses of the men she associated with, her sugar daddies?"

"Can't say that I do," I said.

He seemed surprised at my answer, perhaps forgetting that I'd only moved back to town last summer, before that trial, but I was still travelling back and forth to Toronto every week for treatment on my leg . Anyway, he barged on. "One of the investigators mentioned it at her first trial last October," he said. "I badgered every cop I know for info about that damn book but got nowhere. And during Evelyn's appeal a few months later there was no reference to it at all. Somebody's got it under lock and key, Max. Somebody who's got a strong incentive to throw that key away."

His furtive manner and his concern with the Black Book puzzled me. "So what?" I asked. "It's only an address book, isn't it? It's well known that Evelyn was friendly with lots of men. Hell, I've seen pictures of her dancing at the Brant Inn and here at the Circus Roof, all those fancy joints. And usually with a different man."

"True. We've run some of those pix in the *Spec*. But the lead I'm following points to something more than that. I heard that book contains the names of a couple of judges, some very rich businessmen, a few of our renowned gangsters and even a clergyman or two. People who would shit a brick if their names were made public."

"And you think Myers might be one of these guys?"

"I don't think anything yet," he said. "So far it's all rumour and speculation. According to the scuttlebutt, there's some kind of connection between Dominic Tedesco and your pal Myers. And I've seen pictures of Evelyn and Tedesco looking pretty chummy at some swishy charity event. Therefore ..."

I pulled back as though he'd kicked me in the shins. "Hold on just a minute, Unc. You mean Tedesco the crime boss?" An image of the man flashed through my mind. Tall, dark-complexioned, slicked-back hair – a smooth operator but as corrupt as he was handsome. He was well-known as top dog of Hamilton's Mafia organization, with strong links to other crime families here and in the US. And I sure as hell couldn't imagine him having anything to do with a prissy little guy like Myers. But Myers and a scarlet woman such as Evelyn Dick? Never. "You're shittin' me, aren't you?"

He shook his head. "Not so surprising, my boy. Some of these new Mob guys are a helluva lot more sophisticated than the old-line gangsters like Rocco Perri and that crowd. They're buying up legit businesses to launder their dough, joining the fancy golf clubs, contributing to charities and community events. Tedesco's a perfect example. Know what his speciality is?" He was on a roll and didn't wait for my answer. "Real Estate. Big plans to build some monster apartment buildings and he's buyin' up acres of land along the Queen Elizabeth highway near Burlington. Before long these guys'll look like model citizens of the god-damn community."

The same waiter stopped at our table and deposited a couple more beers, tapping his toe, waiting to be paid. I counted out the correct change and slid the coins toward him through a puddle of beer. He swished the money off the table and said, "Jeez, he can count. Thanks, Sport."

We drank in silence as I considered our conversation, get-ting a little steamed because of the direction in which Scotty was taking it. I set down my glass and asked him, "So you're not interested in Jake Benson's murder?"

"Not today."

"But you want to pump me for info about Myers because you think he's connected to Tedesco who's linked to Evelyn Dick. And maybe this so-called Black Book will tie everything togeth-er and keep you on the front page with a series of exclusives."

"Well, I wouldn't put it that way."

"There's no other way to put it," I said. "You're using me and it pisses me off."

Always the actor, he let his jowls droop and he slumped back as though I'd kneed him you-know-where. "That's a low blow, Laddie." He grasped my arm again. "We've got a common inter-est here, don't you see? Just exchanging information. Now settle down, listen to me for a minute."

I held up my hand, resigning myself for another assault on my good nature. "Alright, Unc. You've got two minutes." I took an exaggerated look at my Bulova.

"That's more like it," he said, again lowering his voice as if the noisy drinkers surrounding us gave a damn. "Now, lookit … I've been covering this story since March of '46 for God's sake and there's still a helluva lot we don't know. Here we are in July '47 and what've we got?" A dramatic pause. "Questions, that's what we've got."

He fumbled for his cigarettes and lit one, took another swig of his beer. His eyes took on an evangelistic spark, a look I knew only too well. He was preparing to talk me into something and I warned myself to hang on for another edition of the gospel according to Scotty Lyle.

"Here's what we know," he began. "Evelyn is a beautiful babe, twenty-five years old, likes to go first class, nothing but the best. She's got a stable of rich boyfriends who wine and dine her. One of them even set her up in that swanky apartment building up there on James South, at the foot of the Mountain. She's livin' the high life and lovin' it.

"Then she up and marries John Dick, a nobody. No ... worse than a nobody, he's a damn streetcar driver for Chrissake. So why'd she get married? And why John Dick? Nobody knows. A few months after the wedding poor John turns up dead – shot, chopped into pieces, some burned up, the torso tossed from the Mountain, all that stuff.

"So Evelyn is charged with murder along with her father, who allegedly helped with the cutting and burning. And one of her boyfriends is charged, too. At her trial last October Evelyn is found guilty and sentenced to death by hanging in January of this year. As a result, her father's trial and the boyfriend's are postponed.

"She appeals her sentence, gets a new lawyer and they do it all over again in February. But this time her fancy mouthpiece from Toronto gets her off. He's one slick character in the courtroom and he shows how badly the cops screwed up the investigation. And let me tell you, the case against Evelyn is a mess from the start; cops didn't even search her house or her father's place until weeks after John Dick's murder. By then, of course, much of the evidence has disappeared. Evelyn is kept in the Barton Street Jail for months before the trial and during that time she gives the cops three or four voluntary statements – all different. Just to keep 'em runnin' around in circles. And it works a treat."

He stopped for a moment to catch his breath and slid off his heavy-framed glasses to polish them on his necktie – a wrinkled orange monstrosity spattered with food stains. Finished with that, he leaned forward again. "And if all that ain't sensational enough for you," he said, "the cops finally find something in Evelyn's attic." Then his voice dropped to a creepy whisper as he said, "The body of a newborn baby boy, encased in concrete, hidden in a suitcase found in the rafters.

"The second trial's a circus, newspapermen from all over the country crowding into the Hamilton Courthouse for the biggest show in town. Evelyn is acquitted in the death of her husband but found guilty of killing her baby and is given a life sentence. Later, her boyfriend's acquitted on all counts because he's been charged as a result of Evelyn's jailhouse statement. But she has a sudden case of amnesia and refuses to speak at his trial. Her father is also acquitted on the murder charge but receives a jail sentence as an accessory."

Scotty drank down the last of his beer and leaned back, taking another breather.

"It's a helluva story, Unc. And you deserved that newspaper award you won."

He waved away my compliment and moved in again, not finished with his spiel. "But there's so much more we don't know, my lad. Who really killed John Dick? And why? At one point Evelyn had convinced the cops that gangsters from out of town had done it, but that was a dead end. Was Tedesco questioned? Was his name in the Black Book? Nobody knows that either."

The waiter delivered another couple of drafts and selected the correct change from the pile of coins in front of Scotty. When he'd gone, Scotty whispered again, "I'm thinkin' the fix is in. Where's that goddamn book and who's responsible for 'losing' it? And another thing – Evelyn's hotshot lawyer from Toronto? I heard his fee was over a hundred grand. Who paid his tab? And why?"

"Here's an idea," I said. "Why don't you visit her in jail? Maybe she'll answer all your questions."

He shook his head. "Tried that. Visitors restricted to family only."

I pushed my chair back, preparing to leave. "Well, this is all very interesting, but it's got bugger all to do with Jake Benson's murder. Maybe Myers' name is in Evelyn Dick's book or maybe it isn't, but so what? I can't see how Benson could be connected to that. As for Myers having links with the underworld, well, even though he may be a selfish little shit, I think that's a real long shot."

He threw up his hands. "Alright, Laddie. Let's give it a rest for now. I'm just sayin' there's a helluva lot more to this case and I ain't quittin' yet." He gulped down his beer and extended his hand. "I'll be in touch," he said and we shook on it.

I got up to leave and he waved me back. "By the way," he said. "There's a story in today's paper about the appointment of two prominent businessmen to the St. Joe's Hospital Building Fund Committee. Guess it's just a coincidence their names are Tedesco and Myers, eh?"

CHAPTER FOURTEEN

NEXT MORNING WAS SATURDAY AND I sat at my kitchen table catching up on paperwork. I welcomed the break when Frank Russo called. "Sounds like you're at the cop shop, Frank. Working weekends now?"

"We never close, Bud, you know that. Listen, I got hold of Benson's brother, Simon, first thing this morning. A terrible shock for him."

"I guess so."

"And he's anxious to arrange for his brother's burial right away. He caught the early train and I just picked him up at the station. Now he wants to talk to you. Wants to hear first-hand what the super-sleuth dug up. Hope you don't mind but I gave him your home phone number."

"Fine," I said. An image of Jake Benson's body refrigerating in the morgue flitted through my mind. "Did you go through his apartment yet?"

"Yeah. We stopped there on the way to his hotel and I gave the place the once-over. Clean as a whistle, far as I could tell. But I'm sending some guys over to take a closer look. I explained to Simon that his brother's killing had the appearance of a Mob hit and he almost went berserk. Swears that Jake was always a square shooter, would never be involved with criminals. Told him we'd investigate but warned him it might be difficult to find the killer if organized crime's involved. You know that drill, Max. No prints. No clues. Nobody talks. It ain't easy."

"For damn sure. How long will you stick with it?"

"Just a couple more days. Captain's already pushing me to wind it up."

Shit. A couple of days wasn't long enough to get to the bottom of this case. I understood why the police brass didn't devote a lot of resources to the Mafia's so-called internal settling of accounts. But it just didn't feel right that Jake Benson might be connected to the Mob. I hoped meeting his brother might give me more to go on. "Okay, Frank. Thanks for the info."

"There's something else. Angela's doing her special osso buco for dinner tomorrow. How about joining us?"

My spirits lifted right away. "Mmmm, I can smell it now." I made some snuffling noises. "What's that sauce called again?"

"Gremolata. And don't make a pig of yourself this time."

I laughed, as he expected me to. "Sounds swell, Frank. But Angela's sister—"

"I know, I know. I told Angie that Rosa came on too strong. But you know what it's like for an unmarried, older sister in these big Italian families."

I cringed at the memory of Rosa, a supersized version of Angela, whose desperation for a husband and children oozed from her pores like extra-virgin olive oil. *Mamma mia*. I said, "Yeah, I know."

"Oh, and Maxie." He paused as though he were choosing his words. "I know you mean well, but forget the Ontario wine. Your company is gift enough." And he cackled like a big brother before he hung up.

I was sipping a cup of coffee, still brooding over Jake Benson's too-early death, when Isabel phoned.

"Sorry to bother you at home, Max. Hope you weren't sleeping in."

I pretended to yawn and fumbled with the phone as though I were just awakened. "Hello, hello," I said and waited for her apologetic reaction.

"Now cut that out. I just called two minutes ago and your line was busy."

Good grief. It was becoming harder and harder to stay ahead of her. So I decided not to try. "Morning, Isabel."

"That's better. I just got off the phone with my father."

Yikes! I hadn't mentioned my summons from her old man. Did he spill the beans? I realized I had no idea how she might react. "And how's Dad?" I said.

"Well, he invited me to an artist's reception at his home tonight, said I could bring that detective fellow if I wished."

"Oh? And what did you say?"

"Said I'd let him know." A smirk in her voice. "Are you interested?"

I squirmed in my chair. What was O'Brien's game? I give him some advice on parenting, obviously unwelcome, and he invites me to a party. I scratched my head. Another thought: maybe he believed I was encouraging his daughter to defy his wishes and he planned to discredit me as a buffoon at his fancy party. Was that too far-fetched? "I don't know, Iz," I finally said. "I'm not the art reception type."

"C'mon. It could be fun. Your chance to see how the swells live."

I had an uneasy feeling about O'Brien. Something ... slippery about him. But why the hell not? I thought.

So I said, "Why the hell not?"

We arranged to drive together to his reception later that day.

With nothing else to distract me I sweated over my stack of paperwork, wishing I were at the beach. Earlier the weather guy on the radio had enthused about breaking a heat record today: "Maybe a hundred degrees, Folks."

The phone again. Holy cow, I should've gone into the office this morning instead of enjoying this quiet time at home. This time it was Simon Benson and we agreed to meet at Duffy's at the end of the morning.

Heading up King Street toward Duffy's, I noticed an animated crowd chattering in front of the *Hamilton Spectator* building, excited about something in the afternoon edition now being posted in the big windows. I elbowed my way to the front to investigate; the detective's curse, I called it, too damn nosy for my own good.

A banner headline: ROYAL BETROTHAL OFFICIAL TODAY. And beneath it, a four-column picture of Princess Elizabeth and someone in a naval uniform.

I was squished beside a tiny, white-haired woman. "See that, Sonny? It tugs at your heartstrings, so it does." Her sapphire eyes sparkled up at me. "Says right there in the *Spectator*, 'The twenty-one–year-old princess will marry the man she loves, Lieutenant Philip Mountbatten.' So romantic, isn't it?"

I grinned at her, trying to think of something nice to say, when an infantry sergeant in uniform stuck his head between us and said to her, "She coulda done a lot better than a navy guy, Lady."

I left in a hurry. Little old ladies with canes could be dangerous. The thermometer outside The Pagoda Chop Suey House read ninety-six degrees. What the old-timers called a typical summer day in Hamilton was strangling the city in its energy-sapping embrace. Shoppers and downtown workers seemed to trudge along the sidewalk in slow motion, as though wading through waist-deep water. I swam with the crowd to the next block, where I spotted a thin, sharp-featured man with short black hair who wilted beside Duffy's. His suit jacket was folded over his arm and he mopped the sweat from his eyes with a damp handkerchief. He was watching a couple of workmen stringing up a banner over the entranceway with the enticing message, COOL INSIDE.

Had to be my guy, so I approached him. "Mr. Benson?"

He pumped my hand. "Thanks so much for meeting me, Mr. Dexter. You're right on time."

We paused inside the dark entryway, letting the cool air envelop us. I led him through to the dining area, quiet at this time of day, where we settled at a corner table. "I thought you might need a cold drink about now," I suggested.

"You're a mind reader."

A sassy waitress took our order and headed for the bar, where Liam caught my eye with a small salute.

"I'm sorry to meet under these circumstances, Mr. Benson. I wish there were something I could do to help."

Benson studied me as he polished his wire-rimmed eyeglasses. He was the scholarly type, conservative suit, neat and tidy despite the circular sweat marks beneath the armpits of his shirt. "I'm still in shock," he said. "It's impossible that Jake might've been involved in any criminal activity, as that detective suggested. True, he said it was only a possibility but ... he must be wrong. This is all a mistake." He spoke in a precise manner and took the opportunity to catch his breath while the waitress delivered our drinks.

I described my brief investigation into his brother's disappearance, including the reported embezzlement from H. B. Myers Investments Ltd.

"I just don't believe he had anything to do with that," he said. "Jake was incapable of such a thing. This doesn't make any sense at all." He took a long, bracing drink and fiddled with his damp coaster. "Detective Russo told me the police might have difficulty closing this case. I can't tell you how frustrating that is." His narrow features pinched tight and his jaw muscles pulsed. "My innocent kid brother is murdered and the police won't investigate."

"When you talked with my assistant you said Jake visited you a couple of weeks ago."

"That's right."

"Did he have a special purpose for his visit?"

He frowned at me. "No. He came to Toronto every month or so. We'd go to a show, sometimes an opening at one of the galleries. Nothing special."

"So he didn't seem upset or depressed about anything?"

"Quite the opposite. He was a great jazz fan and last month we saw the Count Basie band at the Casino Theatre."

He drained his drink and I signalled the waitress to bring him another. "Tell me about Jake; it sounds like you thought a lot of him."

His dark eyes seemed to search my face for something, then he sighed and sagged back in his chair. "You're a perceptive man. I admired Jake a great deal, Max. May I call you Max? It's a good Jewish name, you know."

A good Jewish name? Where did that come from? I waited as he gazed into the distance, an occasional smile flickering across his thin lips. "I was twenty-three years old and Jake was seventeen when we learned we were Jewish," he said.

He explained that his mother's family were German Jews who'd moved to England in the early 1900s. During the First World War, his mother married an Englishman, non-Jewish, which caused her to be ostracized from her Orthodox congregation. Then Simon's parents immigrated to Canada in the early thirties, seeking a brighter future for their two young sons. In the depths of the Great Depression they settled in Hamilton, where they pinched every spare penny for their boys' education. Disaster struck in 1938 when his mother died from tuberculosis. Simon had just graduated from the University of Toronto and begun work in the curatorial department at the Royal Ontario Museum. Jake was in his last year at Central High.

"My poor father," he said, taking a sip of his drink. "He'd doted on my mother and missed her terribly. After high school Jake won a full scholarship to McMaster University but continued to live in the apartment with Dad to make his meals and keep him company."

Throughout their married life, he continued, his father believed he'd been the cause of his wife's exclusion from her Jewish congregation. As his last loving act for her, he decided to have her buried in a Jewish cemetery and was comforted to find that it was possible. Since neither parent had been religious, the sons were stunned to learn of their own Jewishness. Then with the war against Germany and the news coverage of Nazi persecution of the Jews, these revelations took on a new and deeper meaning for Simon and Jake.

"For some time after my mother's death," he said, "I wanted to proclaim my newfound identity as a Jew. I met with a rabbi in Toronto and read all the books he recommended. I had even begun to attend services at a synagogue. It was such an eye-opening experience for me, Max. Because my father wasn't Jewish and my mother never spoke of her past, I'd never known any Jews. So I was oblivious to the long history of anti-Semitic behaviour which continues even now."

I nodded my understanding. "You mean the death camps and ..."

He waved his hand, cutting me off. "Not only the camps. I mean the discrimination here in Canada. You probably aren't aware, as I wasn't, that Jews are still refused admission to many Canadian universities, barred from some professions, associations, country clubs and even some resorts."

"But that doesn't happen here in Hamilton," I said.

"Oh, you bet it does, Max. In Ontario there are so-called 'restrictive covenants' which prevent Jews and others from buying homes in certain neighbourhoods. So, right here in Westdale, for example, it's illegal to buy a house or any property if you're a Negro or Eastern European or a Jew."

"Jeez," I said. "I didn't know that."

"Neither did I for a long time. The ideal in our society is to be white, Anglo-Saxon and nominally Christian. And due to my upbringing I simply floated along with the mainstream, not aware of the difficulties I would've encountered if I'd been raised as a Jew."

"But you're a member of a Jewish congregation now?"

"No, I'm not." He took a long sip of his drink, maybe fortifying himself. "When my father suffered a stroke in '42, I lost all hope that there was a God, Jewish or otherwise. How could a just God allow my mother's death in the prime of her life? My father's lifeless coma? Another World War of monstrous proportions? The unspeakable evil of Hitler's regime? I'm ashamed to admit this, but I buried myself in my work and tried not to think about it."

He withdrew a clean handkerchief, making a production of blowing his nose, catching his breath. "And now with Jake's murder ..."

His entire body seemed to wilt as though the enormity of what he'd just described had shrivelled his very being. After a long pause he gathered himself and went on to describe how, after their mother died, Jake had devoted himself to his father. Following the stroke, Jake spent every Sunday afternoon at his father's bedside in the nursing home, keeping up a one-sided conversation as though he were understood. And Jake had become interested in Judaism, meeting often with Rabbi Fackenheim at Anshe Sholom Temple over on Hughson Street.

He drew in a deep breath and exhaled in a soundless whistle. "I saw the rabbi before I came here. He said he'd been encouraging Jake to join his congregation. And he thinks he would have."

A few early lunch patrons were seating themselves nearby and their muffled conversations seemed to bring Simon back to the present. He removed his glasses again and massaged his reddened eyes. "I'm sorry to have gone on so long. You're a good listener."

I waved him off. If I couldn't be a good listener, I had no right to be in this game. But another matter had occurred to me and I asked him, "Did you and Jake serve during the war?"

"Well, yes and no," he said. "I attempted to join up in '39 but didn't pass the physical. My father had a lifetime pulmonary condition which Jake and I inherited. So no overseas service for me but I was able to work in the Toronto office of the Canadian Red Cross Society until '45. Jake's lungs were better than mine but he was still in school in '39 and later he was deemed to be the sole local support for my sick father."

I was folding and refolding my paper cocktail napkin while he spoke, feeling awkward about probing into his private business. "Sorry to be so nosy," I said. "Goes with the job." I stuffed the crumpled napkin into my pocket. "So what do you plan to do now?"

"Well, I've thought of nothing else since speaking with that police detective," Simon said. "I'd like to hire you, Max. My brother was a decent, law-abiding young man. A far better son than I could ever be. He was never, ever a criminal. It's important to me that his reputation, in fact the family name, be cleared."

Damn. My heart went out to this guy and I wanted to help him; his family history paralleled mine in some ways. And I, too, was having trouble fitting Jake Benson into a criminal's clothes. But the last thing I wanted to do was step on the toes of the Hamilton cops during an ongoing investigation, especially Frank Russo's: I often depended on his inside info, not to mention his friendship. I'd have to be extra careful if I took this case.

It didn't take me long to make up my mind and I leaned toward him. "I can't do much without your help, Simon. And the sooner we get started, the better."

"To be honest, I'm not sure I'm up to it today. Jake's burial will take place in the morning if Rabbi Fackenheim is able to make arrangements on such short notice. We're hoping that my brother's body will be … laid to rest in the same cemetery as my mother's."

I gulped, able only to guess at the distress of burying your kid brother. But the early days during any investigation were crucial and time was moving on. I reached over to grip his arm. "Would you mind if I attended the service?"

His eyebrows rose to a point and his face brightened a little. "I'd welcome that."

We finished our drinks and stepped out onto King Street, where the supersaturated air smacked us like a Joe Louis punch to the kisser. Pedestrians sweated past us in both directions as though they'd escaped from an out-of-control steam bath.

Simon removed his necktie and rolled up his shirtsleeves. "Thanks for listening, Max." He shook my hand again. "I'll call you tomorrow. Maybe we could drive out to the cemetery together."

I watched him cross over to Gore Park, where he paused to observe a dozen dripping kids playing tag in the fountain. What was he thinking? Was his spirit being refreshed at the sight of the youngsters' boisterous game? I didn't think so. And I wondered how, or even if, you ever returned to normal after your family had been almost wiped out.

CHAPTER FIFTEEN

BACK AT MY APARTMENT, I was writing up my notes on my meeting with Simon Benson when Ed Zielinski phoned.

"Change of plan, Max," he said, not even bothering to say hello. "Big snafu in Toronto so I'm squeezing in a quick visit to Hamilton today. You free for a late lunch at the Connaught?"

We agreed on a time and I rang off. I wondered if the snooty maitre d' at the fancy hotel might upgrade me to the status of frequent customer. Maybe add my name to the hotel's Christmas card list. Holy moley, my mind was a jumble: from the depths of contemplating the Benson family's tragic history to fantasizing about Christmas cards in July.

I rubbed my head hard until my fingertips ached, my usual method of straightening scrambled thoughts in my noodle. Right away I felt better.

The royal blue carpeting along the wide corridor leading to the Connaught's dining room looked newly vacuumed and I noticed a dark-skinned woman in a maid's uniform coiling the cord of a Hoover. When I approached the entrance, the maitre d' cocked an eyebrow behind me. "Looks like you've been followed by an invisible tracker," he said. "Perhaps with a limp on his right side."

I glanced over my shoulder at the faint footprints I'd left on the carpet and fixed the guy with a hard stare. Everyone was a comedian these days; I blamed it on the radio. "Good line," I said. "Was that from a Boston Blackie episode or was it The Thin Man?"

He forced a smirk, but I'd scored a hit. "Your party awaits you, Mr. Dexter," he said. Then he led me through the crowded room to a private table in the rear, managed a stiff bow and departed.

Ed Zielinski folded his copy of *The Toronto Daily Star* and extended his hand toward a chair. "Sit down, take a load off," he said, all business. In a dark blue suit, starched shirt and striped tie, my former RCMP boss appeared to be anything but a cop. I hadn't seen him since our squabble last year over my application for reinstatement and I still nurtured a righteous grudge against him for his lack of support.

We settled at the table and I appraised him more closely. His close-cut hair was a little saltier, his jowls fleshier, but his grey eyes still pierced with a hard intensity, his only feature that revealed he wasn't the middle-aged high school principal he appeared to be.

"Couldn't help noticing your little exchange with the maitre d'," he said. "A bit surprising that an anti-capitalist like you would be recognized at this fancy joint."

"I'm not against capitalists. I just don't like the snobs and crooks among them."

A busboy poured water and left menus. Then Longo appeared at our table, bowed and said, "Gentlemen."

After we ordered, Ed tried a little small talk, not his specialty. "About that so-called private eye operation you've got. Think you'll find enough divorce work and credit checks to keep the wolf from the door?"

I felt my hackles rising and wondered what the hell he really wanted. On the way here I'd vowed not to let the bugger get under my skin, so I swallowed my annoyance at his snide remark. "I'm getting along just fine. Couldn't be better."

Before long, the aroma of grilled sole signalled Longo's arrival. We both had the three-course capitalists' special, after which Ed motioned with his head toward the bar. "Let's have coffee where it's quieter."

"So what's all the secrecy about?" I asked after we'd arranged ourselves in a corner booth.

He glanced around the near-empty room. "First off, I'll tell you why I'm here." Sounded like he was giving me the lowdown, but I was wary. "You remember before the war when you worked on the Organized Crime Task Force: all the ground work, compiling lists, contacts, incident reports, statistics. Now we've established international links with agencies in the US, Britain, France and other countries. Lots of intel reports whizzing back and forth. Some of it even useful."

Did he think I'd ever forget that time? Plowing through endless reports from RCMP staff in the field, contacts we'd cultivated in various government departments, local cops on both sides of the 49th parallel as well as a small army of snitches. In particular, we'd worked with the FBI to track the growing influence of American crime families in Canada.

He sipped his coffee. "I can't give you the details, but it looks like members of the Magaddino family in Buffalo are beefing up their connections here in your backyard."

I recalled Scotty's reference to Dominic Tedesco and it made me wonder. "Tedesco's operating on behalf of the Magaddinos nowadays?"

He sent me a sharp look as though I knew more than I should, but he nodded. "Yeah, but he tries to fly under the radar, masquerading as an upright citizen. Here's the thing, Hamilton is becoming the main entry and control point for heroin and other narcotics in Ontario. It could become a helluva big operation so I'm meeting with your mayor and police brass to discuss it."

I'd heard rumors about the Mob's expanding influence, but not to this extent. However, with all the commotion about the postwar boom, it wasn't surprising that entrepreneurs in the drug business were preparing to take advantage of it too. "When you say discuss ... you mean you'll tell them what the RCMP is going to do whether they like it or not?"

His face squeezed into what passed for a grin.

"Maybe, but there's another reason for my visit."

I pointed my coffee spoon at him. Finally, I thought, the purpose of this meeting.

"Guess you've heard about the war crimes investigations, eh? And the treasures looted by the Nazis during the war?"

"Not much. I remember reading that when the Nazis sent Jews to the camps they seized their property. I guess that amounted to a fair bit, did it?"

"It did. And the Nazis were very systematic about it. In France, for example, wealthy families with large art collections – and you're right, many of them were Jews – weren't able to ship them out of the country before the Nazi occupation. And in 1940 Hitler set up a special unit to seize what they called 'abandoned' works of art. By war's end, this loot filled an entire museum in Paris. Since then many of these paintings, as well as other objects – sculptures, furniture, jewellery and the like – have found their way into museums and private collections around the world."

Zielinski was well known within the RCMP for his thorough and sometimes long-winded briefings. I scratched my head and wrinkled my nose. "So what's the connection? You think the Mob is involved with this art?"

He refilled his cup from a tall carafe and pushed the stylish container toward me. "We don't think the Mob's directly involved," he said. "But we don't know that for sure."

His features betrayed some sort of inner debate, as if he were wondering how much inside information to tell me. He shifted on the leather banquette. "Seems some former Nazis and their supporters are peddling this stolen art to finance new lives for themselves in South America or Egypt or wherever."

"Well, no one ever accused the Nazis of not planning ahead."

"Right. And a number of governments have been tracking this activity. Especially the Americans."

"The American spies and spooks."

He nodded. "For the record, they call themselves intelligence agents. Anyway, near the end of the war the OSS set up the Art Looting Investigative Unit, which issued its final report last year. It identifies captured Nazi officials and agents who were interrogated about their involvement in looting. It also includes lists of stolen paintings and other works of art. And now the Americans are leading the Allied effort to root out these people and to return the artworks to their rightful owners." He drew a deep breath and narrowed his eyes at me, as though judging my level of interest and perhaps even my trustworthiness. "The Yanks are now squeezing us to co-operate with them because some of this art has surfaced in Canada."

I leaned back, trying to digest this story. "And you think some of it will show up here? In Hamilton?"

"That's what I'm told. I'm assigning a couple of men to look into it, sniff around a bit, touch base with local Customs and Immigration officials and see what we can dig up. And it wouldn't be a bad idea to have someone on the ground here in Hamilton, someone who's known to us."

I felt my eyebrows lift as I stared at him. So that's what I'd now become? Someone who's known to the RCMP? I was stunned. "You're enlisting me as a spy?"

"Nothing that dramatic."

"But I didn't think your unit did this type of undercover work."

"Times change. We're just trying to stay a step ahead of the bad guys."

I puffed out a long breath and sat back as though I'd been pushed. "Jeez," I said. "I dunno. What would you want me to do?"

"Can't answer that yet. Depends on what our initial review uncovers. But someone who's known around town might be able to ferret out a little more than one of my agents from Toronto."

I twirled my coffee cup in its saucer. Everything I knew about espionage I'd learned from the movies and you could write it on the back of a matchbook. But it wouldn't be that difficult for a professional detective, right? And it wouldn't hurt my new business a damn bit to be part of an international investigation. A sudden chill shot along my spine. Was I nuts for even considering this job? Working for goddamn Zielinski again, even though it was at arm's length? And on something involving Nazis?

What the hell, I thought, and flipped a mental coin. "Okay, I'm interested," I said. "But when did you want me to start? I'm tied up on a case right now."

"Soon," he said and checked his watch as he made ready to leave. "I'm already late for my meeting with the mayor and the police, then I'm heading right back to Toronto. I'll call you in a few days and we'll work out the details."

I folded the bill for lunch and slid it across the table. "I heard about your promotion to Inspector," I said. "I'm sure you'll insist on picking up the tab."

CHAPTER SIXTEEN

EARLY EVENING WAS WARM AND humid and I was beginning to sweat as I waited for Isabel outside my apartment building. I wore my new suit, the blue one with a fine red stripe, a tie that almost matched, and a clean white shirt. Even polished my shoes for the occasion. Earlier, the guy in my bathroom mirror, shaved and showered, hair combed just so, had adjusted his tie in a Windsor knot and said, "Sharp."

A snazzy Studebaker coupé, a brand new '47 with the wrap-around rear window, chirped to a halt and Isabel wiggled her fingers in my direction. I slid in beside her, inhaling that indefinable new-car smell. This model was made in the US but production would begin in Hamilton next year. Was I jealous? Maybe just a little bit? Of course I was. "Nice jalopy," I said.

She grinned. "And you look spiffy, too."

My head snapped back as she shot away from the curb and manoeuvred through the city streets as though she were piloting a Ferrari through the Italian Alps. "Guess we're late, eh?"

She gave me that look women use instead of a smack on your head, but she eased off the gas as we mounted the hill toward Ancaster. At this slower speed I could unglue my eyes from the road and relax my stranglehold on the armrest. I shifted in my seat for a better view of the driver: a body-hugging black cocktail dress, the hem hiked up to mid-thigh for ease of driving, black high heels abandoned on the floor so she could shift gears like a race driver, and an easy smile on her face as she maintained a light grip on the steering wheel, eyes shifting between the roadway ahead and her mirrors. A single strand of flesh-toned pearls, almost invisible, circled her neck. "Do I pass inspection?" she asked.

"Sorry to stare," I said. "Guess I'm a bit nervous. I don't get around to many society wingdings."

"Try to relax, Max. Just remember they all put their pants on one leg at a time." She winked. But a moment later her features became contemplative and her voice softened as though she might be talking to herself. "Don't get me wrong, Max. It's nice to be rich, have a lovely home, possessions, travel. The price of things really doesn't matter, because Daddy, or Hubby or someone else pays. Except there's always a price. One I refused to pay."

"Being poor has a price too."

"No doubt. But I can't live comfortably in the world of the rich. Society women know their proper place and they do their boring duty. As for the men, well, most of them are driven by greed. Money, status, acquisitions, they're all just counters in a big game. And the goal of that game is power. That's not for me, Max. It makes you lose sight of the world outside your closed little circle." Her eyes flicked over to me and she frowned. "And it actually makes you less than human."

I regained my hold on the armrest as she took charge of the roadway again, passing three cars in a row.

"I tried to escape a couple of times before," she said. "But this time, I'm going to make it."

She sounded proud of her resolve and I saw a sparkle in her eye. I recalled her father's warning that Isabel was enjoying a little fling at my expense. I hadn't believed him then, and now, seeing the firm set of his daughter's jaw and hearing the determination in her voice, I was certain that what he'd told me was an elaborate smokescreen, something he'd manufactured, perhaps to cover his failures as a father. "I'm sure you'll make it, Iz." I could see her grin as she concentrated on the road ahead.

"I met Simon Benson today and he's hired us to clear his brother's name," I told her. "So I'm counting on your help with this case."

She glanced my way, eagerness in her eyes. "Oh, I'm so pleased we're helping Simon." Her right hand slid off the steering wheel and grasped my wrist in a quick squeeze. "You can depend on me, Max. A hundred per cent."

She slowed through a turn at the crest of the long hill and we drove down a leafy lane, past homes the size of Dundurn Castle. Driving by the Hamilton Golf and Country Club, I spotted a couple of old duffers wearing plus-fours who were scurrying to finish their rounds. Around the next bend she pulled into a paved driveway, past an acre of lawn, and parked near a Cadillac Fleetwood beside a four-car garage.

We followed a curving walkway topped with fine red gravel to the double-door entrance of a stone manor house. "Be warned," she said as she pushed the doorbell. "My father will want to show off for you before the reception begins."

A middle-aged man in a tux, maybe a butler, opened the door, nodded to Isabel and gave me the once-over. "Nice to see you, Miss Isabel," he said in an icy voice, his manner betraying that if he never saw her again it would be too soon.

We stepped into a large foyer, its coved ceiling painted to depict the entranceway to heaven, cherubs in each corner pointing toward an elaborate gate where St. Peter wrote in his ledger. I wondered if old St. Pete was the patron saint of chartered accountants.

O'Brien bustled in from an adjoining room, leaned toward his daughter and gave her a stingy peck on the cheek. He turned to me without the slightest hint that we'd met before and pumped my hand with both of his, as though he expected that water might flow from one of my openings. "Great to meet you, Dear Boy." I had no idea what he might be thinking, but to onlookers he might appear to treat me like one of his golfing buddies. "Isabel's told me about you, Mr. ... Fletcher, is it?"

I took a close look at him: big smile, red crinkled face, a handful of freckles scattered across his drinker's nose. Pretty smooth, a crafty old bugger, trying to back me into a corner already. "Dexter," I said. "Call me Max."

"Of course, of course ... Well, do come in. Glad you're early. Gives me a chance to show you around a bit."

He led us into the room from which he'd come and spread his arms, encompassing dozens of paintings covering the walls and more displayed on free-standing easels. "All these works will be showing at the Art Gallery of Hamilton," he said. "Promising young artist named Bruce. Part of Hamilton's famous Bruce family. You know, his great-uncle painted at Giverny when Monet worked there." He jabbered away as we toured the cavernous room, perhaps larger than the Art Gallery itself, which occupied the upstairs space of the old Hamilton Public Library. "I often invite some of my associates for an advance showing of good exhibitions," he said. "We buy a few pieces to support the artists. And we raise a few bucks for the Art Gallery Building Fund." Talking down to my level now, trying to be one of the boys, speaking about bucks. But why would he try to impress me? Was this just a clumsy effort to influence his daughter? Get her to return to the fold? Or did he have some other dodge?

The doorbell had sounded several times and voices murmured from the foyer. O'Brien grabbed my arm and gave my hand another thorough shaking. "You'll have to excuse me now. Isabel can show you the other rooms on this floor, Mr. ... Specter." And he hurried away.

She grinned at me. "Mr. Specter, eh? That's one of his oldest tricks. Is he putting you down? Or is he just forgetful? He convinces himself that you're too lamebrained to figure it out."

Men in tuxedos and their fashionably-attired escorts began to drift into the gallery room and the volume of chatter rose. Two bartenders sporting black pants and white shirts with black leather bow ties manned a serving bar in one corner; women in white blouses and black skirts began circulating with silver trays of hot canapés. We lacked only the dapper little man with the monocle to make it a scene from the cover of *The New Yorker.*

An hour later, fifty or sixty like-minded citizens gossiped, nibbled and drank. And a few even glanced at the paintings. Then O'Brien clinked a cocktail fork against his champagne flute as he stood atop a small stool to bellow across the room. "Thank you, my friends. I'm sure you're enjoying the wonderful paintings during tonight's preview showing. Now please welcome our featured artist, who'll say a few words. Ladies and Gentlemen, Robert Bruce."

A smattering of applause petered out in a hurry while O'Brien changed places with a thin young guy, round-shouldered and bespectacled, his bushy brown hair hanging past the collar of a too-large tux that shouted "Rental".

"Thank you, Mr. O'Brien. Ladies and Gentlemen, I appreciate your attendance here tonight and your generous support of the Gallery Building Fund." His reedy voice didn't stand a chance against this crowd. "I'll be available for the rest of the evening if anyone wishes to discuss my paintings." He jumped down and stationed himself beside an imposing landscape that might have been a view of the Niagara Escarpment. No one seemed to have noticed that he'd finished speaking, and I wandered over to him, standing alone.

"Nifty speech," I said. "Just how I like 'em."

He looked me up and down, then waved his arm toward the crowd. "You're the only guy in a business suit, Bud, lookin' like he doesn't belong here. What are ya, hired muscle? Keepin' O'Brien's pals in check so the assholes don't get too drunk or challenge someone to a duel?"

I stared at him, startled by his hoodlum-speak. "You sure you're an artist?"

His hollow face relaxed and a crooked smile appeared. "Of course I am. For your info, all artists don't live in garrets and commune with otherworldly forces through their belly buttons."

I laughed. "Is that what I thought?"

"I don't know what the hell you thought." A look on his face like a carnival barker playing with a rube. "I noticed you earlier, sort of slinkin' among the swells, keepin' your ears open, tryin' to be invisible, maybe even casin' the joint so you'd know the layout when you returned with a lock-pick and a truck." His hazel eyes focused on mine and his small mouth twitched as he tried to suppress a grin.

"Is this stuff worth stealing?" I asked, and he couldn't hold back a guffaw.

"Not my stuff," he said, wiping his brow with the back of his hand. "Well, maybe after I'm dead and my brilliance has been recognized. But I understand O'Brien has quite a valuable collection. Including a few Old Masters ... so they might be worth the risk."

"I thought Old Masters was a brand of cigar."

He squinted at me, I guessed in pity. "Who the hell invited you anyway? I saw you talkin' to O'Brien's daughter earlier so you must be known to someone. But doncha know nuthin' about art?" He moved a bit closer and his voice took on a schoolmarm tone. "The Old Masters were the great European painters of the sixteenth and seventeenth centuries. Rembrandt, Titian, Velazquez, all that gang."

"Worth a few bucks, then?"

He huffed out another burst of laughter. "Let me tell you, Bud. It's a sure bet you don't have the dough tucked away under your mattress that those babies fetch. If they're ever for sale."

I grinned. "How do you know I couldn't afford it?"

He bent his head and gave me a sharp look over his wire-rimmed specs. "You? Why, you're still wearing your Army-issue dress shoes, for Chrissake."

I looked down at the evidence of my budgetary limitation and back up at the artist. "You're smarter than you look, Buster," I said. "And I like your gangster act. What's your name again?"

"Roger Bruce."

"I thought O'Brien introduced you as Robert."

"He's a horse's ass."

"So why are you here?"

He rubbed his chin with his fingers, eyes squeezed half-shut, appearing to puzzle over whether or not to tell me the truth. "It's the horrible part of being an artist," he finally said. "I love to paint. Jeez, I *live* to paint. But I'm making my own way, not relying on family money. So I have to sell my work to eat. That means appearing at functions like this, smiling at people who attend these shindigs only to be seen. One or two paintings might sell, but the matrons here are looking for something nice in lilac or chartreuse to match their wallpaper." He drew a deep breath into his skinny chest and made a show of blowing it out. "It's a shitty life and then you die."

"Sounds like fun."

"Yeah, there's no life like it." A goofy grin on his face now.

A chubby woman overflowing a pink gown shouldered me out of her way, stepping on my foot as she planted her painted face close to the artist's startled features. "What's that red and white painting beside the door supposed to be?" She spoke with a sneer, as though he were a slow-witted clerk at Woolworth's.

I leaned around her and gave him a friendly slap on the back and said, "Good luck, Pal."

I shook my head at the artist's lot and angled across the room to where Isabel was in conversation with a handsome woman wearing a low-cut gown and evening gloves.

A tap on my shoulder halted me and I turned to find H.B. Myers holding up his whisky glass and gesturing toward the bar. "Let's have a drink, Mr. Dexter. I'd like a word with you." My, my, what a surprise. My generous former client and person of interest to Scotty Lyle in his quest for Evelyn Dick's Black Book. What the hell does he want, I wondered.

I followed him to the serving area where the barman reached beneath the table and refilled his glass from a dusty bottle with a thistle on its yellowed label. "Will that be all, Mr. Myers?" A respectful bow.

Myers turned to me with his eyebrows raised.

"Beer, please," I said to the barman. "Anything cold."

From a cooler filled with ice chips, he extracted a green bottle and worked its lever-action spring to lift its white ceramic stopper. He poured its contents into a pewter mug with a glass bottom. "What brand is that?" I asked him.

He allowed me a polite smile, letting me know that my question revealed me as an outsider in this fast company. Maybe wondering, like the artist, what the hell I was doing here. "Grolsch lager, Sir. Imported from Holland."

Myers tugged my sleeve and we stepped behind the bar through a pair of glass doors partially concealed by a heavy curtain. Outside on a deserted flagstone patio a dozen or more wrought-iron chairs were grouped in twos and threes around circular cocktail tables. Myers flicked his handkerchief over the furthest seat from the door and arranged his tuxedo jacket before sitting. Observing his actions, I thought Scotty must be cuckoo. This is the last guy in the world I'd imagine hobnobbing with Evelyn Dick, loose woman about town. I plopped down across from him and breathed in the country club air of freshly-mown grass, noting the thunderheads building in the western sky. "Looks like rain," I said.

He regarded me without expression. "O'Brien tells me his daughter works for you." Not wasting time on niceties like the weather.

I returned his gaze, certain he knew this. So why was he asking? "You met her at my office the other day," I said, not giving anything away either.

"Ah." He stroked his almost-moustache. "I hadn't realized that was her. Of course, I should have ... the colouring, the fine features ..." What passed for a smile came my way. "Sorry for the intrusion into your business, Mr. Dexter. But I hadn't met Miss O'Brien before ... and I wondered why you might require a chartered accountant. But, no matter. It's just my idle curiosity working overtime."

His idle curiosity. Now he'd raised mine: why would it interest him that O'Brien's daughter worked for Max Dexter Associates? Was he just a nosy bugger?

Whatever he was, I didn't have to sit here and listen to him so I pushed my chair back to leave. "Don't think it hasn't been nice, Mr. Myers. By the way, I may need to contact you again about Jake Benson. His brother's hired me to look into his death."

He, too, had begun to rise from his chair but he stopped in mid-motion, his face as dark as the approaching storm. "But I thought we'd agreed that you'd drop the investigation because of the obvious criminal connection, now that it's a police matter."

"You and I agreed, Sir, that I'd stop looking into the matter on your behalf and you paid my fee, along with a generous bonus, for which I'm grateful. Now I'm working for another client."

The chill in his eyes made me shiver. "Jake Benson's brother, you say."

"Correct."

"But doesn't he understand that further investigation will only bring more unfortunate facts to light? The theft from my company, perhaps his brother's involvement with criminals, gambling or worse?" He sat and stared into the remains of his drink. "The poor man's wasting his money, he can only buy more grief,

I'm afraid." He took a long pull on his whisky and set the glass down precisely in its former position.

I followed his fastidious movement with my eyes, then told him straight, "My client believes his brother is innocent, Mr. Myers." I paused a beat. "And so do I."

A bland expression on his mug now, no doubt an ace poker player. "I see," he said, tapping one finger against his glass.

I tried reading his mind. No luck. Why was he so concerned about my keeping the Jake Benson pot boiling? Was Scotty correct that he might have some connection to the Mob? And was O'Brien involved in this … whatever it was? Honest to God, I was baffled – but I kept my trap shut.

Myers again focused on me. "Of course, I'm concerned that more probing might create unfortunate publicity for my company. And despite what you say, you must know, at the very least, Young Benson was a thief. So what good could come from further inquiries?"

I raised my beer mug, able to see his distorted features through its glass bottom as I sipped the tangy brew. Should I tackle him on his contention of Benson's guilt? Or wait until further investigation yielded something? "I can't answer your question today, Sir. Perhaps our efforts will be in vain. But my client wants the satisfaction of knowing that he did everything within his power to clear his brother's name."

Myers drained his glass in one long swallow. "I wish you well, Mr. Dexter. And if you're able to avoid embarrassment to my company, well, I'd be pleased to show my gratitude."

He was one cool customer alright, I had to give him that. Then he rose, straightened his jacket and returned to the reception, followed by a limping detective who suspected Myers' interest was a helluva lot more than he'd stated.

When I returned to the gallery room, the high-pitched chatter had increased by fifty decibels, punctuated by an occasional outburst of raucous laughter. It sounded like Duffy's Tavern after the Tigers won a football game. Except these birds were adorned in fancier feathers. A cloud of cigarette smoke drifted above the cream of Hamilton's society like the weather front outside, but carrying with it the spicy tang of cocktail sausages and Swedish meatballs.

I scanned the exuberant crowd for Isabel and spotted her across the room, standing before a six-foot painting, nodding her red curls while the artist showed her a section high in one corner. Elbows poised, I gritted my teeth and dove into the melee. When I emerged from the scrum, there was Old Man O'Brien who required a second try to link his arm with mine. His sweaty face close to my left ear, he shouted, "C'mon with me. I'll show you the good stuff." Alcohol fumes and second-hand garlic assaulted my nose and I backed away from him as best I could.

When we'd cleared the crowd I shook his arm free and he led me down a wide hallway to a carved oak door, which he opened with a key. Another gallery. A vast space for a private home, about forty feet by twenty or so. One of the shorter walls was bookshelved, floor to ceiling. The other three held more paintings than I'd ever seen, hung one above the other, three and sometimes four high. An oversized desk and a grouping of chairs sat near the short wall, the rest of the room's floor space taken up by a variety of display cabinets, glassed on all four sides to allow close-up viewing of exquisite glassware, carved boxes, jewellery and similar objects. This was a windowless room, indirect lighting filtering down from the ceiling, spotlights mounted over specific paintings while the cabinets were lit from within. A breathtaking sight, especially for a guy from the North End of Hamilton whose knowledge of paintings consisted of a copy of *The Last Supper* hanging on the main altar of St. Mary's Church, and a picture of a snooty-looking kid in a blue velvet suit which Mrs. Mosca, our old neighbour on Napier Street, had clipped from a magazine and pinned over her kitchen sink.

O'Brien waved an arm around the precious room, throwing himself a bit off-balance. "I call this my library, Mr. Specter." His speech was slurred and my incorrect name came out "Schpecter". He walked over to a sideboard and poured brandy into two snifters and passed one to me. "My private retreat and sanctuary." With his glass he gestured toward a painting with a cushioned bench stationed in front of it. "Let's do the royal tour." His face glowed even redder in the presence of his treasures.

Why was this crafty man acting so friendly toward me? Had he forgotten about our tense meeting concerning Isabel yesterday? Not bloody likely, I thought.

He directed me to the bench and snapped on the narrow lamp above a picture of a man. I gazed at a head-and-shoulders view of a middle-aged gent, dressed in an old-time costume with a wide-brimmed hat, his intelligent eyes holding my attention. I smiled up at O'Brien, standing beside me, puffed up like a peacock. "Recognize the signature in the top corner?" he asked me.

It was difficult to read from this distance. "Remhart, something like that?"

"Tut tut, Mr. Maxner. It's signed by Rembrandt himself, a wonderful self-portrait. I admire its brilliance every day."

"One of the Old Masters," I said, remembering the term the artist had mentioned earlier.

"Now you've got it." He clapped me on the back then led me to a corner grouping which included a small mounted panel showing a Crucifixion scene. "Rubens," he said with a self-satisfied grin. "Another master."

We toured the jewel-box room, O'Brien rhyming off the titles of paintings, the names and dates of painters in a rapid-fire commentary. "Watteau here ... Fragonard there ... Frans Hals over there ..."

The grand tour finished, he guided me toward the sitting area. Even a complete nitwit in the field of art couldn't help being impressed by his collection. "I guess such beautiful and expensive paintings don't come up for sale very often." More of my friendly artist's wisdom.

After he'd poured himself more brandy – I took plain soda – we settled into a pair of red leather club chairs. "That's right," he said. "I attend the auctions in Toronto and I get over to Europe from time to time. Private collectors also buy and sell artworks to each other. My Rembrandt, for example, I acquired from my dear friend Henry Myers, who has many magnificent paintings in his collection." He buried his beezer in his snifter and snorted its bouquet with a well-on-the-way-to-being-soused smile.

My dear friend Henry Myers. That stopped me in my tracks. So these guys were pals, but what the hell did that mean? No question they were a couple of arrogant rich guys and it made sense that birds of a feather ... But what else might it signify? I recalled Scotty's interest in Myers and wondered if O'Brien might've been along for that ride, too.

He interrupted my reverie with a nudge, almost upsetting my soda water. "I thought about your advice on raising my daughter," he said. "And decided you might have a point." He leaned forward in his chair, making sure he had my attention. Was he changing his tune or was it just the booze talking?

"She's intelligent for a girl, even if she does want to work with you." He covered his mouth with his hand and burped several times. He found his smile again, wriggled forward and grasped my arm in both his hands, hoisting himself upright. "Time to rejoin my guests." He propelled me toward the doorway with a hand on my back and pronounced his words with great care. "No reason why we can't be friends, eh, Mr. Daxton?"

CHAPTER SEVENTEEN

BACK IN THE MAIN ROOM, Iz grasped my hand just as her father waded into the sea of society, not appearing to notice my sudden absence.

"Had enough fun yet?" She had to shout to be heard.

"More than enough to last me 'til next time," I said.

She was still holding my hand and squeezed it now. "Then let's get out of this hothouse." Her mouth was close enough to my ear that a tingle shot up my spine. I turned my head, noting her smile had something extra in it. And I wondered . . .

The artist, stationed near the doorway with no customers to entertain, waved as we swept past him and called out the Hamilton football cheer "Oskee-Wee-Wee". I glanced over my shoulder at his grinning mug and he thumbed his nose. What a joker.

"You all right to drive?" I asked as we approached her car.

She slid behind the wheel, her dress riding up, as I dropped into the passenger's seat. "I'm fine, Max." A slow head turn and a foxy wink. "Don't I look fine?"

"You always look fine." The words popping out of my mouth.

"You're a smooth-talking guy when you get a couple of drinks in you, Mr. Specter." Then she backed down the driveway one-handed, spun the wheel and we were back in Hamilton in Le Mans qualifying time. On Main Street she slowed to turn right at Longwood Road, passed the sprawling Westinghouse plant and drove down Aberdeen, a ritzier part of town. Another turn into a narrow street with a steep incline to the foot of that mole-sized hill which Hamiltonians call their Mountain. She pulled into the driveway of a Tudor mansion and parked beside a two-storey carriage house partway along the drive. We sat in the dark, trying to read each other's minds.

"Come in for a nightcap," she said. "I'll drive you home later."

I gulped. "Sure this is a good idea?"

She tilted her head close to mine, her perfume sneaking up on me like wispy fingers, enticing me. "You're a veteran. I'm sure you can handle it."

We entered through the front door and she flicked on the lights in a wide entry hall, the living room off to the right. She plopped her purse on a low table and stooped to turn on a floor lamp. "Sit down and put your feet up," she said, indicating a long leather couch. "I'll fetch something to drink." On her way out she stopped before a Philco radio/record player and twisted a couple of knobs. A record released from the changer and the Glenn Miller band with Tex Beneke and the Modernaires bounced along to *Don't Sit Under the Apple Tree With Anyone Else But Me*. I had a theory that you could learn something about a person's character from the type of music they listened to when they were alone. And since she hadn't replaced the platter now spinning on the turntable, this tune revealed something about her. Well, I didn't say it was a perfect theory.

I sat as instructed, dragged a leather hassock closer, propped up my leg and sank into the creamy embrace of the sofa. Ice cubes clinked in the adjoining room and I noticed several doors giving off the central hallway. Tastefully-decorated spaces, fresh-cut flowers on the coffee table. I chuckled to myself; how did she manage it on her Max Dexter Associates' salary?

She returned with a silver tray carrying a bowl of ice cubes, two glasses, Beefeater Gin, Schweppes tonic. "Something funny?"

I shook my head, still smiling.

She moved the flowers aside, set the tray down and spoke in a throaty Lauren Bacall voice, "I love a G and T before bedtime." Then she kicked off her slingback shoes, sat down close to me and busied herself with the drinks.

What did that mean, before bedtime? I cleared my throat. Thought I needed to blow my nose but changed my mind. "You … uh … live here … alone?"

She handed me a drink, then tucked her feet beneath her on the couch, taking her time, making me squirm. When she faced me, she said, "This was my father's estate before he moved to Ancaster. He sold the big house at the end of the lane. Renovated this carriage house for me when I joined the family business." She took a long sip of her G and T, examining me over the rim of her glass. "Does it bother you that I have money?"

"Of course not." My response was too hasty. "Well, maybe." I loosened my tie. "I'm not sure. I haven't thought about it, I guess."

"Tell me what you're thinking right now."

I felt as if my fingers and toes were attached to electrodes and Peter Lorre was saying, "Should I or shouldn't I?" at the control switch. The first time I'd felt a buzz like this had been on a Saturday afternoon in the back row of the Capitol Theatre when Maureen O'Connor squeezed my hand and said, "I like your style, Sport." Of course, Isabel wasn't holding my hand. But I wasn't fourteen years old either. "Uh … what was the question again?"

Slower this time. "Tell me what you're thinking."

I fidgeted in my seat before setting my drink on the table. "I'm thinking about you, Iz. You're a beautiful, smart woman. And a rich one, I suppose. It's been a long, tiring day, we've had a few drinks, we're winding down on a big soft sofa in a quiet comfy room and you look … relaxed … curled up beside me." Her eyelids drooped, her lips parted and she sipped again. "But I'm a bit uncomfortable because … Well, you're my associate and I don't want to jeopardize our good working relationship."

She stared at me for half an eternity, her green eyes boring into mine and I began to melt from the inside out. With one hand resting on my chest, she leaned in closer and her feathery lips settled on mine like a butterfly landing on a rose petal. "You're right," she said. Then she kissed me again, harder and longer this time. I felt like a jellyfish must feel: rubbery, limbs drifting and tingling in the current, waiting for the tide to swoosh me away.

She set down her glass, picked up her shoes by their straps and swung down the hallway, calling over her shoulder, "I'm slipping into something more comfortable. Be with you in a jiffy."

My head was aswirl. Was this really happening to me? Every guy's fantasy: a rich, beautiful woman appears to welcome your attention. *So what the hell am I waiting for?* I blew my nose, then straightened my tie. Then loosened it again. *This is not a good idea.* I stood up and straightened my tie again, heading for the hallway as Isabel emerged from the far end, wearing a pair of tailored slacks, a light sweater and tennis shoes. She picked up her purse and twirled her keys with a jaunty smile. "I'll run you home now."

I was silent all the way back to my apartment, unsure whether I'd been smacked by a Mack truck from the front or the rear. Maybe both. Did I do something wrong? Or something right? Was she happy, relieved perhaps? Or madder than a wet hen?

When she pulled up to the curb at my place she reached across and touched my arm. "I respect your feelings, Max. And I won't do anything to jeopardize my chance to learn the detective business from you." She gave me a bittersweet smile. "We both had a few drinks tonight and shared an interesting time."

I opened my mouth to reply, with predictable results. So I stepped from the car, closed the door and bent over to wave through the window as she zipped away. "Good night," I said, too late.

A couple of hours later, I sat in my kitchen, working the *Spectator*'s crossword, drinking another cup of cold Maxwell House. I couldn't sleep, couldn't even think straight. Was I foolish to resist a closer friendship with Isabel? One moment it had seemed the right thing to do; then again, it seemed like the stupidest move I'd ever made. Or not made. Lord love a duck!

I snapped on the radio and felt lucky for a moment because I'd caught Oscar Peterson playing from the Alberta Lounge in Montreal. With his thousand-mile-an-hour wizardry at the keyboard he always picked up my spirits when he pounded out a boogie-woogie beat. But it wasn't working tonight and I turned off the broadcast.

I limped into the bathroom and stared at the guy in the mirror. Not the same guy with the clean white shirt and the Windsor knot in his tie. This one was in his underwear, his hair messed, bloodshot eyes and a heavy five o'clock shadow. He drew in a deep breath, which fogged up the mirror when he blew it out. Through the mist I heard him mutter, sounding just like my father, "So what are you going to do now, Hotshot?"

CHAPTER EIGHTEEN

OH-DARK-THIRTY, AND SWEAT TRICKLED DOWN my spine as I paced in my underwear from my sitting room to the kitchen. The bedroom was a steam cabinet, the electric fan succeeding only in swirling the muggy air around the room like warm molasses. I sponged off and returned to bed, struck again at how alike Simon Benson and I seemed to be. Each of us had a dead parent; his father was in a coma, my mother was also out of touch, albeit by her own choice; neither of us appeared to have close family connections; our jobs had become our lives; we'd both rejected the comfort that religions sometimes offered. After a while I drifted off, puzzling as Job did at why shitty things happen to well-meaning people ...

Two goons were beating me with short lengths of hose as I lay shackled to an iron bedstead in the prison camp's dank and foul-smelling interrogation cell. My wounded knee was screaming from the unbearable pressure of a diabolical device clamped to my right leg. I caught a quick glimpse of it when the guards carried it into the cell and attached it to the bed – an oversized, cast-iron vice, its gaping jaws studded with spikes still dripping with blood and bits of bone and flesh from its previous use. The smooth-shaven face of the officer-in-charge betrayed no emotion at all as he tightened the vice until I passed out ... again.

When I came to this time he was hovering over me, his face just inches from mine, a thin smile playing across his mean lips. In his heavy accent he repeated, "You must tell us, *mein Herr.* The movement of your troops." Then he stood to attention and clapped his hands like a circus ringmaster. At this signal, an overhead spotlight pinpointed a sallow-faced and haggard Simon Benson who was slumped on a stool with what appeared to be an oversized ventriloquist's dummy on his lap. But the dummy he clutched in despair was his dead and decomposing brother, Jake. I stared into Simon's eyes: two deep wells of sadness and utter loss.

The ringmaster's well-groomed features loomed before me again. "And now, Sergeant, we show you how we conduct our medical experiments."

I somehow managed to gather the dregs of my strength. I reached out and my fingers closed around something solid and I crashed it into the face of this devil's disciple ...

The impact shot me upright in my own bed. My entire body was dripping with sweat, the single sheet twisted around my ankles, my knee throbbing in pain. I gaped at the mangled electric fan lying in ruins near the open bedroom window. I sat panting on the edge of the bed before limping into the bathroom to towel off.

The haggard mug staring back at me from the mirror looked like I'd gone ten rounds with Jack Dempsey. The rehab doctors had warned that nightmares might return, perhaps for years after the war. And I'd thought I was past the worst of it ... no recurrence for the past few months. To make it worse, tonight was the first time those Nazi bastards had actually caught me.

For ten minutes I stood under a cold shower, then remade the bed and tossed about in a half-sleep until a clap of thunder bolted me awake. I glanced at my alarm clock: oh-four-thirty, and a heavy curtain of ozone hung in the soupy air. And just before dawn, coin-sized raindrops blew in through the window, heralding a break in the heat wave.

I did my deep-breathing exercises and got up to face the day. I flicked on the mantel radio in the galley kitchen, tuning in CHML, and ate a bowl of Grape-Nuts Flakes while standing at the sink. The static caused by the rainstorm threatened to drown out Vic Copps as he ran through the sports news: Hamilton was two points behind Batavia in the PONY League after beating Jamestown two-nothing last night; the racing season was scheduled to open Saturday at the Hamilton Jockey Club. Then he launched into a long rigamarole about the merits of merging the Wildcats and the Tigers football clubs and "the benefits which would accrue to our fair city". Sometimes Vic sounded more like a politician than a sportscaster.

The phone rang and I snapped off the radio. Simon Benson confirmed that arrangements had been made for Jake's burial at Beth Jacob Cemetery this morning. "I've rented a car so I could pick you up at nine if you're still interested in going with me."

I agreed and rang off, sat at the folding card table in my sitting room and wrote up my notes from yesterday's meetings. Then I waited in the small entranceway of my apartment building until Simon pulled to the curb in a dark-coloured Chevy. I raised my umbrella against the steady rain, limped out to the car, stowed my umbrella in the rear, and slid in beside him. A great day for a funeral.

He reached across the seat to shake my hand, his voice a shaky whisper. "Thanks for coming, Max. It means a lot to have someone with me."

Downtown, we drove in silence along York Street. Simon appeared lost in thought, and several drivers blasted their horns at his slow pace. "The cemetery's off Snake Road," he said. "Maybe you could keep your eyes peeled so I don't miss it."

We crossed the High Level Bridge over the Desjardins Canal as the west wind howled, rain rattling the car's windows like buckshot. So blustery we could barely make out the giant Neilson's sign ahead at Clappison's Cut. We slowed at the Rock Gardens, turning right onto the winding road down to the water's edge on the Burlington side of the bay. Following the discreet signs to the cemetery, we parked alongside four other cars near a group of men huddling under black umbrellas. When we approached, one of them stepped forward and shook Simon's hand. Before Simon could introduce him, he shook my hand and bowed in the European fashion.

"I'm Rabbi Fackenheim," he said in a heavy German accent. "I'm sorry to meet you under such sad circumstances." Then he withdrew something from his jacket pocket and stepped closer. "It's customary for men to wear a head covering at a service, so I brought these yarmulkes for you."

The other men moved in procession toward an open gravesite sheltered by a canvas tarpaulin. We followed them, the rabbi explaining that, by tradition, only men recited the memorial prayer, the Kaddish, at a Jewish burial service, and that ten men constituted a quorum for prayer. "It is fortunate," he said, "that enough members from the congregation were willing to volunteer."

We hunched together under the tarp to avoid the splatter of the rain. Simon clamped onto my arm, tears streaming down his already damp cheeks as he stared at the plain wooden box holding the remains of his only brother. I concentrated on my sopping shoes and breathed in the loamy smell of the fresh-dug grave, trying but failing to imagine myself in a happier place. Then the rabbi delivered a short eulogy and led the men in the solemn recitation of the Hebrew prayers. When the casket was lowered, we each in turn shovelled a scoop of earth onto it. The men shook Simon's hand, bowed and left. The pain in my leg had intensified during the service, perhaps in sympathy for Jake Benson, so I limped to the car while the rabbi stayed behind in quiet conversation with the remaining Benson brother.

A silent Simon piloted the Chevy back into town while I stared out the rain-streaked window. My body in the front seat, my mind at the gravesite. Back in town, I asked him to leave me at his hotel since I had a few errands downtown anyway. He reached across the passenger seat to grasp my shoulder. "I couldn't have gone through this without you, Max ..."

I nodded and scooted closer to the window to get his hand off my shoulder. I confess I did feel a bit choked up – burying someone will do that to you, even if you don't know the deceased. But I wasn't ready to start weeping in Simon's arms or anything.

After several deep breaths, he got a grip on himself. "I couldn't hold anything down this morning," he said. "I'll try to eat something now. Then maybe I'll rest a while. We could meet this afternoon, Max. I have to pick up a few things at Jake's apartment and I'd appreciate the company."

I cleared my throat. "Sure. I'll be here about three. It's close enough that we can walk over."

I had no errands downtown. But I needed a transfusion of the city's lifeblood to bring me back to life. I'd felt that same need yesterday following my lunch with Ed Zielinski. Cold and calculating, Zielinski always infuriated me the way he regarded people as pawns on his chessboard which he moved at his whim. So yesterday I'd wandered through the outdoor farmers' market, hoping the hubbub of the growers hawking their produce to bargain-hunting shoppers might draw me back from the foul mood Zielinski never failed to leave with me, even if he'd paid for lunch. As I'd strolled through the aisles, I pictured Jake Benson as he might have inhaled the heady, sweet aroma of Niagara peaches mingled with the tang of freshly-cut cauliflower and I listened to the banter of animated shoppers in Italian, Chinese, Yiddish and Hamilton English.

I'd paused beside a stack of wire cages and eavesdropped on an impossible exchange between a cockney-accented poultry farmer and an ancient Chinese woman searching for the perfect bird among the squawkers on offer. She finally chose a fat, white chicken. The farmer yanked it from its cage, snapped its neck and stuffed it into her wicker shopping basket in a fluid, sleight-of-hand motion that Blackstone the Magician would envy. The old lady hobbled away smiling, perhaps at her bargaining skill; the farmer grinned as he slipped her coins into the leather pouch attached to his belt.

But the farmers' market didn't operate on Sundays. And here I stood in front of that same stall, now empty, remembering that vital scene and feeling better for it. How often, I wondered, did I need reminding that death was a necessary part of life?

The rain had stopped and I wandered up to King Street, feeling even better as I absorbed the happier mood of the strolling pedestrians. I stopped under the Connaught's marquee to pick up a Veterans Cab and the doorman sauntered over. "High pressure system moving in fast," he said. "Look at those clouds racing eastward. It'll be clear in an hour. Then the hot stuff'll be back."

Oh boy, another closet weatherman. We had a plague of them in Hamilton. I gave him my withering glare and said, "Could be right, Bub." I waved over a cab from the line at the curb.

Back at my apartment, I propped up my complaining leg and dialled Isabel's number. I told her that I'd attended Jake Benson's funeral with his brother and I described the simple ceremony at the graveside. "It was very moving." My voice croaked, the image of Simon's tortured face still etched in my mind.

"Oh, Max. I'm so sorry. Where is Simon now? We should be with him."

Her compassion touched me and it gave me an idea. "He's at the hotel … resting. I'm going with him to Jake's apartment this afternoon. Interested in coming along?"

She answered right away. "I sure am. We have to find the … whoever's responsible for Jake's death." The determination in her voice confirmed it would be a big mistake to underestimate her strength of will, maybe a quality she'd inherited from her old man. "What time do you want me to pick you up, Max?"

CHAPTER NINETEEN

AT HIS HOTEL, A MORE alive version of Simon Benson greeted us. I gestured toward the stylish woman who resembled an attorney in her tailored grey suit, carrying a black leather briefcase, and introduced them. "This is one of my associates, Isabel O'Brien." They shook hands. "Isabel's an accountant," I told him. "I hope you don't mind, but I asked her along to help us go through your brother's financial records and so on." While we were driving to the hotel, I'd explained to Iz that Simon had hired us to clear the family name since it didn't appear the police would prolong their investigation.

He gave her a shy smile and nodded. "I'd welcome your help."

It was a short walk to Jake's Hess Street apartment and inside the building a strong whiff of corned beef and cabbage mingled with floor wax braced us as we trooped to the end of a dim hallway where Simon opened the door. The first-floor apartment was a basic one-bedroom layout: living room, kitchen with just enough room for a wooden table and two chairs, a good-sized bedroom and a poky bath/shower arrangement.

"Why don't we go into the living room," I said. Simon and I sat on a rock-hard sofa covered in a yellow and green tartan fabric, while Iz settled into a matching armchair. The room had all the charm of the men's lounge at the Bay Street Tavern.

Simon's face was as bleak and drawn as it had been at the funeral this morning, dark pouches sagging under his unfocused eyes; he seemed to be operating on autopilot, pretending to be alive. I glanced at Iz observing his automaton state with misty eyes, and my stomach tied in knots.

I drew a deep breath. "I know this is very difficult," I said, but my mouth dried and I coughed to cover up.

Iz sprang to her feet. "Maybe I can find us something to drink." She bustled into the kitchen, where cupboard doors opened and closed with a rattle.

Simon roused himself and laid a heavy hand on my arm. "I appreciate your help, Max. I just can't seem to do more for myself right now."

Iz poked her head into the room. "Sorry, there's not much choice. Tea or water?"

Simon managed a weak smile. "Water," he said and I signalled the same.

I placed my hand on top of his. "We're going to find out what happened to Jake," I told him. "That might be some comfort, but it's up to you to make sense of your life without your brother."

He raised his head and after a moment his eyes seemed to focus. "You're right." He sounded somewhat stronger. "Thanks."

Iz returned with two glasses of water and a chipped mug of clear tea on a Coca-Cola tray; she placed a plate of dry cookies on the coffee table in front of Simon. His mouth betrayed the tiniest of grins and he said, "Those were always Jake's favourites. Arrowroot biscuits."

I drank my water, lukewarm, but I wouldn't eat an Arrowroot on a bet. "I noticed the desk in the bedroom," I said to Simon. "Would you mind if Isabel took a look at Jake's papers? You'll need to close out his bank account, look after his lease here and so on."

He turned to her. "That would be a big help." Then, with a shrug, "I saw those papers ... but I couldn't bring myself to look at them."

She went into the bedroom with her briefcase and I could hear her shuffling through the contents of the desk. I withdrew my notebook and checked my list. "Perhaps I could look around." I set my glass on the table and stood up.

"Please, go ahead ... I know it's necessary. Maybe I'll go for a walk while you two are busy."

After he'd left I did a systematic search, not expecting to find much after Frank Russo and his boys had been through here.

And I was right: everything you'd expect to find, but nothing you wouldn't. I remembered Doris Arneson mentioning Jake was a jazz fan and, sure enough, pride of place in the living room was given to a framed poster advertising the appearance of the Duke Ellington Orchestra at the Palais Royale in Toronto last year. Duke himself was pictured at the keyboard and seemed to be smiling down at Jake Benson's portable radio/record player on a low table beneath the poster. I riffled through the stacks of 78 records on the table, mostly big bands – Benny Goodman, Dizzy Gillespie, Count Basie, and several others. I checked the record still on the turntable and wasn't surprised to find Duke's theme song, *Take the 'A' Train.*

A bookcase beside the living room window housed a collection of accounting manuals, some of Jake's university texts, several new volumes on Jewish history and even a few detective stories by Dashiell Hammett and Arthur Conan Doyle. I shook through the books but no clues flew out.

In the bedroom I searched the chest of drawers. Nothing unusual, no envelopes or secret codes taped to the drawer bottoms. Next I clanked through the hangers in the closet: no notes in his pants or jacket pockets. But I did find a pair of tickets for Ella Fitzgerald's appearance at the Brant Inn next week and I wondered who he'd planned to take with him.

Iz was busy writing at Jake's desk when I entered his bedroom. "Just about finished, Max. Nothing out of the ordinary, I'm afraid: bank statements, chequing account and a three-hundred-dollar savings account. Can't find a will or any correspondence with a legal firm. Small life insurance policy through his office. Cancelled cheques show he's up to date with lease payments, utilities and all that. No car insurance or ownership papers so I'm assuming no car. Correspondence with the nursing home about his father's care." She snapped her briefcase closed. "Everything looks in order to me." Standing, she smoothed her skirt, a twinkle in her green eyes. "You can always count on a good accountant, Max."

The front door banged open and Simon entered, red splotches blooming on his cheeks and the fine lines around his eyes and mouth seemed less prominent. "Find anything?"

"Nothing unusual," I said, then remembered the tickets. "Oh. I came across a couple of tickets for an Ella Fitzgerald performance at the Brant Inn. Near the end of the month, I think it was. Was he planning to attend with you?"

He shook his head. "No. He didn't discuss it with me."

I handed him the small envelope containing the tickets but he didn't accept it. "Keep them," he told me. "I won't be in the mood for dancing for a while."

Iz showed Simon the stack of papers on the desk. "I've rearranged these and left a list on top showing which items you'll have to attend to first. I hope it helps."

"Both of you have been very kind. If you're finished here, I'm going to drive out to Dundas to visit my father."

We were standing in the doorway shaking hands when Isabel asked about a narrow wooden case, maybe six inches long, attached at an angle to the door frame at about eye level. The same faded colour as the frame, it was almost invisible unless seen in this raking light with the door open.

Simon tapped it, making a hollow sound. "A mezuzah," he said. "For years, Jake and I didn't know what it was; we thought it might be some souvenir my mother had brought from the old country, but she never talked to us about it. After her burial in Beth Jacob Cemetery, of course, we learned about her Jewish background." He stroked the small object with respect. "It held a special meaning for my mother, so Jake continued the tradition of attaching it to the doorpost. I'm so used to seeing it, I never notice anymore." His slender fingers traced the marks etched into the box's surface. "Hebrew letters. Inside is a piece of parchment with passages from the Torah."

Iz moved in much closer, her face inches from the little container before she returned her gaze to Simon, her eyebrows raised in interest. He retrieved a sturdy knife from his pocket and opened a blunt-tipped blade. "Might as well take it down right now, so I won't forget it. Then you could have a closer look."

When he'd removed the screws, he placed the mezuzah in her outstretched palm, opening the case with care to reveal the parchment. And a small flat key. She sent me an inquiring look. I reached over her shoulder and lifted the shiny key, turning it this way and that in the brighter light of the doorway, revealing a number stamped on one side. 472. "Are you thinking what I'm thinking?" I asked her.

"Yep," she said. "Safe deposit box."

Simon's lips moved but without sound, as though he were speaking beside Niagara Falls. Isabel and I exchanged a glance. If this key fit a safe deposit box, where was it and what secret did it hold? The money missing from Myers Investments Ltd.? Other incriminating evidence ... gambling debts ... to the Mob, maybe? Shit in a mitt! If that were true, Simon's world would be shattered. A shudder crept up my backbone.

"I have no idea what this is about," Simon said at last.

"There's nothing in Jake's papers referring to a safe deposit box," Iz said. "I guess we should check with his bank, though."

I closed the front door and we returned to the living room, resuming our former places. Simon voiced the unthinkable. "I can't believe Jake embezzled money from his employer and hid it in a bank vault."

Some fire burned in his eyes and his features contorted like the holdout juror in the movies, frustrated at his inability to convince the rest of the jury of the accused's innocence. And I had to warn him. "We'll need to discover whether there's a box, find it and open it to prove that."

We sat in silence for several moments before he produced a journal from his jacket which contained an envelope. "This came in the mail last week." He passed it to me. "I didn't think it was important. Until now."

Inside the envelope was a single photograph, four by six inches. "Your brother," I said, handing it to Iz. "Standing in front of a building."

"The photo is all I received," he said. "No letter, nothing else. I assumed Jake forgot to enclose his note and thought no more about it." Simon's voice trailed off and he stared at the floor.

"This photo's been taken from an odd angle," Iz said. "Or maybe it's been altered."

I indicated the top section of the picture. "Maybe to conceal the name of the building. From what we can see, it looks sort of familiar. A government building. Or maybe a museum."

"Well, it's not the Royal Ontario Museum," Simon said. "It could be a bank, but why send the photo if it doesn't identify the location?"

"Maybe it was cropped so it would look like just another family snapshot," I said.

"That's all I thought it was ..." Simon began.

"Yes." Iz said. "Maybe to protect the person Jake sent the photo to."

"But why–"

I cut him off. "We don't know yet. Isabel could be right that Jake was attempting to shield you. He might've thought you'd be in danger."

He slumped on the sofa, fidgety now. "What should we do next?"

"Find the building in the photo," I said.

"How?" He seemed unable to think straight.

Iz passed the photo back to me and I tapped it with my finger. "For starters, assuming this is a photo of a bank, we'll visit every damn branch in town until we find it. Then you can open Jake's safe deposit box."

That seemed to make sense to him and he nodded.

"And tomorrow we'll make copies of this photo for Liam at Duffy's Tavern to show to his bartender pals. They might remember seeing Jake the night before he disappeared. Where he was and at what time. Who he was with. And who knows? We might get lucky."

Simon slumped back in his seat, a deflated balloon, and Iz moved to help him to his feet. "C'mon Max. Let's get this poor man back to his hotel."

We walked once more toward the doorway and I placed an arm around Simon's narrow shoulders. "Not to frighten you," I said, "but I think you should take Jake's papers and valuables and return to Toronto. Back to your usual routine until we know what we're up against here. And maybe you should postpone that visit to your father. Let's get you checked out of your hotel. Then we'll take you to the train station."

He began shaking his head as though to object, but stopped. His eyes flitted around the room and he inhaled, perhaps breathing in his brother's presence for the last time. "Alright," he said in a hoarse voice. "Sounds like good advice."

After a short stop at his hotel where I checked the train schedule while Simon packed, we dropped him at the station with ten minutes to spare. He gave Isabel a shy peck on the cheek and shook my hand with more heartiness than he probably felt. "Thank you both. I'll always remember your kindness."

After he'd boarded, we returned to Iz's car and I asked her to drop me at my place, so I could change before heading off to dinner at Frank's.

She turned to face me. "We should talk about last night, Max."

The raking sunlight through the windshield revealed she wore little makeup, highlighting the crop of freckles on her nose and along the tops of her cheeks. I tried out a smile. "Cocktail parties wear me out, Iz. All that standing around."

She extended both hands, palms toward me. "This is all I want to say on the subject. Last night was last night. We're two grown people who enjoy each other's company. Will we become more than friends?" She shrugged. "I don't know. And we'd both have to feel comfortable for that to happen. Or it wouldn't." Throughout this little speech her green eyes were locked onto mine, no obvious signs of embarrassment or hesitation. "I joined you to learn the business, Max. No ulterior motives ... I guarantee it." She gave me her hand and we shook with a firm business-like squeeze and a smile.

"You have a knack for reading my mind," I said. "And saying what I think, better than I can. You know, you did well back there with Simon."

"Thank you. But I'm worried about our client. I hope you don't believe whoever murdered Jake might have designs on his brother, too."

"Just being cautious. Depends where this key leads us. And if Jake's killer thinks his brother might know something ..."

CHAPTER TWENTY

FRANK RUSSO SAT SHIRTLESS AND sweaty on the front steps of his tidy house on Mulberry Street, swigging a bottle of Red Cap Ale, as I stepped from a Veterans Cab at the curb, brandishing a bouquet of red and orange zinnias, fresh from the market. When I limped up the narrow walkway, his dark features split with a white-toothed smile. "Big-shot private eye takes cab to visit poor but pious friends," he said. "Or did your old clunker finally give up the ghost?"

I ignored his smartass remarks and took a theatrical sniff of the bouquet. "No objections to Ontario-grown flowers, eh?"

His mug contorted in feigned pain. "Ooooh. Low blow." He wrapped a hairy arm around my shoulder and kicked open the screen door, bringing me through the darkened living room toward the kitchen. The aroma of braised veal and garlic wafted through the open doorway along with a wobbly soprano voice crooning along with Frankie Laine's hit tune on the radio, *That's My Desire.*

Angela grinned at me over her shoulder while adding white wine to the Italian rice cooking on the stovetop, the rising steam plastering a few ebony curls to her forehead. "Maa-xie." She sang out my name, her dark eyes widening when she caught sight of the posies. "Kiss me quick," she said and leaned her glistening cheek toward me as she continued to stir the risotto.

I kissed her with a loud smack and she tipped her head back with a husky laugh. "Wow, that was a doozie." She motioned to her husband with a wooden spoon. "C'mon over here and watch the rice while I put these beautiful flowers in water." I sat at the kitchen table and she pecked me on the forehead. "Thank you,

Max, they're lovely." She gave her husband the look. "How come you don't bring me flowers anymore, *caro mio?*"

He scowled at me and she snapped off the radio just as Frankie Laine sang, "We'll sip a little glass of wine."

"Speaking of which," she said and took Frank's spot at the stove as she pushed him toward an assortment of wine bottles on the adjoining counter. "Max and I'll have a little glass of the special red."

During dinner I heard much more than I needed to know about the proud parents' year-old twin boys, still napping upstairs after a long afternoon of pampering by their Italian mama.

At dusk we dangled our feet off the back stoop, sipping more of the special red, special because he'd made it himself. Frank lit up a White Owl, sliding the red and gold cigar band onto one of his wife's bare toes as she giggled. Angela spoke with pride about her herb garden sprouting beneath the kitchen window and the morning glories marching skyward on strings along the side of a tarpapered shed at the rear of their thirty-foot lot. She smiled at me through a cloud of smoke from Frank's stogie. "I'm so lucky, Max. What more could a girl from the North End wish for?" She paused and cast a sharp look at Frank. "A hubby who doesn't have to work nights and weekends would be nice, though, but I guess you can't have everything."

Frank smiled and kissed her on the lips. "I think I hear the boys waking up," he told her.

"Bathtime," she said, then bustled through the kitchen, calling over her shoulder, "come up and see them later."

Frank leaned back, balancing on his tailbone by gripping his right knee with intertwined fingers. "This is the life, Maxie." A cloud of cigar smoke circled his head, discouraging a few mosquitoes. "You know, Rosa still asks about you."

I gave him my killer stare. "My big brother. Still looking out for me. Now let's change the subject."

He punched me on the arm and guffawed. "Sure. Guess you wanna squeeze me for info on the Benson case. By the way, did the brother call you?"

I nodded. "Back on the job, Frank."

"Well, I wish you luck. Captain's ready to put the case on ice. Poor Benson's just one more floater, I guess. Same ending as Rocco Perri, eh?"

Rocco Perri. The name blasted through my brain like a gunshot. Perri and his gangsters, the bastards who'd murdered my father. And they got away with it – no arrests were ever made. "I heard he disappeared without a trace."

Frank puffed his stogie and flicked the ashes into the herbs. "Lots of theories kickin' around, Max. But let's just say old Rocco went into the bay and never came out. Now we've got several gangs beatin' the shit out of each other, still competing to replace him as top dog. And the gang leaders keep turnin' up dead. Plus anybody else who gets in the way."

I waved the smokescreen away from my face. Mob killings, wars waged by the criminals seeking to control the rackets: illegal booze, gambling, prostitution and, increasingly, narcotics. Despite this mayhem, the newspapers and radio stations were preoccupied with recovery plans following the war, resettlement of displaced persons and firing up the peacetime economy. The gang wars received scant coverage other than the body count, perhaps because little could be done to stop them. I glanced at Frank, scowling and grinding his teeth. "Yeah," I said. "A crappy situation. But what can you do about it?"

"Sweet Fanny Adams." He sighed. "And the voting public says, look the other way and let the bastards kill themselves." He stubbed his cigar butt into a coffee can half-filled with sand. "Lotta scuttlebutt about the politicians and the police brass being paid off but, shit, you always hear that."

"Pretty discouraging."

"You're tellin' me. But, listen, anything you need on the Benson case, just give me a call. I'll do what I can, and to hell with the captain."

I clapped him on the shoulder. "Thanks, Pal."

There was something else I wanted to discuss with him but I wondered how to get into it without him thinking I was being critical of his department. "Mind if I ask a question about the Evelyn Dick case, Frank?"

He turned toward me with a frown and I could almost feel the tension this subject caused him. I knew that Frank himself didn't have much to do with the Dick case, but it was widely believed the Hamilton cops had botched their part in the investigation, even though the Ontario Provincial Police were in charge. As a result, members of the Hamilton force became pretty damn defensive when discussing the case, especially with civilians. He took a deep breath, taking his time to release it. "What about it?" he said at last.

"Well, I heard that Evelyn kept a notebook or address book whose contents could embarrass some high-profile people if it became public."

"Oh yeah? Where'd you hear that?"

I reached over and squeezed his arm. "Frank, I'm not accusing you or your mates on the force of anything, so don't freeze me out. Scotty Lyle told me Evelyn had such a book and I wondered if it's true."

"Scotty Lyle." Frank spit the name out like he'd taken a swig of panther piss. Most of the cops I knew had a similar reaction; some referred to reporters, especially Scotty, as masters of the misquotation or lying bastards or a helluva lot worse. But Frank wasn't usually that extreme.

"C'mon, Frank. Scotty's my uncle."

"Yeah, I know. But those press guys were all over us during the Dick case. Sure, some mistakes were made but a lot of the reporting was just bullshit in order to sell their stupid papers."

"I know that goes on," I told him. "But Scotty does his homework and he's usually accurate. He claims Evelyn's book contained names of big shots and maybe other info. One of the investigators referred to the book during her first trial, but then it disappeared."

I saw the cords in Frank's neck begin to relax and he nodded. "I heard that too, but I don't know any details." He looked me straight in the eye and I believed him. "So what's your interest?" he said. "I thought you were gung-ho on the Benson case and that's got nothin' to do with Evelyn Dick."

"That's what I thought, too. But the rumour is that Tedesco's name is in that book. And there may be a link between him and our pal Henry Myers."

"What? Are you nuts, Max? No chance in hell a slick Mafia guy like Tedesco would give that shrimpy little society snob the time of day."

I flicked at a mosquito buzzing around my face. "I know, Frank. But they do know each other. Scotty told me they're both serving on the St. Joe's fundraising committee."

Frank puzzled over that for a few seconds, then snorted. "Humph … Yeah, well. Doesn't mean nuthin'."

We brooded for a while until the darkness brought on squadrons of mosquitoes, driving us indoors. Frank clapped me on the back and flipped on the lights as we passed into the living room. It felt cosier in here but my shitty mood persisted and Frank picked up on it. "You seem down in the mouth, Maxie. What's up?"

"Had a helluva long day," I said. Then I described my sleepless night, the Benson family's unlucky lives, and the burial service at the cemetery that morning. "So I'm making an early night of it."

"Wait a minute," he said. "You said the burial was at Beth Jacob Cemetery? Does that mean this Benson was a Hebe?"

I gave him a sharp look. "Well, his mother was Jewish. So he was allowed to be buried there." I wasn't surprised he'd referred to Simon as a Hebe; you often heard Jews called kikes or sheenies or hymies as well. Frank was my closest friend but, like most people in Hamilton, he carried a heavy load of so-called common knowledge with him. So "everyone" knew that Jews were rich and powerful and sneaky and stuck to themselves. Just as everyone also knew all about niggers and dagos and Polacks.

I glanced at him slumped in his chair and decided not to get into another long discussion with him about our prejudices. His usually swarthy face was drained of colour and deep furrows plowed across his brow. He raked his big hands through his black mop of hair. "Shit," he said. "You got me thinkin' about funerals. And I've attended too damn many of them." He cleared his throat. Cleared it again. "Our regiment lost so many good men at Dieppe. My God, what a waste when people die so young." He was breathing through his mouth now. "I didn't mention this before but when I saw Benson's face underwater when we recovered him from the bay … Jesus, it snapped me right back to '42. I was slogging through waist-deep waves, almost to the beach, when the body of our lieutenant floated up in front of me, his empty eyes staring, shot in the throat by the goddamn Krauts … same age as Benson."

We sank back on the old red couch, thinking our own thoughts. Frank's grisly discovery of his lieutenant; my Normandy nightmares. In the seconds before my leg was blown out from under me, I'd scrambled to drag a wounded corporal to safety beneath a mud-mired truck. My last memory before blacking out was his scream when his body exploded and I fell backward still clutching his severed arm and part of his torso.

"You know, we'll never forget this shit, eh?" Frank said. "It's my family that keeps me going, Max. I don't know how you manage. Honest to God, I don't."

I turned to speak but when I saw his eyes glistening, the lump rising in my throat blocked my response. I swallowed several times, then blew my nose for something to do. And I admitted, "Sometimes I don't manage, Frank."

He curved one arm around my shoulders and with the other he yanked me to my feet. "Upstairs, Buster." He spoke in a forced, cheerful voice. "It helps to see the next generation."

We heard the commotion from the bathroom as we mounted the stairs. Angela was kneeling at the side of the cast iron tub cooing, the kids gurgling and splashing somewhere beneath the high rim. The smell of baby powder and breast milk hung in the warm room like a fog bank, reminding me of an earlier visit when I'd been stunned by the sight of her nursing the boys, one suckling on each breast. "Don't be embarrassed," she'd said. "Mother at work." And laughed like a loon at my little boy's blush and hasty exit from the room.

Now Frank and I crammed into the narrow doorway, eyes tearing up, stupid grins on our faces. Angela sensed our presence, turned her head and snapped her eyes wide. "What's the matter with you guys?"

Frank bent down and kissed her, motioning for me to approach the tub. Two Michelangelo cherubs lay on their backs, chubby arms and legs pumping like Olympic swimmers, communicating with each other in the secret way that twins do. Holy mackerel! My insides churned like a washing machine gone berserk. Today's events had swooshed my emotions from the depths of Simon Benson's grief and the emptiness of my own life to the pure joy of these newly-minted little people. I gulped. I blinked. I said to Frank, "Good thing they don't look anything like their old man."

CHAPTER TWENTY-ONE

WHEN I ENTERED THE OFFICE in the morning I was greeted with a warm smile. "Oh, hi there, Max," Phyllis said, as fresh as a spring breeze off Lake Ontario. She bobbed her head toward my room. "Isabel's inside."

I glanced in at my assistant/detective-in-training, spreading her papers on another long table squeezed against the wall. I limped to my desk and plopped in the chair. Even a brisk massage of my scalp wasn't doing the trick to clear my cobwebs this morning. I felt the surveillance and looked up to find Iz watching my contortions, her eyes shining and a quirky smile on her lips. I tilted my head toward the newly-decorated wall beside my desk.

"What's this?" I said. "You don't think I can keep track of the date?" She'd thumb-tacked a calendar on the wall containing a colour photo of some young girls trying on dresses.

"Oh, Max," she said. "Isn't it the sweetest picture – those girls are so cute." Iz was glowing. "Don't you just love it?"

I bent down and took a closer look. "Well, maybe love's a bit strong."

She moved over to my desk now for a closer view then gave me a quizzical glance. "I don't understand, Max."

I squirmed while she set her sights on me. "Who isn't crazy about the Dionne Quints?" she said.

"Well ..." I thought about it a moment. "I just wondered if it was appropriate for a business office and–"

"Oh, pish, Max. Don't be such an ickeroo. Everyone will love it, just wait and see."

"Ickeroo?"

"Fuddy-duddy," she said.

Lost another skirmish, I thought, so I scrambled to change the subject. "What's all that paper?" I said.

She waved a dismissive hand. "Pfffft ... just part of my financial analysis. I'll deal with it later. But first things first. We have to follow up on that photo Jake sent to Simon." Full of spunk she was, like a new recruit.

"Sure. I'll have copies made later. For now let's get some coffee and knuckle down here."

When we were settled I opened a package of three-by-five index cards, gave half to Iz, and we headed each card with the name of a person involved or thought to be involved in the Jake Benson case: H.B. Myers, my former client, his generous bonus still niggling at me; Ken Thompson, Benson's former boss and his immediate supervisor; why had he played his cards so close to his too-tight vest? Doris Arneson, dated Jake and maybe more? And other Myers employees: Walter Potts, accountant whose nose was probably clean; Chuck Cysko, whose nose was anything but clean; Miss Carlson, Myers' secretary – beautiful, sure, but I thought her coming on to me was a bit too staged for God-knows-what reason, so I'd already tossed her business card away; Rabbi Fackenheim – Jake had been meeting with him, and he might be helpful; Sister Norbert at the old folks' home, I thought I'd learned all I could from her; J.B. O'Brien, Isabel's successful father and art collector, who'd referred to Myers as a good friend, and that connection had my antenna quivering. Next, for the people we'd already interviewed, we transcribed the main points from our notebooks to these cards. Then we grouped them by category: Jake Benson's office contacts; family members; a number of blank cards for casual acquaintances, social contacts/friends yet to be discovered.

"We don't have that many cards, Max, and no one stands out as a prime suspect." She stopped rearranging them in alphabetical order, staring at one. "Your note about Cysko. 'Investment scam'. What does that have to do with Jake Benson?"

I related my conversation with Jimmy Nolan about Cysko's European reconstruction program. "It's a thread we have to follow. I plan to have another chat with Call-me-Chuck."

"Interesting," she said and continued to sort the cards until she gasped. "My God. You think my father's involved in this?"

I still hadn't told her of my little chat with her old man, not wanting to upset her. Maybe I should have but I said, "Open mind, Iz. We're only on the doorstep of this investigation. We cast the net wide, see what we catch. Then comes the tedious part of ruling people out." I hurried on to the next name. "H. B. Myers," I said.

"Yes. But we don't know much about him. I can't believe he's involved in Jake's murder. I mean, if funds were embezzled and the audit trail led to Jake, wouldn't Mr. Myers report him to the police, try to recover the money and then fire Jake?"

"But he didn't do that, did he? Instead, he hired Max Dexter Associates to find the culprit and avoid adverse publicity. But Jake Benson appears to be a good guy and that raises questions about Myers."

"Doesn't prove anything, Max."

"Of course not. But why did he do what he did? We just don't know yet. Same thing with Cysko. To me, he came across as a blustery windbag with nothing to hide but his stupidity. But his business card turns up in a possible investment scam. Was he in cahoots with someone? Myers, for instance? Or even Jake Benson, who occupied the office beside him? Maybe Jake teamed up with him and embezzled the money from the company to put up his stake in the scheme."

She shook her head at that possibility and returned to a previous card, snapping its edge. "And J. B. O'Brien?"

Damn, I knew she wouldn't let that pass.

"During the art reception he showed me his private collection," I said. "Especially proud of a valuable Rembrandt painting. Said he bought it from his good friend, Henry Myers."

A flash in her green eyes. "So?"

"I don't know. That's the point. There's a connection between Myers and your father and if it's just business, fine. But maybe it's more than that." It flashed through my mind to tell her about Scotty Lyle's suspicion that Myers might be mentioned in Evelyn Dick's Black Book. And by extension, perhaps Myers' good friend

J.B. O'Brien was in it too. No, I decided, too early to stir that pot. Could be nothing at all.

Then it occurred to me that I'd been speaking with more force than I'd intended and I lowered my voice. "Our job is to follow the trail, wherever it leads. Often it takes you up a blind alley, but you can't move on until you've looked into it. And keeping an open mind is never easy."

After an awkward pause she replaced the card bearing her father's name. "Okay. What's next?"

We sipped our coffee and I allowed the space between us to cool a few degrees. "Well ... examining these cards is a good way to identify gaps in the information, connections between various individuals and so on. In a complicated case I like to make a diagram showing just the names and dates from the cards. Sometimes the result is surprising and a link jumps right out at you."

She bounced the eraser end of her HB pencil against the pile of cards. "What about the evidence, the clues or whatnot?"

I lifted my cup in her direction. "Right. I keep a separate list of that info, including the locations of where things took place. Then that list can be plugged into the overall diagram and patterns sometimes emerge. Often not. For example, our evidence list now includes a key, which could fit a bank deposit box, and a photograph that might show a bank. Consulting our cards, we ask ourselves which of those contacts might know something about such a box? So we re-interview and go from there."

She fanned out the array of cards and lifted one, tapping it on the table. "We should talk to the rabbi. You never know, Jake may have trusted him enough to mention something to him."

"Good. And speaking of banks, I made a list of those Jake might've used in this end of the city. On the way to Frank's for dinner last night, I had the cabbie make the tour and none of them matched the photo."

She frowned, staring at the index card as though it might reveal the building's location. Then her features brightened and she pointed the card at me. "Toronto. Remember Simon told me Jake visited him a few weeks ago? Makes sense, Max. A location out of town. Maybe he believed someone was watching him in Hamilton."

"Not bad. But there must be hundreds of banks in Toronto." I reached over to my desk and fished out a Chamber of Commerce map of Hamilton. "Let's finish up here first." I scanned the map. "Can't be that many left to check. Maybe later this afternoon."

"Or Sister what's-her-name at his father's rest home might know something about it." She flipped her hand back and forth. "Mmmm. Maybe not. I think we might have better luck talking to people at Jake's office again. Someone there must know more about him."

"That's what I was thinking. But listen," I said. "You've got your plate full here at the office and I don't want to overload you too soon. Which reminds me, how's Phyllis working out?"

"She's the cat's whiskers, Max. Pleasant personality, hard-working and smart as a whip." Her grin betrayed something, but I couldn't figure out what. "You couldn't have made a better choice," she said.

I almost responded to her jab but decided that was a dead-end street and changed the subject instead. "Alright, let's do this – since I'm known at Myers' company, I'll check back with some of Jake's co-workers. Meantime, why don't you contact the rabbi? See if he can fit you in this afternoon."

She was tapping her foot, anxious to get cracking. I recalled her father's low opinion of her abilities and, so he claimed, her short-lived enthusiasms. All of which was so at odds with her appearance right now. I was pleased I hadn't told her of my little man-to-man audience with him. And if O'Brien were involved in a crooked art scheme ... well, damnit, the scandal would be difficult for her to bear. But even if he did prove to be a shit, he was the only father she had so she'd probably believe she owed him something.

She made a note in her book, maybe about contacting the rabbi. "Lots to do today," she said. "I'd better get on with it." And she breezed out of my office.

I reshuffled the cards for the staff at Myers Investments Ltd. Had I already spoken with someone who'd clammed up on me about Jake Benson? I stared at the top card: ARNESON, DORIS.

The tiniest tingle binged in my brain. The Nordic blonde. We'd had a cup of coffee together and I'd liked her, but ...

I flipped back through my notebook and reread my interview notes. Miss Arneson had confirmed that Benson was a hard worker, stayed late most nights and was liked by his co-workers. She'd told me he treated the secretaries with respect: a nice person. But he was something of a loner who liked to drop into the clubs after work. "Doesn't make time for women," I'd noted, and Doris had seemed disappointed, had hinted that she'd tried to get something going with him.

I tossed my notebook on the desk, propped up my leg and leaned back. The detective in his deep thinker mode. At the time of our meeting, Jake Benson was only missing and Doris didn't seem to be hiding anything. But now that he'd been murdered ...

I picked up the phone and dialled.

"Accounting Department; Miss Pietro."

'Hi, this is Max Dexter. I'm calling for Doris Arneson, please."

"I'm sorry, Mr. Dexter. She's not in today."

"Oh. There's no problem, I hope. I was in last week to see her."

"Yes, I remember you. I'm afraid Doris has been off with a terrible flu. I spoke with her earlier this morning and she's still under the weather."

"That's too bad. Got her number handy? Maybe I'll give her a buzz and wish her a speedy recovery."

"Sure. I'll get it for you."

I dialled her number several times: no answer. My phone book listed a D. Arneson on Queen Street at the same number I'd been calling. It wasn't that far, so why not?

I didn't spot a cab nearby so I boarded a streetcar on King and jerked westward to Queen Street then limped south to a small apartment block a few doors along where I checked the mailboxes in the entranceway:

D. ARNESON
APT. 4

Second floor, right above the entrance. No answer to my repeated knocking, so I pounded the door with the flat of my hand. The neighbour's door cracked open and I saw a grey head peeking into the hallway. Suspicious eyes assessing me over eyeglasses resting on the tip of her long nose, a woman who looked like a Hallowe'en witch said, "She's out, Sonny." And slammed her door. I guessed she hadn't recognized me as a professional detective who would have reached that same conclusion without her help.

Outside, I crossed over to a churchyard where a row of elms flanked the sidewalk and parked myself in the shade to keep an eye on Doris' building. Street traffic was light this time of day: a couple of mothers with babies in carriages wheeled by; three kids on bicycles, carrying baseball gloves, maybe headed to Victoria Park, where at their age I'd won my only game as starting pitcher for the Napier Street Cardinals.

Twenty minutes later a Veterans Cab squeaked to a halt and a handsome blonde wearing a black dress, a wide-brimmed black hat and dark glasses stepped out. She removed her glasses and dug in her purse, also black, then passed money to the cabbie through the open window on the passenger's side. Waiting for her change, she raised her head and glanced toward King Street. You guessed it: Doris Arneson, grey-faced and haggard. As she entered her building, the cab pulled away and I noted the number on its front door panel.

I saw no movement in her front window, no lights came on. Sick with the flu, I'd been told. But from her black attire and desperate expression, she appeared to have attended a funeral. Perhaps unwise to knock on her door, uninvited.

So I returned to the telephone booth on the corner to call her. But first, I deposited a nickel and dialled Veterans Cab. "Lefty, it's Max. I need a favour."

"Anything for our best customer, Sarge. What'll ya have?"

"I'm up near 34 Queen South where one-oh-seven just dropped off a fare. Where'd the driver pick her up?"

"Hang on a minute, I'm lookin' at the sheet. Yeah, here it is, Arneson. She was picked up right there. Herbie's back on days and he drove her out to that Jewish cemetery on Snake Road. Know where that is?"

What the hell? Doris attending a funeral at the same cemetery where Jake Benson had been buried. Helluva big coincidence.

"Ya still there, Sarge?" Lefty yelled into the receiver.

"Yeah … I'm here."

"Well, Herbie takes her out there, waits maybe fifteen, twenty minutes. Then brings her back home."

"Okay, Lefty." My mind was still reeling. "Thanks."

Leaning against the door of the phone booth, I stared at the steady line of traffic inching its busy way along King Street, but saw Doris Arneson grieving at Jake Benson's gravesite. And I couldn't figure why she might've covered up such a close connection to Jake when I'd spoken with her in that dinky coffee shop.

She answered the phone on the fifth ring. "Hello," came a cracked almost-whisper.

"It's Max Dexter calling. Someone at your office told me you were home with the flu. I hope you're feeling better."

She coughed and blew her nose. "Thank you."

"Well, I'm sorry to bother you when you're not feeling well. But I'm still working on the Jake Benson case." She gasped in my ear. "And it's important that I speak with you again," I said.

"But I don't …" Short, quick breaths, "… understand. Who's hired you?"

"Jake's brother, Simon. He wants to clear Jake's name and reputation. And so do I."

A long pause on the line, Doris' breathing slowing, then a deep sigh. "I'm so glad to hear that. Jake couldn't have done anything wrong, Mr. Dexter. I've heard those rumours going around about embezzling money from the company and other nasty things. But it's just not true. Jake could never do that." Another silence before she said, "I'll help in any way I can."

Well, at least she was talking, but she sounded afraid. "Could I come to see you?"

She blew her nose again and cleared her throat. "Yes, of course. How about this afternoon, about three?"

"Alright. And I'd like to bring one of my associates. I think you'll like her."

Doris agreed and we rang off. I crossed the street and caught a streetcar back to the office. From my seat near the front, I observed a slender woman dressed in black seated nearby, clutching her handbag on her lap, an empty stare. Was she in mourning, as Doris Arneson was? The expression on Doris' face while she'd waited for her change from the cabbie had been as haunted and hopeless as this woman's across the aisle from me now. And, I thought, sometimes this world can be a shitty place.

CHAPTER TWENTY-TWO

As I APPROACHED MY OFFICE, I heard Pete the mailman hooting with laughter inside. I paused for a moment then barged through the doorway like a high school principal, giving him my Sister Theresa voice. "It's surprising how long it takes to deliver an armload of advertising flyers, when there's an attractive young lady involved."

His head snapped up, a hesitant smile on his round mug, but he remained bent over a newspaper spread out on the desk, his neck stretched forward like a turtle's. Phyllis stood beside him with a sparkle in her eye.

"Hi there, Max," Pete said. "C'mon over here and lookit these babes."

Stepping around the mailbag which he'd abandoned in the centre of the floor I glanced at a full-page layout of beauty pageant contestants in various poses, some in evening dresses, others in bathing suits with sashes saying "Miss So-and-so".

"Hubba hubba," he said, almost drooling. "It's the Miss Canada Pageant. Right here in Hamilton. Next month." His eyebrows arched and his Adam's apple bobbed as he looked at the pictures.

"And Barbara Ann Scott will be at the opening ceremonies," Phyllis said.

"I'm surprised at you, Pete." I tapped my forefinger on his breastbone in mock outrage. "I thought you'd outgrown your adolescent obsession with ogling women in their bathing suits."

His mouth gaped open and he rubbed his chest where I'd been poking him, his eyebrows reaching his hairline. "Cripes, it ain't that. These are swell lookin' dames, I'll grant ya." He spoke too fast, spittle spraying toward me, and I took a step back. "But ya see, one of the contestants, Miss Central Ontario," his arms were waving now, "is a local girl, a coed at McMaster. So the honour of the city's at stake."

Phyllis' eyes moved from Pete to me and back again. I gave him my medium-hard stare, but he didn't crack. Then we both broke into laughter and began pushing at each other like kids in a schoolyard argument.

Phyllis rolled her eyes as if to say, "Men."

A moment later Pete was on his way, still chuckling, his mailbag slapping against the door jamb. "You're a character, Max," he called over his shoulder. "See ya tamorra, Phyllis."

Phyllis folded the newspaper while she told me Isabel was meeting with Rabbi Fackenheim and would be back after lunch. I ate a sandwich at the table in my office and studied the photo of Jake, still wondering about the building in the background. It wasn't any of the banks in town that I'd checked on the way to Frank's last night, so we'd have to keep looking. Iz had told me Jake held his financial accounts at the Royal Bank, so I called a friend at the main branch.

"Long time no see, Dex. You pumpin' me for info again?" Liz Lipinski was a classmate from Central High days. Lippy was one of her nicknames, with good reason.

"C'mon, Liz, would I do that?" I had to move the receiver away to protect my eardrum from her horse laugh. "You're right," I continued, "I'm checking on one your customers. Jake Benson. Now deceased."

The merriment went out of her voice. "Cops were snoopin' around here this morning. And you know I can't disclose personal information."

"I know, I know. But I'm working this case for his family. In addition to keeping his accounts at the Royal, I wondered if he rented a safe deposit box there, too."

"Well …" Steady breathing, and then she relented. "I guess it wouldn't hurt. Okay. He didn't. Just two accounts: savings and chequing. And you didn't get that from me, right?"

I thanked her and hung up. Shit. Strike that lead.

Next, I called Ronnie at Hamilton Photo and Supplies and after our usual banter got down to business. "Need some copies of a photo, Bud. Chop-chop," I said. "Think you can squeeze 'em in this aft?"

"Jeez, you ain't askin' much, are ya? Who the hell was your servant last week?"

More back-and-forth before he agreed and I arranged to drop off the photo. Later I'd pass the copies to Liam at Duffy's Tavern so he could circulate them among his bartender buddies.

Next I called to arrange an appointment with Chuck Cysko, got Miss Pietro again.

"Sorry, Mr. Dexter. Seems Mr. Cysko isn't in the office today and I couldn't find out when he's returning."

My, my. Another missing employee? Call-me-Chuck was becoming more and more interesting. "Is that usual?"

"Well, yes and no." She snickered. "In Mr. Cysko's case, you never know. But I'll leave a message for him to call you."

I swallowed my frustration and returned to the study of my index cards, feeling like one of those gypsies in her tiny store-front along York Street who divines your future from her tarot deck.

Fifteen fruitless minutes later and my cards still lay before me. None had levitated. None appeared to reveal its secrets from the netherworld. But Cysko's card was back in my hand. I took that as a sign from the great beyond, looked up his home number and dialled. Busy signal. Meaning he was at home? Or maybe he shared a party line.

Not one to leave a stone unturned, I phoned Vera Evans, my ace background checker and mother of the lofty Phyllis now typing like a Thompson submachine gun in the outer office.

"Not fair, Boss," Vera said. "I just got your latest list of names a couple of days ago."

I allowed her a moment to gripe about my unreasonable demands before I threatened to take my business elsewhere. Then she informed me the work was finished, already on its way to my office. This was our regular song and dance. Bizarre to some, perhaps, but a routine we were comfortable with. "Well, aren't you an old dear," I said. "Now do me a favour and read me the highlights from Cysko's report."

I waited while she found her copy, slamming a few cupboard doors for my benefit. "Here we are ... Mr. Cysko. He ain't in great shape, Boss. Reached his credit limit at the bank. Had a mortgage on his house but that was revoked and now he rents it. Credit Bureau rates him as high-risk. One of those bums who's allergic to paying his bills."

So my general suspicions about Cysko appeared to be well-founded. I asked her a few more questions then thanked her. I felt so pleased with myself about Cysko I even ignored her parting jab before she said, "Goombye, Boss."

Some time remained before Iz and I were due to meet with Doris Arneson, so I decided to pay a house call to Call-me-Chuck. Two Cyskos were listed in the street directory, side-by-side houses on Cannon Street, just a ten-minute limp away.

I stood before a pair of well-kept brick homes at 210 and 212 Cannon, identical except for the colour of their trim: one was painted a gleaming white, the other a pukey green. I mounted the stairs of 212 because I could hear Chuck Cysko's voice booming through the screen door, probably on the phone. At that moment, a flick of the curtain in the living room window next door caught my eye.

Vera had said Chuck's mortgage was revoked and now he rented this place. Betcha the folks at 210 were his parents/landlords and my arrival had been noted by his mama. I beat on the frame of the screen door several times before Cysko finished his phone call and clomped his way down the hallway.

I sent him a hundred-watt smile. "Sorry to bother you at home, Mr. Cysko," sounding as sincere as a Fuller Brush salesman.

After a puzzled moment he said, "Oh, it's that private dick." I was hurt that he didn't recognize me right away.

"Max Dexter," I reminded him, stepping through the doorway, shaking his hand and inviting myself into his living room. Mr. Fuller would have been proud of me.

Cysko seemed dazed – caught off guard at home, I supposed. He followed me in without a word and I sank into a worn club chair and waved at its mate. "Have a seat, Chuck. I just have a few questions."

He regained some of his composure, grinned at me then frowned. Poor Chuck: unsure as to which persona to show a guy who barged into his home uninvited. "So what's up?" he said. "I already told you everything I know about Benson. Besides, he's dead now."

What a swell guy, showing me his sensitive side. I just gave him the fish eye, watching him squirm and, courtesy of my chat with Jimmy Nolan, I said, "European reconstruction fund."

His flabby mouth gaped open like a fat grouper on a bed of ice at the Hamilton Fish Market. On his feet now, he was sputtering. "What the hell are you talking about?"

"And I hear the Bank of Montreal's worried about your loan. Might garnishee your wages."

He flopped back down in his chair with a thump. "So? You never had any trouble paying your bills? Goddamn banks are all controlled by the kikes, ya know, and all they care about is screwin' you out of your dough. Not only that–"

I cut him off. "You lost your mortgage and your job with Myers is on the line." I was guessing, of course, but, so far, my arrows seemed to be hitting the target.

"Where'd you get all this shit? Talkin' to my old man next door?"

Bull's eye. I let him stew for a moment. "How long have you been peddling this European reconstruction guff? You try to involve Jake Benson in your racket?"

"What racket?" His head jerked up as if I'd slapped him. "Anyhow, Benson was a goddamn goody-goody. Wouldn't say 'shit' if he had a mouthful."

So how'd he get this sudden reputation as an embezzler, I wondered. I dealt the remaining card from my deck. "Guy I met is interested in European paintings at a good price. Know anything about that? Who a guy might see to make a deal like that?"

He squinted at me as though I'd spoken in Urdu. "Say that again."

I rephrased, and a quirky smile crinkled his fish lips. "Paintings? Do I look like some powder-puff artsy type? Where the hell did you get you that dumb idea?"

I waited, on the lookout for a telltale twitch. But his features gave nothing away, and I didn't believe Call-me-Chuck was a great actor.

Arms outstretched, he said, "C'mon, Pal. What's goin' on here? I don't know what you want from me."

His watery eyes searched mine, and I returned the gaze of this pathetic, greedy hustler who rolled the dice to win a free ride on Easy Street and crapped out. Was he somehow involved in Benson's disappearance and murder? Whatever else he might be guilty of, I didn't think he had the stones for that kind of work. But people did the damnedest things.

I smacked the arm of my leather chair and his head snapped back. "Tell you what," I said. "I'm working with the cops on this Benson case. So I might have some influence, maybe when you're facing fraud charges for your investment scam."

His face was a ball of fire now. "What goddamn scam? You might think you're Hamilton's answer to Sam Spade, Buster, but I've had enough of your phony accusations. Now, get the hell outta here or I'll call the cops."

He was sitting forward, still fuming, when I grabbed his wrist and squeezed, hard. "Go right ahead. Ask for Sergeant Russo, he's investigating the Benson murder. Wants a word with you anyway."

Cysko slumped back in his chair and stared at me.

When I left I made sure the screen door slammed behind me.

CHAPTER TWENTY-THREE

DURING THE CAB RIDE TO Doris Arneson's, Isabel reported that the rabbi was one of the most sincere men she'd ever met, but he knew nothing about a safe deposit box or photo, or anything else that might help us discover why Jake was murdered. Likewise, I recounted my little tête-à-tête with Chuck Cysko. So far, two strikeouts in one day.

We stood in the linoleumed hallway in front of Doris' apartment and a familiar guilt pang knotted my stomach: I was about to intrude upon someone's sorrow and, no doubt, cause them to relive a painful experience.

Doris opened the door with a grim smile and ushered us into the living room, a faint odour of ammonia lay under the heavy smell of cigarette smoke. A high-backed sofa in a floral pattern and matching armchairs were grouped near the picture window facing the church across the street and she seated us there. "I've just made some lemonade," she said. "Be right back."

Iz sprang to her feet. "Let me help you." She linked her arm through Doris' and they entered the kitchen. Glasses clinked and cupboard doors closed, punctuated by murmuring. Iz was putting Doris at ease, allowing me time to wander about with my sensors at full alert. I appreciated my new assistant's innate ability for this kind of work. Or maybe most women had that knack and I was too stupid to notice.

I surveyed the room. Doris was an enthusiastic smoker, judging by the butt-filled ashtray. A few small framed photos: mom, dad and two little girls in frilly dresses posing beside an ancient Hudson; Doris and another young woman about her age lounging beside a pool. No pictures of Jake. But what did I expect, for cryin' out loud? No wiser, I regained my seat.

When she returned, Doris set the lemonade pitcher and a plate of date squares on the coffee table, apologizing for the out-of-season Christmas napkins. Then she settled in what seemed to be her favourite chair, the one nearest the window beside an art deco floor lamp and a side table stacked with magazines. Her reading glasses bookmarked an opened copy of *Redbook*. She sipped her lemonade and set the glass on a coaster beside her, fidgeting in her seat, fingering the seam along the arm of her chair where the flowery pattern was worn bare. She'd changed from her black dress into tan slacks, a white top and sandals: summery attire, wintry demeanour.

"It's been a hard time for me," she said and reached for the box of Virginia Ovals beside the ashtray. She lit her cigarette and directed a plume of smoke toward the ceiling, offering the box to us. We shook our heads, giving her all the time she needed.

She set her cigarette down and turned to me. "I just told Isabel that I'd never met Jake's brother. We'd talked about him, of course, and I know there was a strong bond between them. I understand why Simon would want to clear his family's name." She reached for her glass and drank half the lemonade. "And I'd like to help." Her voice had some resolve in it now.

Iz reached across from her place on the sofa and patted her hand. Another puff on her cigarette and Doris stubbed it out. She twisted her fingers in her lap, her eyes on the space between Iz and me. "Jake often worked late at the office, so I did too. Just to be near him. He was the sweetest guy I ever met."

She withdrew a handkerchief from her pocket and blew her nose, making a production of it. "This was about six months ago, one thing led to another and he asked me out for a drink. We often went to Fischer's Hotel to hear Jackie Washington; Jake loved his music." A faraway look entered her eyes and a smile crinkled her mouth. "Anyway, it wasn't long before we fell in love. But Jake was so private, didn't want anyone at the office to know about us. It would make our lives awkward, he said, and I accepted that. I just loved being with him."

She hunched forward and plucked at some invisible lint on her slacks. "A couple of weeks ago, Jake was working in the department manager's office while he was away for a few days.

Mr. Thompson. I guess you interviewed him, Max." At my nod she continued. "While Jake was looking in the manager's filing cabinet for a report, he came across some information that upset him. Lord knows why, but this led him to search further. One of the file drawers was double-locked and he said he was lucky to locate the keys in Mr. Thompson's desk." Doris dabbed at her eyes and repeated the word "lucky" as though it poisoned her mouth. "Well, he wouldn't show me what he'd found but I'd never seen Jake so disturbed. Said he'd like to put it in a safe place until he understood what it meant. The next day we took a long lunch hour. Grabbed a cab to Dundas, where we went to the Bank of Montreal. You know, the one right there on King Street across from the post office? I waited outside while Jake rented a box to hide whatever he'd found. Then he showed me how to work his camera. A good one, a Leica, I think. And he asked me to take a picture of him in front of the bank, but he wouldn't tell me why." She blew out a long breath.

Iz and I exchanged a hasty glance. I reached into my jacket pocket and handed the photo to Doris. Her eyes widened and she covered her mouth with her hand. "But ... where did you get this?"

"That's the photo you took?"

"Looks like it. But I think it was a wider shot than this."

Iz leaned toward her. "We think Jake had the picture cropped when he had the film developed. Then he sent it to Simon." She allowed Doris a moment to consider the implications.

Doris opened her mouth then closed it again. She turned to me for an answer.

I shrugged. "Perhaps Jake believed this information he'd found might be ... dangerous. To someone else, or even himself. So he hid it in the bank until he figured out what to do with it. He sent his brother a photo showing its location. And we found a key in his apartment."

Iz moved over to Doris' chair and sat on the wide arm, looping her arm around her shoulders. "We're assuming he had the photo cropped to protect his brother. Anyone seeing that picture would think it was just a family photo. In fact, that's what Simon believed, until we found the key. Looks like it's for a safe deposit box."

Our story seemed to crash over Doris like ocean waves, leaving her with the shivers. After a moment I said, "Tell us what really happened before Jake disappeared."

She leaned her head against Iz's arm before she straightened with a determined sigh. "A few days after I snapped that picture, Jake didn't show up for work. Before that he'd become agitated and remote. Worried about what he'd found and what to do about it. He said he spoke to Mr. Thompson when he returned. And then he met with Mr. Myers. But he tried to protect me by sparing me the details; he didn't want me implicated in whatever it was." She finished her drink and Iz refilled her glass.

Doris had my full attention now as she busied herself with wiping the condensation from her glass with a serviette. What did she just say? After finding whatever he found in Thompson's office, Jake met with Thompson and then Myers? That made sense, I supposed, but it was interesting that both of his bosses avoided telling me anything about that. I made a note to follow up.

"Hang on a sec," I told Doris as she was about to resume her story. "Did Jake say anything at all after his meeting with his manager or Mr. Myers? Were they angry that he'd removed something from the files, that kind of thing?"

"Well, you'd think they would be, but I just don't know," she said, shaking her head. "Jake wouldn't talk about it. Of course, I was worried sick when he disappeared. He didn't answer his phone; his apartment was always dark when I went by at night. Then you came to the office, Max, asking about Jake. You were working for the big boss then, so I couldn't admit to knowing Jake well, maybe to protect him ... and myself too. After that, I didn't feel I could go to the police, because I didn't know anything. Hell, I still don't. Except that Jake found something which scared him. He hid it. Then he went missing and ..." Her voice had faded to a whisper. "And now he's dead."

Isabel held her as Doris' shoulders shook with her sobs. We waited while she dried her eyes and relaxed her breathing enough to continue. "There has to be a connection between whatever

Jake found and his . . . death. But, my God, that's so hard to accept. I've worked at the Myers office for seven years and everyone's so friendly. I must be missing something." She paused for another gulp of air. "When I heard the news on the radio . . . that Jake's . . . that his body . . . had been fished out of the bay . . . then read it in the paper, I was devastated. I couldn't return to that office so I booked off sick. I phoned around to all the funeral homes and had a devil of a time finding out that Jake had been buried at Beth Jacob Cemetery." Her reddened eyes stared at me. "I didn't even know he was Jewish."

She rose and arched her back, her handkerchief falling to the floor. Iz retrieved it and returned it to her at the big window, where she now gazed at the churchyard across the street. "I visited Jake at the cemetery this morning." Her voice dribbled out in a ghostly whisper. "I miss him so much."

Iz hugged her, then guided her back to her chair. "Do you have family nearby? Anyone who could stay with you for a while?"

She shook her head, brushing a few stray tears from her cheeks. "Not close by. A sister in Montreal. I was thinking I might go down there for a while."

"That's a good idea," Iz said. "I could phone you with any developments here."

She attempted a grateful smile, which didn't reach her eyes. "Thank you. You're very sweet." She turned to me. "What'll happen now with the investigation?"

I tapped my notebook, where I'd written the name and location of the bank in Dundas. "We'll contact Simon and see what's in the safe deposit box. Then we'll go from there."

She twisted her hands again and spoke as though she were hypnotized. "If whatever Jake discovered led to his death, then whoever's responsible might still be looking for what's in that bank. And if his killer finds a connection between Jake and me, then I may be next on the list."

We sat in silence for a long moment. In the kitchen, a tap dripped. Doris seemed composed now and sat straight, as though a force had entered her body and stiffened her spine. "I guess that's why you'd like me to visit my sister. I can get a train tonight."

"I'll help you pack," Iz said and helped Doris to her feet with both hands and marched her down the hallway before she could change her mind.

I made a couple of quick phone calls from Doris' apartment and, back on the street, we glanced up as she waved from her window.

"You forgot to call us a cab," Iz said.

"Nope. Thought we'd take a little walk first. Then we'll stop by the photo shop and see if those copies are ready for Liam to circulate."

Along King Street car horns sounded, brakes squealed, pedestrians hurried by, shopping or returning from work. A couple of kids on bikes whizzed past ringing their bells and laughing. It felt good to be swept along with the pulse of the city, the tension of our meeting with Doris Arneson easing off. At the corner we stood and admired the beautiful old Scottish Rite Temple, a massive building resembling an oversized castle's keep. The building took up half a city block and was completely surrounded by a high wrought iron fence. "The Freemasons must have been doing pretty well when they put up this pile of stone," I said.

"They're doing too well, according to my father," Iz said. "He says the Masons are in league with the devil."

"Really?" I said, thinking O'Brien must be a member of the Knights of Columbus. I smiled at my new associate. "You know, Iz, you did well today. I'm proud of you."

She looked my way, a pink flush on her freckled cheeks. "Thank you. I liked Doris."

"I could tell."

"It was a good idea to check the train schedule and arrange for a cab to pick her up," she said.

"And the dispatcher will confirm when she's caught her train."

We walked west on King for three blocks and waited for the traffic light at Locke Street before crossing over to Victoria Park where a street vendor had stationed his pushcart, topped by a glass box alive with hot buttered popcorn. I bought two bags and passed one to Iz as we strolled toward the ball diamond.

"What are we doing here?" she said.

"That way." I showed her the bleachers where a few fans watched a kids' baseball game. We sat along the third base line and had to duck as a foul ball zinged past us into the stands. I wiped my buttery fingers on a clean handkerchief and passed it to her. "In answer to your question, this is the site of my boyhood triumph with the Napier Street Cardinals," I told her, pride in my voice.

She finished her mouthful of popcorn, shaking the red curls at me, the green eyes locked onto mine. "Max, my friend," her voice held a tone that you used with the slow-witted, "sometimes I think you're nuts."

Wow. What a dame. Look at her eating her popcorn, a bit of butter dribbling down her chin, relaxed and cool. She thinks you're full of shit, she tells you. And why not?

I placed my finger on my chin and nodded toward the hand-kerchief on her lap. She wiped her chin but didn't take her eyes from mine. "Tell me why you think I'm nuts," I said.

"Well, Max," that tone again, "we're hot on the trail of Jake's killer. The biggest clue we have is waiting for us in a bank in Dundas. And Doris just told us Jake met with Mr. Thompson and Mr. Myers after he'd made his discovery in Thompson's office. So they have to know a lot more than they've told you, don't they, Max? But instead of putting on our stalker's hats and fol-lowing the clues, we're at the park watching a bunch of kids chas-ing themselves around the bases." She heaved a Sarah Bernhardt sigh. "That's why."

At the crack of the bat, I turned my head. The kid at third base muffed an easy fly ball which caromed off his leg and rolled to a stop at our feet. I tossed him the ball and he missed that too. I smiled at him and regarded Iz, waiting with feigned patience for me to explain. I struggled to contain my grin; stalker's hats – that was a good one.

"I have to force myself to stop and relax," I said. "My mind gets clogged with a zillion ideas about the facts and non-facts you uncover on a case, the motives of the people involved. So I've learned from some of my stupid decisions that my brain needs some time, some diversion, so it can do its work."

Shouts from the ballplayers and another foul ball came our way. Iz jumped up, made a one-handed catch and side-armed it with a smack into the third baseman's mitt. The kid gaped at the ball he'd caught and grinned at her. So did I. She returned to her seat, straightened her skirt and resumed our conversation as if snagging a fly ball like Joe DiMaggio were an everyday event. "And what did your brain conclude today, Max?"

"A few things," I said. "First, we have to be careful. Doris is correct to assume she might be in danger if her link to Jake is discovered. Likewise, we might find ourselves in the sights of whoever's trying to find what Jake hid in that safe deposit box. So we need to watch our backs, too."

She nodded, listening to me but watching the kids.

"And I agree with you that Myers and Thompson are hiding something. I'll certainly wear my stalker's hat when I see them again."

She jabbed an elbow into my ribs. "Don't be smart," she said.

"I'll call Simon as soon as we get back to the office. I'd like him to come back to Hamilton tonight so we could be at the bank first thing tomorrow. And I'm wondering when we should tell the cops what we know." I paused a beat. "I believe it should be soon."

She turned to me, folding and unfolding her empty popcorn bag. You could almost see the neurons firing in her brain, if that's what they did. "That all makes sense." A smile tugged at the corners of her mouth. "But I still think you're crazy, Max. But maybe like a fox."

CHAPTER TWENTY-FOUR

THE FOLLOWING MORNING, I ENTERED the coffee shop at the Connaught and found Simon Benson seated at a booth in the rear, his back to the wall and his eyes flicking toward the entrance.

"Do you think I'm being paranoid, Max? I was thinking of registering under another name. I know that sounds pretty damn foolish but I'm scared to death."

On the phone yesterday he'd sounded excited to learn that we had a new lead, so he jumped on the next train to Hamilton, determined to stay here as long as it took to follow any clue leading to the capture of his brother's killer. I hadn't been able to convince him to rent a car this morning and return to the relative safety of Toronto later today.

But now the reality of waking up in the city where Jake had been murdered was beginning to hit home. He hadn't tasted his scrambled eggs, just nibbled at a piece of dry toast, and I watched him spill most of his tea when he tried to pour it from the little silver pot with the Mother Parker's tag trapped in its lid.

I passed him a wad of paper napkins from the chrome dispenser. "It's not paranoid to be afraid of a real threat, but try to calm yourself. All we can do is take reasonable precautions. And we will." I helped him pile the soggy napkins on his plate and he pushed it all aside. He drummed his fingers on the table as he examined the other patrons coming and going. I quieted his fingers with my hand. "The bank opens at ten. If we leave now we'll arrive in Dundas in time to walk to the bank from a few blocks away."

He jerked his hand from under mine, eyes wide. "You think we're being followed?"

"Like I said, reasonable precautions."

At the stand in front of the hotel we picked up a Veterans Cab and Simon slumped low in his seat. I patted his arm and he settled down. "Don't expect to find a note from Jake telling us everything we need to know," I said. "Whatever's in this deposit box is probably just a piece of the puzzle, which will lead to another, and so on. That's often the way these things go." The cabbie drove off and I glanced over my shoulder, taking note of the black Ford which pulled into traffic a few cars back.

When we approached Dundas, I had the driver turn right at Sydenham Street and head up two blocks to St. Augustine's Church, where we got out. "Drive around for ten or fifteen minutes," I told him. "Then park behind the post office, off the street. We'll meet you there."

At the massive door to the old church Simon stepped ahead of me to tug it open. We paused at the entrance until our eyes adjusted to the gloom. The spiciness of incense mixed with candle wax coloured the still air. I directed him down a side aisle where two women shrouded in black knelt in front of a life-sized statue of the Virgin Mary surrounded by votive candles.

"My first time in a Catholic church," he whispered.

"Don't get used to it. If you like to eat meat on Fridays."

We left by a side door near the altar and headed downtown. "You can't see this door from the front of the church," I told him. "So I don't think we'll be followed." I spoke with conviction, hoping I wasn't full of baloney.

He walked with a springier step now and some of the tension around his mouth and eyes had eased. On King Street we paused in the shade of a green and white striped awning lettered "Valley Tea Shoppe" while I scanned the light traffic both ways. Life was quieter here in Dundas; inside the tea shop several old women in flowered dresses and straw hats gossiped and sipped their morning tea. Across the street, a young mother dragged a pair of squabbling kids into Grafton's Department Store, its display windows plastered over with red and white SUMMER SALE banners. In the next block we joined a small knot of customers at the entrance to the Bank of Montreal, mostly businessmen, shuffling their feet and awaiting its opening at ten sharp.

Simon bent his head close to my ear. "Was all that rigama-role back there at the church for my benefit? Nick Carter's basic course on how to shake a tail? Guaranteed to reassure nervous clients?"

I forced a grin, trying to look like the fearless detective. But I felt in my bones that somebody was taking an unhealthy interest in us. Paranoia is contagious, of course, but in my line of work it never hurts to be careful. "Well, do you feel reassured?"

"Yes," he said. "I guess I do."

"That's good, Simon, but stay alert. We lost the follower from Hamilton in the black Ford, but it's interesting that some-body wants to know why we're here."

His eyes widened and he opened his mouth to speak, then closed it again. "Okay," he said after a pause. "Let's go in."

Inside, he asked to see the manager on an urgent matter and we were ushered into a wood-panelled office right away. After explaining the situation, Simon laid out Jake's death certificate, signed by the coroner, and his own credentials establishing his identity to the manager's satisfaction. We stood before the vault where the deposit boxes lined one wall, floor to ceiling: a regi-ment of small stainless-steel drawers, lined up in perfect rows like the crosses in a Normandy cemetery. The manager inserted a key, as did Simon. The manager opened the drawer and with-drew a shallow box, then took us to a claustrophobic room where, seated on two wooden chairs at a narrow table, we waited until he left.

Simon drew the box closer and lifted the lid. Inside were two sheets of paper, folded lengthwise, with a business card clipped to them. The card read:

THE LEVINSON GROUP
WHOLESALE DIAMONDS

39 MAIN STREET EAST
HAMILTON, ONTARIO

The first sheet of paper had been removed from an account-ing ledger and was divided into five columns – names down the left side and across the top the next three columns were headed:

Titles, dimensions, dates. There was a narrower column on the right, containing a list of initials.

We scrutinized the ledger sheet for several minutes. Then I turned to Simon and confessed my ignorance. He tapped it with a finger and said, "This list shows the names of some famous artists, titles and sizes of paintings. But I have no idea what it could mean and why it was so important that Jake would hide it."

A buzzing sensation tingled my scalp. Ed Zielinski had told me the RCMP had been tipped off about artworks showing up in Hamilton which were looted by the Nazis. Was this such a list, maybe identifying their owners? Or just my imagination?

I scanned the column of initials; none meant anything to me. Isabel's father had mentioned that Myers had an extensive art collection, had hinted that he'd sold some pieces to other private collectors. But I didn't see either of their initials. So perhaps this list recorded details of sales between other collectors. If so, why had it been tucked away in the office of the accounting department manager at H. B. Myers Investments Ltd? Could Thompson, like his boss, also be a collector? I zipped through the initials again; his weren't there either. Well, no one had said sleuthing was easy. Of course, the big question was: Had Jake stumbled across this list by chance? Or was he ...

"Max, Max." Simon was shaking my arm and it took me a second to pay attention to him. "Are you all right?"

"Sorry. My mind was running ahead of me." I gave my head a healthy rub, combed my hair with my fingers.

Simon reached for the second sheet of paper and unfolded it. Just two columns on this one. On the left were lines of numbers – about a dozen entries of nine or ten figures each. The second column showed a post office box and city for each entry. For example, a typical entry read: 89023940038 - - - - - - - P.O. Box 582, Toronto. We studied the page for a moment and Simon shook his head. "I've no idea," Simon told me. "Looks like a math problem."

"Yes, it does," I said. "Jake was an accountant, so I presume this information has something to do with Myers' bookkeeping system." I folded the sheets and clipped the business card to them.

"Okay. Let's get a move on. I suggest we leave this information right here in the bank."

Simon slapped his palm over the lists and I gripped his wrist. "Hang on," I said. "This info may well have cost Jake his life. I think we should turn it over to the police." I took out my notebook and flipped to a blank page. "I'd like you to copy those lists into my book. Then I'd feel a lot more comfortable if we went somewhere else to talk. Maybe it's just a hunch, but I'm getting the heebie-jeebies out here."

He clutched my notebook in one hand, the other still covering the lists on the table, eyes swimming in confusion. I got up and stood behind him, resting both my hands on his shoulders. "C'mon, Simon, here's my pen. Copy that stuff and we'll be out of here in no time."

On our way back to Hamilton I kept an eye peeled on the traffic behind, the black Ford not in evidence. I had a quiet spot in mind. I asked the cabbie to drive up the Mountain to the top of the old Wentworth Street incline railway and come back for us in an hour.

At the lookout point we leaned against the guard railing overlooking the mountainside where we could appreciate the ingenuity of the Hamilton planners almost sixty years before. Although the so-called 'Mountain' had a vertical drop of just three hundred feet, it must have seemed like Mount Everest to the farmers navigating their teams of horses, and later their trucks, down the switchbacks with precarious loads of market-bound vegetables. So this short railway was a godsend: a swift and safe means to transport goods and people by steam-powered engines.

"I used to love this ride," I told Simon. "As kids we tried to sneak past the operator and save the fare. Spent hours up here in this park looking for mischief."

He stood upright, gazing at the panoramic view of the tree-lined streets beneath us, the toy-sized sails sparkling on the placid waters of Burlington Bay in the late-morning sun. And beyond, the wide sweep of Lake Ontario. Shifting his weight from one foot to the other, he appeared to examine the rusted railway tracks, now abandoned in the wake of progress. "When Jake and

I were younger my father brought us up here and we'd walk along the top of the Mountain." His voice was almost inaudible.

We crunched along a gravelled pathway and sat on a park bench that featured the million-dollar view. "Sometimes I come up here to think," I said. "And at this elevation, you get a bit of a reprieve from the bad stuff happening down the hill."

He stuffed his hands in his pockets and stretched his legs. "All right, Max, that's enough sightseeing. Let's talk about what we found at the bank."

"Okay." I was relieved he was ready to get down to business. "That card from the wholesale diamond merchant – ring any bells?"

"Nothing at all."

"He never mentioned this Levinson Group? Never had any dealings with them? Maybe bought some diamonds for a lady friend?"

Simon shook his head. "This is my brother we're talking about. He's always been so damn secretive."

"Alright. Those lists." I opened my notebook and passed it to him. "That list of figures and post office box numbers still drawing a blank with you?"

"Yes, but I think you're right – they must be connected to Jake's business. And I'm in the dark about that."

I took a moment to study my client, his features so wrinkled with worry he appeared to sag inside his skin. At that moment I was convinced of his loyalty to his family and I knew he was a man of integrity. I flipped the page to the second list. "You say this shows artists and paintings?"

"That's right," he said, and I reminded myself that he was a curator at the Royal Ontario Museum. "But I don't see any particular relationship between them," he continued. "My speciality at the museum is decorative arts: furniture, ceramics, silverware, jewellery and so on. I could show this list to a friend at the Toronto Art Gallery. She might have an idea." He stopped short, concentrating on his shoes. "On the other hand, I don't want to place her in any danger. So forget about that for now."

"Fine." I'd been mulling over how much I should tell him of my conversation with Ed Zielinski ... maybe better to keep it general for now. "You know, I've read that works of art seized during the war are finding their way into collections around the world."

He squinted at me, maybe wondering how a lowly gumshoe in lunch-bucket Hamilton would know that. "True," he said. "Our museum director briefed all the curatorial staff. We're extra-vigilant now about the provenance of every object offered to us."

"Provenance?"

"Ah. I suppose you could call it a record establishing ownership of an object since it was made. Unexplained gaps in that trail cause collectors to question its authenticity." A wisp of doubt entered his eyes. "Are you suggesting that this could be a list of stolen paintings? That whoever made this list ... whoever's on this list ... might have something to do with those artworks? And that this ties in with Jake's murder?" He sat up straight, his cheeks now flushed. "I think you know a helluva lot more than you're telling me, Max."

"There could be a connection," I said. "But that's a long shot and I didn't want to upset you more than I had to." Then I told him about Doris Arneson, her relationship with his brother, her visits to his gravesite, Jake's discovery of these lists in his manager's office, and how it had troubled him.

Simon listened to my recital as though it were a news report on the radio concerning someone he didn't know. When I finished, he was staring toward Lake Ontario in the distance. "Jake and his damn secrets," he said. "I'd like to meet this woman. She must be broken-hearted."

I didn't know what to say, so I said nothing. He leaned forward, still looking at the water. "So ... we're looking for some connection between Jake's boss and this list. But you don't think Jake was part of this ... whatever it is. Or do you?"

"I just don't know," I replied. "And neither do you. Your brother came across this information in the office of his boss and hid it in a bank deposit box. Why? What did the lists tell Jake? Why did he feel threatened? According to Doris Arneson, he was very agitated after he'd found this stuff. So what are we missing?"

Simon shrugged. "I don't know the reason. But I do know Jake. And he would've kept all this under wraps until he'd decided what to do about it. So who else would know he'd even found these things, let alone kill him to keep him quiet?" His voice caught. "His manager, for instance. Would he go so far as to kill Jake, or arrange his death? It doesn't seem possible, does it? I mean, does this sort of thing happen in the business world?"

Happened more than most people thought, if the stakes were high enough, but if I confirmed that fact I'd risk rattling Simon even more. "Doris Arneson said he didn't tell her much in order to protect her."

Simon twisted around on the bench to face me. "This Arneson woman. Could she have blabbed to someone?"

I replayed my conversations with her. She'd agreed to leave town right away, saying she feared for her own safety. At first, she hadn't admitted her relationship with Jake, and hadn't gone to the cops with what she knew about the safe deposit box. Nor had she mentioned having snapped that photo of Jake outside the bank. But if she was in love with him, it stands to reason she wouldn't betray him. "It's true we don't know a lot about her," I said. "But if she lied to me, she played the part of the grieving girlfriend better than Greta Garbo."

He snapped at me. "Well, maybe you should re-examine her story."

I held his gaze. "Look," I said. "Let's not be too quick to judge Doris. It's possible she mentioned something to others. Maybe she told her sister. But if you could've seen the desolation on her face when she returned from visiting your brother's gravesite, you'd know she loved Jake very much."

He sucked in a couple of breaths of Mountain air and worked his shoulders back and forth, releasing some tension. "Okay," he said. "Let's continue."

I clapped him on the back. "Good man," I said. "There is something else. About the stolen paintings ... before the war I was a member of the RCMP."

His eyebrows lifted.

"The other day, I spoke with Inspector Zielinski, my former boss in Toronto. He's investigating the possibility that some of the artwork looted by the Nazis has arrived in Canada." Simon leaned forward, his eyes glistening. "That's why I think you should turn this information over to the police – to see if there's some connection. If so ... well, receiving stolen goods from a foreign country is a federal offence, so the RCMP would take over the case. At the very least, having them examine that list might show us how it links to Jake's death. If it does."

"But the police might try to implicate my brother in this scheme. I don't want that."

"Would you prefer to keep the list to ourselves? Do our own investigation? You know I don't have the resources the cops do."

He didn't reply right away. "Could I do that? Not report what we found at the bank?"

I shifted on the bench, stretching my bum leg, which was beginning to throb from all our walking. "Look, Simon. Your brother left that information for you. And you can do whatever you please with it."

"But you might report it. Don't you have some kind of obligation to–"

"Listen," I said. "Get this through your head – I work for you. If you tell me to ignore something, my lip is buttoned." Would I really have withheld info from the police? That would depend on the circumstances, but now was not the time to admit that.

He stared at me for a moment, then the flicker in his eyes told me he'd made up his mind to trust me. "Okay," he said. "I think it makes sense to inform the police. When can you contact them?"

CHAPTER TWENTY-FIVE

WE RETURNED TO THE TOP of the incline railway where our cab was waiting, and fifteen minutes later we arrived at Max Dexter Associates. Phyllis had just hung up the phone and I introduced her to Simon.

"I'll get the coffee in a minute," she said. "Oh, and Isabel called in. From Duffy's Tavern, of all places. She said she's following up on something ... went to have a chat with the bartender."

I smiled, pleased that I could rely on Iz to keep the ball rolling.

I guided Simon toward the grouping of new office furniture and settled him on the couch. "I'll be with you in a minute," I said. "I have to make a quick phone call."

In my office with the door closed I called Ed Zielinski, giving him a brief rundown on the lists and the business card we'd found at Jake Benson's bank. "In addition, someone followed us to Dundas but we gave him the slip."

"Interesting," the inspector said. "But I can't spend much time on that case right now."

"What? What the hell do you mean?"

"Settle down, Mister. We've got higher priorities here. You remember I had a meeting with your mayor and police chief the other day? Well, we're moving full speed ahead on the Magaddino file. This is gonna be the biggest drug operation in the history of Ontario."

Shit. I'd more or less promised Simon that the police would protect him and work on solving his brother's murder. "Just a minute, Inspector. What about these stolen paintings arriving in Canada? And the pressure from the Americans to follow up on their information?"

He sounded annoyed when he answered. "I'll just have to put them off, won't I? I told you I'd get back to you and I will. But not now."

"Damnit to hell, Ed–"

"Hold it right there," he said and I heard him take a long breath. "Look, send me a copy of that list by special delivery and I'll have somebody look at it. That's the best I can do right now." And he hung up.

So much for my close connection with a big-wheel RCMP inspector in Toronto. What'll I tell Simon?

I picked up the phone again and called Frank Russo. I filled him in on this morning's excursion to the bank in Dundas and described the contents of the box.

"So how come you didn't bring the damn stuff back with you?" he asked.

"We picked up a tail on the way to the bank but managed to shake him off. Somebody's keeping an eye on him, Frank." I heard him sigh over the phone but I pushed on. "So I thought it was a good idea to leave the papers in the bank for now. In case we were stopped and forced to give them up."

"My God, Max. You're always falling into the crapper. Whaddya want me to do? Drive you guys out to Dundas and hold your hands while you clean out the box?" He sounded like the Frank of my childhood and it always made me feel ten years old.

"Well … yeah. I was thinking you might run us out there after lunch. Simon'll feel a helluva lot safer if you go with us. He needs a spine-stiffener, Frank. He needs to know the police are on his side. Should only take an hour or so."

Frank's big-brother hoot echoed down the line. "Only an hour or so, that's a laugh. Remember that twenty-minute job I helped you with a coupla weeks ago? We spent two goddamn hours locked in the women's washroom at the Honest Lawyer Hotel." He didn't speak for a moment and I heard him rustling papers at his desk. "All right, what the hell. I guess I could get away about two."

We agreed to meet at the Connaught's John Street entrance. "Thanks, Frank. You've saved my life."

"Yeah, yeah. How many lives you got left anyway?"

I kept the phone in my hand, waited for an open line and called Myers' office. I wanted to see him right away – see what he had to say about that meeting with Jake which he neglected to tell me about. Doris Arneson said Jake spoke to his boss, Thompson, when he found those lists in his office, and right away he was passed along to meet with Myers himself. So what the hell was that all about?

The luscious Miss Carlson answered the phone and said, "I'm sorry, Sir," her voice an icicle in my ear. "Mr. Myers is very busy and will be unavailable for the next few days." I hung up the phone. It was my guess she'd received instructions from on high since our last encounter. Then I dialled Thompson's office and the deep-freeze continued. His secretary was downright snippy. "He's out of town, Mr. Dexter. He'll be gone for at least a week."

I drummed my fingers on the phone, thinking about why Myers and Thompson would want to avoid Yours Truly. But maybe Myers really was busy. And maybe Thompson was out of town. And maybe pigs could fly. Nope, I knew a cold shoulder when it rubbed up against me. The golden gates at Fortress Myers had clanged shut.

I brought Simon into my office and he sagged into my visitor's chair like a sack of rice. His eyes were bleary and he was breathing through his mouth. Hard to imagine that this Simon was the same one who had accompanied his father on the incline railway on a sunny Sunday, his kid brother Jake tagging along, maybe chasing the squirrels as they walked along the mountain brow.

"You look beat, Simon," I said. "Why don't you go over to the hotel and rest for a while?"

He removed his glasses and rubbed his eyes. "Maybe I will. But first tell me what the inspector had to say."

Shit, I knew he'd ask me that. But I hadn't had time to think of a satisfactory answer. "Well, he's on a special assignment right now. Up to his neck in a big operation. So we'll send him a copy of the list of paintings and he'll have it checked."

Simon wasn't cheered by this news. "But I called Detective Sergeant Russo," I said. "He agreed to accompany us to the bank in Dundas. We'll meet at your hotel at two o'clock. Then we'll clear out the deposit box just before the bank closes."

"And then?"

"We'll come back here and decide what to do." I stepped behind his chair and patted him on the back. "Come on, I'll walk you to the Connaught."

CHAPTER TWENTY-SIX

WHEN I RETURNED TO MY office, I gobbled a quick lunch at my desk while I puzzled over that list of paintings: legitimate collections or Nazi loot? What significance had they held for Jake Benson? Could he have recognized any of them from their titles? How well versed was he with the art world? Maybe, given his brother's position at the ROM, he shared Simon's love of the arts. Or was it the business card that snagged his interest? Maybe I had time to see my new friend the artist before I met up with Simon at the Connaught.

I limped over to the Art Gallery on Main Street. I mounted the curving staircase to the second floor and found Roger Bruce. Or was it Robert? He was sitting cross-legged on the floor of an empty exhibition space, his eyes closed.

"Am I interrupting the yogi in full meditation?" I asked from the doorway, my words echoing around the open area.

The artist's head turned toward me, his eyelids at half-mast. "Ah, so. The private eye. He dares to enter the hallowed halls of the art world, so far above his humble station in life."

"Busy?" I said, ignoring his guff.

His eyes were wide open now, a smile twitching on his lips. "Of course I'm busy, you dope. I have thirty-three exquisite paintings ready to hang for my new exhibit. And I'm awaiting the spirit of Leonardo da Vinci to suggest the perfect arrangement of these masterpieces. To achieve maximum impact."

What a banana. The kind of guy I enjoyed as a friend.

"He's standing there staring at me, mystified," the artist continued. "Probably never heard of Leonardo da Vinci. Am I right?"

"Didn't he used to play on the offensive line for the Hamilton Tigers?"

He dropped his head, shaking it from side to side. "Jesus wept," he said. "The man's a complete fool."

I approached him and tapped his shoulder. "Robert?"

"Roger."

"I knew that."

He tried hard to glare.

I shuffled my feet. "Can I ask you a serious question?"

He caught my shift of tone and studied my eyes. "Sure," he said. Then he held up one arm and I tugged him to his feet. "Let's go next door."

In the adjoining room his paintings were stacked along one wall, tables and chairs piled against another. Roger Bruce fought with two folding chairs until they opened and we sat facing each other. I withdrew my notebook, found the page listing the artists' information and passed it to him.

He studied it, nodding as he read. "Very nice. Some of the heavy artillery here: Tintoretto, Rubens, Van Dyck. Even a Rembrandt."

He returned the book and my eyes fixed on the last column. At the bank I'd been looking for O'Brien's initials and I hadn't noted an O'B on the list. But here at the bottom were the initials J.B. and I remembered O'Brien's business card was engraved "J.B. O'Brien". Perhaps this list was prepared by someone who knew him well enough to refer to him by his first initials. And that someone could be O'Brien's good friend Myers.

I reached over and tapped a finger on my notebook, "Did you say Rembrandt? I don't see his name here."

He ran his finger down the list, stopping at the last name. "R. van Rijn." A theatrical pause. "Guess what the R stands for?"

Well, I'll be damned. So it was possible Isabel's old man was involved in this mess. But she wouldn't know anything about that, would she? "And the title of his painting?" I stared at the book, the exquisite image featured in O'Brien's private gallery shimmering in my mind.

"*Man with Hat,*" he said and handed me my notebook.

"Could it be a self-portrait?" I'd remembered O'Brien had referred to it as that.

He narrowed his eyes. "It's possible." Another pause. "He painted a ton of self-portraits. Some in costume, some not. Head and shoulders, full length, side view, front view. And don't forget, the records in the 1600s weren't always accurate. This is the stuff art historians go to war over." His arms waving, he appeared ready to launch into one of his fanciful sidebars, but reined himself in. "So, yes, *Man with Hat* could be Rembrandt himself. Now, why are you asking me about this? Something big's going on, isn't it?"

Concern shadowed his intelligent face, a cyclone of tangled hair colliding with the shoulders of his frayed work shirt. Old pants splashed with great gobs of hardened paint sagged around his hips. A treasure disguised as a castoff.

"I can't tell you right now."

"But you're sending me a strong signal that whatever it is, it's serious. And I should keep my trap shut."

I nodded.

"Okey dokey." He stood up, lending me a hand. "I'll walk you out, Mr. Gumshoe."

As we descended the long stairway a thought occurred to me. "Say, there wouldn't be a book with a picture of that Rembrandt painting over at the library, would there?"

"Jeez, what a jughead. Of course there's a book. Let's go."

We crossed Main Street to the Hamilton Public Library where he led me to the art history section. At home among these tomes, he selected a ten-pound volume from several devoted to Rembrandt and hefted it onto a long table.

"*Man with Hat*," I reminded him.

"Shhh." Finger to lips, he wore a mock librarian's scowl as he paged through the portraits. "Humph. First time I've been wrong." He hauled out another hefty book and buzzed through it, waving me closer. "Keep an eye peeled. We'll make a detective out of you yet."

I scoured the pages with him. "What the hell?" I said in a library voice. "How come there're so many self-portraits?"

He sighed like a patient teacher. "Long version or short?"

"Guess."

"Okay. Short version. Scholars don't agree on why he painted so many. More than fifty. Some say they're a form of self-examination. Others claim he was just meeting market demand and saving the cost of hiring a model. I agree with the latter, he painted what he could sell. And a mirror is a whole bunch cheaper than a model."

Two pages later, there it was: the head and shoulders of the artist himself, wearing his old-fashioned costume and wide-brimmed hat. I slapped the glossy paper, producing what sounded like a thunderclap in those hushed surroundings. Two old cronies at the next table glared at us.

Roger Bruce hissed at me. "Not so loud." He touched the picture and whispered, "That's it, Buster. *Man with Hat.*"

"Terrific," I said. "Possible to find out who owns it?"

He bent over the picture again, examining something. "Not in this case," he said. "The book publisher must obtain the rights to reproduce these works. So you often see a line crediting such-and-such a gallery or museum. But this line says it's from a private collection. Means the owners didn't want their names published."

I waved my hand. "That part doesn't matter right now. But this," I said, pointing my chin at the photo. "I think it's an important part of the puzzle."

I clapped him on the back and pumped his hand. "I owe you for this," I told him.

He whacked me on the arm. "Don't think I'm not gonna collect."

At the library entrance he handed me a sealed envelope. "An invitation to the opening of my exhibit at the end of the month. You could bring that good-looking babe, too. She's a helluva lot easier on the eyes than you are."

CHAPTER TWENTY-SEVEN

I WAS ANNOYED WHEN I didn't find Simon Benson waiting for me at the Connaught's side entrance. I limped into the lobby crowded with conventioneers wearing cowboy boots and ten-gallon hats. I had to muscle aside a couple of these Roy Rogers guys to reach Simon, who stood near the house phones. He was facing away from me, scanning the main entrance then rotating his head to radar the crowd.

When I touched his arm he rounded on me, forcing me back a step. "Oh my God," he said. "Am I glad to see you."

"Why? What's happened?" I guided him out of the crush into a corner of the lobby.

His eyes continued to cover the crowd like a lighthouse beacon. "When I returned to my room I couldn't sleep, so I called my landlady to tell her my travel plans. She lives in the duplex beneath mine and keeps an eye on my place." I had to lean closer to hear him. "She said that two men came to see me this morning, large men in dark suits. Thank God, she sent them away, told them she didn't know where I worked. They said they'd catch up with me later."

He gripped my arm. "You'll be fine," I said, hoping I sounded sure of myself. "After all, with the police helping us, we're on the side of the angels." Then I wondered if I'd gotten that wrong – maybe it was: Fools rush in where angels fear to tread.

Frank arrived in an unmarked car and I briefed him on my client's early-morning visitors. He shrugged but appeared to file the information away in his noggin.

Again I accompanied Simon into the bank, this time to retrieve the contents of that damn box.

Frank met us at the front entrance and, driving back to Hamilton, he said, "Been thinking about those guys snooping around your place in Toronto, Simon. And that tail on your first trip to the bank."

Simon leaned forward from the back seat. "I have to admit that it scares the hell out of me, Detective."

"Might be better if you didn't return to Toronto just now. Friend of mine's the chief of security at the Connaught, what some people call 'the house dick'. Be a good idea if he got you another room there under a different name. Then he could keep an eye out for any unwelcome visitors."

Simon turned to me. "What to do you think, Max? I sure don't like the idea of going back to my apartment with a couple of thugs hanging around."

"Makes a lot of sense," I said, pleased that Frank seemed to be on board with us now.

At the hotel, Frank introduced us to Hank Humphries, the security chief. "Hank used to be on the Hamilton Police force," Frank said. "My first partner."

Humphries was a jowly guy with steel-grey hair; mid-fifties but still thick through the neck and shoulders, not someone you'd want to tangle with. "Yeah, that's right," he said, his voice like coarse sandpaper. "They used to team up the old guys with the young pups. Figured we could teach 'em something." He turned to me and jerked his thumb at Frank. "Didn't work in your pal's case."

We chuckled at Frank's expense, which seemed to relieve some of Simon's tension. Then Hank got on the phone and arranged for Simon to move into another room near the rear of the hotel, beside an emergency exit.

Room 928 had a pair of windows on the east wall which afforded a view of the bus terminal in the next block. I peered down over the rooftops at a knot of jostling sailors in white summer uniforms, probably from HMCS *Star*. They were boarding a Greyhound bus, probably headed for Buffalo, and I wondered if they'd have any memory of their leave when they returned to Hamilton.

Between the windows a round table held a coffee service and it was Humphries who stepped forward to pour the java. "On the house," he said. "I've got friends in the kitchen." I imagined Longo, the light-fingered waiter, working some scheme to heist the hotel's fancy food and Humphries tracking him down like a bloodhound.

We drank our coffee as Frank gave the security chief a vague outline of Simon's situation and his need for a watchdog.

"Helluva lot more to this story than you guys are telling me," Humphries said. "But I don't need to know all the grisly details, do I?" He looked over at Simon. "I've booked you in as Thomas Waller. He's my favourite piano player and I always use his moniker when we stash away extra-special guests. That way, the staff here knows to inform me if anyone becomes too interested in a certain Mr. Waller."

Humphries shook hands all round. "Let me know if there's anything else you need," he said, then left the room.

We sat at the small table and Frank got right down to business. "I've gotta get going soon. Let's see what you got from the bank."

After examining the info that might have cost Jake Benson his life, Frank picked up the business card and, holding it between two fingers, motioned toward Simon. "Any ideas about this diamond merchant?"

"Sorry, no."

"And you wouldn't know if your brother knew him? Or had business dealings with him?"

"'Fraid not. Jake never mentioned him to me."

Then we reviewed the list of artists' names and paintings. Simon admitted that he recognized the titles, but he couldn't say what their relevance might be. No, he responded to my question, he didn't think his brother had more than a general interest in art, nor was he interested in collecting it himself. He didn't know if the titles of the paintings might have meant anything to Jake, or why Jake had been so agitated about the list. All he knew, he assured us, was what I had told him: Jake had found the list in his manager's office and for some reason he'd hidden it in a bank deposit box.

Frank scratched his head while examining the second list of figures. "Any ideas?" he asked Simon.

"Not a clue, Detective. Something to do with my brother's work at the office, I suppose."

Frank sat thinking for a moment then he pushed back from the table, ready to leave. He shook Simon's hand. "Don't be worried about staying here," he told him. "Humphries is a good man." He motioned his head toward the door. "We'd better be going, Max. Mr. Waller here looks like he could use a little nap."

CHAPTER TWENTY-EIGHT

WE LEFT THE HOTEL AND were drawn across the street by the commotion of the crowd gathering at Gore Park. An enthusiastic audience was applauding and cheering a pair of jugglers whizzing Indian clubs at each other while balancing on unicycles. A large poster board promoted the Ringling Bros. Circus opening that night at the Barton Street Arena.

Frank nudged me in the ribs. "You'd never see anything like this during the war, Maxie. Look at these people enjoying themselves. Something you could only imagine back then."

Another cheer went up as the street performers bowed and passed around an oversized hat. Frank flipped in two bits and we continued along King Street. "I worked a double shift, Max, so I'm off duty now," he said. "Let's grab a beer at the Grange."

Just this year the government had granted licences for cocktail lounges and the Grange Tavern was one of the first to jump on board. Right in the centre of the city, it operated for years as a Chinese restaurant. And now it boasted a two-story flashing neon sign, smorgasbord lunches and dinners as well as nightly entertainment. I'd been here before for the ninety-nine cent lunch special.

A smiling Chinese lady bowed as we entered and Frank made a beeline for the circular staircase to the Dragon Room upstairs; the sweet-and-sour aroma of Chinese food lingering in the smoky lounge. I hoisted my bum leg up the stairs after him and we sat at a table with a bird's-eye view of the spirited drinkers below us. Frank waved over a waitress and ordered a couple of cold ones. When he leaned back and peeked under the table, he asked me, "Leg's still botherin' you, eh?"

"Only when I climb mountains," I said.

"Ahh ... still the tough guy." A grin lit up his dark mug and he wagged a finger in my direction. "Remember when we were kids? Your fall off the balcony into the back yard—"

"Not a fall. You pushed me, you bastard."

He ignored my interruption, enjoying my discomfort. "After the fall you kept saying, 'I'm fine, I'm fine' and kept pushing me away. Broke your arm in three places and still acting like Superman."

Frank was still chuckling when our waitress arrived and dropped off a couple of Peller's. She put a little extra into it when she sashayed away and I caught him practising his surveillance skills on her rear end. He flicked his eyebrows and said, "Quite a view up here, eh?"

"Cheers," I said. And we clinked bottles.

He was quiet for a few moments then moved his chair closer to mine. "Let's get down to brass tacks," he said. "Like I told you, my captain's on my ass to wrap up this Jake Benson business and get on with my next case."

I gave him a quick rundown on what Isabel and I had done since our last discussion. "Remember my old boss, Ed Zielinski, from my RCMP days?" I asked him.

"Yep. I just saw him at the station house the other day. Got off his throne in Toronto to deliver marching orders to the Chief here. Looks like a big drug push coming up."

I grinned at him. Nothing annoyed the local cops more than the Mounties galloping into town uninvited and throwing their weight around. "Yeah, well, I met with him too," I said. "He told me about some artwork stolen by the Nazis during the war which might've made its way into Hamilton." I briefed him on Zielinski's tip from the Americans and his interest in having me sniff around.

"Jesus," he said when I'd finished. "Nazi loot in Hamilton? That's hard to believe."

"Could be true though. One of those lists Jake Benson squirrelled away might be connected."

He made a face like he'd bitten a lemon. "I don't see how, Buster."

When I told Frank about attending O'Brien's art reception on Saturday night and seeing his Rembrandt painting, his eyes bugged out.

"You shittin' me, Maxie? You were up there in Ancaster hob-nobbin' with those rich buggers, lookin' at their fancy art and chompin' on cocktail weenies?" His head was shaking like I'd told him I'd just had tea with Princess Elizabeth. "You're from Napier Street for Chrissake."

"C'mon, Frank. Don't be a jerk. We're talking about Isabel's father here. Sure, he's rich and so are his pals. Did I feel comfy rubbing shoulders in that crowd? Of course not. But keep your eye on the ball here." I could feel sweat forming in my armpits as I got wound up. "O'Brien shows me a painting and he says it's a Rembrandt. Then he says he bought it from his good friend Henry Myers. Yes, the same Henry Myers who's my former client and owner of the company where Jake Benson worked and where he found that goddamn list. I ain't stupid, Bud, so sure, I think there's a connection. And you will too, if you think about it."

We stared at each other for a long moment; Frank didn't see me lose my temper very often, especially with him. Then he snorted a laugh and punched me on the arm. "Time for another beer," he said and waved at the waitress with the curvaceous derrière.

After my little tirade, Frank was more receptive and I hoped he might loosen up and offer some help. "For what it's worth," he said, "I got the same impression you did when I interviewed Jake Benson's co-workers. He seemed like a good guy. And we only have Myers' word that an embezzlement actually occurred, right?"

"Yeah. And Jake's boss, Thompson, agrees of course."

He fingernailed the label on his Peller's bottle as he thought about it. "So, to prove there was a theft we'd need an audit of Myers' books. But there's no way in hell to get that without some evidence. And don't forget Myers is a pillar of the community, pals with the rich politicians, gives gobs of dough to all the right charities, blah blah blah."

"You're right," I said. "But maybe we'll find something."

Frank flipped through the pages of his notebook until he found what he was looking for. "You know, I got the feeling that this Arneson woman at Myers office knows more than she told me."

I always said he wasn't as dumb as he looked. I told him Doris Arneson and Jake Benson were sweet on each other and that Jake told her he'd discovered the lists and business card in his boss' office. "Doris said it scared the hell out of him," I added. "So he talked to his boss and then to Myers. Then he stashed the stuff away in that bank in Dundas."

Frank made a note. "So Myers and Thompson knew that he found these papers. What're you gonna do about that?"

"I'm trying to get in to talk to them, Frank, but their secretaries are stonewalling me. And now Doris is afraid she could become the next target if someone links her to Jake." Then something else occurred to me. "Oh, and Doris said Jake was a music fan – a regular at the Flamingo, Duffy's, the Golden Rail, those joints. So we're circulating Jake Benson's photo among the bartenders downtown. Maybe get a lead on who he was with, where he was going before he disappeared, something."

Frank scribbled again, looked up.

"That second list full of numbers is a mystery," I said. "Maybe it had something to do with Jake's job in the accounting department. I'm going to have Isabel take a look at it. She's an accountant and it might make some sense to her."

Frank nodded his head. "Okay, keep me posted on that." He waved his hand for me to continue.

"And we're gonna drop in on this Levinson Diamond place, see if that leads anywhere."

He frowned. "Who's we?"

"Isabel and I." I could feel myself becoming defensive as his mouth puckered. "I'm training her as my assistant," I said. "You wanna comment on that?"

He busied himself with the waitress as the next round of beer arrived. When she'd gone, he said, "Sure that's a smart idea, Maxie? I mean, you hardly know this woman and she's part of the high society circle you're trying to investigate. I dunno ..."

"Sure I'm sure. She's smart and she's eager to learn. It's true she comes from the upper crust, but she's no snob."

"Jeez, it ain't that. All I'm tryin' to say is, she's a dame, you know? And this type of work ... well."

I shook my head, thinking of all the times we'd gone round the mulberry bush with this old argument. "All you're tryin' to say is that a woman can't do a man's job. Is that right, Frank? Even though women took over most of the factory jobs during the war for less pay than men, yet they were more productive? Is that what you're saying?"

His hands flew up as though he were blocking my punches. "Don't get your knickers in a knot, Maxie. You know damn well that dames can't ..." He began to stammer when he saw me leaning toward him with a glare. "Ah, shit," he said, spitting out the words like they were a worm in a bite of apple. "There's no arguing with you when you think you're right. And you always think you're right, you dumb bugger."

We sat in silence, cooling off, looking over the railing at three musicians in fancy duds setting up their instruments on the bandstand downstairs. The guy on the clarinet tooted a few bars of *Stormy Weather*. Finally, I reached across the table and tapped Frank's notebook. "You talk to Chuck Cysko?"

He rolled his eyes at the mention of Cysko's name. "Yeah. Now there's a guy who's workin' in the wrong job," he said. He seemed relieved that we were talking again. "He shoulda been a used car salesman."

I grinned. "We had a heart-to-heart chat yesterday," I told him. "There might be more to this guy behind all that bluster."

"Tell me."

"Tip from a friend," I said. "Cysko's peddling shares in a so-called European reconstruction fund to some of the members at my pal's golf club. One of them smelled a rat and my friend told me about it. Not only that, Cysko's credit check showed he's drowning in debt. High credit risk, mortgage foreclosed, the works."

Frank nodded as he wrote. "It figures," he said. "I'll ask around, see if there's anything in our files. Be good to know if he's involved in anything else. 'Call me Chuck', eh? Maybe that's not all we'll call him."

"Might also be an idea to pick up any paperwork he left with the golf club members." I passed him Cysko's business card with the club's number written on the back.

Frank tucked it away and drained his glass. "Gotta go, Bud." Before he stood up, he leaned across the table and said, "I was just wondering ... How did you get this Myers guy as a client?"

I wasn't sure what he was driving at. I thought about it for a moment. "He just walked in off the street. Told me one of his accountants embezzled funds and disappeared. Wanted me to find him. And keep it quiet, 'cuz it would be bad for business."

"Uh-huh. Then his employee turns up dead, a couple of slugs in the head, dumped in the bay. So it stands to reason, since it looks like a Mob hit, he'd stolen the money for some criminal purpose, right?"

"That was the theory," I said.

"All very convenient, Maxie."

"Yeah, I know. Myers made me antsy right off the bat and it wasn't just his snooty attitude."

"No prior contact with him? Work for one of his associates? A referral from another client?"

"Nope. Not that I'm aware of."

"Well, maybe I'm full of crap, but ... think about this. Myers has an employee who discovers a criminal scheme at the office. Maybe he tries to reason with that employee and fails. Myers doesn't see a way around the problem so he has him taken care of. Then he calls in a private dick to look into the employee's disappearance, says he embezzled a sackful of dough. The investigator just starts working the case when the body turns up. The cops are under pressure so they file the case away as just another gangland killing. Very neat and tidy." Frank's eyes were alive and they bored right into my brain. "So I was thinking ... Maybe he set you up."

I felt like the air had been punched out of me and I flopped back in my chair. Shit, was I just a bit player in Myers' plan to cover his tracks and deflect the police? And why hadn't this angle occurred to me before? I felt like a jackass and my face must have said so to Frank.

He came around the table and clamped me on the shoulder. "Don't be so hard on yourself, Pal. It's just an idea. Maybe I'm way off base here."

I took a couple of deep breaths and calmed myself before standing up. "Yeah, but it's a possibility, damnit."

Frank helped me down the stairs and when we parted he said, "Be careful, Maxie."

CHAPTER TWENTY-NINE

AT THE CORNER OF KING and James I watched Frank join a crowd of pedestrians heading east, his parting words about Myers still racing around in my mind. I glanced across the street at the Birks clock – only sixteen hundred hours, just enough time to drop in on my former client at the Pigott Building.

On the way up in the elevator I pictured Myers' secretary, the voluptuous Miss Carlson, and I wondered if her shoulder would still be as icebox cold as it was when we'd spoken on the phone. Hard to believe she was the same babe who'd slipped her phone number into my shirt pocket, zapping me with an electric buzz.

I limped down the hallway toward her desk, my footsteps muffled by the cushy carpeting. She was facing away from me, bending over a file drawer again, maybe her favourite pose. And still a stunning view. When I tapped on her desktop, her head snapped up and her automatic smile sagged into a snappish pout.

"Oh, it's you again," she said, clutching an armload of files to her breast as though I'd made a grab for them. The files, that is. "I've already told you Mr. Myers is not available. He's out of the office. Not here until next week."

As she spoke, I glimpsed a blurry motion through the partially open door to Myers' office. A burly guy in a dark suit was stacking cardboard boxes on a wheeled cart. He caught me watching and kicked the door shut. What the hell was going on here?

"Are you moving offices?" I asked her.

She gave me such a frigid stare that I could feel the goosebumps dancing up my spine. "Not that it's any of your business, Mr. Dexter. But we're having some cleaning done while Mr. Myers is away."

I opened my mouth to reply but she extended the files toward me as though to block my words. "We're finished here," she said. Then turned to continue her filing.

I walked to the end of the hallway looking for Thompson's office, still stunned by the change in Miss Carlson's manner. Was she under orders to give me the bum's rush? Maybe Myers had hoped I'd succumb to her charms so she could keep tabs on me but he'd given up that plan. Or maybe it was personal – she was just pissed with Yours Truly because I hadn't been caught in her web.

Thompson's secretary hung up her phone as I entered her office. Five would get you ten she'd been speaking with Miss You-know-who. "He's not here," she said. "Just like I told you when you called the other day."

I headed for the elevators. I could take a hint.

A couple of sleek businessmen shared the ride down with me. Listening to them, a guy would be crazy to hang onto to his Steel Company shares after the company 'capitulated' when they settled last summer's long violent strike. "We made a killing during the war," one of them said. "Now we'll have to be more creative – there's more than one way to skin a union."

Sometimes I had to fight hard not to believe that all businessmen were greedy bastards.

Back on James Street, the pace of traffic had picked up and shoppers seemed to be in a hurry. Because of the crush I almost missed spotting Bob, stationed on his dolly, selling pencils outside Renner's Drug Store.

He waved me over. "How's tricks, Sarge?"

"Fine," I said. "How come you moved from the Capitol Theatre?"

"Well, I wanted to give the folks at King and James the benefit of my sparkling personality, eh? Besides, my sister Aggie just got a part-time job at the United Cigar Store on the corner there, so it's more convenient for us. And you'd be surprised at all the customers Renner's gets. They got that big cafeteria at the back, and the snack bar. Plus all the drugstore stuff, of course."

"Good for you, Bob. Guess you won't have time to do the odd little job for me, eh?"

"Hey, Sarge. Don't say that. My shingle's always out. Open for business."

I laughed along with him and bent a little closer. "I was hoping you could set up in front of the Pigott Building for a couple of days."

He grasped my arm before I could continue. "Hang on a sec," he said. A handsome woman in a pink flowered dress inspected his display of pencils.

"How much are they?" she asked.

"Five cents each," he told her. "But for a beautiful lady like you – five for a quarter."

She gave him a sly smile, selected five pencils and flipped him a quarter. "Smooth talker," she said.

"Does that work every time?" I said after she walked away.

"More times than not," he said. "Now tell me about the Pigott Building."

"Okay. Guy called Henry B. Myers. Heard of him?"

He rubbed the stubble on his jaw for a moment. "Think I seen his picture in the *Spec*," he said. "Rich guy, gives to charities and all that?"

"That's the one. Owns an investment company on the fifteenth floor. And you won't believe this, but he doesn't want to talk to me."

"Shame on him, Sarge."

"Yeah. Anyway ... I was just up there and it looked like some stuff was being moved out. Maybe he's doing a runner, Bob. Think you can handle that?"

"'Course I can." He withdrew five more pencils from a Duncan's Stationery bag and arranged them in his display. "Did you know," he was wagging a finger at me now, "there's a loading dock behind the Pigott Building?"

I admired the careful way he handled his pencils, laying them out in the same direction, forming a perfect fan shape. You could trust a guy who took that kind of pride in his work, no matter how trivial it might seem. And Bob knew a helluva more about this area of downtown than I'd ever know. "News to me about the loading dock," I said. "Maybe Aggie could drop you off there—"

"That's what I was thinkin', Sarge. Consider it done."

I gave him a light punch on the arm, smack dab on his faded tattoo of a bathing beauty. "Thanks, Buddy," I said. "Talk to you tomorrow."

The Birks clock across the street showed sixteen thirty. On the way back to my office, I decided to check in with Longo at the Royal Connaught.

Passing Aiken's Billiards, I eyeballed a couple of zoot-suiters strutting their stuff just outside the entrance. You didn't see a lot of this fashion around Hamilton; I heard it was something from the States, an outfit adopted by the hipsters during the Thirties in the big cities. But here in this lunch-bucket town these guys were like visitors from another planet; their jackets were very long and wide-shouldered, pants were high-waisted, baggy at the knees and pegged at the cuffs. One of them wore a flamboyant wide-brimmed hat with a long feather in it and a watch chain which reached his knees.

The guy with the goofy hat caught me staring and flipped his cigarette butt on the sidewalk in front of me. "Dig it, Man," he said. "If you ain't mell-o-roonie you're nowhere."

I decided to be nowhere and ignored him.

In the next block, I spotted Longo outside the hotel's John Street entrance, having a smoke with a couple of guys dressed in black pants and white shirts, keeping a close eye on the passing female traffic. "What's this?" I asked him when I approached. "Waiters' convention?"

Longo took a long puff on his cigarette then tossed the butt into the street. "Very funny, Sarge," he said. He turned to his pals. "See you guys later. I've got a little business to transact here."

I grinned at him. "Everything's business with you, eh, Longo?"

"Why the hell not? One thing I learned in the war. If you can make a buck, then you're a hero. And that's all that counts back home, too."

Jeez, he'd fit right in with those businessmen I'd overheard in the elevator at the Pigott Building. "Speaking of business," I said, "got any news for me?"

"In fact, I do. You asked me to keep an eye on Miss O'Brien's father. Last week, remember? Well, he was here for dinner yesterday with another businessman. They had a big argument and the other guy stomped out."

"Hmmm. Did you see the argument?"

He shook his head. "Bartender told me about it when I asked him about the commotion."

"Name of the guy?"

"Got it from the head waiter. Name is Myers."

Well, shit. I'm beating my brains out trying to find the bugger and he's having dinner not a hundred feet from my office. But at least he hadn't left town, so I should be able to track him down. And this argument between Myers and O'Brien had me curious. What was it, a falling-out between art thieves?

"This guy Myers a frequent customer?" I asked him.

"Only seen him once before." He made a subtle head motion in the direction of the hotel. "There's a private section off the dining room upstairs reserved for a special customer. That's where Myers had dinner."

"When was this?"

His eyebrows formed a dark V as he thought about it. "Musta been a couple weeks ago."

"Be helpful if you could get an exact date," I told him.

"I'll check on it, Sarge, and get back to you."

"Okay. And, by the way, who's the special customer?"

Longo glanced around and whispered, "Dominic Tedesco."

CHAPTER THIRTY

As I LAY AWAKE THAT night, fanned by a warm breeze through the bedroom window, I couldn't stop rehashing Frank's words from the afternoon. *"Maybe he set you up."* And now Longo reports that Myers and Tedesco had their heads together in a private dinner a couple of weeks ago. And that was ... a short time before Jake Benson's death. So here we go again with the gumshoe's predicament: when is a coincidence not a coincidence?

Bad enough if Myers had danced me around like a marionette, but my mind kept flashing to Isabel. Replaying her introduction of Myers in my office, her red curls, big green eyes and freckled face came into focus – Iz claiming she'd run into Myers at the building's directory board, both of them confused about my office location until the nice elevator operator showed them the way.

But maybe she'd arrived with Myers. Perhaps O'Brien had suggested that Myers take along his beautiful daughter to bedazzle the private eye. Hit him with a double whammy: Isabel to flirt with him and keep him off balance; Myers to deliver the old flimflam then shut him up with a handsome payoff.

And where the hell was Myers anyway? His secretary insisted both he and Thompson were occupied with some high-level meetings somewhere. But that big bugger tossing boxes around in his office sure had my antenna twitching. Maybe Bob's surveillance would turn up something soon. Then my next step would be ...

My mind kept drifting and the scene shifted to Isabel's living room. There she was, nestled on those soft leather cushions, shoes off, feet tucked under her, smooth fingers on my chest, the world's softest lips kissing mine. My God. Had I lunged at the bait like a largemouth bass and swallowed it whole? Was there a bigger jerk in the entire City of Hamilton? At that moment, in the dead of the night, I was certain there was not.

And to top it off, Frank Russo's high school taunt echoed across the years: "When it comes to dames, Maxie, you're a complete horse's ass."

CHAPTER THIRTY-ONE

I AWOKE EARLY THE NEXT morning, frazzled by my lack of sleep. I stood at the kitchen window, tapping my foot, annoyed because the Royal Oak Dairy guy was taking his sweet time today and I was out of milk for my Grape-Nuts Flakes. I finally spotted the guy in his white uniform, shirt untucked and cap askew as he rapped on the screen door. He was puffing hard, damn near out of breath. I opened the door and he handed me a quart bottle. "Sorry I'm late, Mister," he said, still panting. "Parked my wagon at the curb and the damn horse decided to go back to the barn. Had to run like hell to catch her."

"I thought Royal Oak was switching over to milk trucks," I said.

He shrugged as he turned to leave. "It's what they keep tellin' us. I'll believe it when I see it."

I slumped at the table, dawdled with my breakfast, the sports report blaring from the radio with more scores from the PONY league. But I couldn't concentrate – my mind was churning with thoughts of Isabel. A Mata Hari weaving her wicked web? No, she wasn't like that. But there I went again ... one moment convinced I'd been duped; the next, hoping I was mistaken and Iz was everything I'd believed her to be.

I flipped off the radio and reached for the phone: it was bull-by-the-horns time. After six rings, she answered. "Sorry to call so early, Iz. I'd like to come over now for a talk. Fifteen minutes? It's important to me." She must have heard the urgency in my voice because she agreed right away.

We sat at her kitchen table, coffee pot percolating on the stovetop, the acrid odour of burnt toast lingering. "You sounded so serious on the phone, Max."

Those green eyes pinned me with concern, already dusted with a touch of makeup, her freckles less evident. She wore a crisp yellow dress and her breakfast dishes were stacked on the drainboard. Ready to leave for the office but eager to know my urgency.

I fiddled with my tie: it felt like a noose. How do you talk to your betrayer?

"Tell me," she said. "You're making me nervous."

"Sorry. It's hard to know where to start." I gulped a breath of air. "Well, you know I spent most of yesterday with Simon Benson. We opened Jake's deposit box at the bank." Then I described the lists we'd found with the business card attached. Referring to the information Simon had copied into my notebook, I read off a few of the artists' names and the titles of their paintings. Her eyes shone with interest but didn't widen in surprise or alarm.

I reminded her I'd served with the RCMP in Toronto before the war and told her of my recent discussions with my former boss, Ed Zielinski. "I met with him last weekend and he told me about the possibility of art looted by the Nazis showing up in Canada. Perhaps here in Hamilton."

She straightened, eyes wide now. "And this list Jake found might show some of those paintings? But why would it be in his manager's office?"

"That's the question of the day, isn't it? I spoke with Zielinski yesterday and sent him a copy of the list. He'll have it checked."

Out of her chair now, she was pacing the length of the kitchen. "Stolen paintings could be the motive for Jake's murder?"

I waved her back to the table and slid my notebook across, my finger on the last entry. "*Man with Hat* by Rembrandt," I said. Then I shifted my finger to the last column. "These initials may indicate the owners of the paintings."

She sat down and scanned the page. She kept her finger on the last entry and looked up, her gaze foggy. "You think these are my father's initials?"

"I'm pretty sure he showed me that painting in his library."

She gripped the edge of the table. "I don't understand this. How does it connect to the embezzlement Myers was so sure Jake was guilty of?"

"Dunno. But I saw Myers at your father's reception."

"So you think he's an art collector too?"

"You didn't know that?"

"My father's art collection has never interested me. And I told you, I hadn't met Myers before my first day at your office, Max."

Her eyes searched mine, her expression earnest yet calm. Waiting for some sign from me? God knows I ached to believe her and to say so. Sure, it was possible her showing up with Myers was a coincidence. Or was that wishful thinking? And why was I having such a helluva hard time deciding?

She tapped her fingers on the page, then poured two cups of coffee. "So now you're wondering if I know where my father got this Rembrandt? And my answer to that is no, I don't."

"In fact, I already know. He told me himself. He bought it from Myers."

Isabel's lips formed an "O" then her mouth closed. She lifted her coffee cup but returned it to the table unsipped. Her eyes shifted toward the kitchen window, drawn by the blurred arrival of a ruby-throated hummingbird at a feeder suspended from a nearby limb. Her brow furrowed as she seemed to concentrate on the tiny bird's stationary flight while it fed. My mind reading ability wasn't on a par with hers, but maybe she'd guessed I was wondering whether Myers and her father were in cahoots. I'd have been angry if the shoe were on the other foot but her appearance was almost contemplative. "Talk to me, Iz. Is your father involved with stolen art? With Myers?"

She turned toward me, sadness in her eyes. "I don't honestly know, Max. It's possible, I suppose." She released a lengthy sigh. "But he's a rich man, successful career, wide circle of friends. Why would he have anything to do with stolen paintings?"

I waited for her to think it through; her desire to believe in her father's innocence clashing with the possibility that he was an art thief. "If the paintings on that list were stolen and if my father bought the Rembrandt from Myers ..." Leaning on her elbows, chin resting on her hands, she scoured the list with her accountant's eyes. "I don't see Myers' initials here."

"I noticed that too."

Another silence, then her eyes flicked to the window, as if the hummingbird's sudden departure had left an emptiness behind. Then she whirled back toward me. "Max, I'm the one who brought Myers into your office."

Her eyes were moist and pleading but the tears held in check. Either she was in the dark about her father's activities or it was an Academy Award performance.

I nodded, "Yes, you did."

I stood at that proverbial fork in the road: the left one leading to Heaven; the right one to Hell. Or was it the other way around? God knows, I wanted to believe she knew nothing about any of this. But I'd lose my business and everything else if I were duped by a gang of art thieves ... or worse.

I leaned back and stared at the ceiling; the shallow saucer of the light fixture became the moon face of my tough old CO in the Provost Corps and his words came out like a short burst of machine-gun fire, "Shit or get off the pot, Sergeant Dexter."

I blinked and the image disappeared, replaced by the woman across the table, her head bowed. "Isabel," I said.

She looked up, her jaw set.

I reached across to touch her hand. "I trust you," I said, just a little wobble in my voice.

The breath she was holding came out in a soft sigh and a tentative smile made its way to her lips. "Thank you, Max." After an intense moment, she squeezed my hand, hard, then stood up, brushed her skirt and reached for her purse. "Time for work, Boss."

I spotted Tiny glancing our way from his perch in the elevator when we arrived together at the Wentworth Building. He made a show of checking his watch when we entered and he winked at Isabel. The little weasel barely gave me a nod. He worked the controls and the doors clanked closed.

As the car rose he wheezed in his radio accent, "You're both pretty keen this morning, Sarge."

I poked him in the ribs and said, "'T ain't funny, McGee."

Isabel's eyes flashed between Tiny and me. "What's going on, Max?" she said. "You're not teasing Tiny, are you?"

We both grinned at her and she dismissed us with a woman's shrug as the car jerked to a halt on the third floor.

Inside my office, I'd just flopped into my chair when the phone rang.

A hurried voice barked in my ear. "Don't have much time, Max. On my way to a meeting."

It was Ed Zielinski from the RCMP and I hoped he had some info on the list of paintings. Before I could speak he barged on.

"Just got a cable from American Intelligence about that list you sent. They've confirmed that three of those paintings were looted by the Nazis."

"Which three?"

"Let's see ... there's one by Renoir and another by Monet," then he gave me their titles in butchered French.

"And the last one?" I held my breath.

"Just a minute ... yeah, here it is, *Man with Hat* by Rembrandt. Gotta go now. I'll let you know if I hear more."

"Wait a minute, Inspector. I've seen that painting–"

"Hold it right there, Dexter. That case is on the back burner for now. We've just begun a big drug operation with the US And there's no goddamn time for this painting business."

"But what about Jake Benson's murder? It must be connected with those paintings and it was you who approached me about them in the first place."

"Listen up, Mister. I can't discuss RCMP priorities with civilians. You know how it is." And he slammed down the receiver.

Shit – the dial tone droned in my ear like a bully's taunt. I knew too damn well how it was. Well, to hell with Zielinski and the RCMP. And to hell with the back burner.

Jake Benson was still on my front burner.

CHAPTER THIRTY-TWO

MY NEW ASSISTANT AND I cut across Gore Park, heading toward James, when we were slowed by a dozen or more people who were milling about, some window-shopping and others waiting to meet their friends 'under the clock at Birks', a Hamilton tradition. I looked up at the fanciful English timepiece suspended from the corner of the building. At the stroke of the quarter-hour a row of jousting knights galloped around the clock's exterior. Three small kids and their mother were staring up, entranced by the jousters.

I stopped when one of the kids, head back and cheering for the red knight to ride faster, bumped into me. "Sorry, Mister," he said, but he didn't look too sorry until his mother tugged his ear.

Iz nudged me and tilted her head. "Let's go, Max. You can play later."

We passed the Pigott Building and turned left toward a massive stone office building at 39 Main East. The directory board in the foyer showed the first floor was occupied by The Levinson Group and I pocketed the business card Jake Benson had hidden in the Dundas bank.

The main office was at the rear of a dark lobby, guarded by a massive oak door. I tried the brass knob and found it locked. Isabel pressed a small buzzer fastened to the door jamb. At the answering click she glanced at me with raised eyebrows and grinned like a kid about to enter a forbidden room in her grandparents' spooky old house.

Inside, we stepped into the sepia splendour of the late 1800s. Straight ahead, a long hallway revealed a series of doors along each side, all closed. To our right was a spacious reception area boasting a high-backed sofa and matching brocade chairs, deep oak baseboards, cove moldings and picture rails, an oriental carpet on the hardwood flooring. On the facing wall were several pictures of high-collared, whiskered gentlemen, and an oak desk behind which a handsome, middle-aged woman smiled at us.

"How may I help you?" she asked, her voice a cultured purr.

I stepped forward, feeling miles out of my depth in these plush old surroundings and I wondered if we were in the right place. Maybe that business card had nothing to do with those lists and Jake had picked it up elsewhere.

I handed my card to the receptionist, if that's what she was. "Name is Max Dexter, Ma'am. I'm a private detective. I'd like see to see the owner if he's available."

She studied the card and her puzzled look told me I'd need something a helluva lot better to enter the magic kingdom. I was about to speak when Isabel stepped forward.

"Excuse me," she said, extending her hand toward the receptionist. "I work with Mr. Dexter and we're undertaking a discreet investigation into quite a delicate matter." Iz moved closer to the desk and lowered her voice. "Your company's name has come up, in a perfectly legal way mind you, and it's important that we clarify a few details with Mr. Levinson."

The woman gave Isabel the once-over, taking in her fashionable summer dress and sincere manner, then smiled "What's your name, Young Lady?"

Iz returned her smile. "It's Isabel O'Brien. I'm a chartered accountant, formerly with my father's company. My father is J.B. O'Brien of O'Brien Associates. I believe Mr. Levinson may be acquainted with him."

"Yes, of course." The woman pressed a button on her phone and turned aside to speak quietly for a moment. Then she stood and said, "Follow me, please."

As we walked in single file to the end of the hallway, Iz glanced back at me and I pretended not to notice her snippy I-did-better-than-you-did grin.

A tall gent in a tailored grey suit rose from behind his desk and shook our hands. A robust guy in his sixties, I guessed, who looked more like a retired British guardsman than a diamond merchant. But what did I know about diamond merchants, never having met one? My image of them was a mixture of boyhood impressions from movies and comic books. And Levinson looked nothing like that hunchbacked old guy peering through his eyepiece at a sparkling mound of loot.

He motioned us toward a pair of leather visitors' chairs facing his desk. "I'm pleased to meet you both," he said. "Especially you, Miss O'Brien. I've met your father a number of times. An astute businessman."

The careful way he pronounced "astute" made me wonder if he meant more than that. But after we were seated, he said with a smile, "Now, how can I help with this 'discreet' investigation of yours?"

I started off. "I wonder, Sir … do you happen to know anyone by the name of Jake Benson?"

His brow furrowed, thinking about it. "No, that name doesn't ring a bell."

"How about Mr. H. B. Myers?"

"Well, of course, I do. Quite a prominent citizen. And," he turned toward Isabel, "he has a magnificent art collection."

He must have presumed Isabel would be well versed with her father's collection activities and his art friends. She gave him a sweet smile in return.

He eased back in his chair and, whether he realized it or not, lobbed me a bombshell. "Mr. Myers used to be a good customer of mine," he said.

I couldn't keep my eyes from flickering but I waited a long beat before asking, "Used to be?"

"Well, yes. Over the years he purchased a number of very fine diamonds from me. He's quite knowledgeable in that field as well as art."

"I see. And then?"

"Well, as sometimes happens between businessmen, we had a disagreement."

My goodness, a disagreement. The wheels in my brain were spinning and I wondered how snoopy he'd allow me to get before throwing up the barricades. The worst he could say was, "Mind your own business," – right?

"Must have been quite a serious matter, Sir, if he's no longer a customer. Do you mind telling us about it?"

He sent me a hard stare, then swivelled his chair toward Isabel. "What about you, Miss O'Brien?" A tiny grin twitched the corners of his mouth. "Are you just as inquisitive as your friend here?"

She dazzled him with her hundred-watt smile. "No, Sir, but I'm just learning the detective business. Max says it won't be long now before I'll be a Nosy Parker, too."

Levinson laughed out loud, leaning back in his big chair. "That's a corker," he said. Then he lost the smile and sat forward, arms resting on his desk. "Now I'd like you two to level with me. What's this all about?"

"It's about Jake Benson," I told him. "He was an accountant in Mr. Myers' office. But last week he was murdered; you may have read about it in the paper."

He mulled that over while he stroked his upper lip with his forefinger in the manner of a man who'd recently shaved off his moustache. "Yes," he said. "Yes, I did see that. But why come to me about it?"

"Well, Jake Benson's murder appears to have been a gangland killing, the type of crime which the police have little chance of solving because there are usually no witnesses. And they don't spend much time on such cases. So his family has hired us to inquire into the circumstances of his death. It's a puzzling case because Mr. Benson appears to have been a law-abiding citizen, well-liked by his friends and co-workers and no history of criminal activity. Not your usual candidate for a murder victim. So far, we've found a few unusual items among his possessions, including your business card. So we're following up every lead–"

Levinson held up his hand, stopping me there. "I'm sorry about the young man's death, Mr. Dexter. But he may have acquired my card any number of ways. I told you I didn't know the man. So I really don't see how I can help you."

"You're right about the card," I said. "But you told us Mr. Myers used to be one of your customers. Before your disagreement, you said. And it's probably just a coincidence that Jake

Benson worked for his company, but maybe you could tell us what you disagreed about."

He paused for a moment, his eyes searching my face, maybe for some sign of an ulterior motive. "All right," he said at last. "He offered to sell me a painting from his collection."

What the hell, Levinson's another art collector? Seems like they're coming out of the damn woodwork. "Do you collect art as well, Mr. Levinson?"

"Indeed I do," he said. "In fact, I've acquired some wonderful paintings over the years. Including a couple I bought from Mr. Myers before the war."

I leaned back in my chair, considering his reply, and I managed to catch Isabel's eye. We seemed to be on the same wavelength and somehow she knew it was her turn at bat.

"I have a little confession to make, Mr. Levinson," she said and leaned forward in her chair. "I think you might have assumed earlier that I was familiar with my father's interest in collecting art. Well, I don't really know that much about it."

Levinson made a dismissive motion with his hand and smiled at her.

"So I wondered . . ." she continued, "is it common practice for collectors to sell pieces to one another?"

"Oh, yes," he replied, eager to instruct this charming visitor. "Usually, people will collect the work of particular artists or periods in art history, or only contemporary work and so forth. And when you come across something outside your area of interest, you might advise other collectors. Or, if you change from one area to another, you might sell off a few works. It's quite common."

"Thank you," she said, then a frown wrinkled her forehead. "But . . . you had a falling-out with Mr. Myers over a painting he offered you. Do you mind talking about that?"

Levinson swivelled in his chair again, this time clutching the arms as though he intended to stand and I thought we'd lost him. After all, why should he reveal his private business to these two nosy strangers, even if the beautiful one was well-connected? It surprised me when he turned back and relaxed in his chair.

"All right," he said. "I don't see how it could be useful to your murder investigation but I'll answer your questions. Mr. Myers offered me a beautiful painting, quite old and very valuable. We went back and forth on the price for some time and I think we might've agreed eventually. But there were other considerations and, in the end, I turned his offer down."

"Other considerations?" I put in.

The spark in his eye when he glanced my way seemed to say, I thought you'd say that. "It's complicated," he said, stroking his invisible moustache again. "I was concerned about the painting's provenance – that is, who owned it, who sold it, its history, in fact. You see, Mr. Myers had become evasive on that point. And he wasn't able to provide the usual certification of authenticity one requires in these deals. So in the end, I refused the painting and he got quite upset. Then he threatened to take his diamond business elsewhere so I suggested he do just that. And that was the end of it."

I slumped in my chair. Shit. That couldn't be the end of it. Myers offers a painting to Levinson. Then he sells one to O'Brien. Jake Benson works for Myers and he finds that list of paintings, then he hides it, then he's murdered. Way too coincidental for my liking. My mind was trying to make sense of this sequence when it hit me. "By the way," I asked him, "what was the painting Mr. Myers offered you?"

"It was a self-portrait. By Rembrandt."

Holy hell. I shot a sideways glance at Isabel; she was staring straight ahead, gripping the arms of her chair with white knuckles. Earlier, I'd told her about Zielinski's phone call confirming that her father's painting had been looted by the Nazis. She had to know now that he was involved in this business. For her sake I didn't want to ask Levinson but I forced myself. "Do you recall the title of that painting?"

"I do," he said. *"Man with Hat."*

It wasn't a complete surprise to me. When Levinson said it was a painting by Rembrandt I was pretty sure it was the one which O'Brien had paraded in front of me. But poor Iz, she must be devastated to know her not-so-dear old dad was mixed up in this mess.

I half-turned from Levinson and whispered to my partner. "You all right? Want to leave now?"

She unclenched her hands from the chair. I saw the colour beginning to return to her face and she forced a thin smile. "I'm okay," she said. "Keep going." I gave her arm a light squeeze.

Levinson observed our little huddle and raised his brows. "Is there a problem, Mr. Dexter?"

"Not at all," I told him. "We were wondering if you might verify that painting for us if we were able to locate a photograph?"

He was out of his chair in a flash. "I can do better that," he said and strode to the bookcase behind us. It took him a moment but he returned to his desk and opened a large volume so that it faced us. "That's it," he pointed. "Right-hand page."

I took a close look. Jeez, Louise. Same pose, shoulders facing right, head turned to the viewer. I remembered the moustache and wispy beard. And that spectacular hat I'd seen in O'Brien's gallery and in the picture Roger Bruce had shown me in the Hamilton Public Library.

Isabel reached forward and closed the book with care. "We appreciate your time, Mr. Levinson." She extended her hand and he clasped it with both of his. "You've been very helpful," she said. He came around his desk and walked us to the door. I felt his eyes following us all the way down the hallway and I imagined him wondering what the hell we were really after.

CHAPTER THIRTY-THREE

WE WALKED UP JAMES TO Gore Park again, where we sat in silence on a bench well away from a crowd of kids cheering for a Ringling clown who twisted balloons into animal shapes. Isabel hadn't spoken since we'd left Levinson's office and I'd managed to keep my trap shut, giving her time to think about her father's predicament and God knows what else.

After a few moments she began taking deep breaths and stretched her arms and legs as though she'd just arrived on the train from Vancouver. Then she touched my arm. "It pains me to say this, Max, but my father might be a crook." Her eyes searched mine, looking for ... agreement, denial, comfort? Maybe a bit of each?

"It was his decision," I said, "to do what he did." I covered her hand with mine. "Now, what should we do about it?"

She stayed quiet another moment. "That's the hard part, isn't it, Max? But I'm still wondering, are you absolutely sure that was my father's painting?"

"It's been confirmed," I said. "And the Americans say there are two other looted paintings on that list."

I gave her time to reach her own conclusion. "There may be other ..." Her words sputtered to a stop. She removed a handkerchief from her purse and dabbed at her nose. "That means there could be other ... stolen paintings in my father's collection."

"Yes. And if not, the man who sold him the Rembrandt may have two more for sale."

She turned to face me, still clutching her handkerchief. "Mr. Myers," her voice shaky. "And he seemed like such a nice polite little man."

"They say Hitler could be very polite when it suited him."

Another silence, her handkerchief now a small white ball in her fist. "Wait a minute, Max. Maybe Mr. Myers didn't know the paintings were stolen."

I shook my head. "He knew. Remember, Levinson told us Myers was evasive and couldn't provide the usual documentation that accompanies such sales. So he must have known, Isabel. And so did your father."

She slumped back on the bench, staring through the old fountain's misty spray toward the statue of Queen Victoria beyond it. But I'd bet she saw neither. Then she startled me by springing to her feet and walking around the bench. She circled it three times then clapped her hands with a smack before sitting beside me again. "There," she said.

"Witchcraft?"

"No ... well, maybe. It's something my mother used to do when she had a difficult decision to make. Irish superstition, I suppose."

I gave her more time, watching her lean forward, head down, swinging her feet in slow circles. She seemed to be examining her slingback shoes, but my guess was she was weighing her father's motives for buying stolen art. And finding them out of balance.

"I just can't believe it, Max. He's my father, for Pete's sake. Why would he ... ?" She planted her feet on the ground and leaned back. Her upright posture told me she'd reached a conclusion.

I turned to face her. "What do you think we should do?"

"Sometimes it's so difficult to do the right thing, Max. Whatever the right thing is."

I waited a beat. "You need to walk around the bench again?"

She gave me a weak smile. "No. But I feel like such a traitor. Or at least disloyal to my family, such as it is."

I didn't speak.

She edged forward on the bench and clutched her purse, making ready to go. "There's no way around it, Max. We have to tell the police."

CHAPTER THIRTY-FOUR

"YOU'RE PULLIN' MY LEG, MAXIE." Frank was sputtering like my old Ford as he squeaked his chair away from his desk and glared at us.

Isabel and I had walked over to Central Station on King William Street, just a block and a half from my office.

"You've asked me to do some stupid-ass things before," he said, "but this takes the biscuit."

We were perched on a pair of mismatched wooden chairs in front of his desk. "C'mon, Frank. Isabel's had to screw up her courage to come here. How easy do you think it is to report your own father?"

"Yeah, but J.B. O'Brien? You want me to stride right into his fancy boardroom, maybe interrupt his meeting with the mayor or some other big shot, and clap him in irons?"

Sometimes my big brother could be a real pain in the ass. "Jeez, Frank, be serious. You're on solid ground here so just look at the facts." I paused a moment, wondering how to bring him on board. Logic wasn't always successful with Frank, but what the hell, it was worth a try.

"We saw Levinson at his office this morning," I said. "Turns out he's an art collector, too. He told us Myers tried to sell him a Rembrandt painting titled *Man with Hat*. That's the same painting O'Brien showed me in his home gallery and said he'd bought it from Myers. Now, here's a helluva coincidence: it's also the same painting shown on the list Jake Benson found in his boss' office. And the kicker: it's been verified by the American Intelligence report as looted by the Nazis."

I sat back on the hard chair to catch my breath and glanced over at Isabel. She'd transported herself to some other place, staring straight ahead. Ashamed of her father's actions? Ashamed of her own for reporting him?

Frank was writing in his notebook now; maybe I'd finally gotten through to him. Then he looked up, shaking a stubby pencil at me. "So you want me to arrest him for buying what you say is stolen property? No proof on my part, of course, no evidence in my hot little hand. And he's probably got a valid bill of sale. But if you're right, you know damn well this is a federal offence. So I've got no jurisdiction here anyway."

We didn't speak for a moment; then I caught my second wind. Isabel was fidgeting in her chair now but, so far, she was still a silent witness to this meeting.

"Frank," I said, "let's not quibble about jurisdiction. You know damn well that all this art stuff is just a sideshow for me. My main interest here is to find Jake Benson's killer."

"But that's got nothing to do with J.B. O'Brien," he said.

I gave myself a damn good scalp rub and felt calmer. It occurred to me that maybe Frank's definition of logic was different from mine. "Okay. One more time." I scootched my chair closer to his desk. "Jake confronts Myers about those lists he found at the office. He ends up floating in the bay. Some of the paintings on the list prove to be looted by the Nazis and Myers sells one to O'Brien. That's your jurisdiction, Frank. That painting opens the door for you to get after Myers. Now I don't know if he planned Jake's murder or arranged it or what the hell, but damnit, he's involved." By this time I was standing, waving my arms, sounding like Sam Lawrence at civic election time. "You've gotta see O'Brien, Frank. That painting is the key to Myers' jail cell."

I flopped into my chair, out of breath, facing the silence from my audience.

After a moment, Isabel opened her mouth to speak. Nothing came out. She coughed into her handkerchief and tried again. Her voice came out a wobbly croak. "I agree, Frank," she said.

We waited an eternity, watching the gears in Frank's brain slipping and sliding before they finally meshed. "All right," he said at last. "I'll have a word with your father, Isabel." He walked us to the door where he grabbed my arm and pulled me aside, his words coming out in a growl, "Call you later."

CHAPTER THIRTY-FIVE

WE WALKED UP MARY STREET on the way back to the office, passing the Century Theatre. *My Favorite Brunette* with Bob Hope and Dorothy Lamour was held over, according to the marquee.

I glanced at my glum-faced assistant and gestured toward the movie poster. "We should see this picture sometime," I said. "It's about a bumbling guy who's mistaken for a detective and investigates a murder. Remind you of anyone?"

She gave me a weak smile and touched my arm. "Thanks for trying to cheer me up, Max. I'm just disappointed in my father. I'll be all right."

It took some urging, but I convinced Isabel to stop for lunch. We got a window seat upstairs at the Pagoda Chop Suey House with a view of the post office across King Street and the busy lunch-hour crowd beneath us. After a short wait, a thin Oriental woman brought us a heaping platter of the chow mein special and we devoured most of it without a word between us.

I set my chopsticks down and drank some green tea. "We need a plan," I said.

Isabel passed me her cup and I filled it from the china pot. "It's hard for me to make plans when I don't know what'll happen to my father," she said.

"I know, I know." I hoped I didn't sound insensitive but I had to tell her. "Whatever happens with him, Iz, we can't stop our investigation. Both Myers and Thompson are making themselves scarce. And Frank won't be on the case much longer. We've got to make our move now. On our own, if we have to."

She sipped her tea, staring past the crush of traffic creeping across King Street, horns blaring at the daredevil pedestrians dashing between cars. She extended her teacup for another refill.

"You're right, Max." Her voice stronger now, some energy in her eyes, too. "What did you have in mind?"

I'd been doodling on the paper placemat trying to organize my thoughts, little arrows pointing this way and that. "I'm worried about Myers," I said. "He might be planning to skip town."

Her eyebrows arched and she moved her plate aside. "Really?" she said. "What makes you think so?"

I told her about my icy reception at his office the previous day and spotting that big guy packing boxes in the inner sanctum. "Remember meeting that veteran selling his pencils in front of the Cap?"

"Bob." She was nodding her head. "Nice man."

"Well, he's moved up to King and James now and I've got him keeping an eye out for Myers at the Pigott Building. Bob's wife works downtown and she'll help, too," I said. "But that's not enough."

"Whatever you want me to do, Max."

I ripped off the corner of my placemat. "I'd like you to call Miss Pietro at Myers' office. She's in the steno pool, friend of Doris Arneson." I jotted down her name and extension number, passed Iz the scrap of paper. "Sweet-talk her a bit. She'll get you Myers' and Thompson's addresses."

She took a moment to think about it, then leaned forward on the edge of her chair, eager now, the old Isabel setting aside for now her concern for her father. "Then what, Max? Are we going to stake out their houses? Maybe break in and search for clues?"

"Hold your horses, Partner," I said, glad she was back in the game. "We're not going anywhere near them. I want you to call George Kemper and have him put a surveillance team on each of their places for a couple of days. Myers and Thompson are supposed to be out of town on business. But I think that's baloney."

"All right. But I don't know if George will do that for me, Max."

"Of course he will," I said. "He was crazy about you when we met the other day. If he gives you a hard time, tell him he'll have to answer to me."

She sipped her tea, set her cup down. "I'm not very good with threats." But her half-closed eyes and hint of a smile were combining in that special way women have to get what they want.

I noticed it feeling warmer in the room and I squirmed in my seat. "Well, do what you have to," I said. "We need to find those guys."

CHAPTER THIRTY-SIX

IZ RETURNED TO THE OFFICE and I walked over to James Street to see Bob. If nothing else, this case was giving my gimpy leg more exercise than my rehab sessions.

I couldn't find him at the entrance to the Pigott Building. Not in front of Renner's Drugs either. That wasn't like Bob; he was as dependable as heartburn after a meal at the White Spot Grill.

I crossed the street and entered the United Cigar Store, where I waited for Aggie to make change for a customer in front of me.

"Bob's home now, resting," she said, before I could even say hello. Then it all spilled out in an angry torrent, spittle forming at the corners of her mouth and fire flashing in her eyes.

"Slow down, Aggie," I said, grasping her arm. I brought her to the end of the counter and she signalled to the other clerk on duty to take over.

We huddled out of earshot near the walk-in humidor, stacked with Monte Cristos and other expensive stogies. "Now take it easy and tell me again," I said.

She started to shake and I gripped both her hands in mine. It took a few moments before she began again. "I dropped him off at the Pigott Building, y'know, about eight this morning; that's when my shift starts. I always take him in the wheelchair from our apartment to wherever he sets up downtown. We built a shelf under the chair to store his dolly. Then, y'know, I get Bob fixed up and I keep his wheelchair wherever I'm workin'."

She stopped speaking, gave my hands a hard squeeze. "I'm scared, Max. It's been an awful shock, y'know."

"You're doing fine. Take your time."

"Okay." She gulped a deep breath and started again. "I don't know how he did it but somehow he pushed himself, y'know, around to the back of the building." A proud smile lit up her face, like a parent who was pleased as punch with her child's straight-A report card. "There's that insurance company on the corner beside the Pigott Building? Well, a friend of ours is one of the janitors there and he goes out back to the alley between the old Public Library, y'know, with the Art Gallery upstairs, and that leads to the dock behind the Pigott Building.

"Anyway, he's out there and hears Bob and this big bozo shoutin' at each other. The big guy's loadin' up a panel truck and all of a sudden, wham bam, he rushes over to Bob, y'know, and kicks him right off his dolly, the big shit. When Bob hit the pavement he got some real bad scrapes on his arms and hands. Banged his head, too."

Tears now and she was shaking again. I reached behind the counter and grabbed a couple of Kleenexes from an open box. While she mopped up I slipped my arm around her shoulder. My God, what kind of creep would kick a legless veteran? Little wonder Aggie was so upset. "So what happened then? This friend got in touch with you?"

She blew her nose again, catching her breath before she answered. "Came right down to the store and got me. After he made sure Bob was okay, 'course."

"What about his cuts and bruises?"

"Yeah, I brought the first aid kit from the store and patched him up. Pencils scattered all over the place; we lost some of those."

I shook my head, still trying to understand why the guy attacked Bob, and I blamed myself for his being there. "Are you sure he's okay? Should we take him to the hospital?"

She waved my questions away. "He won't go near any hospital. Hates 'em all. And he's such a stubborn guy, y'know, he'll be back at work tomorrow."

I still had my arm around her, leaned closer and gave her a peck on the cheek. "Nobody could have a better sister, Aggie. You're a real Florence Nightingale."

She rewarded me with a faint smile, a hint of colour in her cheeks. "Why don't you drop in and see him, Max?"

"I'm heading there right now," I said. "And if there's anything else you need, just let me know."

They had a small flat behind Family Cleaners, a couple of blocks north on James. I put my leg in gear again and arrived there ten minutes later. The summer swelter was back after a one-day holiday. The big *Toronto Daily Star* thermometer on the newsstand at the corner showed ninety-two degrees.

My army trainers had drilled into me the value of forward planning and preparation. So I chose to approach Bob's place via the alley to his side entrance, thereby avoiding the fumes from the dry cleaners' shop. Those trainers hadn't said anything about wind direction.

I pounded on the screen door, waited a few seconds, then entered, still holding my nose. Found Bob in the bedroom, propped up on a pile of pillows, listening to the radio, a sappy version of *The Old Lamplighter* by Sammy Kaye and his orchestra. "Like that better than music?" I asked him.

He gave me a lopsided grin which probably hurt like hell. A red welt streaked from his mouth to his left ear. Bandages on his arms and a melting ice pack on his head. He grimaced as he reached over to snap off the radio and said, "What's new, Sarge?" Trying to sound like we'd met by chance in the street and he hadn't had the shit beaten out of him.

"Not much," I said, keeping up the pretence. "Happened to be in the neighbourhood ..."

My God, what a pitiful sight he was. Aggie was right, the guy who did this really was a big shit. I stared in silence, unable to speak for a moment, knowing I'd gotten him into this fix. "I'm so sorry," I said at last. "I shouldn't have asked you ... too dangerous—"

He stopped me there, lifting an arm, which made him cringe. "Cut it out, Sarge. I screwed up. All my fault. I let the sonovabitch get to me and I lost my temper."

"Tell me."

He was about to speak, but coughed, then nodded toward a glass of water beside the radio and I retrieved it, holding it to his lips.

"That's better," he said and laid his head back on the pillows. "Well ... Aggie dropped me off at the entrance to the Pigott Building and I got to thinking about that loading dock at the rear, like I told you yesterday." He signalled for another sip of water and drank it. "So I wheeled around there and spotted that big bastard tossing cartons into a truck. And I called out to him, friendly I thought, like, 'Hi there, Bud. Whatcha doin'?' – that kind of thing. Well, damned if he doesn't leap down from the platform and come chargin' over to me, cursin' and swearin', gets right in my face and I can see he's got this ugly red birthmark down one side of his neck and it's lit up like a neon sign. Then he screams at me, 'Piss off.'"

I grasped his arm, slowing him down, forcing him to rest a moment. "Easy does it," I said. "What do you think got him so riled up?"

"Dunno. But I wasn't gonna take his crap without a fight. That's when I lost my temper and started shouting back at him, y'know."

"Jeez, Bob. You could've gotten yourself killed."

"Damn near did. He grabbed me by the shirt, tore off the buttons, said if he caught me snoopin' around again I'd be sorry, then he booted me right off my dolly. Don't mind tellin' you, Sarge, I was scared shitless. Didn't know what he'd do next."

I patted his hand, careful to avoid the scrapes. "Still brave old Bob, eh?"

He tried to scowl at me but it came out as a grimace. "Yeah, well. Stupid, I guess. Sometimes I go too far, Sarge."

"That's what soldiers do," I said. "Sometimes we all go too far." I plumped up his pillows, gave him another drink of water. "Do you want to call the cops? See if they'll charge this guy? Thirty days in the cooler?"

He shook his head, taking no time to think about it. "Hell with that, Sarge. Go through all that rigamarole, for what? My word against his and it would come to nuthin'."

"You're probably right," I told him. "But you were a big help. You got this mover guy, or bodyguard, or whatever the hell he is, pretty damn jumpy. Proves we're on the right track, making them nervous."

"Well, I didn't do a helluva lot."

"You kiddin'?" I said. "They know we're onto them now, probably running for cover."

He got a kick out of that, managed a small grin. "Always the optimist, eh, Sarge? Well, go get the buggers."

I left by the front door this time.

CHAPTER THIRTY-SEVEN

LATE AFTERNOON BY THE TIME I limped back to my office, my knee putting up a squawk about all this recent walking. Phyllis gave me a big smile and stuffed a wad of messages in my hand, URGENT scrawled across the top one. Isabel was at her desk, telephone receiver propped in the crook of her neck while she made notes. She waved, signalling she'd be in to see me in a moment.

The urgent message was from Scotty and I returned his call; he wasn't available and I left a message of my own, wondering if this was about his crusade for Evelyn Dick's Black Book. I pulled out my bottom drawer and had just hoisted up my leg when Iz bustled through the door.

"We're all set with the surveillance, Max. I was just finishing up with George Kemper on the phone. And you were right, he's tickled pink to help us out."

"You mean he's tickled pink to help you out."

She batted her eyes at me. "Well, you told me to do what I had to."

I made a get-on-with-it motion with my hand, which – surprise, surprise – caused her to take her sweet time: dragging a chair over to my desk, arranging her papers just so and smoothing the wrinkles in her skirt. I was coming to the conclusion that she might be as contrary as I was – but in a ladylike way, of course. Why do women get away with this stuff?

I was ready to burst a gasket when she said, "Ready to talk now, Max?"

"Whenever you are, Isabel. Take your time."

She looked straight at me, sunlight from the window highlighting the smooth planes of her face, her gaze as serene as the

Virgin Mary's. "I love working with you, Max. You're so easy to bait."

Before I could ask what the hell that meant, she said, "Ask me about George Kemper."

Off balance again, I counted to ten, taking my time to think of a snappy reply. "All right," I said and sat a little taller. "Tell me about George Kemper."

She reached across the desk and patted my hand. "Well done, Max." She referred to her notebook, flipping a few pages, back to business. "George agreed to start surveillance at Myers' and Thompson's places tonight. He'll assign two teams of two men each on twelve-hour shifts. How's that sound?"

"Sounds fine. Where do they live?"

"Mr. Myers has a house overlooking the mountain brow. Do you know where Bull's Lane is?"

I shook my head.

"Well, you take the Jolley Cut. I've got directions when you get to the top. And Mr. Thompson lives close to St. Joe's Hospital." She turned another page. "Here it is. On Charlton West, near the corner of Park."

"Good work. Have any trouble getting George to agree?"

She gave me that smarty-pants look I was becoming familiar with, as though the question didn't deserve an answer. "He's a cream puff, Max."

"Right," I said. "What about taking a little drive this evening? Be good to see their places, get the lay of the land, check in with the watchers."

"Great idea, Max. I already told George we'd probably do that."

I leaned back in my chair and the spring mechanism made a terrible screech. Same kind of screech I wanted to make but the rules of polite discourse prevented that, didn't they? So I took a moment to stretch my leg, to get comfortable, and said, "Ask me about Bob."

She did, and I related the unhappy events in the alley behind the Pigott Building this morning, as well my visit to Bob and Aggie's apartment. When I finished she was almost in tears.

"Why, that's terrible news, Max. What kind of man would assault a veteran? Especially one in his condition? I can't believe it."

I thought about her question for a moment, and the nasty side of the detective business. "These aren't nice people we're after," I said. "Crooks will do whatever's necessary to stay in the game. Look what happened to Jake Benson. And now Bob. But there's a bright side, if you could call it that – their roughing up Bob shows that we're making progress, the bad guys are on the defensive."

Iz gasped. "Oh, Max. That sounds so heartless."

"Not heartless," I said. "I care about Bob. But he was warned off for a reason. So you have to be pragmatic. It's the nature of this work, part of the package."

She was silent for a long moment, fidgeting, sometimes frowning, perhaps considering whether this business was going to be her cup of tea. "Something I need to know," she said at last. "What time should I pick you up tonight?"

CHAPTER THIRTY-EIGHT

AFTER SUPPER FRANK CALLED ME at home. "Told you I'd give you a buzz after I'd seen O'Brien," he said. "Just got back from his place. Boy, that's sure some mansion he's got there, eh? Helluva long way from Napier Street."

"Stay for dinner, Frank?"

"Wasn't invited, Smartass. He had some big function at City Hall tonight so I only had a half-hour of his precious time."

"And what did the great man have to say for himself?"

"Said what they all say: 'I didn't do anything wrong, Officer.'" We laughed at his cop joke, which we both knew wasn't a joke. "Gotta lot of horseshit from him at first and I waited 'til he talked himself into a corner. Told him we had a reliable witness who was offered that same painting and refused to buy it because of the lack of documentation. Then when he heard that business about the American investigators proving his painting was looted by the Nazis, well, that finished him off."

"The other two paintings on the list, any sign of them?"

"Nope. I asked about those; he said he refused to buy them when Myers offered them. Too expensive or didn't suit him, or some damn thing. Then he showed me his big exhibit room and gave me the grand tour, but I didn't see those paintings on display."

"How the hell would you know what they looked like, Frank?"

"Hey," he said testily. Then a pause on the line and I could picture him wagging a finger at me over the phone. "I've got photos of all three of those paintings, don't I? Hot off the press from the US of A. Called your old buddy Inspector Zielinski and he sent them on the express bus. What do you think of them apples?"

"Oh," I said. "Well, what about the Rembrandt?"

"Wrapped it up and took it with me."

"Jeez, man, it's worth a zillion bucks. What did you do, throw it in your trunk?"

He let loose with one of his horse laughs, the kind he reserved for stupid remarks. "Don't lose any sleep over it, Pal. It's locked up tight at the station house. In the evidence vault."

"So, that's it for O'Brien? No arrest, not even a rap on the knuckles?"

"Charges could be pending, eh? We'll do our usual thorough investigation." Giving me the company line, like he was talking to a snoopy reporter. "What are you doin' here, Max? Tryin' to get your new girlfriend's old man in hot water? What'd he ever do to you?"

Ouch, that stung. But was he right? Was I vying with Isabel's father for her attention ... or affection? I didn't want to think about it. "Frank," I raised my voice to cover my chagrin. "That painting's connected with Jake Benson's murder, so that's what I'm trying to do here."

"Okay, okay. Don't get your arse in a knot. Here's what I'm gonna do. In the morning, I'll notify the RCMP that we've seized the painting and we're investigating. Zielinski will probably want it shipped to Toronto for authentication and all that. Then I'll pay a visit to Myers and we'll have a nice chat about those other paintings. See where that leads."

"O'Brien?" I said.

"Don't worry about O'Brien. I scared the piss out of him. He's a chiseller, yeah, but I'm sure that's all he is. Just another greedy sucker who didn't wanna know the dirty details while he made a shady deal. People do that all the time, Max, you know that. So we confiscate the painting, he loses his money and maybe he'll get a suspended sentence or a fine if the case ever gets to court, him being a rich guy and all. But I'll betcha he ain't gonna do it again. Wouldn't want to risk losing his precious social standing. Not to mention the effect on his business."

See? I knew he wasn't as dumb as he looked. "Okay," I said. "But it won't be easy to get your mitts on Myers. I can't reach him and his office is giving me the runaround." I told him about Bob and my suspicion that Myers was on the move.

I didn't mention George Kemper's guys on surveillance duty. Frank was my best friend and all that, but I find that cops can become very territorial with us civilians.

CHAPTER THIRTY-NINE

I WAS FLIPPING THROUGH THE *Spectator* at the kitchen table, putting in time until Isabel picked me up to snoop on our snoopers.

You can learn things reading the paper. Mind you, these things are often so goofy they appeal only to certain people.

On the local news page, for example, was a story about the first-ever Miss Canada contest, which took place last year during the celebration of Hamilton's centennial. Some of the contestants complained that a number of the girls were wearing falsies. The *Spec* quotes Phyllis Webb of Toronto (a non-winner): "I don't mind losing to girls who have it, but this phoney business shouldn't happen in a beauty contest." I smiled, thinking, *Sour grapes, Phyllis.*

And on the next page, another fashion flash – Christian Dior was in the US today defending long skirts against all critics. He said, "Nothing can stop the new fashion. If anything, skirts are going to drop to the ankles." Did he mean ...? Made me wonder if he'd been misquoted.

I'd just turned to the funnies for relief when Scotty phoned. "Busy?" he asked.

"You could say that." I folded the newspaper, tossed it on the pile. "I'm finishing up some paperwork."

"Sorry to bother you at home, Laddie. Tried to call this afternoon but you were out. Just wanted to chat."

I didn't like the sound of that and I said, "I can feel your hand in my pocket already."

He tried a polite chuckle to get on my good side, which made me even more suspicious. "C'mon, Unc. What's this all about?"

"Well, since you ask ... a little birdie told me you've got Isabel O'Brien workin' in your office now."

"What?" I was stalling for time, trying to figure where the hell he was going with this.

"Your new employee. Don't be coy with me, I know you too well."

I could hear him sorting papers, probably still at his desk at the *Spec*. "You know Isabel?" I asked him.

"No I don't. But I know her old man. Well, not quite true; I know about him. Not as though we're buddy-buddy or anything," he said. "Anyway, you know I'm still diggin' around on the Evelyn Dick case, eh? Well, I heard that O'Brien and your former client Myers are pals. And since you're still interested in that guy who was murdered ... what's his name?"

"Jake Benson."

"Yeah, Benson, who used to work for Myers. Well, that gives us a mutual interest here. We could help each other out."

"How do you figure that?"

"It's obvious. I told you Tedesco's name was in Evelyn Dick's Black Book. And he and Myers are serving on the hospital fund-raising committee, right? Now, I know you pooh-poohed this idea before, but I'm still trying to establish a connection between those two boys and Evelyn.

"So, two things. First, I'm havin' trouble seeing Myers, his office keeps givin' me the bum's rush. You could help me with that 'cause you've probably got some good connections there. And second, if we strike out on that score, young Miss O'Brien could talk to her daddy, get me together with Myers through him. Sound good to you, Max?"

"Hell, no. It sounds crazy. Why should I use my influence so you can win another damn newspaper award? You're my uncle, yeah, but I think you've got a helluva nerve."

"Whoa ... keep your shirt on, my boy. You do me a little favour and I do the same for you. Like we agreed the last time we talked, remember? It's the family way." He paused then, trying a new tack. "Say, you sound a little tense, Lad. Have a bad day, did you? Want to talk to your old uncle about it?"

I didn't respond, letting the silence build on the phone, still wondering what his dodge was, and annoyed that our so-called family sharing was all one-way. "Why this sudden interest in Myers?" I said at last. "What's happened?"

"Well ..." He didn't speak right away and I figured he was returning my dose of the silent treatment. But he continued, "One of my sources at the cop shop has come through for me. He talked to a guy who talked to a guy. Seems that Henry Myers was in Evelyn's book of celebrities after all, along with his unlisted phone number. Then I called in a couple of favours and, whaddya know, Myers has been paying the rent for an apartment on James South since 1944. And not some forty-bucks-a-month third-floor walk-up, either – the Lower Park Apartments."

He stopped again, treading water, waiting for me to beg him to continue. "Don't be cute, Unc," I said. "Tell me what it means."

"Guess who occupied the apartment for most of that time?"

"Goddammit, Scotty, enough with the striptease, just tell me the story. I've gotta go out in ten minutes."

"All right, then. Jeez, you're an anxious young lad, should learn to control that. Anyway, yes, it was Evelyn Dick who lived there until the autumn of '45. That's when she bought a house on Carrick Avenue, $2,500 down. Pretty damn good for a girl from a working-class family who didn't have a job, eh? Now you're wondering, where did she get her dough? And the answer is, from all those men-about-town listed in her Black Book. Including your pal, Myers."

Well, shit. Was that all there was to Myers' nasty little secret? He wasn't a married man, after all, so keeping a mistress wasn't that big a deal. But maybe there was more. "What happened to the apartment? After Evelyn moved out?"

"Knew you'd ask that," he said. "Myers still rents it. Some other babe is in there now but I haven't tracked her down yet."

"No shit? What's the apartment number?"

"You know something," he said, barking out the words.

"I don't know a goddamn thing, Unc. This is all news to me. So give me the number, just in case."

"In case of what?"

I began counting to ten – out loud. "One. Two. Three–"

"All right," he said. "318 James South. Apartment 6A. "

"Fine," I said and slammed down the phone.

CHAPTER FORTY

I WAS SITTING ON MY front steps, letting off steam after my phone call with Scotty. A tenacious guy, but what a pain in the ass. And he might get to Myers before Yours Truly. Maybe I should be tailing him, for Pete's sake.

A gleaming red Studebaker glided to a stop and Isabel stepped out, holding the driver's door open. "My car or yours, Max?"

I glanced at my Model A Ford and winced. Sixteen years old now, rusting, dented and tired, it dozed in the shade at the end of the side drive and seemed to be abashed, hiding its boxy old-style shape from the streamlined beauty at the curb with the driver to match. I felt like a traitor but I said, "Since you're blocking the drive, we might as well take yours."

From my apartment, she took Hunter Street over to James, passing the busy T.H. & B. railway station. I smiled, remembering the ramshackle clubhouse our gang of kids had built alongside the tracks, not far from here. For us those initials didn't stand for Toronto, Hamilton and Buffalo but, rather, To Hell and Back, which was where a guy had to go to join our club.

Iz snapped me back from the past. "Something funny, Max?"

I turned toward her, patting my chest. "No. Just a bit of gas, I think."

When she turned onto James Street I asked her, "What'll it be? Thompson's or continue up the Mountain to Myers' place?"

She made a right turn on Charlton, drove three blocks and, *voilà*, we were looking at Thompson's home. Iz stopped behind a new green Chevy parked on the street a few doors away. "Guess we'll stop at Thompson's, Max. Since it's on the way."

"And the guy in the car ahead is one of Kemper's boys?"

"That's what George said – green Chevrolet, nearby. Think we should go over to talk to him?"

"Not necessary. If I know George's guys, once he spots you in the rear-view, he'll be here in a flash." I hadn't quite finished speaking when the guy left his car and hotfooted it back to us. I signalled to him with my thumb to get in the back.

He jumped in and when I leaned over the seat I recognized McGuire, ex-cop and ex-army, the kind of guy George Kemper always hired for this type of work. I stretched my arm over the seat to shake hands with him. "Long time, McGuire. Got a sitrep for us?"

"Not until I meet your driver, Sarge. This job's gotta have some perks."

I introduced him to the driver and he almost swooned when she made a fuss over him. "Pleasure, Miss," he said. "Mr. Kemper asked me to give you an update on our surveillance. So here goes …" And he stammered to a halt.

Oh, brother. I could see he was going to stretch this one-minute job into a half-hour, so I cut him off. "Get on with it, McGuire. We're on a tight schedule here." Why do guys make such fools of themselves in the presence of a beautiful dame? Present company excepted, of course.

He shot me a dark look but I glowered back and he turned to Isabel. "Began our shift couple of hours ago, Miss. My partner's around back in the alley. No activity to report, far as we know the subject's not in the residence."

Isabel turned on the charm again. "That's wonderful, Mr. McGuire, keep up the good work. Any change and you give us a call. You've got our numbers, right?"

He left, bobbing his head like a trained dog as she smiled him out of the car.

"What do you think, Max?" A triumphant grin, like she'd climbed Mt. Everest.

"I think he's a boob."

"Oh, c'mon. I meant, do you think we'll learn anything from this stakeout?"

"It's a bust," I said. "He's flown the coop."

She was quiet, tapping her fingers on the steering wheel, glancing around the neighbourhood, taking it all in, maybe giving some weight to my words of wisdom. I congratulated myself once again for hiring such a smart cookie. I was the one who'd done the hiring, right?

"You might be right, Max. Let's push on."

We turned around and drove past St. Joe's Hospital – I didn't notice any new members of its fundraising committee lurking about.

At the top of the Jolley Cut Isabel made a sharp right, glanced at her handwritten directions, and after a couple more quick manoeuvres we arrived at a secluded roadway, quiet and leafy and exclusive. "Bull's Lane," she said. "Keep your eye out for number 7, Max."

Iz pulled over behind another green Chev parked alongside the low wrought-iron fence surrounding the property. We leaned over for a closer look at the house and way in there, clinging to the edge of the mountain brow, we glimpsed a low-slung modern building of limestone and glass spread out over a couple of city-sized lots.

"Wow." Her voice a whisper, as though we were trespassing. "Can you imagine the view from there, Max? Bet you can see all the way to Toronto."

We jumped at the tap on the window behind us. I wheeled around and saw George Kemper's guy take a step back from the car.

"Sorry," he said when I rolled down the window. "Didn't mean to startle you. Name's Trepanier. Mr. Kemper said you might come by."

"Don't worry about it," I said, giving him some bluster. "We were just admiring the scenery. Get in the back seat and tell us what's happening."

He slid in and we looked him over. A replica of the first guy, McGuire. I wondered where George found these guys; they looked like they'd dropped off an assembly line at a security agent factory.

"So, Trepanier," I said, tasting his name. "You from Quebec? I noticed a bit of an accent."

He gave me a hard look, on guard. "From Quebec and proud of it," he said. "Will that be a problem for you?"

I could feel Isabel shifting in her seat and I knew she was giving me the eye. "Hell, no. I served with Quebecers overseas, good soldiers. I believe a guy should be judged by what he does, not by where he was born."

Trepanier smiled and I saw his shoulders relax. "Good," he said. "So do I." He stuck his hand out and I shook it. Isabel did the same.

"Very pleased to meet you," she told him. "I think your accent is cute."

He shrugged at her remark, trying to look nonchalant, as though being observed by a beautiful woman, one who thought his accent was cute, was a daily occurrence. And maybe, for Trepanier, it was.

"Your report," I said.

He unclamped his eyes from Isabel and turned to me. "Sure. We got here about five. My partner is out there somewhere, working his way to the front of the house. So far there is only small traffic here. One car went in the neighbour's at the end of the road, did not come out. And a delivery van drove by, went to the end of the road and drove out again. Maybe the driver was lost."

"He didn't see you?" I asked.

He shook his head. "No chance. I was a soldier, too," he said. "Van Doos." It sounded different spoken in French and I noticed Isabel's eyelids flutter.

It was almost dark by the time we drove down the Mountain and I was still thinking about our visit to Myers' place. "Trepanier seemed like a nice fellow," I said.

Isabel didn't take her eyes from the road but I saw her head bob. "I thought he was sweet," she said. "But let's not get side-tracked, Max. Do you think the watchers will learn anything?"

Trepanier? Sweet? I pushed his image from my mind and concentrated on her question. "Probably not," I said. "But it's worth a try for a couple of days."

CHAPTER FORTY-ONE

AFTER WE LEFT MYERS' PLACE we drove down James South and at the base of the Mountain I motioned toward an impressive apartment building at number 318. I asked Isabel to pull in and park. "The last row," I said. "Back in the shadows."

She parked, switched off the engine and slid around in her seat so she could face me. "What's going on, Max? You know someone here?"

I shook my head. Was she always this suspicious? Or just since she joined Max Dexter Associates? "Don't know a soul here," I said. "Just wanted a quiet spot to talk."

She stared at me, hard and steady, and I noticed the leery twitch of her eyebrows. "Okay, Max. Talk."

I gave her chapter and verse of Frank's visit to her father's home earlier this evening, sparing no details. She listened to me grim-faced, hands clasped in her lap, from time to time shaking her head. Sometimes she moved her lips without a sound and I'd bet she wasn't praying.

We remained silent for some time after I'd finished. Bad news was like army food – hard to stomach.

At last, Isabel got out of the car and walked around it three times, clockwise this time, then got back in. She sat statue-still, the kind of calm that signalled deep disappointment and probably a lot of anger. And it warned off any comments on my part. "Will he go to jail, Max?"

"I don't think so," I said. "He's a rich man. His lawyer will work something out. I'm sure you know more about the old boys' network than I do."

She turned to face me now, a kind of defeat in her eyes, and sadness. "I just don't understand why he did it, Max." She bowed her head and whispered, "I feel so let down."

I reached forward, touching her hand and we sat quiet like that until she began to relax. "Ready to get back to work?" I asked her.

She sent me a tentative smile and took a deep breath while she pushed her hair back with both hands. "It's the best medicine, isn't it?" She dabbed at her eyes and nose with her handkerchief, then returned it to her purse, straightened her skirt and looked me in the eye. "Okay. Shoot."

I grinned at her spunk. And got back to business. "Evelyn Dick had an apartment in this building. 1945."

She stared at me, eyebrows raised. "So?"

"One of her many sugar daddies paid the rent."

"All right."

"Henry Myers."

Her eyes widened and she leaned toward me. "Our Henry Myers? I know he sold that painting to my father but ... no, no, no, Max. Not with Evelyn Dick. I don't believe it."

"Neither did I," I said. "At first."

Then I told her about Scotty's research on the Evelyn Dick case for the *Spectator* and the mysterious disappearance of the Black Book because it named such high-powered individuals, including Myers. "Scotty also found a connection between Myers and Dominic Tedesco, the Mafia chief. He's in Evelyn's book, too."

She grasped my arm, staring at me. "The Mafia chief ..."

"And here's another curious thing ... Myers and Tedesco had a private meeting at the Connaught just a few days before Jake Benson's murder."

"Wait a minute ... How would you know that?"

"Longo, the waiter," I said. "I asked him to keep an eye open for me. And he saw them having dinner together." I was quiet while she mulled that over, then I added, "That was right after Jake had found that stuff in his boss' office and spoken to Myers about it."

"Oh, Max. You're not suggesting–"

"It's the sixty-four dollar question, isn't it? Was it Myers who arranged Jake's murder?"

We left the car and walked down the block toward Aberdeen Avenue.

"I need this fresh air, Max. To clear my mind." Her arms behind her back, hands linked, she strolled like a nun saying her prayers. "What you say sounds so ... so far-fetched that it just doesn't make sense."

We ambled along in silence, onto Aberdeen, which was downhill and easier on my leg. Isabel stopped at the corner of Bay and turned toward me. "I guess you're thinking that Jake Benson might have argued with Myers about those papers he found. And that Myers was doing something illegal and thought Jake would be a threat to him. Not to mention his precious business. So he arranged with Tedesco to ... take care of the problem."

"That's exactly what I think."

"But that list showing the Rembrandt painting ... my God, Max. My father may be part of this, too."

I held up both my hands. "I don't think he had anything to do with Jake Benson. Yes, he let his greed get the better of him when he bought that painting. But I'm sure that's all he did."

We walked another block, Isabel deep in thought, then turned back toward the car. "I believe you're right, Max," she said at last. "But what he did was bad enough." And that seemed to be all she had to say on that subject. Looking at the set of her jaw, I shuddered for J.B. O'Brien if he had any hopes that his daughter would forgive and forget.

Back in the car, I stretched out my leg, giving it a well-earned rest. I glanced over at my assistant, bending low now, craning her neck to look up at the Lower Park Apartments. Then she eased herself back against the seat, settling in.

"See something?" I asked.

She moved her head side to side, tiny movements, and in a tiny voice said, "I know Evelyn Dick."

"What?"

"Evelyn Dick. She attended Loretto Academy when I did. Couple of years behind me but ... I knew her."

I sat up straight and faced her. "What was she like?"

"Hmmm. Not an easy question, Max. I'd say she was like many different people, all rolled into one." She paused, straightened her skirt again. "Loretto's a private girls' school operated by the Loretto Sisters. Many of the students come from well-to-do Catholic families. But there were a few exceptions and Evelyn was one of them. I guess the families of those girls scraped together the tuition somehow because a good education along with the religious training was important to them."

"Not to mention the contacts they'd make among the upper crust," I said.

"Yes, I guess that's true. It certainly seemed to be the main reason Evelyn was sent there for her high school years. I heard that her mother was very ambitious for her only child. And she always seemed to have lots of money. At school we had to wear uniforms, but after school she wore the latest in fashionable clothes, even had a fur coat and hat. And she bought lavish gifts for her friends, gave parties at the best restaurants."

"Trying to buy acceptance," I said. "But that must have cost a fortune."

"I'm sure it did, Max. We didn't know this at the time, but it came out last year during her trial – her father worked in the office of the Hamilton Street Railway and had been stealing money from them for years. To finance his daughter's future."

"What about later on, after she left school?" I asked. "Did you still see her then? I understand she had quite an active social life."

She glanced at the apartment building again, then back to me. "Well, that's an understatement. By then, she was way out of my class. I was the studious type, nose in my books, getting my degrees, trying to please Daddy, all of that. Oh, I went to the odd dance and had a couple of part-time boyfriends, but my life was almost monastic compared to Evelyn's. I guess you've heard all the stories, her stable of generous men who showered her with gifts, parties, travel, you name it. They say she could adopt whatever personality the situation demanded. And she must have thought she was on top of the world. Until she wasn't."

We stayed quiet for a while; I was struggling with the idea that Jake Benson's murder was related in some way to the Evelyn Dick case but I couldn't make the connection. And Isabel, well, I wasn't sure what she was thinking. By now I'd admitted to myself that she was often a step ahead of me but ... well, I was just stumped.

What a great detective, eh? Clueless.

A white Lincoln convertible rolled into the lot, a fashion plate behind the wheel, her blonde hair ruffled by the breeze. She parked near the entrance and waited while the canvas top retracted and snapped into place. Talk about a luxury automobile, it probably came equipped with electric-powered windows, too. She stepped from the car, a tall woman in an off-the-shoulder white gown, classy. She glanced around as though expecting applause, then swivelled toward the Lower Park Apartments.

We sat in silence for a long moment after she'd disappeared into the building. "Mitzi Slater," Iz said.

"You know her?"

"Her family lived two doors from us. Before my father moved to Ancaster. She was in my class at Loretto."

Holy Dooley! Were the gods working overtime up there in Valhalla or wherever they had their office? Or was this a real coincidence?

"In case you were about to ask, Max, I haven't seen much of Mitzi since high school. But I can tell you that she's become quite the party girl, very popular around town. Last time I saw her was New Year's Eve at the Royal Connaught. My father arranged a date for me with one of his protegés and we were up there at the Circus Roof. Festive, very gay, you get the picture. Mitzi stopped at our table for a while, the life of the party, danced and smooched with all the men."

"Sounds like fun," I said.

She gave me a nudge. "Don't be smart, Max, I'm not finished yet. Later that evening, I spoke with a woman who told me Mitzi had become the queen bee of the nightclub set. Now that her close friend was in jail."

CHAPTER FORTY-TWO

Isabel sped east along Main Street, not much traffic this time
of the evening. Took her only ten minutes to reach my place from
the Lower Park Apartments, home of the new darling of the
night, Mitzi Slater. Before we'd left there, I dug out my notebook
to check Evelyn Dick's apartment number which I'd squeezed
out of Scotty. Iz walked into the lobby to verify the occupant of
Apartment 6A. You guessed it.

Now we sat on my tiny front porch, looking out at the dark
street, discussing what we'd learned tonight. More like what we
hadn't learned.

"There's too much to think about, Max. My mind feels sea-
sick. Myers and Evelyn? And now, Myers and Mitzi? It's just ...
too absurd."

I was in the same boat; this case kept getting murkier. And
more difficult to stay on target – was any of this stuff connected
to Jake Benson's murder?

"Doesn't seem like we're making much progress, Max."

And I thought, ain't that the truth, but I didn't say it. Instead,
I said, "Sometimes it's like that. All this info we've been gathering seems contradictory, doesn't it? It won't fit our theory of the
case. And that's the hard part of this job – do we need more facts
or less theory?"

"So where do we go from here?"

I'd been thinking about that most of the evening. "We'll call
George Kemper in the morning, see what his men have come
up with, if anything. Couple more days of surveillance should
be enough. And Frank'll be on the job another day or two; he's
following up on the stolen paintings and trying to track down
Myers."

She turned to face me, frowning. "Doesn't seem like we're doing enough."

"How about contacting Mitzi?" I said. "Maybe that's a way to get to Myers."

Quiet now, she was looking off in the distance, then showed me a tiny smile. "I like it, Max. I'll get on it first thing."

After she left, I limped into my apartment and put on the kettle. I'd acquired a taste for tea in England, mainly because that's all they drank there. Or was it because I used to enjoy a "cuppa" with Ruth Greer at the nurses' station on the fourth floor of the Rehab Centre in the southwest of London and I still carried a torch for her?

I shook off that memory and looked in my book for the extension number of Simon Benson at the Connaught. "Sorry to call so late," I said, "but I just got home." Then I filled him in on developments to date, sounding more hopeful than I was.

"Keep your fingers crossed," I told him. "I've got a feeling things'll be coming to a head soon." He'd never know how much I hoped that were true.

I assembled my notes on the kitchen table and tried to manufacture a new theory. After a frustrating hour and a couple of cups of tea, I gave up and hit the hay.

At oh-three-hundred the phone woke me and I stumbled against the bedroom door, stubbing my big toe in my haste to answer it. Phone calls this late were never good news.

"Maxie, Old Pal." A chirpy voice. "You busy?"

"What the hell do you want, Frank? You know what time it is?"

"Yeah, I know. Get your clothes on and I'll pick you up in five minutes. Tell you about the explosion on the way there."

CHAPTER FORTY-THREE

YOU COULDN'T SEE THE FIRE trucks from where we parked but their rotating red and white lights strobed through the stand of trees and brush as we approached the corner of Bull's Lane, where a city cop stopped us at a barricade. Behind it Myers' mansion swarmed with firefighters, smoke belching from one wing. Frank spoke with the cop on duty, who tilted his head toward two men in suits with their heads together standing beside a red car labelled Fire Chief.

We were making our way there, stepping over the snakes' nest of hoses stretching from the nearby hydrants and the pumpers, when I spotted our lookout guy, Trepanier, at the edge of a crowd of gawkers.

"I'll catch up, Frank. Someone over there I need to talk to."

Trepanier stood with the neighbours behind the police line, most of them hastily-dressed or clutching their nightclothes around themselves, craning for a better view and asking each other what caused the big bang. One woman, her white hair in curlers under a pink bandana, said, "Why, it almost rattled the dishes out of my china cabinet."

He shook my hand when I reached him and said, "Just another boring surveillance job, eh?"

I grinned at his black humour. "Not quite," I said. "How's your partner? You both okay?"

"For sure. My partner was in the car when the end of the house blew up." He looked in that general direction but our view was blocked by a couple of fire trucks. "We parked far enough away so there was no damage. Me, I was around the front there, moving past the neighbour's place, along the edge of the Mountain."

Trepanier was becoming antsy now, his speech speeding up and his French accent more pronounced. I clapped him on the shoulder. "Take it easy," I said. "Slow down and tell me what happened."

He gulped a couple of deep breaths and I could see his shoulders loosen. "Okay. When I heard the big bang I hit the ground and rolled. But I was close to the edge of the Mountain and fell through a gap in the small bushes there. I slipped over the side and dropped maybe two, three feet, landed on a flat space. It was a small trail."

"But you're all right? Don't need to see a doctor?"

"No, I am fine. Just some bruises. It's because I was over the side of the Mountain that the blast missed me," he said. "But I will be sore tomorrow, for sure."

"That trail–"

"It's what I was thinking," he said. "I follow it and it goes along the front of these other houses and back to the end of the lane. So I am thinking, someone could do this explosion and escape along the trail. We could not see him from the street. Not from the front either, if he bent down on the path, he will be under the level of the yards and gardens."

I looked closer at Trepanier, seeing past the handsome exterior and thinking, this guy could make a damn good detective. "But neither of you saw anyone? Going in or coming out?"

He shook his head. "Nobody."

"And before the explosion? No suspicious noises? Lights going on or off in the house?"

"No noises. No lights. No warning, like I said."

"Good man, Trepanier." I slapped him on the back. "Thanks very much for your help. Now, why don't you and your partner pack it up here. I don't think we'll have any more excitement tonight. I'll call George Kemper in the morning."

He was about to leave but turned back. "I hope you don't mind that I ask a question," he said. "That lady who was with you before – is she single, is she going with somebody?"

What the hell? I stared at him; he'd just had a lucky escape, could've been blown to smithereens or fallen down the Mountain and he's wondering about Isabel. And why did I care so much?

I took too long to answer. "Well ... she's single. But I don't know much about her personal life, so you'd have to ask her."

He gave me an odd smile and tapped me on the arm. "Thanks," he said. "Maybe I will."

I was still thinking about that nervy Trepanier when I caught up with Frank. "Spoke with the Chief," he said. "Going to meet the fire captain. Follow me."

We high-stepped our way over the hoses toward the west wing of the mansion, which now appeared to be gutted. The roof here had collapsed and the surrounding area was muddy, soaked from the high-pressure spray. But no flames now, just white smoke billowing in clouds, stinging our eyes when the wind swirled in our direction. The centre section of the house and the opposite wing had escaped the blaze because the roof and walls there were wet down as a precaution.

Frank pulled me aside. "Who was that guy I saw you talking to?"

I waved away his question. "Just somebody I used to know. Army guy." And before he could ask more I said, "What's the captain say, anybody trapped in there?"

He shrugged. "Dunno. They're still searching the building. But a place this big you'd think he'd have some staff, cleaners, a cook, whatever. But maybe they didn't live here, just worked days." He waved his arm toward the east wing. "Three-car garage over there. Two empty bays and an old pickup truck in the third."

We'd reached the far side of the burned-out section now. The fire was out and wispy smoke curled from roof timbers as firemen cleared through the debris with their axes. A tall man in a white fire helmet directing the crew waved us over. He gave Frank a quick nod. "Chief said you'd be over. Sergeant Russo, right? Well, make it snappy."

Frank got right to it. "We'll be quick," he said. "We're interested in the homeowner here. Any news?"

The guy seemed to appreciate Frank's direct style; he backed away from his crew and tipped back his helmet, wiping the sweat from his face with his sleeve. "Bad fire," he said. "Hotter than hell on a bad day." He looked around as though he might be overheard and moved closer to us, a sour mixture of smoke and sweat coming off him. "Got a dead body in the basement here. Fried to a goddamn crisp."

Holy shit. My head snapped around to Frank, a dark scowl on his face as his eyes drifted toward the sound of the firemen chop-chopping through the smoking ruins beside us.

Then Frank stepped in closer. "No chance of identifying the body?"

The guy shook his head. "Not my job, Bud. I rescue the living and put out fires. Then it's over to you."

Frank gave him a grim smile. "Right," he said. "Now tell us what you think happened here."

"Looks like arson to me, so I've called our fire investigation team. Can't verify that until they're finished. But it could've been an explosive device detonated in the basement here. That's where we found the body." He lowered his voice. "Don't often see a body burned up like that. Must've been doused with gasoline or something. A helluva mess." He put on his helmet, ready to leave, signalling to his men to finish up. "I'm gonna call the coroner's office now."

Frank grabbed his coat sleeve. "Hang on a sec. Tell us about the layout of this place."

The fire captain hesitated, anxious to leave. "Sorry, we've got a lot of work–"

"C'mon," Frank said. "It'll just take a minute."

The guy shrugged, taking a deep breath. "Okay," he said and gestured with his arm toward the other end of the building. "Place is built in three sections. Far side is the kitchen, utility rooms, garage. In the centre, there's a living room facing the mountainside and a bigger room beside it, seems to be some kind of art gallery. This wing here had a big bedroom and a couple of smaller rooms, maybe offices. And a huge basement."

Frank was still looking away. "The other two sections aren't too bad."

"Right. Some smoke damage. There'll be water damage, too – had to keep the hoses on the roof so it wouldn't spread." Then he reached over and shook Frank's hand. "Good luck with your investigation," he said and hurried away.

Frank's face looked as grim as I felt, staring at the devasta-
tion in front of us: this wing a burned-out shell, and somewhere
in there a blackened corpse. Looked like a case of arson, the
man said. Frank was shaking his head from side to side and I'd
bet a sawbuck that our thoughts were identical: Myers had been
torched in his own home. What a shitty way to go.

But why was he hiding out here? I'd tried to contact him at
home by phone but never got an answer. Not at his office either.
And our surveillance guys saw nothing. So the big question was,
who set the goddamn fire?

"Russo!" We turned toward the booming voice.

Frank stepped in front of me, grabbed my arm, pushing me
toward the front of the building. "Make yourself scarce," he said
in a hoarse whisper. "My Chief's here."

I disappeared in a hurry so the Chief of Police wouldn't crap
all over Frank for consorting with the enemy. In my experience,
most of these old-line cops did their best to avoid civilians. And
they were the guys in charge. Here's my theory: when they'd
been inducted into the police service I think they swore a blood
oath never to share information with the public. And the young
cops who crossed that line got a kick in the ass by the brass.

I stood alone on a vast patio stretching across the front of the
house. It was quiet here, moments before dawn, a fresh breeze
from across the bay, which I couldn't quite see in the dim light.
Small birds began to flit among the branches of a long boxwood
hedge close to the mountain brow. I took the opportunity to
snoop around, since the firemen were packing up their gear on
the other side of the house.

I approached the hedge and peered over the brow: a steep
incline, scrubby bushes near the top, piles of fallen rock and
some taller trees further down. But just a few feet below me, a
narrow pathway seemed to meander all the way to the end of the
block. This must be the trail Trepanier told me about. A dangerous route, so close to the lip of the slope, but you could get
in or out of Myers' house without being seen during the day if
you crouched down. No need to navigate that path at night, you
could make your way along this line of shrubs. And there, near

the edge of the neighbouring property, was a gap in the hedge, a few feet wide. Must've been where Trepanier took his tumble. Damn lucky he didn't kill himself.

A voice behind me: "Don't jump!"

I almost pitched forward into the hedge. But Frank had extended an arm, ready to stop my fall. "Shit, Man. You startled me," I said.

"Brother, have you got the jitters. And what're you looking at anyway?"

I showed him the overgrown trail, our eyes following its zig-zaggy direction through the bushes to our right.

"Whoever set the blast used this path?"

"Possible, isn't it?"

"Maybe." I'll get someone to look around down there."

We looked off into the distance for a moment, admiring the first glittering reflections of the rising sun on the bay. Isabel was right: the view from up here was spectacular.

I turned to Frank. "Chief got a bee in his bonnet?"

"The usual," he said. "Don't talk to the press. Just keep your trap shut and do your job. Arson, what arson? Said he'll be issuing a short statement this afternoon. The party line will be: this was a tragic accident, one of the city's leading citizens, blah blah blah."

"He's not going to wait for the coroner's report?"

"That's why he's holding off his statement 'til this afternoon."

"Shit," I said. "Too early for that."

He delivered a soft punch to my arm. "Good thing you didn't join the boys in blue here, eh?"

The fire captain called from the corner of the building, waving us back to Myers' bedroom wing. We met Dr. Crandall, the coroner, a well-dressed older man with a crisp and efficient air who was buttoning up a pair of black coveralls. The captain guided us through a gaping hole in the wall where a pair of French doors had been blown out across the side lawn. At the end of a short corridor we came to the bedroom, the entire centre of the floor had imploded, leaving a giant crater through which the shattered contents had plummeted into the basement.

I peered over the crater's edge and my mind spun like a pin-wheel, crowded with images of the London blitz: the detritus of bombed-out buildings, homes reduced to smoking debris and charred bodies. Frank had to grip my arm to steady me. And there, poking out of the pile of timbers and smashed furniture beneath us was a tangled black corpse, its arms folded on its chest in a grotesque parody of prayer.

CHAPTER FORTY-FOUR

AN INSISTENT RINGING IN MY ears jolted me upright in my bed and for a moment I was huddling with a crowd of Brits in a tube station, an air-raid siren wailing above us. Then a vision of Myers' corpse, fried to a crisp, forced my eyes open. I fumbled with my alarm clock, oh-nine-hundred. Frank had dropped me off a couple of hours earlier but I was too busy today to waste my time in bed.

The ringing continued. It was the damn phone. I groped my way to the kitchen, stubbing my toe again.

"Rise and shine, Max. Time's a-wastin'." Isabel's voice was an ice pick in my ear. "Your uncle Scotty called twice already. He's anxious to talk to you. And I have some news of my own."

I held the phone away from my ear, massaged my scalp with the other hand and yawned. "Okay. Scotty called," I said. "Any word from Frank?" I yawned again.

"Not yet. And don't go back to sleep, Max. I'm picking you up. Ten minutes."

I wasn't timing her but she arrived at oh-nine-eighteen. I'd just finished showering and when I stepped from the bathroom I spotted her in the kitchen, fixing coffee. I guess I'd forgotten to lock my front door. Relieved, though, that I'd remembered to wrap myself in a towel. I mumbled a greeting as I headed to the bedroom. "Morning. Be right out."

We sat at the kitchen table while I ate my Grape-Nuts Flakes and sipped my coffee. "Busy night," I said when I'd finished. Then I told her about the fire at Myers' place and the discovery of his charred remains in the ruins.

Isabel's face was chalkier than the Dover cliffs as she fidgeted in her chair, not speaking right away.

I kept quiet, too.

"Dead," she said at last. "Are you sure it was him?"

"Can't be sure until the autopsy later this morning. But who else would it be?"

She shrugged her shoulders. "The cause of the fire, Max? Do you know what happened?"

"Fire inspectors will investigate," I told her. "But arson's suspected."

"Arson? Good grief. What are we mixed up in? Jake Benson is murdered, Mr. Myers is ... well, maybe murdered, too. Who's doing all this?"

I reached across the table and touched her hand. "We're going to find out," I said. "But we have to be careful." I held her eyes with mine. "Are you with me?"

It took her a moment before she gave my hand a hard squeeze. "Yes, I am," she said. "What's next?"

I got up and refilled our coffee cups. "First of all, you said you had news."

"Right. Well, it's not as shocking as yours, and ... it also concerns Mr. Myers. But I guess that doesn't really matter, now that he's ... gone." She took a long sip of coffee, then another before continuing. "I went back to Mitzi's apartment after I dropped you off last night. Made up a little story about seeing her driving up James Street and parking her car, so I thought I'd drop in, get reacquainted. She's so full of herself, Max, she wasn't suspicious, didn't question my story at all. Just gave me a big hug, showed me around her apartment and then we drank a bottle of wine." She raised her eyebrows at me as though I might not believe she was capable of such a ruse.

"You rascal," I said.

She shrugged as though she'd a long history of being a rascal. "Well, one thing led to another and we got talking about men, of course. She told me that after Evelyn went to jail she and Mr. Myers got together, and she moved into that apartment. Says they're madly in love, Max. And they're planning to go away together. Or they were planning to ..."

"Did she say where they were going? And when?"

"Going today. To Niagara Falls."

That didn't make sense. Why Niagara Falls? It billed itself as the honeymoon capital of the world but Myers didn't strike me as the romantic type. Maybe he simply intended to cross the border to the US and the Falls was closer than Buffalo–

Isabel wasn't finished. "Mitzi's father is a big-time real estate developer. He's planning to build a luxury hotel overlooking the Horseshoe Falls. And tonight there's a big announcement party, unveiling the scale model of his project, all that stuff. At the General Brock Hotel. Mitzi said Mr. Myers was already there and she was to drive down later this afternoon and meet him."

I jumped to my feet. "Hang on a sec. She said he was already there? In Niagara Falls?"

"That's right, Max." She stopped, locking her eyes on mine. "But if that's true, then who ...?"

CHAPTER FORTY-FIVE

WHEN WE ARRIVED AT THE office, I returned Scotty's call.

"The fire," he said, not even hello. "Tell me everything, Laddie."

I gave him a taste of his own medicine. "Spiro's," I said. "Ten minutes."

Isabel and I sat at the corner table, the furthest from the chit-chat at the counter. I gave her the lowdown on my famous uncle and we developed a small plan. Scotty rushed through the door a moment later and stood beside our table. Didn't make a move to slide onto the bench across from us. Just stood there scowling, hands on hips.

"Thought this was a private meeting," he said.

I stood up. "Isabel, this is my polite uncle, Scotty Lyle. Say goodbye to him. We're leaving now."

He moved to block me, making soothing sounds. "Come, come, Laddie. Don't get your feathers ruffled." He pushed me into my seat and reached across me to shake Isabel's hand. "Pleased to meet you, Miss. I understand you're working with the great sleuth now. Who's too busy to talk to his uncle."

She took his extended hand and drawled, "Charmed, I'm sure."

His eyes darted to me. "Ah. Two of a kind, eh?"

I ignored him and waved at Spiro, signalling for three coffees. He looked the other way and Isabel stepped over to the counter.

When she'd gone, Scotty bent his head to mine. "What the hell, Max? I can't be doin' business with a woman, even if she is a stunner. Now, what's this all about?"

"I meant what I said. We're working together. She's learning the business. So it's all or nothing, Buster. Uncle or not."

He leaned back on the bench and sulked until Isabel returned with Spiro, three cups of coffee on his tray. "Anything else you need, just wave," Spiro told her. "I'll be right over." I gave him a dirty look. ·

We creamed, sugared and stirred, then sat there sipping. Not a peep from Scotty. Isabel gave it about fifteen seconds, set down her cup and leaned toward him. "Max was at the fire last night. He's got all the juicy details. He told me you've probably got the results of the autopsy on the body from the fire scene. From your guy on the inside at the morgue. I believe it's what you call your 'tit-for-tat' situation. So go ahead, let's hear it."

His mouth had fallen open while she was speaking and he'd turned a nice shade of red, but I give him credit. He recovered himself in short order, whipped out his handkerchief and pretended a little coughing fit, then blew his nose. "Pardon me," he said. "Summer cold. They're hard to shake."

I noticed Iz cover her smile with her hand as we waited for him to make his next move.

"All right," he said. "But Max goes first."

I gave him a complete rundown; he made notes, asked questions, some of which I answered. After ten minutes of that I ran out of gas and said, "Your turn."

He made a long production of arranging his coffee cup just so, then his napkin with the spoon exactly in its centre. Satisfied at last, he looked up with a smug smile on his face. "It's not Myers." He leaned back against the bench, intent on our reactions.

Isabel stared at him, straight-faced. But I couldn't cover my surprise. "What the hell, Scotty? What do you mean, it wasn't him?"

He grinned now, one up on me. "So, Laddie. Seems you don't know everything after all, does it? When the coroner finished his work he noticed there was a discrepancy with the information your pal Detective Sergeant Russo provided. That corpse was several inches taller than Myers and quite a bit heavier. Doc Crandall's called for Myers' dental records for confirmation."

I lifted my cup, saw it was empty and studied the coffee grounds forming a tiny trail from the bottom to the lip. Reminded me of the path along the mountainside at Myers' house. Had he used it to escape the fire? Or had someone else done the dirty work? The description of the corpse sounded like it might be Thompson. But most of the men in Hamilton were taller and heavier than Myers, weren't they? I guessed Frank would have the coroner check Thompson's dental records, just in case, since he was still AWOL.

Of course, I hadn't told Scotty anything about the surveillance at Myers' and Thompson's places or Trepanier's discovery of that trail. And if Myers was still on the loose we sure as hell weren't going to find him by sitting around in the White Spot Grill drinking Spiro's shitty coffee.

"Well, thanks, Unc. That's interesting but it doesn't get us any closer to solving Jake Benson's murder."

"I'm not interested in Jake Benson," he said and thumped the table with his fist. "Something big's going on with this Myers guy. And I told you about his connection with Tedesco and my Evelyn Dick investigation."

Isabel turned toward me and lowered her voice, but not low enough. "It just hit me, Max. This means that Mr. Myers will be meeting Mitzi in Niagara Falls after all."

A stunned silence settled over the table, as though the world had suddenly taken a time-out. Isabel held a hand to her mouth, her eyes saying, Oh, Max, I'm so sorry.

But Scotty was squinting now, his jaw set, a sure sign his brain was in overdrive.

I was about to give him a line of malarkey but he spoke first.

"What's this about Niagara Falls, my boy? Someone taking a little trip?"

I nodded toward him, making it up on the fly. "Yeah, we picked that up yesterday but it turned out to be a rumour, just some gossip. I told you I've been talking to Jake Benson's friends and co-workers and someone mentioned that Myers might've gone there. Turned out it was a blind alley."

He gave me the fish eye and I knew he wasn't buying it. "And who is this ... Mitzi, is it?"

"Just a friend of a friend. Anyway, it was nothing. We've gotta go now. Busy day."

Scotty slid along the bench, one hand on the table, the other on the seatback and pushed himself up. "Well, thanks for the info on the fire, Laddie." He bobbed his head toward Isabel. "Pleasure, Miss." His face said it was no pleasure at all.

He shuffled away and we continued to sit there beside each other, looking straight ahead and not speaking.

I broke the silence. "He knows. When he figures out who Mitzi is, he'll learn about her father and his announcement party tonight. We'd better get there before he does."

CHAPTER FORTY-SIX

A LIGHT RAIN WAS FALLING when we left Spiro's and returned to the office. I figured we had a few hours lead time before Scotty tracked down Mitzi, probably sometime this afternoon.

Frank answered his phone after four rings; I'd bet he hadn't gotten to bed last night and his voice sounded like Bela Lugosi.

"Helluva a night, eh?" I said.

"Roger that. What d'you want?"

"My, my, Frank. Is that any way to greet a citizen?"

He made a sound with his lips like a spouting whale and I held the receiver at arm's length. When he finished, I said, "That bad, eh?"

"Ten to one you want the results from Doc Crandall, right?"

"Well, if you've got them handy …"

"You wouldn't believe what it's like around here, Maxie. Damn Chief's got the entire place buttoned down. No contact with the press or the public on the subject of, and I quote here, 'the unfortunate fire which occurred at a private residence on the Mountain last night. Fire officials are investigating and their findings will be released in due course.' End of goddamn quote."

"Shit," I said. "Makes you wonder who's applying the pressure. I don't think Myers had that kind of clout. Maybe it's coming from Tedesco."

"Can't say, Max. Not if I want to keep my job."

"Jeez, why's the brass got such a burr up its ass?"

"Blame it on the Evelyn Dick trial. The department took a lot of heat last year and we're still under the microscope. 'Sloppy investigation work, missing evidence, incompetence', all that bullshit. So the Chief's main concern is our image. Or maybe I should say, his image. And he can't tell the public that citizens are being murdered and torched in their homes, can he?"

My heart went out to my long-time pal. I'd never heard him sound so disillusioned about being on the job. "Not gonna do anything rash, are you Frank? Like leaving the force?"

"No, no, not today. But if it stays like this ..."

When I hung up the phone, I pushed back from my desk and propped up my foot. I hated to hear Frank so tied up in knots. He would have told me about the autopsy if he could, and I understood his dilemma. But it wouldn't have made him feel any better if I told him I already knew, especially since my source was the hated press.

I placed a quick call to George Kemper to call off his surveillance teams. "Top-notch guys," I told him. "I'm impressed with their work, especially Trepanier. He's got the makings of a good detective."

"Discontinue at both places, Max? Or do you want them to carry on at the Charlton Avenue address?"

"Both places," I said.

"Trepanier called me first thing this morning," George said. "Sounds like you had an exciting time on the Mountain. Want to tell me about it?"

"I'd like to but I can't. Police Chief's got the force clammed up and I don't want to jeopardize my best source there. Maybe you could ask your guys to keep mum too, just for a couple of days. Should be over by then."

I hung up the phone as Isabel entered my office and I stifled a yawn.

"You must be dog-tired, Max. Why not go home and grab forty winks before we leave? I'll arrange things here with Phyllis, get a change of clothes and pick you up after lunch."

The rain misted the windshield when we merged with the traffic along the Beach Strip onto the Queen Elizabeth Way, Canada's first inter-city divided highway, which connected Toronto, Hamilton and the Niagara Peninsula. Most of the locals still referred to it as the 'new' highway, although it was opened to traffic in '37. And despite the complaints about the QEW – too much traffic, people drive too fast, too many trucks, et cetera – it was still a helluva lot faster than meandering along Highway 8 through Winona, Grimsby, Beamsville and the other small towns dotting the fruit belt. True, it was far less picturesque, but you could get to the Falls in only a little more than an hour on the QEW, and we were on a mission.

Isabel settled in behind a line of cars and glanced at her purse on the seat beside her. "I forgot to show you the letter Mitzi gave me. And so much has happened in the meantime. Help yourself."

I didn't make a habit of opening women's purses but I glanced at Isabel's. It was on the small side, unlike some I'd seen which could hold two or three of the Dionne quints. Even so, I was nervous about it. After all, who knew what type of feminine item might tumble out and embarrass a guy?

But I'm a veteran, as Isabel reminded me once, so I opened her purse and found the envelope on top. Whew. It was addressed to Mitzi, but not at her current residence. I withdrew the letter and the first thing I noticed was the signature – a flamboyant scramble of letters jumping off the page in green ink which spelled *Evelyn*. It was written last December, after her first trial but before the second one in February.

December 15, 1946

Dearest Mitzi,

Thanks so much for your wonderful gift, I just adore Yardley soap. Everyone's been so kind, really. Remember Flo, hostess at the Town Casino in Buffalo? Well, she sent some nylons and a Toni Home Permanent, which I'm just dying to try. You know me, always up for something new.

Your note was so touching, Darling, really sweet. But silly you, to wonder if Mr. M. is still standing behind me – he's in love, my dear!!! He's looking after the lawyers and everything else. You know, he told me I'd be found guilty at my first trial, it's what the politicians wanted. But I'll win on appeal because he's hiring that young hotshot lawyer from Toronto. This murder charge is just temporary bad luck, Mr. M. calls it. And by the by, if you happen to see him, do keep in mind he's far more complex than he appears.

You asked about "that place". Really, Darling, no need to be coy, my friends must face the facts along with me. I'm in the Barton Street Jail and it's old and noisy and smelly. As for meals, it certainly isn't the Connaught dining room. The guards? Well, they're mostly bored, but Mrs. Johnson on the night shift is a sweetheart (she's giving me the Toni tonight). The very worst thing is that I can't go out when I want. Oh God, how I miss all of you, cocktails and dancing at the Circus Roof, the floor shows at the Brant Inn. Remember when we did the rumba with Xavier Cugat? Oh boy, what a night that was.

Love and kisses,
Evelyn

P.S. Are you still seeing that nice Justice What's-his-name?

When I'd finished reading I lowered the letter onto my lap and stared out the window. The E.D. Smith food processing plant outside Winona whizzed by. And several other low buildings. Then acres of fruit trees and grapevines.

Sonovabitch, I thought, another connection to Evelyn Dick. And man-oh-man, talk about a plotter; she'd put Machiavelli to shame.

I returned the letter to Isabel's purse and said, "I wonder why Mitzi gave it to you."

"I told you we shared a bottle of wine, remember? She drank most of it and was in a very generous mood by the end of our visit. I told her I was ever-so-fascinated by Evelyn's exciting life and couldn't even imagine such a femme fatale existence. So Mitzi took pity on naive-little-me and said, 'Well, Darling, take this letter with you as a memento.'"

I grinned at my partner, enjoying her la-di-da accent. "Did she tell who Mr. M is?"

"No, she didn't. But my money's on the Mr. M. who pays the rent on her apartment."

"So is mine," I said, placing the purse on the floor between us. "What about Evelyn's little reminder that Mr. M. is more complex than he appears? Think she was warning Mitzi off him?"

A quick hunch of her shoulders and she said, "Perhaps not, Max. Maybe they were sharing him."

Holy cow, that hadn't occurred to me. But I couldn't imagine his attraction to one woman let alone two. I changed the subject. "You wouldn't happen to know who 'that nice Justice What's-his-name' is, would you?"

I saw her red curls moving side to side. "'Fraid not, Max."

Closer to Niagara Falls, the rain was still spitting and the wind had picked up. Isabel slowed so we could read the highway signs. The one we'd just passed directed us to stay right for the Rainbow Bridge to the USA in five miles.

The graceful new carillon tower was the first thing you noticed as you neared the bridge but, contrary to its name, no rainbow lit the sky above it today. The rain continued to drizzle and a heavy cloud of mist massed above the falls, carrying its spray toward the gorge and past the bridge.

I glanced at the driver as she ducked her head for a better view of the tower.

"Rain, mist and gloom," I said. "Think it's a bad omen?"

CHAPTER FORTY-SEVEN

A BLOCK FROM THE BRIDGE we turned onto Falls Avenue to the General Brock Hotel. Isabel drove along the ranks of cars parked near the entrance to the stately hotel until she found a vacant space and was about to turn in. I touched her arm and she stopped. "Why don't you tuck it in behind those tour buses at the back of the lot," I said. "In case someone's interested in us."

She did as I suggested and turned off the ignition. "What's next, Max? Put on our disguises and sneak into the hotel?"

Her goofy remark seemed to relieve some of the tension we'd been feeling as we got closer to a possible confrontation with the elusive Myers. Maybe.

"When you were a kid," I asked her, "were you a member of the Girl Guides?"

She shook her head, giving me that kind of bemused smile you might use with your four-year-old nephew who's shown you for the umpteenth time how well he could tie his shoes. "Okay," she said. "I'll bite. Yes, I was a Guide and our motto was 'Be Prepared'. So I was about to ask you, Max, why don't we develop a little plan before we barge in there and make fools of ourselves?"

Then, to top it off, she gave me the three-fingered Guide salute.

My lips were probably pinched but I wasn't aware of it. Too busy thinking: Shit, I was about to suggest the same damn thing with my 'Be Prepared' line. But she was a step ahead of me again and making a habit of it. I regrouped and said, "Good idea."

"So what's your plan?"

In fact, I didn't have what you might call a full-blown operational plan. What I was itching to do was barge into the hotel, find Myers' room and beat him to a pulp for what his bodyguard did to poor old Bob. Then throw the bugger out the window, and I hoped his room was on the top floor. But I recognized such direct action had a fair chance of attracting unwanted attention from the local coppers. So I proposed to go with my usual plan: barge in, find Myers, then play it by ear. But I didn't announce it yet, thought I'd wait to hear if Isabel had something better.

"Ladies first," I said.

"I've racked my brain, Max. Best I could come up with is tip-toe around and see what happens."

"Good, we agree," I said. "Let's go."

We entered the hotel's lobby through a massive set of revolving brass doors into a vast marble foyer, gleaming like Solomon's temple. Quiet strains of classical music played in the background from hidden speakers. A majestic air about the place.

Behind the reception desk a group of eager staff members in snappy blue uniforms could hardly wait to serve us. My first thought was, Spiro could learn a helluva lot here. Then I amended that to could but wouldn't.

Isabel's voice was maple syrup when she leaned close to the first clerk in line, a smile on his mug, fountain pen uncapped and at the ready. "We're meeting up with friends for the big party tonight," she said. "And I thought they might be early. Mr. and Mrs. Abbott? They'll have a suite on an upper floor."

The guy bent at the waist, bowing as though she were royalty. "Of course, Miss. Let me check that for you."

I shot her a glance, my eyes asking, who the hell are the Abbotts?

While the clerk was riffling through his files Iz whispered, "Mitzi told me she and Myers always registered under that alias when they travelled. In case anyone became nosy."

See, I told you she was a mind reader.

The clerk was back in a flash. "Sorry for the delay, Miss. Mr. Abbott has checked in but went out for the afternoon. And Mrs. Abbott is expected later this evening."

"That's very kind of you," she said. "Do you have the suite number handy?"

He shook his head and every hair stayed in place, obviously a Brylcreem man. His expression remained respectful but he adhered to the company line, "I'm afraid we don't divulge that information."

Iz looked him in the eye, didn't speak right away and I wondered how she'd play it. Surprised me when she said, "That's fine. Thanks anyway."

She turned toward the entrance and paused. I approached the clerk and slid my hand along the counter, a brown two-dollar bill peeking between my fingers. He glimpsed it, wrote something on the back of a business card and palmed the bill faster than Mandrake the Magician.

We strolled toward the coffee shop at the rear of the lobby and I passed her the card.

"Ten-oh-nine, Max. Great view from up there." And she changed direction, heading toward the elevators.

"Think this is wise?" I said as we joined a small group of damp tourists staring up at the floor numbers blinking on and off. "We might bump into him."

She finished scanning the directory and turned to face me. "We're just going up to the Rainbow Room, Max. Top of the hotel, windows all around, it's a sightseer's paradise. What could be wrong with that? Especially if we tag along with this tour group."

When we boarded, Isabel said to the cute teenaged operator, probably working a summer job, "I hope the Rainbow Room's open this afternoon."

She bobbed her head, almost dislodging the blue cap which matched her uniform. "Sure is, Ma'am. We've been taking tour groups up. But the big room at the back is closed – they're preparing it for a party tonight."

We left the elevator and hooked onto the group making a beeline for the floor-to-ceiling windows. Isabel knew what she was talking about – this was a view to end all views.

We melded with the tourists at the windows, marvelling at the majesty of the scene below. A zillion gallons of water cascading over the falls, sending a towering spray toward the cloud cover above. And way down there, bobbing like a toy boat in a bathtub, was the *Maid of the Mist*, thrilling passengers with a water-soaked cruise so close to the falls you were sure you'd be sucked under.

I asked Isabel, "Guess you've been here before, eh?"

"My first time was with my Grade 8 class. It was so much fun, Max. I've been back a few times since, but it was never the same."

I'd only seen the Falls once, and that was before I went overseas in '39. Some of my pals thought it would be a good idea to take me here for a going-away party. I remembered the cruise on the *Maid of the Mist* alright. But after that it wasn't such a good idea – we'd toured most of the bars on the American side and my mind's a blank for the period between the raid on the strip joint and waking up on the train to Halifax.

Our perky guide was now delivering her spiel to the American tourists. I could tell they were Americans because several of the men strutted around with small US flags stuck in their hats as though they'd won the war single-handed. Another clue – the old guys wore multicoloured shorts and the women snapped off their Baby Brownies as though they were loaded with free film. The guide raised her voice and stretched out her arm. "Straight across from us are the American Falls." She paused for the oohs and aahs. "Then if you look over to your right you'll see the Horseshoe Falls, on the Canadian side of the border."

I overheard one old buzzard say to the guy beside him, in that sloppy kind of drawl some Americans use, "Shit, Wilbert. Their Falls is twice as big as ours. Soon as Ah git home, Ah's writin' mah congressman."

Iz nudged me in the ribs, inclining her head toward an exit door. We separated from the group and went through the door to the stairway. "Down one floor," she said.

On the tenth floor, she peeked through the small window in the emergency door with a view down the hallway. Then she stepped back to let me see: a half-mile of plush carpeting, paintings hung along both walls, small tables with art deco lamps and baskets of candies for the pampered guests, elevators halfway down. Myers' suite was right across the hall from us. As I stared at his door, thinking of a plan, it opened.

I ducked away from the window, signalling to Iz with a finger to my lips. We waited a few beats then took a careful peek. There was Myers, his back to us, heading for the elevators, striding along in quick short steps, as stiff and erect as a pint-sized guardsman.

"Reminds me of a toy soldier," she said in a whisper.

"My very thought. Now let's get the hell out of here." I headed toward the stairway.

"Oh, Max. You can't walk down ten flights."

"No choice," I said. "Can't take the chance of seeing him in the lobby. We'll find a rear exit."

CHAPTER FORTY-EIGHT

OUTSIDE, WE LEANED AGAINST THE wall at the rear of the hotel, bending over, gulping in air. My partner had linked her arm through mine for most of the race down the stairs but, even so, my leg was throbbing like an abscessed tooth. "I'll be fine in a minute," I said, using my favourite lie. "Maybe you could get the car–" I stopped for a breath. "And pick me up here."

When she returned, she held the door for me then found a parking spot with a clear view of the front entrance. "I guess we don't have to wonder if Mr. Myers is planning to attend the party tonight, Max."

I was still panting from our rapid descent, and rested my leg across the car seat. We'd decided to park here to watch for Myers or Mitzi, or anyone else of interest. "I'm not sure he'll stay for the party. Could be he's just waiting for Mitzi, then he'll disappear across the border."

"And leave Mitzi here?"

"I don't know, Iz. Maybe she's just coming for a last farewell. But I'm sure if he wanted to take her, his friend Tedesco could probably pull the strings to get US documents for them both. Whatever he does, he'll do it soon because he knows it won't be long before the police discover it wasn't his body in the fire."

She was quiet then, tapping her fingers on the steering wheel, watching the hotel. "So what's your plan, Boss? What'll we do when Mitzi arrives? Or Mr. Myers leaves?"

"Call the cops," I said. "We'll have to do it soon. I've never been a big fan of the citizen's arrest. Good way to get yourself killed. But the cops would have laughed at us if we hadn't verified Myers was actually here. And I give you full credit for that,

Partner. Let's give Mitzi another half-hour and, whether she shows or not, we'll call in the cavalry."

I leaned my head against the seat back and felt a sharp pain searing along the left side of my head. My eyes spun out of control and when I could see again, a black pistol was now jammed against Isabel's neck, its owner kneeling on the floor behind us, staring into my face from inches away. "One peep out of you," he said, spraying me with his spittle, "and your girlfriend's head goes through the window."

He was a big bugger, judging by the size of the hand gripping the gun. His face was too close to bring into focus but I had a blurry image of bushy hair, piggy eyes and a boxer's flattened nose. At that moment, I wished my fist had done the flattening.

I opened my mouth to speak and he moved even closer. "One peep," he said in a breathy voice, and the heavy stench of yesterday's garlic made my eyes water.

When I tried to look at Isabel, he kept his head in front of mine, blocking my view. She hadn't cried out, not a word, not a sound. I thought she might be frozen with fear, scared witless.

Then the big guy leaned back a few inches, giving me some breathing room. "Okay," he said. "I think we understand each other." He eased the pistol away from Isabel, leaving a vivid red O on her neck. But he kept it close, making sure I saw it. "Here's what's going to happen – I'm takin' you two into the hotel and up to the room. Peckerhead here walks two steps ahead of me. And the broad walks beside me so I can hold her arm. Try to pull any Lone Ranger tricks and I'll plug the dame. We clear on that?"

He gave me a nasty look and I nodded. When he turned to Isabel, I was able to glimpse her face; no outward sign of strain or fear, and her eyes were hard and determined.

"I'm clear on what I have to do," she said and the words came out so coated with frost I was damn glad she wasn't directing them at me.

The hotel lobby was buzzing with activity; hordes of excited tourists raised the noise level by a hundred decibels as they flooded in from a line of tour buses at the curb. Piles of luggage and hotel handcarts were scattered everywhere and, in the confusion, our kidnapper was able to move us around the edge of the crowd without suspicion. And the bugger kept shoving me in the back toward the elevators when I didn't limp fast enough for him. I noticed too, he was keeping an eye on the exit doors on this side of the lobby so if I did try to wrestle Isabel away from him, he could shoot her and still make a clean getaway. Not as stupid as he looked.

On the tenth floor, he used his pistol to tap on the door at 1009. He waited a moment and tapped again, then used his key.

Myers' suite was a feature page from *House Beautiful* or one of those mags. In the living room, floor-to-ceiling windows like the Rainbow Room above us. And plush furniture grouped to show off nature's wonder, thundering in the distance. An adjoining dining room and a long corridor to the bed and bath rooms.

He shoved us into the dining room, placed two chairs back to back and said, "Sit."

From a black leather satchel he removed a coil of rope and strapped us together so we couldn't see each other. When he'd finished, he stood in front of me, a couple of steps away, and for the first time, I noticed the bright blotchy birthmark on the side of his neck. I could feel the anger bubbling up from deep inside me and, with it, the image of poor old Bob, beaten, bloodied and bruised by this bastard.

Madder than hell, I spit my words at him. "Pretty damn brave, aren't you, Big Guy? Brave enough to beat the crap out of a legless veteran. And now it's a woman and a gimpy guy. Who's next, one of the little old ladies in the lobby?"

His entire face mimicked the colour of his birthmark; his fists clenched and I held my breath. When the punch in the gut came, it was so powerful it knocked both our chairs over and we toppled into the table with a helluva crash. I gasped and sputtered and couldn't breathe fast enough but I didn't throw up as I thought I might.

We lay in a jumble like that, dazed and defeated. Until then, Iz hadn't made a sound. Then I heard her whisper, "You okay, Max?"

I couldn't speak yet. Concentrated on breathing. Glad I was still alive. When I was able to, I said, "Yeah. I'm okay."

We remained on the floor for an hour or more, still tied back to back but on our sides now, struggling with the ropes knotted behind us but making no headway. The big bugger stayed in another room, but checked on us every ten minutes, nudging us with his feet, making sure we stayed uncomfortable.

I had a partial view of the sky out the dining room window, gray clouds were thickening over the falls and raindrops were running down the pane, relentless as sand in an hourglass. I hoped our luck wasn't headed in the same direction.

It was late afternoon when someone entered the suite and I heard voices murmuring from another room. Then Myers strutted into the dining room and smiled. "Ah, visitors," he said. "I'm so glad you could drop by." He walked slowly around the overturned table several times, bending down to peer at us from close range, testing the tightness of our bindings, enjoying himself. A fisherman pleased with his catch.

Myers stopped beside me and stared, studying the abrasion along the side of my head like a surgeon. He knelt on one knee and traced a tiny finger along the bloody cut, taking his time, watching my eyes wince in pain. He could have been that Nazi torturer who tormented me in my nightmares. But I was damned if I would give the little bastard the satisfaction of crying out. When he'd had his fun, he stood and withdrew a handkerchief and wiped my blood from his hands.

He called for his houseboy or whatever the hell he was. "Bruno, come in here." When he arrived, Myers told him, "Clean up this mess. I'm going to change my clothes and when I come back I want them seated at the table. But keep their feet tied, they won't be going anywhere."

Myers left and Bruno did what he was told. Enjoyed his work, too, pushing us around like sides of beef, stepping accidentally-on-purpose on our arms and legs, and fondling Isabel when she couldn't squirm away from him. But she made him howl when she damn near bit his finger off as he tried to run it along her lips the way Myers had done to my head wound. That cost her a solid thwack across the face, the imprint of his fingers livid on her cheek.

Goddamn Bruno. He reminded me of Bluto in the Popeye cartoons. Big, fat, ugly and mean. I'm sure he was unaware that he was piling up a heavy debt at the Bank of Max Dexter Associates. And I can't tell you how much I looked forward to collection day.

CHAPTER FORTY-NINE

ISABEL AND I WERE SEATED at the dining room table, our ankles cinched tight, the comic-strip Bluto across from us, his big black gun aimed in our direction. Myers had returned in a chirpy mood and sat at the head of the table, arranging himself like he was preparing to carve for Christmas dinner. And Yours Truly was the turkey.

"I'm impressed with your initiative, Mr. Dexter," he said. "Do tell how you managed to track me down."

"Wasn't that difficult," I said. "You're not as clever as you think you are, judging by the company you keep." I flicked my head toward the bruiser. "Who is this bozo? One of Tedesco's goons? The same bum who tried to follow Jake Benson's brother and me around town and he couldn't even do that right?"

Bruno's mug scrunched up, his eyes bugged out and he managed to sputter, "Chuck you, Farley." Then his feet were shuffling and he started to reach across the table when Myers grasped his arm. "Save that for later," he told him. "Mr. Dexter believes he's a witty man – it amuses me to hear him chatter."

He smiled in my direction and withdrew a gold case and a cigarette holder, making a fussy production of fitting a cigarette into the holder and firing it up with a gold lighter. He lifted his hand away from his body, about eye-level, gripping the holder with his fingertips, palm upward like an upper-class poofter in a British movie. Maybe this was the real Myers, I thought. And he was using Mitzi as camouflage.

I motioned my head toward Isabel and said to Myers, "Perhaps my associate could tell you about her meeting with a friend of yours at the Lower Park Apartments."

He glanced her way and puffed a cloud of smoke at her. "Ah, the chatty Miss Slater," he said. "One of her less appealing habits. It could lead to her downfall."

Isabel sent him a frigid glare and waited for his complete attention. Then she said, "Is that what led to Mrs. Dick's downfall?"

Myers flinched as though she'd smacked him, and his prissy manner fell away, revealing, just for a snapshot moment, a hard-eyed vicious little man who'd stop at nothing to get what he wanted. Another puff on his cigarette and he became the cool customer, in control again. "Here's a life lesson for you, Miss O'Brien, with my compliments." A short dramatic pause. "Sharp-tongued women are supremely unattractive."

Her face flamed – redder than red, a volcano inside. "You're a supercilious little prig," she said, spraying her words at him. "And it doesn't surprise me at all that you have to buy your female companions."

I had to admire his self-control: his stone face remained in place, not a muscle flinched. And by his non-reaction I knew she'd scored a direct hit with her 'sharp tongue', not so much with the 'supercilious prig' but the small man's dreaded reminder that he was 'little'. He did his best to ignore her; busied himself with his cigarette, took a last puff, removed it from the holder and stubbed it out in a clamshell ashtray beside him.

After wiping his hands, he turned his chair so it faced mine; Isabel no longer existed for him. "Well, Mr. Dexter, let's get down to business, shall we? We have plans for you two a little later. I've arranged a short sightseeing excursion which I hope you'll enjoy. I know I will." He glanced out the window at the steady rain, looking past Isabel, not seeing her. "Despite the inclement weather," he said. "I'm sure you'll find it interesting."

"Can't wait," I told him. "Let's go."

He dismissed my bravado with a flick of his hand. "Soon. I must attend a short meeting before leaving."

I noted the twitchy curl of his lips and I guessed he was annoyed at having to wait for his meeting, probably with Mitzi Slater.

"Then we have time for a little chat," I said. "As you know, I've been fascinated with your business ventures and the interesting people you've made, let's say, certain arrangements with. Maybe I could ask you a few questions – to satisfy my idle curiosity."

He gave me one of his thin smiles, perhaps recalling he'd used that same phrase when he'd tried to pump me for information at the art reception in O'Brien's home.

But it seemed to me he might be receptive so I jumped right in. "Perhaps you could tell me about those papers Jake Benson found in his boss' office. And why he had to die."

He paused for just a moment before making up his mind. "I don't mind talking about these things, Mr. Dexter. You know, I'm proud of what I built, and you won't have a chance to do anything with this information anyway."

From the corner of my eye I noticed Isabel was about to speak and I made a small movement with my fingers in her direction.

"Young Mr. Benson was a bright lad," Myers said. "Too bright for his own good. He wouldn't listen to reason when I made him a generous offer, so he had to be removed. You can see he was responsible for his own downfall, can't you?"

It didn't escape my notice that enemies of Myers had a habit of downfalling. I grappled with his twisted rationale, gave up, and continued. "That list showing account numbers ... or something ..."

His lips turned upward at the corners, just a little. A smile, I supposed. "It doesn't surprise me you couldn't figure that one out. But you're on the right track there. In fact, they are account numbers. Also on that list were post office box addresses where proceeds could be mailed. You see, these were accounts I maintained in private for my special friends to shelter their funds from the punitive tax system."

I pursed my lips, thinking about that, and I sensed my partner was champing at the bit to join the conversation, since this was her field. I flashed her a let's-keep-him-talking look and she remained quiet.

"Money laundering," I said to Myers.

"That's a very crude way of putting it. You see, governments are no longer as friendly to business as they were in the old days. Taxes are much too high and spiralling higher. And there's an unfortunate trend toward socialism – taxing the hard-working businessmen to support those people too lazy to work. The politicians in Ottawa are at fault, of course, Mackenzie King and his half-baked theories of social harmony. And communists are infiltrating everywhere – even sitting on Hamilton City Council and the Board of Control. Last year, for example, our shameless Mayor Lawrence marched in favour of the Steel Company strikers. So you see, Mr. Dexter, I've been forced to adopt certain measures even though my methods may seem unorthodox."

I marvelled at this little twerp. He was a goddamn crook, period. And here he was feeding me this feeble line of bullshit to justify his getting into bed with the Mob and stealing, cheating, even murdering whoever got in his way. I didn't dare look at Isabel. I knew she must be ready to explode and I hoped she might sit on it for a minute longer.

"Tell me about the list of paintings," I said. "And the business card."

"What business card?"

"Levinson's. Wholesale diamonds."

Myers took a moment to think about it, scratching his head. "I don't remember any card but I did some business with Levinson in the past. And I sold him a few paintings from my collection, but not recently. A very stubborn man. But he's a Jew, you know." He paused another moment. "I must admit it surprised me that Thompson was keeping a file on my private affairs. He confessed to me later that it was insurance, something he could use against me if necessary. I blame myself for not being aware of that. So after young Benson found the file, Thompson came to me, told me it wasn't a serious matter, just some scribbled notes he'd accidentally left in a file. But when I spoke with Benson on my own, he told me in detail what he'd found. Then he became very righteous about those accounts and just wouldn't let it go. Well, you know what happened to him. By then, of course, I realized the full extent of Thompson's treachery and I was forced to take care of him too. So it's my guess, Mr. Dexter, he kept Levinson's card for insurance as well. Not that it did him any good."

What a cold little bastard, probably a psychopath. Jake Benson was removed, he says, as calm as you please. And Thompson was torched, tut-tut. Telling me his dirty secrets in the same casual tone he might use to dictate his grocery list. I wondered how many other bodies he'd left in his wake. Not to mention Isabel and me – now on his to-do list.

I reached under the table, located her hand fidgeting on her lap and squeezed hard. She returned the pressure and I didn't doubt she was feeling the same sense of revulsion toward this sawed-off little monster as I was.

Somehow I found the will to continue with my questions; he was in a co-operative mood, so what the hell? "Those paintings," I said, and I felt the tension throb in Isabel's hand.

"Yes," Myers continued and I think he was pleased to have an audience. "Some wonderful pictures. I acquired them quite by accident. My good friend, Mr. Tedesco, has a contact in New York with a connection to the so-called Nazi government in exile – a fanatical group of Hitler's boys down there in South America. They're selling off their looted treasures to finance their return to power. So far, I've only received a few canvases, but it's a very profitable sideline."

As if it were against his better judgement, he looked at Isabel. "You may be surprised to learn that your illustrious father is the proud owner of a very fine Rembrandt portrait."

"Is that so?" she said. "And I suppose he also dabbles in your other little enterprises, does he?" I saw the tension in her eyes as she waited for his answer.

He shrugged and redirected her question. "I don't think he's ready for that. Yet."

Myers glanced at his henchman and jerked his thumb toward the entrance door. "Run down to the desk," he told him. "Check on my meeting."

Bruno stood, stuffed his pistol into his waistband and left the room. As soon as I heard the door snap closed, I placed my hand on the tabletop and moved to get up.

Myers reached into his pocket and whipped out a small .32 calibre pistol. He placed it on the table, pointing at my chest.

I sat back in my chair, finding Isabel's hand again. "You know how to fire that peashooter?" I asked him.

"Try to leave, Mr. Dexter, and I'll show you. And do take note – that's a silencer attached to the barrel."

Isabel's hand was shaking and moist; I gripped it tighter. "I'm not ready to go," I said. "I still have another question." I thought I'd cast another line in the water; see what I could catch for Scotty. "I heard you were listed in Evelyn Dick's Black Book, one of her special friends."

Something, I couldn't put a name to it, flickered in his tiny eyes – anger, contempt, annoyance. Then it was gone. "There is no Black Book."

I released Isabel's hand, rested my arms on the table and leaned toward him. "Ah, but there is. It was mentioned at her first trial."

"That's correct," he said. "And there was talk of such a book disappearing from the police evidence locker. But I can assure you it no longer exists."

If he was trying to impress me with the reach of his influence, he did. I flicked through my mental file to the next question: "Mrs. Dick had a new lawyer for her appeal," I said. "Did you pay his tab?"

He answered without hesitation. "It was part of the deal."

This guy was full of surprises. What deal? I was beginning to wonder if he was on the level or just toying with me. And did I really want to know? Damn right I did.

So I asked him, "And what deal was that?"

"I had an arrangement with Mrs. Dick," he said. "I agreed to pay the expenses for a first-rate trial lawyer and certain other costs she'd incurred. On her part, she agreed to make no mention of my name before, during or after the trial, whatever its outcome. For life."

Myers picked up his gun and walked over to the window. Of course he knew, with our ankles tied, we couldn't make a move on him without being shot. He looked out at the Falls, seeming to forget we were there. I reached beneath the table, feeling the outline of the jackknife in my pants pocket. Useless against a gun, of course, but its presence reassured me somehow. I clutched the small knife in my closed fist now, hoping for a chance to use it later.

Isabel stared at his back, concentrating. Her voice was surprisingly soft when she asked, "Did she also agree to keep the identity of her baby's father a secret?"

Myers spun around, his eyes dark and flinty. "I didn't know the baby was mine until after she'd killed it."

Isabel caught her breath, her hand covering her mouth. My mind was whirling, trying to remember what Scotty had told me, something about a newborn baby ... yes, a tiny body discovered in the attic of Evelyn Dick's home, encased in concrete and stuffed in a suitcase. I could understand why Myers would want to suppress that.

"Evelyn already had a young daughter who lived at her parents' home most of the time," Myers said. "So it was obvious another child was out of the question. She agreed to dispose of the baby and I never knew how she did it until the evidence came out at her trial." He looked away, appearing to have a dreamy moment about this 'disposal'. "Evelyn was always an inventive girl," he said. "And her father helped her, of course."

'Inventive' wasn't the first word that sprang to my mind but I suppose Myers had been besotted by her. By the way he spoke about her now, it sounded like he still was.

The door opened, Bruno clomped into the dining room and plopped in his chair. It took Myers a moment to notice him. "My meeting?" he said.

"Not 'til seven p.m.," Bruno said.

Myers' expression turned sour, the type of guy who hated to change his plans. "Collect the visas and passports?"

Bruno nodded. "All set."

"Okay. Get these people up, untie their feet but bind up their hands. We've got time for our excursion right now, so you can send up the service elevator as we planned. I'll meet you in the basement in five minutes."

Bruno bound our wrists once more, then released the ropes from our ankles. He took no notice of what I might have clutched in my right hand. It wasn't a helluva lot but it was better than nothing. When he left on his errand, Myers herded us down the hall, gripping Isabel's arm, his pistol jammed into her side.

At the end of the hallway, we huddled against the wall until the elevator arrived. Myers shoved us inside, had us face the back wall and gave each of us a sharp tap with his pistol, reminding us who was boss. "Don't try to be heroes," he said. "Either one of you."

Isabel and I slumped together, contemplating the 'excursion' we were about to take.

When we jerked to a stop in the basement, the doors opened onto an interior loading bay. I turned around and saw a row of cars and trucks parked along the left side, a few small pickup trucks on the right with a couple of men off-loading crates of vegetables and other kitchen supplies. Straight ahead, a huge overhead door was open to the rain-soaked parking lot. On an inside wall, an electric sign over a pair of glass doors indicated the way to the visitors' elevators and the hotel above.

I spotted Bruno behind the wheel of a new black Packard parked beside a delivery van, nose facing the exit, ready to roll. Myers stood at the elevator door, making sure the coast was clear before bringing us out to the car.

Then I heard a mighty uproar, several men shouting and yelling at the top of their lungs.

Myers was distracted, swivelling his head, looking for the commotion, and I moved behind him, lined up my foot with the centre of his back and stepped forward with a hefty kick, sending him out the elevator doors where he sprawled face-down and dazed on the concrete floor.

In that moment, Isabel dashed to the control panel and jammed the "Close Door" button with her finger. I grabbed her arm and pulled her to the floor in the back corner of the elevator. Now I opened my clenched fist, showing Isabel my pocket knife. By taking turns we were able to saw through the ropes binding our wrists, sustaining only a few nicks on our skin.

The shouting had stopped, replaced by the muffled pounding of running feet. That's when the gunshots began. Four or five quick blasts, no pause between them, bang, bang, bang. Everything went quiet for a minute and I wondered if it was all over.

The engine of a big car rumbled to life and I jumped up and pressed the button to open the doors. I held Iz close beside me at the control panel and peeked out. Myers was up and stumbling to the passenger door of the Packard while Bruno revved the engine. Ten seconds later he was in the car and it screeched toward the exit door.

We stepped out and, on our right, two guys were down on the floor near the pickup trucks, one of the guys groaning and holding his leg with bloody hands. The other lay still; I couldn't tell if he was dead or unconscious.

I turned Isabel toward the open doorway, where Myers' car was picking up speed. "Run after them," I said. "See which way they turn when they leave the parking lot, then get back here. I don't think they'll be looking for anyone to follow, but if they spot you, take cover. Run into the hotel."

She was off before I finished speaking. I didn't feel good about sending a woman into battle but my foot-race days were over.

As I limped toward the two guys on the floor, a third man stepped from behind a truck and came toward me. I tensed up, anticipating an attack; he sure as hell had the drop on me, out in the open without a weapon, two guys down nearby. He kept coming, then raised a hand. "Whitey Johnson," he said. "Friend of Scotty's."

I let out a big puff of relief. Shit, that was a close call but … what did he say? "Friend of Scotty? Where is he?"

Johnson motioned toward the floor behind me and I whirled around. He was the bleeder, still clutching his leg with both hands. I knelt beside him and he opened his eyes; his breathing was laboured, but he managed to speak. "Good day, Laddie. I'm here to save you."

I stared down at him and laughed. "And you did, you old bastard."

I turned to his friend. "I'll look after him. Check on the other guy. He came with you?"

He nodded and I watched him turn his mate over, face-up; the guy was breathing, his eyelids beginning to flutter.

"Through those doors there," I told the guy, tipping my head in that direction. "One floor up to the registration desk. Tell them we've got two injured and need an ambulance PDQ. And hurry."

The guy hustled away and I knelt beside Scotty. "You're going to be okay, Unc. Help's on the way."

I carefully peeled back his hands where he'd been clutching his hip. An open wound, dark blood oozing like oil. I put his hands back right away. "Press hard," I said. "It's only a flesh wound." That's what they said in all those war movies and it seemed to make the victim feel better. But it didn't work here.

"Shit, shit, shit. Hurts like hell. Think I'm gonna die."

"No, you're not, Unc. Medics'll be here any second. Hang on tight now."

I heard someone running, looked up and saw Isabel at the entrance door. "Get the car," I called out. "I'll come up and meet you."

I bent over Scotty, took a clean handkerchief from my pocket and wiped the sweat from his face. "Gotta go now," I told him. "Myers is on the run. When I get back I'll give you an exclusive. Story of the year, I promise."

He gritted his teeth, some blood in his mouth where he might've bitten his tongue. "Go get 'em," he said. Then he forced a grin. "And get in a lick for me."

CHAPTER FIFTY

A STEADY RAIN PELTED THE car as Isabel made a left turn when we drove from the General Brock Hotel, then she made a quick right at the next corner. "They headed this way, Max," she said. "Toward the Rainbow Bridge. Maybe they'll cross the border here."

As we neared the bridge, I saw long lines of cars snaking through the Canadian Customs stations. "He wouldn't have stayed here," I said. "Stalled in a lineup for twenty or thirty minutes, he'd be a sitting duck. And that's not his game."

Iz pulled over to the curb and I made a quick study of the street map I'd picked up at the hotel. "Let's take a left at River Road," I said. "It's only a mile or two to the Whirlpool Rapids Bridge – probably won't be as busy."

We turned onto River Road, which followed the Niagara River along the gorge and the whirlpool. From there it became the Niagara Parkway and went north to Lake Ontario. In the other direction it was about twenty-five miles to Buffalo. That could be Myers' Plan B.

"Will Scotty be all right, Max?"

I'd given her a quick report about what I'd found after she sprinted out of the hotel after Myers' car. "I think so. He'll get treatment right away and if the bullet didn't do internal damage he'll be limping around in no time. Just like me."

"That's a relief," she said. "But I was wondering ... how do you think he found us so quickly?"

"He's a suspicious guy; it's his job. So when he heard 'Mitzi' and 'Niagara Falls' in the same sentence, well, I bet he learned about her father's announcement party at the hotel in no time.

Don't know why he brought those guys with him, probably his drinking buddies, along for the ride. Some ride."

"But if it he hadn't shown up, Max ..."

"Yeah. It's my guess he spotted Myers' car going into the loading bay and followed it. We were damn lucky."

She reached across the seat and delivered a soft punch to my arm. "Back there in that elevator, when all hell broke loose?"

"Uh huh?"

"I saw Sergeant Dexter. On the battlefield. And I was proud of him."

I didn't know what the hell to say. It was always like this – since Grade 8 when Kathy Daly kissed me on the cheek and said I was a killer-diller. So I did the same thing as I did then; turned red and mumbled, "Thanks."

Then I gave myself a frisky head-rub, both hands, and got back to work.

On our right I noticed a low stone wall, maybe three feet high, between the road and the lip of the gorge, then a steep drop of a couple of hundred feet down to the whitewater of the rapids. I felt the car sway in a gust of wind and said to the driver, "Makes you wish they had seat belts in passenger cars, eh?"

She kept her eyes on the road, watching her speed, concentrating hard in these wet conditions. "Not a bad idea, Max. But you'd have to force people to wear them." She eased through a tight bend in the road. "Any sign of them yet? Make sure you check these side streets, in case they pulled off."

"I've been watching. And we're not far from the next bridge."

A White Rose gas station was coming up on our left and I surveyed its lot. Beside the pumps, a smaller building housed a car wash facility, no customers because of the rain. And tucked in beside it was a long black car which crept forward as we passed. A Packard. "There they are," I said, too loud, too excited. I twisted around, looking out the rear window. "Pulling in a few cars behind us now."

She sped up as much as she could and at that moment a startling clap of thunder set our nerves jangling. I yelped out loud when a zigzag of lightning ignited the overcast sky; I was still on lookout duty and almost fell over the back seat. "They've passed one more car. Want to pull over? Live to fight another day? You didn't sign up for this kind of duty, Iz."

"We're in it now, Max, so we're going to finish this." I turned to my new partner, impressed by her coolness under fire, both hands on the wheel, strong and determined, fully alive. She could have been on the beach in Normandy, part of the landing party.

I looked behind again. "Only two cars between us," I said. "Holy Hell! He's pulling out to pass. Is he crazy?"

We were approaching another curve and, rather than slowing, Isabel sped up. "Don't worry, Max. My Studebaker's a lot more manoeuvrable than their big boat. And I'm a better driver."

How'd she know I was worried?

"I don't believe this," I said, almost shouting because of the thunder. "There's an arm sticking out the passenger window ... and ... shit, they're firing at us."

I flipped around and slid down in my seat, just peeking over the back now. "No chance of hitting us in these conditions," I said. And then a bullet whanged off the trunk and ricocheted against the rear window, causing it to crack all to hell.

"Lucky shot," she said.

The Packard was gaining on us and Isabel gave it the gas coming out of the tight turn. The car's rear end drifted slightly, just like she'd planned it I bet, and she zipped well ahead. I was watching behind but they didn't come ... and didn't come. And neither did anyone else.

Isabel slowed and pulled into a driveway of a small bungalow. "Let's give it a minute," she said. And we waited for two.

She backed onto River Road and we reversed our course. Saw the line of cars backed up in the other lane. Saw the drenched people, some in raincoats, some under umbrellas, looking over the stone wall toward the gorge. We joined them, asked what happened. Nobody seemed to know much ... "A big crash ... too stormy to see ... a black car ..." One of the truck drivers who'd stopped was looking toward a fenced-off part of the wall and we moved closer.

"Stupid bugger was goin' way too fast," he said. "Look at those broken barricades near that gap in the wall. Musta been under repair and that big black car just sailed right through it and disappeared."

We got as close as we could, but we couldn't see the side of the gorge wall where it went down to the river. "Let's follow along downstream," Isabel said. "They may have gone in."

Back in the car, she turned around and continued in our original direction. But a lot slower this time so we could find a clear lookout spot. We reached the Whirlpool Bridge and parked.

Standing on the bridge we had a clear view of the gorge wall and the churning rapids beneath us. Isabel brought an umbrella from the car and we huddled under it. Drops of water clung to her cheeks as we stood transfixed next to the guardrail, watching for any sign of the big Packard. It felt like time stopped as we stood together in the rain, my arm around Isabel's trembling shoulders. We soon saw it. Down there, bobbing around the bend in the river like a kid's toy boat, was a big black car. Upside down.

Then the current got its clutches on that car, swirled it around and tossed it into the rapids, where it banged its way under the shuddering bridge and out the other side. Without a word we ran across the empty road and stared as the battered machine filled with water and, with surprising speed, sank from sight.

EPILOGUE

A WEEK LATER ISABEL PICKED me up in her now-repaired Studebaker and we attended Roger Bruce's opening at the Art Gallery of Hamilton. Iz wore a stunning white cocktail dress, shimmering with tiny sparkly things, and her red curls were arranged in an upswept hairdo I hadn't seen before. Boy, what a showstopper! In my blue suit, I looked like her bumpkin cousin who'd ridden into the big city on his bicycle from Binbrook Township.

We mounted the wide staircase strung with a ten-foot banner:

IMPRESSIONS OF THE ESCARPMENT
An Exhibition of Paintings by Hamilton Artist
ROGER BRUCE

A group of dignitaries formed a receiving line to greet the cream of the city's society, resplendent in gowns and tuxedos. Almost overlooked in all this glitter was the artist himself, slouching beside the gallery's distinguished director.

I shook hands down the line, nodding and smiling until my cheeks were sore. When I got to the star of the show I couldn't restrain my grin, even though it hurt. "Still with the too-big tux rental, huh?"

His eyes twinkled as he grasped my hand. "Well, well, if it ain't Superman and ... yes, there's Lois Lane right behind him."

Isabel approached and clutched his hand. "Lois Lane, eh?"

He leaned forward and gave her a peck on the cheek. "Thanks for coming," he said. "I was just explaining to your slow-witted friend here how stunning you look this evening."

She gave him a sweet smile.

"And I've been reading about your exploits in the *Spectator*," he continued. "Keeping the city free from crime and fighting for the rights of the downtrodden."

"All bullshit," I told him. "That story made us look like heroes because the *Spec* reporter is my uncle. And you must have noticed he served up a heaping spoonful of glory for himself – 'writing from my hospital bed in Hamilton General', and all that guff."

"Yeah, but scribes are like that," he said.

"The main thing," Isabel said, "is the bad guys got what they deserved. Mr. Myers and his driver are … gone. And that other man in the fire."

Roger Bruce nodded in agreement. "Now I hear the cops are after Tedesco, but good luck with that."

At that moment a gallery guide, keeping the line moving, hustled us along to the bar.

"You weren't teasing him were you, Max? Before I arrived?"

"No, it was the other way around."

Drinks in hand, we made the grand tour of the exhibit. Most of the paintings looked like landscapes to me, but they seemed a little – different. They might have been inspired by scenes along the Niagara Escarpment, but to me they looked out of focus. Artistic licence, I guess you'd call it, and I was surprised as hell that I liked the mood these images captured. My pals at Duffy's Tavern would never believe it. And I'd never tell them.

"Is your father coming tonight?" I asked Isabel.

"He's not, Max. He's been lying low since giving up his Rembrandt, staying at home and licking his wounded ego. I don't think he realizes how lucky he was to lose just the painting. It could have been so much worse for him."

I decided not to think about her old man. It wasn't a difficult decision. A greedy turd, if you asked me, and he should have gotten more than a slap on the wrist, even though it was an expensive slap.

We stood in silence before the last, and largest, painting in the exhibition – a vivid impression of the Niagara Gorge, frothy with fresh memories for Isabel and me. That fearful, storm-drenched race from Myers and his henchman still popped into my mind, but not with guilt at its outcome. I leaned toward my partner and whispered. "How are you feeling?"

She gave me a direct, clear-eyed look and there was a satisfied calmness about her, a woman at peace with herself. "I feel just fine," she said and returned her gaze to the painting. "I'm over the shock of those evil men dying when they crashed into the gorge. As Mr. Myers was fond of saying, 'They were responsible for their own downfall.' We didn't cause their deaths, Max. We pursued them on behalf of their victims and I'm proud of us for that."

We left the exhibit area, heading back to the bar.

"I was speaking with Simon Benson today," I said. "He's satisfied the record's been set straight and his brother's reputation restored. But I think it'll be a long time before he can trust a system that allows crooks like Myers and Tedesco to operate under their own set of rules."

"He's not the only one, Max, whose trust has been shaken."

We stopped walking and looked at each without speaking for a moment and I think we came to some sort of telepathic agreement on that subject.

"Something else," I said. "Simon reminded me about those tickets he gave me. Remember we found them at Jake's apartment? They're for Ella Fitzgerald's performance at the Brant Inn. Tonight."

"I forgot all about those," she said.

"So did I ... but, I thought ... well, maybe ... " and I withdrew the tickets in their tiny envelope from my shirt pocket with a hopeful little flourish. "I know I'm no Fred Astaire but ..."

Her green eyes opened wide and she studied me like a specimen under a microscope. And I confess, at that moment, I had no idea what she was thinking. Against all odds, I kept a brave face although my hopes were beginning to evaporate.

Then her smile lit the space between us. "I just love Ella," she said as she slipped her arm through mine and we floated down the stairway and out the door.

END

ACKNOWLEDGEMENTS

I'M INDEBTED TO MANY PEOPLE for their help in bringing Max Dexter to life.

To my publisher Maureen Whyte at Seraphim Editions for taking a chance on another new writer. And editor George Down for the thoughtful and knowledgeable way in which he massaged my manuscript. I'm also grateful to Trudi Down for her hard work promoting and publicizing my novel. And a tip of the fedora to Julie McNeill of McNeill Design Arts for her designs on Max.

To Catherine London for her editorial support and snappy ideas.

Also to Brian Henry for his editorial insights – Shalom.

To the late Brian Vallee for his excellent book, *The Torso Murder: the Untold Story of Evelyn Dick.*

To archivist Margaret Houghton at the Hamilton Public Library's Local History and Archives Department, who knows everything about Hamilton and then some.

And, of course, to my first reader and favourite artist, my wife Michèle LaRose for her support that never ends.

Finally, my thanks to our grandchildren in Montreal: Max, Dexter and Isabel, whose names were just right for these characters.

Chris Laing is a native of Hamilton, Ontario. He worked in private business for twenty years before joining the Federal Public Service, where he served in the Department of the Secretary of State and National Museums of Canada until his retirement.

In the past few years he has expanded his long-time interest in detective stories from that of avid reader to writing in this genre. His short stories have appeared in *Alfred Hitchcock's Mystery Magazine* and *Hammered Out* as well as online journals including *Futures Mystery Magazine*, *Mystical-E Magazine* and *Flash Me Magazine*. His short story "Golden Opportunity" will appear in the anthology *Best New Writing 2013*, to be published by Hopewell Publications. *A Private Man* is his first novel.

He now lives in Kingston, Ontario with his wife, artist Michèle LaRose.